"Marry me, Penelope . . ."

. . . he whispered, his mouth still brushing hers.

Her resistance was rapidly waning. "I don't think I should," she whispered back in honest anguish.

"Nonsense. Trust how you feel," he breathed, and his lips settled on hers. Penelope inhaled in surprise, and he touched her chin, nudging her lips apart and proving beyond all doubt that there was far more to kissing than she'd thought.

"Do you want me?" It was a weak basis for marriage, but she was trapped and she knew it. Any little comfort would be very welcome.

"Desperately." He glanced at the door. "Enough to commit every last wickedly pleasurable act we're accused of, right here on this sofa, if only your parents weren't outside the door."

Heat flooded her face, and not at the thought of her parents. If she married him, he'd make love to her. "What acts?"

His eyes glittered and one corner of his mouth curled upward. "Marry me and find out . . ."

By Caroline Linden

CAROLINE LINDEN

Love in the Time of Scandal

AVONBOOKS

An Imprint of HarperCollinsPublishers

This is a work of fiction. Names, characters, places, and incidents are products of the author's imagination or are used fictitiously and are not to be construed as real. Any resemblance to actual events, locales, organizations, or persons, living or dead, is entirely coincidental.

AVON BOOKS
An Imprint of HarperCollins*Publishers*
195 Broadway
New York, New York 10007

Copyright © 2015 by P.F. Belsley
ISBN 978–0–06–224492–5
www.avonromance.com

First Avon Books mass market printing: June 2015

Avon Trademark Reg. U.S. Pat. Off. and in Other Countries, Marca Registrada, Hecho en U.S.A.
HarperCollins® is a registered trademark of HarperCollins Publishers.

Printed in the U.S.A.

10 9 8 7 6 5 4 3 2 1

To Marnee, a wonderful writer and a great friend.
This is going to be your year, I know it!

Prologue

1805
Stratford Court, Richmond

Perseus lay in pieces on the floor. His arm, divorced from his body, held out the severed head of Medusa as if to ward his attacker off, and indeed, Benedict Lennox thought it might well have turned him to stone.

Before he fell, Perseus had held the head aloft, poised in mid-stride. The Gorgon's face was twisted with rage and her eyes seemed to follow a person. It was hideous, even frightening, but Benedict's father said it was a masterpiece, and Father knew art. As such it was displayed in a prominent position on the landing of the main staircase of Stratford Court, with a large mirror behind it to display the rear. Benedict always tried not to look right at it when he passed, but there was no avoiding it now. The base rested against the remains of the mirror, while Perseus and his trophy were scattered in pieces across the landing, amid the glittering shards of broken glass.

"Do you know anything about this?" The Earl of Stratford's voice was idle, almost disinterested.

His son swallowed hard. "No, sir."

"No?" The earl rocked back on his heels. "Nothing at all? Do you not even recognize it?"

Oh no. That had been the wrong answer. He searched frantically for the right one. "No, sir. I didn't mean that. It's a statue of Perseus."

Lord Stratford made a soft, disappointed noise. "Not merely a statue of Perseus. This is one of the finest works of art by a great sculptor. See how exquisitely he renders the god's form, how he encapsulates the evil of the Gorgon!" He paused. "But you don't care about that, do you?"

Benedict said nothing. He knew there was no correct answer to that question.

Stratford sighed. "Such a pity. I had hoped my only son would pay more attention to his classical studies, but alas. Perhaps I should be grateful you recognized it at all. Our entire conversation would be for naught otherwise."

Benedict Lennox gripped his hands together until his knuckles hurt. He stood rigidly at attention, mesmerized by the shattered glass and stone before him.

His father clasped his hands behind him, rather like Benedict's tutor did when explaining a difficult point of mathematics. "Now, what else can you tell me about this statue?"

"Something terrible happened to it, sir."

"Was it struck by lightning, do you think?" asked the earl in exaggerated concern.

The sky outside the mullioned windows was crystal clear, as blue as a robin's egg. "Unlikely, sir."

"No, perhaps not," his father murmured, watching him with a piercing stare. Benedict longed to look away from that stare but knew it would be a mistake. "Perhaps it was a stray shot from a poacher?"

Stratford Court was set in a manicured park, surrounded only by gardens, graveled paths, and open rolling lawns. The woods where any poachers might roam were across the river. Benedict wished those woods were much closer. He wished he were exploring them right this moment. "Possible, but also unlikely, sir."

"Not a poacher," said Stratford thoughtfully. "I confess, I've quite run out of ideas! How on earth could a statue of inestimable value break without any outside influence? Not only that, but the mirror as well. It's bad luck to break a mirror."

He stayed silent. He didn't know, either, though he suspected he was about to be punished for it. Bad luck, indeed.

"What do you say, Benedict? What is the logical conclusion?"

His tongue felt wooden. "It must have been someone inside the house, sir."

"Surely not! Who would do such a thing?"

A flicker of movement caught Benedict's eye before he could think of an answer. He tried to check the impulse, but his father noticed his involuntary start and turned to follow his gaze. Two little girls peeped around the newel post at the bottom of the stairs. "Come here, my lovely daughters, come here," said the earl.

Benedict's heart sank into his shoes. Suddenly he guessed what had happened to the mirror.

Samantha, who was only four, looked a little uncertain; but Elizabeth, who was seven, was pale-faced with fear. Slowly the sisters came up the stairs, bobbing careful curtsies when they reached the landing.

"Here are my pretty little ones." The earl surveyed them critically. "Lady Elizabeth, your sash is dropping. And Lady Samantha, you've got dirt on your dress."

"I'm sorry, Father." Elizabeth tugged at her sash, setting it further askew. Samantha just put her hands behind her back and looked at the floor. She'd only recently been allowed out of the nursery and barely knew the earl.

"Your brother and I are attempting to solve a mystery." The earl waved one hand at the wreckage. "Do you know what happened to this statue?"

Elizabeth went white as she stared at the Gorgon's head. "It broke, Father," piped up Samantha.

"Very good," the earl told her. "Do you know how?"

Elizabeth's terrified gaze veered to him. Benedict managed to give her an infinitesimal shake of his head before their father turned on him. "Benedict says he does not know," Stratford said sharply. "Do not look at him for answers, Elizabeth."

In the moment the earl's back was turned to them, Elizabeth nudged her sister and touched one finger to her lips. Samantha's green eyes grew round and she moved closer to Elizabeth, reaching for her hand.

Stratford turned back to his daughters. "Do either

of you know?" Elizabeth blinked several times, but she shook her head. "Samantha?" prodded their father. "It would be a sin not to answer me."

Samantha's expression grew worried. Benedict's throat clogged and his eyes stung. He took a breath to calm his roiling nerves and spoke before his sister could. "It was my fault, Father."

"Your fault?" Fury flashed in the earl's face though his voice remained coldly calm. "How so, Benedict?"

What should he say? If the earl didn't believe his story, he'd be whipped for lying, his sister would be punished for the actual crime, the nursemaid would be sacked for not keeping better watch over her charges, and his mother would be excoriated for hiring the nursemaid at all. Of course, confessing to the crime would get him whipped anyway. All over an ugly statue that everyone tried to avoid seeing.

A fine sweat broke out on his brow. Boys at school told of lying to deny their misdeeds, but how did one lie to claim a crime? He would have to ask, next term. Not that it would help him now.

His breath shuddered. "It was a cricket ball, sir. I was tossing it and—and it got away from me so I lunged to catch it—" His stomach heaved. He'd be whipped hard for this. "I apologize, sir."

For a long moment Stratford stared at him in the narrow-eyed flinty way he had. Like a hawk, he seemed not to need to blink. "When did this carelessness occur?"

"Not long ago, Father." His heart was pounding painfully hard, but he made himself continue. Elizabeth looked like she would cry, and that would help neither of them. "I was trying to find a maid to fetch a broom so I could sweep it up."

The blow on the back of his head made him flinch. "Viscounts do not sweep," snapped the earl. "Fetch a broom, indeed!"

"No, Father," he whispered.

"Nor do they lie and attempt to conceal their sins!" The second blow was harder, but he was ready for that one. The earl paced around him, his coattails swinging. "Elizabeth, where is your nursemaid?"

"In the garden, Father." Her thin voice quavered.

"Return to her with your sister, and do not wander off again." He turned back to Benedict. "Come with me."

Elizabeth shot him an anguished glance as she took Samantha's hand. He saw Elizabeth stoop and grab a doll, lying almost out of sight one step down, as they hurried down the stairs. It was her favorite doll, with the blue silk dress and the painted wooden head with real hair. He hoped she shook the broken glass out of the doll's clothing.

It was a long walk to the earl's study. Benedict counted every step to keep his mind from what was to come, his gaze fixed on his father's heels striding in front of him. Twenty-two steps down to the ground floor. Forty steps to the north. Eleven to the west. Six to cross his father's study and stand before the wide, polished desk with the ornate pen and inkstand.

"I cannot abide liars, Benedict." The earl walked around his desk to the wide windows that looked out toward the river. "You should know that by now."

Benedict stole a glance out the windows. The river glittered placidly, invitingly. It was a beautiful summer day and he'd finished his lessons early, planning to take the punt across the river to the wilder bank. His friend Sebastian was probably sitting up in the old oak tree right now, dangling his feet over the water and waiting for him to come. They'd recently begun a determined search for a long-lost legendary grotto. Everyone said it had been filled in years ago, but Lady Burton, who owned the estate where the grotto had been—and hopefully still was—had granted them permission to look for it. Benedict was secretly sure that grotto would prove the perfect spot to hide when his father was in a fury. If he knew where it was, he'd run from the room right now, call to his sisters to follow him, and row them all across the river. They could stay in the grotto indefinitely; Sebastian would smuggle them food from his house, and they would never return to Stratford Court again. After a while they would send a note to their mother, and then she, too, would run away and join them in the woods. The four of them could live there forever, climbing trees and washing in the river, and never facing another thrashing over a broken statue or anything else.

The earl lifted the thin rod that stood against the window frame, bursting the moment of wishful thinking. "Not only a liar, but a careless one as well. That statue is irreplaceable. And yet you didn't come to confess at once. I must have been remiss, if you thought that would escape my notice." He circled the desk. "Nothing escapes my notice."

"No, sir."

"Well?" The rod slashed down and made a loud crack against his lordship's boot. "What are you waiting for?"

Benedict cast one more longing glance at the river and the distant woods before closing his eyes. It would be at least a week before he could escape to them now. Gingerly he laid his hands flat on the desk and braced himself.

"I grow tired of this, Benedict. I expect more from you."

"I know, sir," he whispered, ashamed that his voice shook. His father despised weak, fearful people.

"No," said the earl quietly. "I don't think you do—yet." He raised the rod and began.

It was dark when his bedroom door opened. "Ben?" whispered Elizabeth nervously. "Are you awake?"

He raised his head, wincing as his back throbbed anew. "Yes."

There was a rustle and the door closed with a quiet click. "I managed to save a bit of milk." She crouched down next to his bed and held up the cup. "I think Nanny looked the other way on purpose."

He pulled himself toward the edge of the bed. From his shoulders to his hips, he ached. Awkwardly he sipped from Elizabeth's mug.

"I don't think it's fair that you got a whipping and shall have only bread and water for a week."

Benedict sighed, resting his cheek on the mattress. "It doesn't matter what we think."

"I know." Her eyes filled with tears. "I'm sorry, Ben. Samantha wanted to hold my doll Bess, but I was selfish and wouldn't let her. She pulled on Bess and I pulled back, and we both bumped into the statue, and Nanny was calling us, and—and—"

"Don't worry." He reached for her hand. She scrambled nearer and leaned her head against the bed frame beside his, clasping his hand to her cheek. "Make sure Samantha knows not to tell about Bess."

She nodded. "I will. I told her to pretend she had a nightmare and go cry in Nanny's lap while I sneaked in here with the milk. Are—are you badly hurt?"

He made a face even though his back felt like it was on fire. "Not much."

"Mother will come see you tomorrow, won't she?"

He hoped. Sometimes his punishments included being sequestered from everyone else. Elizabeth was only able to come to him because his room was still in the nursery. Benedict thought he could bear this much better if his mother would come and stroke his hair and lay cold compresses on his back and read to him. She did that when the earl was away from Stratford Court. Of course, when the earl was away, he wasn't whipped at all.

"I wish he would go to London," whispered his sister, echoing his thoughts.

"So do I." He wished the earl would go to London, or anywhere else, and stay there forever.

"You should go back to bed before Nanny realizes you're here."

She held up the cup so he could finish the milk. Greedily he sucked the last of it, then gave her a little push. "Good night, Ben," she whispered next to his ear. "Thank you."

He closed his eyes as she slipped out of the room. If he hadn't taken responsibility, their father would have begun to suspect the girls. Stratford never whipped his daughters—Benedict wondered if he would when they grew older—but he would punish them in other ways. If Stratford had seen Bess lying on the stair and realized the truth, he probably would have burned the doll. That would have broken Elizabeth's heart; she loved Bess and took very gentle care of her.

In a few days his back would stop hurting. A week with only bread and water would be miserable, but he was ten, nearly eleven—almost a man—and his little sisters needed their milk and good food more than he did. With any luck, his mother would find a way to come see him and make the days pass more quickly. And on the bright side, he would be allowed to recite his lessons here, instead of standing in the schoolroom.

But he wished, deeply and intensely, that he had been born the son of anyone other than the Earl of Stratford.

Chapter 1

1822
London

Some people were born with an acute appreciation of the little things in life: a good book, a beautiful garden, a quiet peaceful home. Nothing pleased them more than improving their minds through reading, or practicing an art such as painting or playing an instrument, or helping the sick and infirm. Such people were truly noble and inspiring.

Penelope Weston was not one of those people.

In fact, she felt very much the opposite of noble or inspiring as she stood at the side of Lady Hunsford's ballroom and glumly watched the beautiful couples whirling around the floor. She wasn't envious . . . much . . . but she was decidedly bored. This was a new feeling for her. Once balls and parties had been the most exciting thing in the world. She had thrilled at sharing the latest gossip and discussing the season's fashions with her older sister, Abigail, and their friend Joan

Bennet. None of the three of them had been popular young ladies, so they always had plenty of time to talk at balls, interrupted only occasionally by a gentleman asking one of them to dance.

At the time, they had all openly wished for more gentlemen to ask them to dance, and to call on them, flowers in hand, and beg for their company on a drive in the park. No one wanted to be a spinster all her life, after all. Whenever Joan fell into despair over her height, or Abigail fretted that only fortune hunters would want her, Penelope loyally maintained that there existed a man who would find Joan's tall, statuesque figure appealing, and a man who would want Abigail for more than her dowry.

Well, now she'd been proven right. Joan had married the very rakish Viscount Burke, and Abigail was absolutely moonstruck in love with her new husband, Sebastian. Penelope was very happy for both of them, she really was . . . but she was also feeling left out for the first time in her life. Her sister was only a year older than she, and they had been the best of friends her entire life—and now Abigail was happily rusticating in Richmond, cultivating the quieter society that made Penelope want to run screaming from the room. Joan's bridegroom had swept her off on a very exciting and exotic wedding trip to Italy, which Penelope envied fiercely but obviously could not share. And that left her alone, standing at the side of ballrooms once more, but this time without her dearest friends to pass the time.

"Miss Weston! Oh, Miss Weston, what a pleasure to see you tonight!"

Penelope roused herself from her brooding thoughts and smiled. Frances Lockwood beamed back, cheeks pink from dancing. Frances was on the brink of her first season, still starry-eyed at the social whirl of London. "And you, Miss Lockwood. I hope you are well."

The younger girl nodded. "Very well! I think this is the most beautiful ballroom I've ever seen!"

Penelope kept smiling. Just three years ago she'd been every bit as wide-eyed and delighted as Miss Lockwood. It was both amusing and disconcerting to see how she must have looked to everyone back then. "It is a very fine room. Lady Hunsford has quite an eye for floral arrangements."

"Indeed!" Miss Lockwood agreed eagerly. "And the musicians are very talented."

"They are." Penelope felt much older than her twenty-one years, discussing flower arrangements and musicians. Her mother was probably making the very same comments to her friends.

Miss Lockwood sidled a step closer. "And the gentlemen are so very handsome, don't you think?"

Now Penelope's smile grew a bit rigid. Frances Lockwood was the granddaughter of a viscount. Her father was a mere gentleman, and her mother was a banker's daughter, but that noble connection made all the difference. Penelope's father had been an attorney before he made his fortune investing in coal canals, and the grime of that origin had never fully washed away. The Lockwoods were received everywhere; Frances, with her dowry less than half the size of Penelope's, was considered a very eligible heiress. Not that Penelope wanted Frances's suitors—who were silly young men with empty pockets, for the most part—but it set something inside her roiling when she saw the way they fawned over her friend.

"There are many handsome gentlemen in London," Penelope said aloud. There were, although none near this part of the ballroom, where the unmarried ladies congregated. If Joan were here, they could discuss the scandalous rakes lounging elegantly at the far end of the room, closer to the wine. But Frances was only seventeen and would fall into a blushing stammer if Penelope openly admired the way Lord Fenton's trousers fit his thighs.

Frances nodded, a beatific smile on her face. She edged a little closer to Penelope's side and dropped her voice. "Miss Weston . . . may I confide in you? You've been very kind to me, and I do so look up to you for advice—well, you know, on how to deal with gentlemen who are only interested in One Thing."

Oh dear. Frances meant the fortune hunters who clustered around her. Penelope tried not to heave a sigh. Unfortunately she had too much experience of those men, and too little experience of real suitors. She was probably the least suited person to be giving advice, but Frances persisted in asking her. "Is another one bothering you? If so, you must send him on his way at once. Such a man will never make you happy if all he cares for is your fortune or your connections."

"Oh no, I know that very well," replied Frances earnestly. "I've turned away Mr. Whittington and Sir Thomas Philpot and even Lord Dartmond, although my mama was not very pleased by the last one. Only when I explained to her that you had turned him down as the very lowest of fortune hunters did she relent."

The Earl of Dartmond was at least forty, with a pernicious gambling habit. Mrs. Lockwood was a fool if she even considered him for her daughter, earl or not. "I'm sure you'll be very happy you did, when you meet a kinder gentleman who cares for you."

The younger girl nodded, her face brightening again. "I know! I know, because I have met him! Oh, Miss Weston, he's the handsomest man you ever saw. Always so smartly attired, and the very best horseman I've ever seen, and a music lover—he listened to me play for almost an hour the last time he called, and said I was a marvel on the pianoforte." Frances looked quite rapturous; she was very fond of the pianoforte and practiced for an hour each day, something Penelope couldn't fathom surviving, let alone enjoying. "And what's more, he's heir to an earl and has no need of my fortune. Mama is so pleased, and Papa, too. He's been calling on me for at least a fortnight now, always with a small gift or posy, and he's the most charming, delightful gentleman I could imagine!"

Penelope nodded, hoping it was all true. "How wonderful. I told you there were true gentlemen out there. They just require some hunting."

Frances laughed almost giddily. "There are! My other friends were so very scandalized when I refused to receive Mr. Whittington, because he's the most graceful dancer even if he is horribly in debt, but you were entirely correct. I credit your wise advice for the happiness I now feel—indeed, for the very great match I'm about to make! May I present you to him? He's to attend tonight."

For a moment Penelope felt like saying no. It was bad enough that she had to feel old and unwanted next to Frances. Her friend was sweet and kind, but also somewhat silly and naïve. It was bad enough to see Joan and Abigail marry deliciously handsome men; Penelope loved them and wanted them to be happy. She also wanted Frances to be happy, but tonight it just felt a bit hard to see Frances find her ideal man and be swept off her feet in her very first year in London, while Penelope had been overlooked for three years now by all but the most calculating fortune hunters.

But that was petty. She mustered another smile. "Of course. You know I always like to meet handsome men." Frances's eyes widened at the last, and Penelope hastily added, "I'm especially pleased to meet one who adores you."

Frances's smile returned. "He does, Miss Weston, I really believe he does! He's even hinted that he means to speak to my papa soon." A very pretty blush colored her cheeks. "How should I respond, if he asks me about that?"

"If you want to marry him, you should tell your father that he's the man for you. And stand by your conviction," she added. "Parents may not always understand your heart, so you must be sure to tell them emphatically."

"Yes, of course." Frances nodded. "I hope you approve of him, Miss Weston."

"Your approval is what matters." Penelope

wondered if she had ever been so anxious for someone else's validation of her opinion. She would have to ask Abigail, the next time she saw her sister.

"I see him," said Frances with a little cry of nervous delight. "Oh my, he's *so* handsome! And his uniform is very dashing! Don't you think so?"

Penelope followed her companion's gaze and saw a group of the King's Life Guards, making their entrance with some swagger. Instinctively her mouth flattened. She'd met a few of them last summer, when one of their number, Benedict Lennox, Lord Atherton, had courted her sister. Penelope was sure he'd never been in love with Abigail, and when Abigail confessed her love for another man, Lord Atherton reacted like a thwarted child. Penelope hoped he wasn't in the crowd, but then she caught sight of his dark head.

She repressed the urge to walk the other way. She hadn't seen him since they last parted, when he'd reluctantly helped solve a years-old mystery that had tarred the name of the man Abigail loved. Sebastian Vane had stood accused of stealing a large sum of money from Lord Atherton's father, and Atherton himself had done nothing to disprove it—even though he'd once been Sebastian's dearest friend. Penelope grudgingly admitted that Atherton had been fairly decent after that, but she still thought he was insincere and always had an eye out for his own interest, whatever truth or justice demanded.

It wasn't until Atherton turned and looked toward them that Penelope realized she was staring at him. She quickly averted her gaze and turned her body slightly, hoping he hadn't actually noticed her. However, that only gave her a good view of Frances's face, which was glowing with joy.

Because . . . Penelope closed her eyes, praying she was wrong. Because her brain was fitting together details, just moments too late, and they were adding up to one dreadful conclusion. Atherton was heir to the Earl of Stratford, who was a very wealthy man. He was appallingly handsome, which Penelope only acknowledged with deep disgust. And when she stole a quick glance under her eyelashes, she saw that he was heading directly for the pair of them.

Oh Lord. What could she say now?

"Miss Lockwood." Penelope gritted her teeth as he bowed. His voice was smooth and rich, the sort of voice a woman wanted to hear whispering naughty things in her ear. "How delightful to see you this evening."

"I am the one delighted, my lord." Blushing and beaming, Frances dipped a curtsy. "May I present to you my good friend, Miss Penelope Weston?"

His gaze moved to her without a flicker of surprise. He'd seen her, and was obviously more prepared for the meeting than she was. "Of course. But Miss Weston and I are already acquainted."

Penelope curtsied as Frances gaped. "Indeed, my lord."

"I—I didn't know that," stammered Frances, looking anxious again. "Are you very good friends? Oh dear, I wish I had known!"

"No, we hardly know each other," said Penelope

before he could answer. "It was a passing acquaintance, really."

Atherton's brilliant blue eyes lingered on her a moment before returning to Frances. "The Westons own property near Stratford Court."

"Then you're merely neighbors?" asked Frances hopefully. "In Richmond?"

"A river divides us," Penelope assured her. "A very wide river."

Atherton glanced at her sharply, but thankfully didn't argue. "Yes, in Richmond. Unfortunately I'm kept here in London most of the year. I believe my sister Samantha is better acquainted with Miss Weston."

"Indeed," said Penelope with a pointed smile. "I hope Lady Samantha is well."

"Yes," said Lord Atherton after a moment's pause. "She is."

Too late Penelope remembered about Samantha. In their zeal to clear Sebastian Vane's name so Abigail could marry him, the Weston girls had inadvertently resurrected a dark secret of Samantha's, one her brother had claimed would lead to dire consequences for her. Penelope hadn't wanted to cause trouble for Samantha, but Sebastian had been accused of murder and thievery; Abigail's happiness depended on exonerating him, and Samantha was the only person who could help. Penelope cringed to have brought it up, but Atherton did say she was well, so the consequences must not have been as bad as he'd predicted. Still, she did truly like Samantha—far more than the lady's brother—and she was sorry to have been so cavalier with her name.

For a tense moment they seemed frozen there, Penelope biting her tongue, Frances looking troubled, and Atherton staring at her with a strange intensity. He shook it off first. "Miss Lockwood, I hope you've saved me a dance."

Frances's smile returned, although a little less brilliantly than before. "Of course, my lord. I am free the next two."

"Excellent." He gazed warmly at her, and Frances seemed to sway on her feet.

Penelope had to work hard to keep from rolling her eyes. How could she escape this? Thankfully she caught sight of a familiar face across the room, causing her to smile widely in relief. "You must excuse me, I see a dear friend just arriving. Miss Lockwood, Lord Atherton." She bobbed a quick farewell and all but ran across the room.

Olivia Townsend was one of Penelope's favorite people in the world. She was only a few years older than Abigail, and had been like an older sister to the two Weston girls for as long as Penelope could remember. Olivia's family had lived near the Westons and all four children had been fast friends. But while Penelope's family had prospered—greatly—since then, Olivia's had not. At a fairly young age, she'd made a hasty marriage of dubious happiness to a charming but feckless fellow, Henry Townsend, who managed to run through his modest fortune with shocking speed before his death a few years ago. Since then, Olivia had lived very modestly. It was a surprise to see her here tonight, in fact, as she didn't often attend balls.

"Olivia!"

Her friend was scanning the room and didn't seem to have noticed her approach; she jumped at Penelope's exclamation. "Oh," she said in a constricted voice. "You startled me."

She blinked. "I can see that. Whom were you expecting, an ogre?"

For a moment Olivia's face froze, as if she had in fact been on guard, but then she smiled ruefully. With a shake of her head, she turned her back to the room and squeezed Penelope's hand. "Forgive me; I was woolgathering. Are you enjoying the ball?"

"Well enough." Penelope peered closely at her. "What's wrong? You looked worried."

Olivia waved one hand. "It was nothing. How kind of you to leave your friends and join me."

Penelope barely kept back her snort. "I don't know how I could have stayed. You'll never guess who Miss Lockwood's new suitor is."

"Who?"

"Lord Atherton," whispered Penelope, after a cautious glance backward. She'd already let her temper get the better of her once tonight, and wouldn't put it past him to overhear every slighting word she spoke about him.

Olivia looked surprised. "Atherton? The gentleman who courted—?"

"The same," said Penelope grimly. "And my sister felt so cruel to turn him down! I shall have to write to her at once and assure her that, far from suffering a malaise, he's found a younger, sillier girl to marry."

"Now, Pen, you don't know that. He may be deeply attached to her."

She couldn't stop the snort this time. "She is certainly attached to him. He's the perfect man, in her telling. I don't know how I could have held my composure if I'd known who she was talking about. He sits and listens to her practice the pianoforte—can you imagine?"

"Perhaps he enjoys it." Penelope widened her eyes in patent disbelief. "Perhaps he's so smitten with her, he would be content just to sit and gaze at her," Olivia added. "It could happen."

"Huh." Penelope made a face. Just the thought of Lord Atherton sitting and staring at her was enough to make her skin prickle.

"Well, it's Miss Lockwood's cross to bear," said Olivia practically.

"But if he marries her, I'll have to see him from time to time." Frances might be young and naïve, but she was endearing all the same, and Penelope did like her.

Olivia laughed and tucked Penelope's arm through hers. "Perhaps she'll become disenchanted and change her mind about him."

She caught sight of Lord Atherton, leading Frances about the floor in a quadrille. Frances was fairly radiating adoration as she gazed up at him. It took Penelope some effort to quell the urge to run over and warn Frances not to fall for his very handsome smile, or athletic figure, or disgustingly perfect face. "For her sake as well as mine," she grumbled, "I hope so."

Chapter 2

Benedict Lennox had never thought he was one to take things for granted, but he was quickly revising that opinion.

It was a very rude surprise that Frances Lockwood was friends with Penelope Weston. Partly that was because he didn't know much about Miss Lockwood yet, but partly because what he did know indicated that she was utterly unlike Penelope. Miss Lockwood was anxious to please, listening to his every word as if it had the gravity of Scripture. Miss Weston also seemed to regard his words as biblical, but rather more as she might view the hissings of the serpent in Eden. Miss Lockwood liked the simpler pleasures of life, such as playing her pianoforte and dancing. Miss Weston craved excitement and adventure, and nothing daunted her, as Benedict had seen all too well; there was something wild and unconventional about her. Seeing them together was like seeing Hestia stand shoulder to shoulder with Aphrodite.

He tried not to think of another way they were

different. Miss Lockwood was round-faced and pretty in a girlish way, while Miss Weston seemed to blaze with an internal heat that rendered her mesmerizing. Miss Lockwood's looks were perfect for a wife: pleasant to look at but not distracting. Miss Weston's future husband, whoever the poor blighter was, would need a strong stomach to be able to endure the way other men watched her.

Benedict banished all those thoughts. He needed to keep his wits about him tonight as he struggled to decide how seriously he wished to pursue Miss Lockwood. After two weeks of companionship, he ought to have a sense of the girl and how she felt about him. He'd already had one marriage proposal rejected—by Miss Weston's sister, of all people—and he didn't plan to suffer that humiliation again.

"You look lovely this evening," he told Miss Lockwood, leading her out for a quadrille. Miss Weston had disappeared into the crowd, although if pressed, Benedict would have wagered a large sum that she was still watching. His skin seemed to prickle, as if he could feel her searing blue gaze on him.

"Thank you, sir." Miss Lockwood blushed, although her smile was delighted.

Benedict started to relax. This was a girl with no artifice or vendetta. He needed to stop thinking of Penelope Weston and direct his attention to the girl he was considering marrying. "Are you enjoying the ball?"

"Oh yes, especially now that you're here." She modestly averted her eyes, but he could hear the eager happiness in her voice.

He leaned his head down to hers as the musicians began to play. "Then I apologize for not arriving sooner, if my presence has added to your pleasure."

She looked up at him with her heart in her eyes as they made their opening courtesies. It gave him a twinge of something that was half satisfaction, half unease, as if he'd won something without even trying for it. Which was absurd. Miss Lockwood was an heiress; she had her pick of gentlemen, and he was not her only suitor. If she chose him, it would be because she wanted him. And he was hardly some worthless scoundrel with nothing to offer a woman. Unfortunately many of his advantages were related to his father—the wealth, the title, the estates he would someday hold—but Benedict knew he was a handsome fellow with a pleasing manner. He'd never had any trouble winning a woman when he set his mind on her . . . with the notable exception of Abigail Weston, much to her sister Penelope's fiendish delight.

No. He was not going to think of that frustrating female again. The dance brought him back to Miss Lockwood and he smiled anew.

"Have you known Miss Weston for a very long time?" she asked.

Silently Benedict cursed. "Not at all."

"I've only known her a few weeks, but I find her very amusing and clever." She glanced up at him curiously. "What do you think of her?"

I try not to, he thought. "She's all you say, as well as loyal and devoted to her family."

Miss Lockwood nodded as though relieved. "She is, isn't she? I had no idea what to do or how to act at balls, but she was so kind to me. Why, I would have made a silly fool of myself if not for her!"

Benedict took a deep breath to calm the spike of apprehension this inspired. In his experience, Penelope Weston's interference was not a good thing. "I'm sure you wouldn't have. You're a very sensible young lady."

She glowed at his words. "You're so kind to say so." She lowered her voice. "One gentleman who called on me was not as gallant; he implied Miss Weston would be a bad influence on me. But I learned later that he was desperately in debt and had a mistress as well, so his motives were far from honorable."

"How did you learn such a thing?" Benedict asked, although he had an idea.

Miss Lockwood gave the answer he expected. "Miss Weston told me! And when I asked Miss Drummond, she confirmed it was true."

The dance parted them again, and Benedict went through the steps while his thoughts ran down some grim lines.

Obviously Penelope Weston had significant influence over Miss Lockwood. That was unfortunate for a number of reasons, the foremost being that Penelope despised him. He could tolerate that—she had a knack for getting under his skin, too—but he couldn't let her spoil his budding courtship of Frances Lockwood. What business was it of hers whom Miss Lockwood married? The girl deserved to make up her own mind without being swayed by Penelope's sharp tongue.

This called for a preemptive strike. He escorted

Miss Lockwood to her mother's side when the dance ended and exchanged more pleasantries with Mrs. Lockwood. With any luck, Miss Lockwood would pay more heed to her mother than to her friend, for it was clear to see Mrs. Lockwood approved mightily of him. After securing an invitation to call on them the following day, Benedict drew Miss Lockwood aside.

"Would you be distressed if I asked your friend to dance?"

She blinked, a trace of alarm returning to her expression. "You wish to dance with Miss Weston?"

"Only because she's your friend," he replied, stressing the last two words and giving her a small, private smile. "I wish to be on good terms with your friends, my dear."

Miss Lockwood almost trembled with delight. "Oh," she breathed. "Yes, of course. Miss Weston did say it was important for—"

"Yes?" he prompted when she gasped and fell silent.

The girl wet her lips as if confiding a secret. "She advised me to look askance on any gentleman who didn't care for my friends, or of whom my friends disapproved. Her opinion is that no one man is worth giving up my friends. Do—do you disagree, my lord?"

"Not at all." It *was* sound advice. He just had to make certain it worked to his benefit in this instance. "But I wouldn't wish you to wonder at my asking her."

She gave him a look of devotion, and some of Benedict's tension eased. "You are a true gentleman, sir."

He brought her hand to his lips and took his leave, telling himself he was, and would be, a gentleman. He bore Penelope no ill will. Once upon a time, they'd even seemed to share a joie de vivre, when she dared him to prove Hampton Court was haunted and they laughed together in dusty corridors about ghostly legends. The memory quickened his step; when Penelope was in a good humor, she had a sly wit and a laugh that made men stop and listen. All he had to do was rekindle enough of that good feeling between them so she wouldn't try to turn Miss Lockwood against him.

It took him a few moments to locate her. Unlike Miss Lockwood, who was always watching the dancers as if she couldn't wait to be one of their number, Penelope had retreated to a corner. Benedict made his way through the crowd without hurrying, giving her plenty of time to note his approach. He could tell the exact moment she did. She raised her chin, leveled a cool glare at him, and deliberately turned her shoulder to him.

Damn. This would take some effort—and for some reason he felt an unwonted thrill at the prospect.

He summoned his most charming smile as he drew near. "Miss Weston."

She faced him the way Queen Elizabeth must have faced the Earl of Essex before sending him to the block. "Lord Atherton. What an unexpected pleasure." She glanced at the woman beside her. "May I present to you my friend Mrs. Townsend? Mrs. Townsend, this is Lord Atherton, whose father has a very beautiful property in Richmond near ours."

"It is a pleasure, Mrs. Townsend." He bowed.

"How do you do, sir?" Mrs. Townsend curtsied, shooting a fleeting, curious glance at Penelope.

For some reason he suspected that they had been speaking of him, and he had the sudden desire to charm Mrs. Townsend mercilessly, just to see what Penelope would do. He checked the impulse—he wanted to win her over, not antagonize her further—and kept his easy smile in place. "We didn't have a chance to speak earlier. Would you honor me with a dance, Miss Weston?"

"How kind of you to ask, my lord. Are you certain Miss Lockwood can spare you?" she asked, somewhat archly.

"Miss Lockwood encouraged me," he replied.

Penelope raised one brow. "Did she? Well then, how could I possibly refuse?" With a vaguely ominous smile, she gave him her hand. "Shall we?"

They joined the dance figures forming on the floor. Unlike the other couples, many of whom spoke to each other or at least exchanged a glance, Penelope gazed straight ahead as if no one stood beside her.

"I hope your family is well," he said, thinking to start cordially.

"Yes," she said. "They are all very well." Finally she looked at him, an almost sly glance through her eyelashes. "My sister especially."

Benedict absorbed the hit without a flinch. He'd expected it. "I am delighted to hear that. I always wished her well."

"She's married now, you know," she went on. "It was a lovely wedding, small and private. I don't think I've ever seen a man so in love as my new brother-in-law."

He clenched his jaw but kept his expression composed. "Vane was due for some good fortune and happiness. I'm glad to hear he's found it."

Penelope smiled that dangerous smile again as the music began. "He most certainly has."

They turned and made the courtesy to the couples on either side of them, then faced each other and did the same. The next several steps separated them, but when she took his hand and they turned, Penelope's eyes shone in a way that put him on guard. When the dance moved on to the other couples, he discovered why.

"Have you known Miss Lockwood long, sir?"

"A few weeks. She's a charming young lady."

"She is," agreed Penelope warmly. "I'm very fond of her; she's like a younger sister to me."

Benedict took that as a warning. "She's fortunate to have secured your friendship."

Her eyebrows went up. "She considers herself more fortunate to have attracted *your* notice."

"I can hardly comment on that."

"No? You never seemed one to ignore your own advantages, my lord."

Fortunately the dance sent her away from him, before his temper could slip from his grasp and cause him to say something rash. She seemed to know it, though, for she sent him a simmering glance as she moved around the other dancers. He could barely control his impatience for her to be back at his side. Such a comment could not go unanswered.

"Are you accusing me of misrepresenting myself?" he asked as soon as she took his hand for the next turn.

She tipped her head as if pondering it. "I don't know. How highly *do* you think of yourself?" He looked at her incredulously, and she smiled, with a tiny shake of her head. "Never mind that. Tell me instead what you love best about dear Miss Lockwood."

For a moment he didn't reply. He couldn't. All thoughts of Miss Lockwood, his potential bride, had been driven out of his head by the infuriating woman at his side, with her gleaming blue eyes and secretive smile that always rattled his equilibrium. He scrambled to control his thoughts and say something sensible. "Her warm and kind spirit."

Penelope nodded. "Of course. She's inclined to see the best in people, even when it's not warranted."

By only the thinnest of margins did Benedict not ask if that explained her fondness for Penelope. She was trying to provoke him. He should have been prepared for that. Her delight in needling him had been amusing at first, but he was growing tired of it—and unlike before, when he had brushed it aside, there was something very real at stake this time. If she decided to poison Miss Lockwood against him, he wasn't sure he could tolerate it with good grace.

"That is surely the mark of a true lady," he said softly, "to be the sort of woman everyone admires and likes."

The barb struck home, he could see it in her eyes. For the briefest moment they darkened as if in hurt, but then the sparkle was back—and this time they glittered like the finest sapphires. "Indeed! What a revelation, sir. I have always thought gentlemen were far more interested in a woman's other attributes."

Without thinking his gaze dropped. Penelope wasn't as slender as Miss Lockwood, and she had been skipping about in the dance. Her bosom rose and fell against her exquisitely cut bodice of blue silk in a very tempting display. Her skin was flushed a perfect pale peach, and her locket had nestled right between the swells of her breasts. Benedict had meant to set her back on her heels, and instead found himself almost mesmerized. "One must consider every part of a woman."

"Some parts more closely than others, I see," she shot back furiously as she turned away in the dance.

He cursed inside his head as they performed the next several steps. What about this woman always caught him wrong-footed? Benedict barely remembered going through the rest of the dance. It felt as though little jolts of lightning coursed along his nerves, his every sense as sharp as a razor and focused solely on Penelope Weston. From the smoldering look she gave him, he wasn't the only one who felt the tension. Before he knew it, the music was ending and she was beside him again. He offered his arm to escort her from the floor, and she took it with a hand that trembled.

He didn't think it was upset. He had a feeling it was fury. To be honest, the same feeling had a strong grip on him. The temptation to pull her into a quiet room and have a proper blazing row was overwhelming. For a moment his steps strayed unconsciously toward the door before he caught himself.

Damn. This was not going as planned.

"Miss Weston," he said as they made their way through the crowd, "I asked you to dance in the hope of rediscovering the easy companionship we felt at Hampton Court last summer. I would very much like for us to be friendly once more." In spite of himself a note of warning crept into his tone. "I've grown very fond of your friend. If I manage to secure her regard, I hope you would wish us both well."

She stopped and faced him. For a moment she simply studied him, all coyness gone. "You say you're very fond of her, but is it merely fondness? Is fondness enough for marriage?" She noticed his faint start at the last word. "Miss Lockwood anticipates a proposal any day now. Is that what you intend? Do you really love her enough to pledge your troth to her from now until death?"

"That must be between me and Miss Lockwood," he replied coolly.

"So you say," she retorted. "But she's my friend. Do you think I won't hear of it if she's unhappy?"

Benedict's jaw tightened. He could hardly swear to make Miss Lockwood happy at all times; it wasn't possible. Marriage wasn't designed for happiness but for security, status, and money. If one was fortunate, it also provided contented companionship, which he supposed led to happiness. On the other hand, if he admitted the possibility of unhappiness, it would hand Penelope a weapon to skewer him, and he had already seen how quickly she would do it.

"I don't want to make her unhappy," he said.

"Yet what you love about her is her tendency to think too well of people—including, perhaps, gentlemen who call on her. A man truly in love would surely be able to declare it openly, with no need for prevarication. One doesn't even need to ask Sebastian if he loves my sister; it's written on his face when he looks at her—something he does all the time." She made a dismissive motion with one hand as Benedict's expression hardened into stone. "I haven't seen you glance once toward Miss Lockwood. Instead you've been watching me like a cat watches a mouse, as if you'd like nothing more than a chance to wring my neck."

"A cat," he bit out, "does not wring a mouse's neck. He eats the mouse. Do you seriously convict me of not caring for Miss Lockwood because I'm not consumed with jealousy over her every move? Quite aside from the fact that I have been paying attention to you, my partner in the quadrille, what sort of marriage would it be if I never allowed my wife to dance with another man or do anything at all out of my sight? You advocate something more like possession than marriage." He didn't care that he had all but admitted he was planning to propose to Frances Lockwood. Something about Penelope Weston made his blood run hot and reckless.

"You needn't be consumed with jealousy," she scoffed. "But consumed with passion for her . . . That is something every woman wants from the man she marries."

He almost lost his temper. *Every* woman? Not even half, by his accounting. Just in this ballroom alone, Benedict could see more than a dozen women who had married for money, for rank, for power. If they wanted passion, they must have found it outside their marital beds, because he knew a great many married couples in London who could hardly stand the sight of each other.

"Such charming idealism," he said in a stony voice. "What a romantic haven you must inhabit. Either that, or you're too naïve to understand marriage among the upper classes."

Her eyes widened. "It is not idealism!"

He gave her a cynical look. "Then you've not seen enough *ton* marriages."

"Perhaps not," she retorted. "Perhaps I've seen too many *happy* marriages, like my sister's." She gave him a scathing look up and down. "Perhaps that's the difference between us, Lord Atherton. I believe a man should love the woman he marries, and she should love him. I don't believe it's enough to simply 'get on well together' and enjoy each other's company."

The edges of his vision burned red. Even if he hadn't remembered speaking those words, the scornful lilt Penelope gave them would have reminded him of the occasion. He hadn't been desperately in love with Abigail Weston when he proposed to her, but neither had he lied and claimed he was. He'd been honest with her, and now Penelope was flinging it in his face as if it were some sordid insult. Someday, someone would give her a well-deserved comeuppance, and he hoped he was there to see it.

"I expect it's but one of many differences between us." He bowed. "Good evening, Miss Weston." He walked away, and felt her gaze boring into his back with every step he took.

His fellow Guardsmen had congregated at the far end of the room, closer to the card room and the wine punch. Sick of female companionship for the moment, he rejoined them, still thinking how he could have charmed his way back into Penelope Weston's good graces—assuming she had any, which he was beginning to doubt. Those flashes of affinity between them must have been figments of his imagination.

"What were you up to?"

He started at Lieutenant Cabot's question. "Dancing."

Cabot snorted with laughter. "We saw! How did you make out?"

Benedict lifted a glass of wine from a nearby footman's tray. "What do you mean?"

"The Weston girl," said Cabot, lowering his voice. "The cit's daughter."

"Ah." Benedict took a drink. *Her.* "I'm not pursuing her."

Corporal Hollander eyed him closely, a teasing grin lurking about his mouth. "No? You couldn't take your eyes off her."

Benedict shot an annoyed look at him. "How dull it must be, standing here watching other people dance. Couldn't find a partner of your own?"

"Not one with that kind of dowry," returned Hollander. "Nor that pretty a face. And you act like a man hell-bent on finding a wife. If you're determined to get yourself leg-shackled, why not pursue an heiress?"

"I'm not determined to get married." Not to the wrong girl, at any rate.

Cabot rested his elbow on Benedict's shoulder, probably for balance as much as to lean closer. There was wine on his breath, and he swayed a bit on his feet. "I don't blame you. She's quite fetching. I hear she's got a tongue like a dagger, but the rest of her is quite fine."

Against his will, his mind conjured up the image of her breasts, pale and perfect above the bodice of her gown. He felt again the charge that seemed to leap between them when she glanced at him in that coy way. Penelope Weston was very fine, indeed. God help him. He drank more wine and shrugged off Cabot's elbow.

"She's pretty enough," he said.

Hollander snorted. "Pretty enough! She's a dashed beauty. I'd like to have my way with her. The spirited ones are always the most invigorating to bed."

Oh Lord. Such a thought did nothing for Benedict's peace of mind. He waved one hand at the footman to bring more wine. "You'd better keep your wits about you if you mean to try." The accommodating servant put another full glass into his hand, which he promptly raised to his mouth, trying to wash away the thought of taking Penelope to bed, all her crackling energy and spirit channeled into more passionate outlets . . . A man would need to hold her down . . . or tie her down . . . or lie back and let her ride him hard . . .

"For twenty thousand pounds I certainly could," said Cabot with a laugh.

"For twenty thousand pounds you could buy some wit to keep about you, too," added Hollander.

"Who are you setting your sights on, Cabot? The Weston girl?" Bannister, a strapping subaltern new to the regiment, joined the conversation. "I'd advise against it."

"I never asked for your bloody advice," said Cabot petulantly. He hiccupped in the middle, though, slurring his words, and no one paid him much mind.

"Atherton's eyeing her." Hollander gave Benedict a sly look.

"I am not," he said through his teeth. The wine was not, as hoped, mellowing his temper.

"Oh! He might have a chance, but the rest of you lot . . ." Bannister grimaced. "Her father's ambitious and wants an earl at least."

"The devil you say!" Cabot blinked, steadying himself on Benedict's shoulder again. "An earl! On what grounds?"

"Forty thousand pounds, that's what grounds." Bannister nodded at Hollander's quiet whistle of astonishment. "Had it from Mrs. Harrow herself."

"What's her interest?"

"Well." Bannister smiled slightly. "I might have admitted a wealthy wife would enable me to maintain certain pleasures that would otherwise strain my purse."

Hollander chuckled. "Bannister, you scoundrel. Asking your mistress to help you find a wife so you can keep supporting her? What brass, man."

Bannister ignored him. "But you've set your

cap at her, Atherton? I thought you were after the Lockwood girl, but if you've moved on, I don't like to trespass on a fellow officer's interest . . ."

Benedict silently said a very colorful curse. The Guardsmen had apparently turned into a group of gossiping old women tonight. "As a gentleman, I refuse to discuss any lady in such vulgar terms. I had the pleasure of making Miss Weston's acquaintance last summer, and I assure you all she despises nothing as much as she despises insincerity."

"Oh, I intend to be sincere," murmured Bannister, his eyes roving the room like a hunter's. "My father's a marquess, after all, even if I'm not the heir. Is she here?"

"She danced with Atherton just a few moments ago."

Someone really needed to draw Cabot's cork. The man chattered worse than a little girl when he was drunk. "It was only a quadrille," said Benedict coldly. "And this entire conversation has grown rather tedious. Good evening." Ignoring the chuckles and teasing, he walked away.

It didn't occur to him until much later that he could have ended the matter simply by admitting he was courting Frances Lockwood. He was growing certain that she would be a suitable wife. In fact, his mates had seen him dance with her before; they just hadn't teased him about her. He told himself that was because Miss Lockwood hadn't exercised her wit on as many gentlemen as Penelope had done, shaping society's view of her. Or perhaps it was because Penelope's dowry dwarfed Miss Lockwood's, while her pedigree did not. He told himself it was not because Miss Lockwood looked quiet and ordinary next to Penelope, and that all Hollander's enthusiasm for a spirited girl was just the ramblings of a man with too much wine in his belly. Because a spirited girl of fiery beauty was not what Benedict wanted.

Not at all.

Chapter 3

"There's simply got to be a way to stop him!"

"I don't see one that won't land you in trouble," Olivia remarked.

Penelope fumed. She'd been fuming ever since the previous evening's infuriating dance with Lord Atherton, when he baldly admitted he wasn't in love with Frances Lockwood but meant to marry her anyway. She wished he'd never asked her to dance. Then she could have listened to Frances's raptures about him and told herself they might be true. She could have held her tongue and simply agreed that he was handsome and danced well and was a very eligible match. That was all true, and she could tell herself that Frances had a mother and a father who were very capable of advising her on which suitor to choose.

But now, curse him, all she could think about was that he appeared to be intent on dazzling Frances into a hasty marriage without much care for how happy they would be after the wedding. Unfortunately for Atherton, Penelope had seen him do that before. Last summer she'd watched him focus that same charming smile on her sister, Abigail. She'd watched him ignore any hint that Abigail didn't return his interest. Penelope had reached the unpleasant conclusion that Lord Atherton was either not very bright or not very honest. Since no one else seemed to think him dim-witted, it must be that Atherton had pursued Abigail for his own mysterious—and therefore vaguely nefarious—reasons. Fortunately Abby had already lost her heart to another, better man, and Atherton's charm had bounced off her.

Poor, sweet Frances would never see through him, though. Much like Penelope's own parents had been, the Lockwoods were plainly delighted by his courtship of their daughter. They would give her to him without a moment's hesitation. It would only be later, when Atherton's lack of real affection became apparent, that Frances would realize her mistake.

Unless someone . . . like Penelope . . . told her sooner.

As if she could read Penelope's thoughts, Olivia nudged her. "It's not your place to save her," she admonished. "Indeed, there may be nothing terrible to save her from! Just because you don't care for him doesn't mean she can't."

She scowled and swung away from the window display Olivia had been studying. Penelope had been so caught up in her grim thoughts she hadn't even seen the bonnets within. "I don't want to interfere! I wish she would notice how insincere he is on her own, and I wouldn't need to say a word. But Olivia, what if she doesn't?"

Her friend linked her arm through Penelope's,

prodding her to resume their stroll down Bond Street. "Sometimes there's no saving someone from what they want to do. If she wants to marry him and he wants to marry her, what can you say? You're not her mother, nor even her sister. Your approval isn't required."

"I know," she admitted on a sigh. "I don't want to spoil her happiness! But it can't make me pleased to see her so easily convinced."

"Perhaps it's best if you don't discuss him with her."

"That would definitely be best, but it may not be possible."

Olivia smiled in sympathy. "Try."

"Believe me, I will," said Penelope fervently. "He's the very last person I want to talk about." They were passing Madox Street, and on a whim she paused. "May we stop in a shop down there?"

"Of course." Olivia turned with her. "Which one?"

The bookshop was only a few doors down. It was small and had a slightly dingy air about it. If Mrs. Weston discovered Penelope had come here in search of a certain banned pamphlet, she'd be furious—but since Olivia was with her, her mother wouldn't be suspicious at all. Olivia was so respectable and trustworthy, Mrs. Weston hadn't even sent a maid with them.

Of course, that didn't make this any less daring. If Mrs. Weston did find out, not only would Penelope be exiled from London for months, Olivia would no longer be trusted, either. Penelope knew all this, but recklessly set any worries aside. She needed something to distract her mind from seething over Lord Atherton's latest attempt to dupe a kindhearted girl into marrying him, and there was nothing more distracting than *50 Ways to Sin*.

When she indicated the bookshop, though, Olivia gave her a wary glance. "What do you want in there?"

"Nothing much." Penelope tugged her onward as Olivia's steps noticeably slowed.

"Penelope," warned Olivia. "Don't be foolish!" Penelope gave her a look, and Olivia bit her lip. "Then let me ask for it. You'll be in such dreadful trouble if your mother discovers this . . ."

"I don't care," said Penelope, pushing open the door. At that moment, she really didn't. London had grown dull and monotonous. Abigail was rusticating in Richmond. Joan was enjoying the beauties of Italy. Penelope was going mad with boredom; witness how upset Atherton's courtship of Frances had made her. As much as she didn't want to care about anything he did, she couldn't stop herself, and it irritated her to no end. Hopefully something else, of a deliciously scandalous nature, would help her forget about him.

A bell tinkled as they went in. The bookshop was small and dim, and it smelled musty and dry. She looked around with interest, but Olivia pulled her behind a bookcase before she could see much of anything.

"Look for something else. I'll ask for *it*."

"It doesn't much matter who asks for *it*," Penelope whispered back.

"No, but if you buy something else, you can

honestly tell your mother you came in search of that, and had nothing to do with the other."

Penelope felt like cursing. If she were married or widowed, she wouldn't have to worry about her mother's approval, and could buy as many naughty pamphlets as she wanted. Of course, she didn't seem in danger of being married, let alone widowed, any time soon. Before long, seventeen-year-old Frances Lockwood would probably be married, too, leaving her marooned once more at the side of every ballroom, bored and alone. Other ladies were either scandalized by Penelope's adventurous tastes or too snobbish to associate with someone of her low birth. Gentlemen often stared at her, but the only ones who asked her to dance were friends of her brother taking pity on her, or conniving rogues who only had their eyes on her father's money or, occasionally, down her bodice. All her mother's instructions in propriety and decorum felt fussy and constricting, and following them hadn't won her anything anyway. It felt like life was passing her by.

"Olivia, if my mother thinks to ask me about this, it means she's already suspicious and I'm done for." She raised one brow at her friend's expression. "If she discovers you bought it for me, she'll ban me from seeing you. It was hard enough to lose Abigail and Joan; if I can't see you, I don't know what I'll do."

"How would she ever discover I bought it for you?" asked Olivia in a harsh whisper.

Penelope rolled her eyes. "How will she ever discover I bought it myself?" Her companion didn't look reassured. "If you want to keep us both from getting in trouble, find a book of your own and distract one of the clerks. If anyone saw us come in here, by a most unfortunate chance, I can say you were looking for that book."

Her friend sighed. "I feel like a wicked woman, contributing to the misbehavior of a young lady."

"You're not contributing. You're merely failing to stop me from misbehaving, something both Abigail and Joan also failed to do."

"And I feel worthy of any lawyer in London, drawing that distinction," retorted Olivia. "I don't know why I let you talk me into these things."

"Because you're the best sort of friend." She grinned and squeezed Olivia's hand. "And because you always want to save me from myself, even though it's hopeless."

"I certainly hope not," murmured the other woman. "Well, get on with it before my conscience gets the better of me."

"Do you require assistance, ma'am?"

They both jumped at the question. A thin young man, almost a boy, was beaming at them. "Oh! Er . . ."

"We have some novels over here," he said, holding out one hand. "Poetry as well."

"Have you anything for travelers?" Olivia asked, recovering first. "Perhaps Italy?"

The young man nodded, bobbing on his feet once more. "We do, we do indeed have a selection of books about Italy. Would you care to come this way?" He headed toward a back corner of the shop.

"Try to be quick," Olivia breathed before following him.

Penelope took a quick peek around the book-case. The shopkeeper, a rotund, pink-faced man, was attending to a tall man in a greatcoat. She remembered from Joan's report that one had to ask specifically for the pamphlet, which meant she had to wait. Keeping her ears attuned to the murmur of conversation, she turned to the shelves in front of her. The books here were old and well-worn. In some cases the titles were rubbed off the spines entirely. She took down one, only to find it was a medical text, with horrifying engravings of bones. The next one she opened released a puff of dust that made her sneeze. She put it back with a grimace. What did her sister see in bookshops? Abigail could happily visit one every day, for some utterly unknown reason.

The bell sounded; the shopkeeper was escort-ing the tall man out the door, bowing and scrap-ing all the while. He must have bought a great many books, from the shopkeeper's solicitous manner. Her heart unaccountably hammering, Penelope stepped into his path as he turned back toward the counter.

He stopped at once. "Good day, madam. May I help you find something?"

"Yes," she said, striving to sound very cool and poised. "Have you any issues of *50 Ways to Sin*?"

"Ah." He rocked back on his heels and patted his ample stomach. "I'm not certain. Very popular, those are. But if you'll pardon me a few moments, I'll have a look in the back."

She nodded, and he hurried off. As he disap-peared through the curtain behind the counter, she exchanged a glance with Olivia, who was studying a collection of books laid out on the counter by the clerk. Her friend gave a tiny nod, and asked the clerk if he had any more recent editions.

Penelope stationed herself at the other end of the counter and affected great interest in the button on her glove, straining her ears for any exclamations of discovery from the back room. She could hear rustlings and mutterings, but nothing that sounded like success. A few feet away, Olivia kept asking for other choices of travel memoirs. Penelope knew her friend was trying to draw it out as long as possible, to provide an excuse in case anyone came in. This shop was only a few steps from Bond Street, where any number of busybodies might be strolling right now, eyes alert for improper behavior.

Penelope knew she was risking extreme punishment; *50 Ways to Sin* was the most wicked thing she'd ever read. In lush, erotic detail it recounted the many adventurous love affairs of Lady Constance, a lady of very flexible morals. Penelope's mother had caught her reading it once before, and her wrath had been terrible to behold. First had come a long lecture on decent, modest behavior, all of which Penelope had already heard though she didn't dare point that out. Then had come the stern reminders that even if she had no care for her own good name—which would only demonstrate what a feckless, silly girl she was—she should bear in mind her family's reputation and how it would reflect on them. At the time Abigail had also been unwed, and it gave Penelope an honest pang to think she might tarnish her sister by association, but now Abigail was happily married, so that worry was eliminated. Even better, Abigail had married a man who endorsed her readings of *50 Ways to Sin*, contrary to her mother's dire warnings that it would disgust gentlemen, so Penelope doubted she was hurting her chances of marriage by reading it.

Her mother had finished the lecture with an expression of deep disappointment that, after all her father had done to give her a comfortable life, Penelope had recklessly gone her own way and indulged her most prurient curiosity. To that, there was no argument. However much she might wish her life was more exciting, Penelope adored her father and didn't want to disappoint him. She had sat in penitent silence, promising that she wouldn't buy any more copies of the shocking story if only Mama wouldn't tell him. To her relief, her mother had agreed, and then imposed a harsh sentence of social restriction that lasted for almost two months. Finally her penance had ended, though, and Penelope was allowed to go out without her mother or a trusted maid following her.

And here she was, breaking that promise only a few weeks later, almost tempting fate to punish her again. A part of her felt guilty, but that part wasn't big enough to overrule the rest of her, the part that felt trapped in a box that seemed smaller every day. This visit wasn't just about *50 Ways to Sin*, although it was the most deliciously wicked story imaginable; no, it was more about Penelope's longing for excitement. Love and adventure seemed to be happening to everyone except her or to Olivia, although Olivia expressed no interest in being the center of an illicit love affair or a clandestine adventure or anything exciting. As much as Penelope knew she was wrong to feel such urges, she couldn't stop them, and sometimes they simply had to be indulged or she would burst.

Hence, here she was, doing something no decent young lady in London would dream of.

Finally, after what felt like an eternity, the shopkeeper came back with a flat package tied with string. "Here you are, madam. Number thirty-four." He winked as he laid it on the counter.

She blinked, fighting to keep her voice calm. "Oh? Have you any copies of issue thirty-three as well?"

"No, I'm sorry to say I don't. These do sell quite quickly, you know."

"Yes." She smiled, hoping her expression was still cool and poised. "I understand they do." At the other end of the counter, Olivia was paging through a book. Penelope knew she wouldn't buy it; Olivia rarely had funds to spare. Today, though, Penelope felt in such good charity with the world, she impulsively told the shopkeeper to add the cost of the travel book to her own purchase, and she paid for both before her friend could protest.

"Thank you, a hundred times thank you!" Penelope all but clapped her hands in glee when they were back in Madox Street. "Oh, wasn't that a jolly trick?"

"I presume you were successful." Olivia eyed the package in her hand.

Penelope laughed. "More than successful! I've

read through issue thirty-two, but this is thirty-four. There's another one out there." It was at once thrilling and disappointing. Finding it would be a challenge, but on the other hand, she knew there was an issue to search for. It was surely a sign of how mundane her life was that she was this delighted at the prospect.

Olivia gaped at her. "You've read through—? Goodness, Penelope, where are you getting them?"

"Never mind that. What did you choose?"

"I ought not to have let you buy it," her friend said. "It was unnecessary."

Penelope waved it off. "In thanks for overlooking my scandalous behavior. What is the book?"

Real gratitude warmed Olivia's eyes. Often she resisted Penelope's and Abigail's efforts to treat her to small indulgences, no matter how hard they argued that her company was worth far more to them. "A travel book about Italy. Very decent and apt to improve my mind."

She grinned. "One can hope."

"It can hardly hurt." The other woman regarded her package almost wistfully. "I'm not likely ever to see Italy, so I hope it's an engaging account."

"Nonsense! Someday a handsome man will sweep you off your feet and carry you away to Italy, and France, and even India for all you know."

Olivia sighed. "It's a lovely dream."

"Well, why can't it come true?" Penelope raised one hand in question.

Her companion gave a rueful laugh. "That's what I adore about you, Pen; your constant quest for adventure and your certainty that something exciting *will* happen to you."

"You mean like this outing?" She made a face. "That's quite a small adventure. It's a bit sad, really. Nothing like Lady Constance's adventures, and she never even leaves London."

"What do you find so appealing about . . . her?"

Penelope glanced over in surprise. "What do you mean? You've read her stories, haven't you?"

A deep scarlet suffused her friend's face. "One or two."

They turned back into Bond Street. The wicked pamphlet was wrapped in plain paper, concealing the title, but it still felt daring to carry it right through the heart of fashionable London. Penelope fixed a pleasant look on her face and lowered her voice. "Then you know why. They're shocking. They're delicious. They're so wicked and yet so intriguing—is that really the way of it, between a man and a woman? No one wants an unmarried girl to know, which only makes us wild to discover the truth. And besides . . ." She gave a guilty little shrug. "Everyone else is reading it, why shouldn't I?"

"I doubt everyone is reading it," murmured Olivia, still red-faced. "Doesn't it seem a bit farfetched to you?"

Penelope lowered her voice even more. "Joan told me they're accurate. Even Abigail admitted it. They would tell me the truth, now that they're married and in a position to know. And that means—"

"What?" Olivia asked when she stopped.

Penelope cleared her throat. "That means I ought to read them. They're instructional."

"Instructional?" Olivia gaped at her, then choked on a laugh. "You're incorrigible, Penelope."

"Absolutely," she agreed, although her own smile was forced. Yes, *50 Ways to Sin* was even more intriguing for being accurate, but Penelope would have wanted to read them anyway. Right or wrong, they were the closest she'd come to actual passion. Combined with her growing feeling that there wasn't a man in London she wanted to marry, Penelope thought it would be wise to learn a little something before she broke her mother's heart and embarked on a life of sin. She might well be a spinster forever, but she needn't be a virginal lady that long. Lady Constance seemed to have worked it all out; she managed to live among the *ton* in London, enjoy a talented new lover whenever she chose, and make a fortune on the retellings of her erotic adventures. If even half the people who whispered about *50 Ways to Sin* behind their fans at balls were buying issues, Constance must be making more money than she could count. It all sounded thrilling to Penelope, an intoxicating mixture of freedom and indulgence.

That didn't mean she wouldn't welcome something more. Every time she saw her sister exchange a glance with her new husband, Penelope felt a stab of envy. As shocking and delicious as Lady Constance's adventures were, Abigail had done one better: she'd found a man who offered her not only passion but also companionship and love. Constance herself admitted her heart was untouched by any of her lovers, which seemed a little sad to Penelope—wild and wicked and thrilling, but in the end, more lonely than not.

She gave herself a shake. Wanting more didn't change the fact that she currently had none of those things. She wasn't completely out of hope, but Penelope had never been good at waiting patiently. It would probably take another year or two before her mother accepted defeat and stopped making her brother, James, introduce her to gentlemen. She felt sorry for those men, who were always polite but also uninterested in her. She wished her brother would grow a spine and tell Mama that no one he knew wanted to court her, but failing that, she'd just have to wait it out. If Lady Constance kept writing, and Frances miraculously decided to reject Lord Atherton, she would probably be able to endure it.

Chapter 4

Of course, fate must have overheard her silent wish and set out to thwart it at the first opportunity. Not two days later, Frances Lockwood drew her aside at a Venetian breakfast.

"I have tremendous news," she began, her face glowing.

Please don't say Atherton, Penelope thought. "Indeed?"

"It is the best sort!" She gripped Penelope's hand. "Lord Atherton has spoken to my father!"

Of course he had. Penelope kept smiling and said nothing.

"He hasn't proposed to me yet, but oh, Miss Weston—I can scarcely breathe, thinking of it! What shall I say to him? How shall I respond? Please tell me, I am in terrible fear of making a fool of myself!"

She took her time replying. Olivia's advice echoed in her mind: *Just because you don't care for him doesn't mean she can't.* It was possible, she supposed, that Lord Atherton would fall deeply in love with Frances as he got to know her, as they lived together and spent time together and had a family together. She had to take a deep breath at the thought of him taking Frances to bed and making passionate love to her. "You must respond as your heart directs," she settled for saying. "Do you care for the gentleman enough to spend the rest of your life with him?"

Frances blinked, her perfect little mouth dropping open as if she'd never thought of anything past the wedding. "Oh. Oh my. Goodness, that does sound a bit daunting."

"That's why you should be absolutely certain of your regard for him, and his for you, before you accept."

"Well, yes," said Frances slowly, then more firmly. "Yes! I've never met a handsomer, more charming gentleman, I'm certain of it."

That wasn't what I asked. Penelope bit it back. "If you're sure of his love, too, then you should say yes."

Her friend's forehead creased. "Why . . . I—I don't quite know if he loves me." She hesitated, then added as if to assure both of them, "But my mother says love is not paramount in such matches, and I should choose a man who is amiable and polite. Is that not sound advice, too?"

Penelope racked her brain for a plausible reason to excuse herself and bolt from the room. She was having an increasingly difficult time holding her tongue. "Those are indeed very admirable qualities."

"But not the most important?" asked Frances anxiously. "Oh, I want to make the right decision!"

Ask him why he wants to marry you. "I'm sure you will."

Frances was quiet for a moment, which was rare. "You don't like him, do you?"

She started. Why oh why couldn't Frances have attracted any suitor other than Lord Arrogant Atherton? "What? Er . . . Whatever gives you that idea?"

Frances bit her lip. "My other friends gasped with delight when I told them he'd spoken to Papa. None of them urged me to consider his affection for me. They assume it, if he intends to propose marriage."

"Never assume anything about Lord Atherton." The words flew out of her mouth before she could stop them. Frances's eyes rounded in shock, and Penelope could have smacked her own face. She rushed to repair the damage. "I mean, a lady should never assume anything about any man. Choosing a husband is the most important decision she can make . . ." Her voice trailed off and she wished she hadn't spoken.

"What do you mean?"

"Nothing," muttered Penelope. She tried to smile. "Don't pay me any attention, I might have a headache coming on . . ."

"No! Please tell me." Frances stared at her in worry. "This is the rest of my life at stake!"

Penelope took one last agonizing look around for anyone who could save her. But this breakfast was filled with drawling lords and proud ladies who would never have invited her if not for Papa's fortune, and even that couldn't make them speak to her. Olivia wasn't here, her mother was off sharing a gossip with some of the less snobbish matrons, and that left Penelope to her own devices—a situation that had rarely led to anything good, even when she was really trying to behave, as she was now.

She said a quick prayer for tact. "If you don't know his feelings for you, perhaps you should ask him. A man in love will have no hesitation in declaring himself."

"Declaring himself?"

"Yes. You know, going down on one knee and swearing he couldn't live without you, or some such thing."

Frances blinked. "Oh yes, I—I see. That *would* be very flattering and romantic . . . Is that what you expect?"

"Absolutely," said Penelope with relish. This was much safer conversational territory. She had never hidden her preference for romance and drama and grand gestures. "I want nothing less." A faint smile crossed her face as she pictured her imaginary lover, passionate and devoted. "A man who would fight a duel for me. A man who would die for me. A man who has no hesitation telling me he loves me, desperately and passionately, every day of our marriage."

"That—that doesn't sound like something most Englishmen would do," protested Frances, her brow knit in worry.

"Then they aren't for me," declared Penelope. "I shall have to wait for a foreign cavalier, or a dashing privateer. No milk-and-water man for me, I want a man of passion and action. A man who won't leave me in doubt of his feelings, but who would sweep me away for an ardent kiss, and damn the consequences."

Frances seemed dazed. "Goodness . . ."

Penelope calmed down from her fervent speech, and smiled at her friend. "Now you must see why I'm relegated to the spinsters. None of these English gentlemen have the dash and passion I prefer."

Her companion was quiet for a moment. "But how would you know such a man? Why, if a gentleman tried to sweep me away for a kiss, my mama would intervene. How can one find a passionate suitor when one always has a chaperone?"

"I don't know," said Penelope, uninterested in such logical details, "but a determined man would find a way."

"Yes," said her friend slowly, "yes, of course he would. A man in love would not be deterred."

"Nothing would stand in his way," Penelope agreed.

"A man in love would be overcome with passion at least once, wouldn't he?"

"I hope so," she replied with a laugh. "Or it's not a very exciting sort of love."

"Of course." Frances's face grew serious. For a moment she appeared deep in thought, then her expression cleared. "If Lord Atherton wants to marry me, he must love me, mustn't he?"

"Ah . . ." Too late Penelope realized she ought to have held her tongue. Still, she was only speaking the truth as she saw it. "He certainly should."

"And if he loves me, he should prove it," went on Frances, more eagerly.

Since Penelope thought it highly unlikely that

Lord Atherton was in love with anyone except possibly himself, she didn't say anything.

"But he hasn't." The younger girl looked at her and demanded, "Should I tell him he must?"

She coughed. She cleared her throat. "I don't know . . . If you have to tell him to do it, how will you know it sprang from his true desires and not merely from the urge to please you?"

For a moment Frances's gaze grew sharp and probing. "Do you think he won't want to?"

Oh Lord. "I have no idea what Lord Atherton wants."

"But you are acquainted with him."

"Slightly," Penelope stressed. "Very, *very* slightly, for a brief time. It was hardly a month! It's somewhat shocking to me that he remembers me at all." It was also somewhat annoying. Penelope certainly wished she could forget him. But Frances still looked troubled, and she didn't want that. She could easily picture Mrs. Lockwood calling on her own mother to accuse Penelope of stirring up trouble in Frances's betrothal, and there would be another friend lost.

She took a deep breath and squeezed her friend's hand. "Don't let me divert you from what you feel in your heart. If he loves you, and you love him, that is what matters. If he loves you, he'll have no difficulty confessing it. I expect that will lead to other proof of his love, and then you'll know how you should answer his question."

"You really think so?"

Penelope beamed, pleased that the other girl sounded relieved. All Frances needed to hear was a word or two of affection from Atherton, true or not, and she would be satisfied. Surely even he wasn't such an idiot as to omit that entirely. "Of course! Oh—you must excuse me, my mother is looking for me."

"Thank you, Miss Weston," said Frances fervently. "I'm ever so grateful."

"Just remember to trust your own heart," Penelope said, "and never mind what other people say."

"I won't," Frances assured her. Penelope smiled once more and hurried away, never so glad in all her life to see her mother waiting for her.

Chapter 5

Every time he thought about her, Benedict Lennox reached the same conclusions: Frances Lockwood was sweet, pretty, and honest. She was young, granted—ten years younger than himself at least—but that was hardly a fault. They got on well together, and he doubted there would be much discord between them. She had good connections as well. In short, she met every criterion he had set for a bride.

Furthermore, to his relief, she hadn't mentioned Penelope again. Perhaps that was yet another sign that this courtship would be smoother than his last. He'd spoken to Mr. Lockwood and received a very gracious blessing. Mrs. Lockwood beamed every time she saw him, as did Frances herself. All the signs were encouraging.

The only thing he didn't know was why he was still hesitating. If anything, he ought to move quickly to settle the matter, but instead . . . He scanned the drawing room at yet another party, irate at himself. Instead of taking swift action to secure the bride he'd chosen, he was still stewing over Penelope Weston's last words to him. A man should be consumed with passion for his wife! *In what society?* he quietly fumed. Certainly not this one. He watched Lord and Lady Rotherham enter the drawing room and immediately part ways, the viscount heading for the card room and his wife joining the Earl of Wilbur, who was widely known to be her lover. Both Rotherhams would enjoy their evening, even though they likely wouldn't see each other again before morning. That was normal marriage, not some dramatic passion Penelope had read about in women's novels.

Not that he intended to be like Rotherham. Benedict wanted a wife he could respect and like, and he didn't want to be a cuckold. That was why Frances was perfect for him. There was enough affection between them to rule out troublesome complications like lovers and mistresses, but not enough to cause strife within their marriage. Passion was far from vital. It was all well and good for Penelope to talk of it with approval, she of the high spirits and exuberant temperament and daring sense of adventure; of course she would want passionate encounters and dramatic declarations. She would be the sort of wife who drove a man wild, who made love in carriages and on picnic blankets and on the dining room table and—

He reined in his thoughts. It didn't matter to him where Penelope would make love to her husband, who was likely to be a broken, if sated, man after a few years with her. That was none of his concern. Benedict forced himself to survey the room again. This time he saw Miss Lockwood, so he headed toward her.

She was as pleased as ever to see him, and after a few minutes' conversation he led her out on his arm. Their conversation was limited during the country dance, but when it was over and he asked if she would take a turn with him in the quieter corridor outside the drawing room, she eagerly agreed.

"Thank you for walking out with me," he said as they strolled, her hand nestled in the crook of his arm.

The smile she flashed him was different than usual—more flirtatious, even coy. "I'm sure you had good reason for asking me."

"I did," he agreed. It was time to cross the Rubicon. "A very special one."

Miss Lockwood seemed to lean a little closer on his arm. "Perhaps we should find a quieter place?"

"Very well," he said after a startled pause. It wasn't like her to suggest that; usually she was very conscious of propriety and decorum. But then he had spoken to her father already, so perhaps her parents had given her permission to bend those rules. After all, he meant to propose, and although a quiet alcove would suffice, more privacy was always welcome. At the turn of the hall he tried a doorknob and showed her into a small music room, bathed in silvery light by the full moon hanging low over the neighboring rooftops. He left the door open, but she reached behind her and nudged it almost closed.

He gave her a curious glance, but she just tipped

her head to one side and waited, beaming back at him. Benedict shook off his hesitation; if she meant to refuse him, she wouldn't have closeted them. It was a good sign. He reached for her hand. "Miss Lockwood, it's been a very great pleasure becoming acquainted with you."

"I have also enjoyed your company, my lord."

"We get on well together, don't we?" He eased a step nearer. "And share so many interests."

She leaned toward him almost playfully. "Are you mad for me?"

"I beg your pardon?" Benedict frowned in bemusement. "I am deeply fond of you and expect we will only grow closer as time goes on. I believe we would be happy together, and I very much hope you agree."

"But now," she said, a little insistently. "At this moment, are you madly in love with me? Would you fight a duel over me? Would you *die* for me?"

"Die for you," he repeated in disbelief. "What on earth are you talking about?"

"I want to marry a man who adores me," she exclaimed, clasping both hands to her heart. "A man who declares his undying love for me every day!"

Suddenly he knew what had happened. "Did Miss Weston tell you to say that?" he asked, thin-lipped.

"Do you love me?" she boldly demanded. "If you do, you should have no trouble saying so!"

"That interfering little baggage," he said under his breath. "Miss Lockwood, this is not what I expected from you—"

"Perhaps this is how I really am." She put her hands on his chest and stepped closer, thrusting her face up almost accusingly. "You've never even tried to kiss me. Don't you want to?"

He wanted to wring Penelope's lovely neck. Benedict's temper strained at the seams. How dare she instill her extravagant romantic notions into a proper young lady's head? Where was the sweet, anxious-to-please Frances Lockwood he'd decided to marry? If he wanted this bold, demanding sort of woman, why, he might as well marry Penelope herself.

With jerky motions he took her hands in his and removed them from his chest. "Forgive me," he said, controlling his voice with great effort. "Something seems to have come over you—"

"I just want to know if you love me." She pulled free and raised her chin. "I thought you must, because you spoke to my father. You led him to believe you want to marry me. If you want to marry me, you must care for me, and yet you won't say it."

"What am I supposed to say?" he snapped. "What reply did Miss Weston tell you to demand?"

Her expression became almost mulish. "This has nothing to do with her. Why are you always asking about her?"

He shoved his hands through his hair. "Christ! She's the last person I want to speak of!"

"Your language, sir," she gasped, but Benedict had had enough.

"I cannot guess if this is your true self or if you're just acting some part you think would amuse Penelope Weston, but I must tell you, it's not very appealing. You want me to fight a duel over you? Over what? Do you expect to carry on with all sorts of men without even bothering to be discreet about it? Because that's what drives men to duel, my dear—a faithless woman who doesn't give a damn about the consequences of her actions. And if you intend to be that sort of woman, I most certainly will not be swearing my undying love to you, let alone risking my life for you."

Her blue eyes were perfectly round, glistening with shocked tears, and the plume in her hair quivered with her every breath. "You—you—you heartless *monster*. I don't want to see you ever again!" She turned on her heel and stomped across the room with her hands in fists at her sides. The door crashed against the wall when she flung it open, and he listened to her footsteps patter rapidly down the hall.

"Damn it!" Benedict stalked back and forth across the room. "God bloody damn it!" He slammed his fist into the wall, cursing again as pain jolted up his arm. He shook out his fingers and seethed.

She was the devil. That was the only explanation. A golden-haired, blue-eyed devil with a siren's smile, whose sole mission in life was to undermine his plans and then gloat over the smoking ruins of his hopes. He could just imagine her satisfied little smile when Frances Lockwood told her the news: he'd been rejected once more and lost yet another prospective bride. In honesty, he didn't think Abigail Weston's refusal had been Penelope's doing, but there was no question that she had instigated Miss Lockwood's little drama tonight. *Would you die for me?* Was that what women wanted these days? What the bloody blazes was the world coming to?

Benedict flexed his aching fingers and told himself to think. So Frances Lockwood didn't want to see him ever again. Perhaps that was a mercy. Even if she changed her mind, the damage was done; there was a side of her he'd never seen before, and he could only be glad she had revealed herself before it was too late. But it was incontrovertible that Penelope Weston had wrought some mischief, and he positively burned to confront her about it. If he didn't, she might take it as a sign of cowardice or weakness. It was all too easy to imagine Penelope blithely telling every young lady of the *ton* that he was a coldhearted scoundrel whom everyone else had already refused to marry.

"Damn," he muttered once more. It wasn't remotely true, but two rejected marriage proposals were bad enough, and rumors like that could dog a fellow for years—and he didn't have years to spend on finding a bride. He really hadn't thought it would take *this* long. England was full of ladies in search of a handsome nobleman to marry, and at least a few had plump dowries. It just appeared none of them wanted him.

Unlike many of his mates, Benedict felt more than ready to marry. Not out of any poetical yearning for love or because he was eager to settle down, but because he was tired of being jerked back and forth by his father's whimsy like a puppet on a string. The Earl of Stratford kept a tight rein on his family, controlling his wife and children through every means at his disposal. Benedict had managed some level of escape, but he was still tied to his father by the purse strings. More than once the earl had cut off his funds with no warning. More than once Benedict had had to go crawling back to beg for money, which was given only after a period of penance and some act of contrition. For years he'd endured it, but his father's demands grew too punishing. Stratford had set him every objectionable task possible: sacking loyal servants of long standing, making unreasonable demands of solicitors and tradesmen, snubbing acquaintances who displeased the earl, bullying art dealers who didn't meet the earl's standards. Enough was enough.

For a gentleman in Benedict's position, though, independence wasn't easy. He had no profession except soldiering, and that hardly paid well—if anything, it cost a great deal. He had no capital to invest, not even a small sum he could have used to take himself to America or the West Indies, where a man might start from nothing. He had no head for politics, no exceptional talent, nothing except his name and his face . . . which were both, to be blunt, very appealing to ladies. Obviously the answer was a wealthy bride.

Unfortunately heiresses seemed to be in short supply this year. Even including scandalous widows and the daughters of merchants, he'd met only a few women who seemed tolerable. Benedict didn't really want to exchange his father's tyranny for a wife's, but every woman of reason and property had half a dozen suitors already. When his sister wrote to him last spring that a wealthy man with two beautiful daughters had bought an estate near Stratford Court in

Richmond, it seemed like a gift from heaven. A quick journey home proved him right. Abigail Weston was beautiful, kind, modest, and sensible. To his delight, they got on well together. He could envision a companionable life with her. For a few short weeks last summer, everything had seemed within his grasp.

If only he had known that courting Abigail Weston would wind up being a colossal mistake. It certainly hadn't appeared to be one at the time. No one had told him she was secretly in love with another man. No one had warned him he'd lose her to Sebastian Vane, who had once been his dearest friend before his father had managed to ruin that, too.

Losing Abigail's hand hurt, and not merely for the sting of being found wanting next to Sebastian. In her, he thought he'd found the perfect solution: a wife he could care for and respect, with a fortune that would render him, finally and for all time, independent of his father. Instead he had been rejected, rather strongly, and then he'd had to endure his father's contempt over his failure, because he must have cocked it up very badly if the lady preferred a man with a bad leg and a deranged parent.

And to top it all off, it seemed he'd somehow earned Penelope Weston's animosity, which apparently hadn't faded in the slightest.

The thought of Penelope revived his temper. That minx. Did she plan to bedevil him forever? No, he vowed at once; he couldn't let her. He ignored the fact that his attempt at cordial reconciliation hadn't gone well. This time she wouldn't be left to gloat at his predicament without consequence. And so even though he knew he shouldn't—even though he suspected no earthly good could possibly come of confronting her about her actions—he set off to find her.

Chapter 6

After some thought, Penelope decided it was better if she avoided Frances Lockwood's company for a few days.

Partly it was cowardice. She didn't want to listen to raptures about Frances's engagement to Lord Atherton, or her excited wedding plans, or long, dreamy odes on how very handsome he was. As much as she wanted Frances to be happy, she didn't think she could bear to listen to her friend go on and on about how Atherton adored her or the way he kissed her. Just the thought made her feel like flinging herself off a balcony.

But it was also partly discretion. She had a bad feeling she'd spoken too rashly, too recklessly at the Venetian breakfast. Penelope knew she was very fortunate to have parents who indulged—or at least tolerated—her dramatic tendencies and natural cheekiness. Frances was not as lucky, and if she followed Penelope's lead, she could find herself in terrible trouble. Therefore, avoiding Frances wasn't merely for her own sake, to avoid hearing Atherton's name, but for Frances's sake as well.

When they reached the Gosnold rout, she stuck by her mother instead of seizing the relative freedom she was afforded at parties to mingle with other young ladies. Her mother gave her a mildly surprised look, but took it in stride. Penelope stood at her mother's side, a polite smile fixed on her face and feeling absolutely certain that her brain was slowly softening like butter left in the sun. Married ladies talked about nothing: Mrs. Archer shared a long anecdote about a vexing situation with a maid; Mrs. Heathcomb described, in minute detail, her new set of china; and Lady Danford couldn't resist any opportunity to mention her daughter's recent engagement to Baron Redmaine.

She knew they talked about more exciting things when they were alone. After all, she'd started reading *50 Ways to Sin* after overhearing a tantalizing bit of conversation among these same ladies. It had taken her a whole week of surreptitious searching to find her mother's copy of the wicked story, which was even more risqué than she'd expected. For a few minutes she indulged in imagining what would happen if she asked them all what they'd thought of issue thirty-four, where Constance found her pleasure in a carriage.

Thankfully, a familiar face caught her eye before she could give in to the dangerous urge. She leaned toward her mother. "Mama, I see Olivia over there. May I join her?" At her parent's nod, she slipped through the crowd, keeping a careful distance from the dancers, who had recently included Lord Atherton with Frances Lockwood. Resolutely she kept her gaze away, focused on

Olivia. It was a surprise to see her here, although a welcome one. Olivia wasn't always invited to routs and balls, and Penelope suspected she didn't even attend all the ones she was invited to. Abigail had once told her Olivia couldn't afford the wardrobe for it, which was partly why the sisters made a point of buying small gifts for her. Mr. Weston could well afford the purchase of another bonnet or pair of gloves, and it enabled his daughters to see their friend more often.

But there was something off about Olivia tonight. She stood alone near the doorway, and instead of wearing her usual warm smile and air of enjoyment, her face was pale and almost grim. Now that Penelope thought about it, she'd seen that look on Olivia's face before, especially when she thought no one was watching her. Penelope frowned; what was wrong? Tonight Olivia seemed to be searching for someone. Her gaze was roving over the room, but then stopped. She gave a tiny nod before turning and slipping out of the room.

Penelope craned her neck, trying to deduce at whom Olivia had nodded. There was a cluster of gentlemen in the general area, some of them frightfully handsome and rakish. Questions blossomed in her mind: Was Olivia having an affair? She started to smile in astonishment at this possibility, but then remembered her friend's expression. That made her frown. Surely Olivia would have looked more pleased—even eager—if she was meeting one of those handsome rogues for a tryst. Still frowning, she followed her friend out of the drawing room.

The Gosnold house was spacious and grand,

with the staircase in a sweeping central hall.
Penelope just caught sight of Olivia as she vanished down it. It took forever to descend against
the flow of guests still arriving and going up. At
the bottom Penelope turned left, but that only led
toward the servants' stair, so she went through
the hall and down the opposite corridor.

This part of the house wasn't open for guests.
It was quiet and rather dim away from the rout.
Penelope hesitated, then heard a door open and
close ahead somewhere. Curiosity and a trace
of concern propelled her forward. She'd be careful; the last thing she wanted to do was interrupt
something amorous, but her imagination was capable of supplying many more unpleasant possibilities. Someone could be blackmailing Olivia, or
threatening her, or simply harassing her.

At the door Penelope stopped to listen. A faint
murmur of voices came through the wood, a man's
deeper voice and after a long pause a female voice.
Penelope strained her ears. There was another silence, then a gasp . . . and then a sob. Her eyes
grew round and she listened even harder, pressing her ear to the wood. "Please," she made out
Olivia saying. "Don't make me do this . . ."

Without hesitation Penelope grasped the doorknob and turned it.

Olivia stood facing the door. The man behind
her had one arm around her waist, and his other
hand around her throat as he pressed his face to
the side of her neck. When Penelope opened the
door, the sudden burst of light made her friend
turn away, but not before Penelope saw the anguish on her face. Any worry that she'd interrupted

a romantic rendezvous vanished from her mind. She stepped boldly into the room.

"Olivia," she said brightly. "There you are! I've been looking everywhere for you."

Olivia wrenched free and stumbled several steps forward. For a moment she just stood, visibly trembling, her hands pressed flat to her skirt. She kept her chin down, but not far enough to hide the red imprint of fingers on her neck. "Yes. Here I am."

The man who'd been holding Olivia slowly raised his head and glared at Penelope. With a shock of disgust, she recognized Simon, Lord Clary. He was only a viscount, but had excellent connections. His wife was a duke's daughter, and his mother came from an illustrious naval family. He was widely regarded as a handsome man: black hair, expertly brushed around his high, pale forehead. Deep, dark eyes. A long, aristocratic nose. A mouth that looked carved from stone. He was aloof, mysterious, and always wore an expression that suggested he was faintly bored by everyone nearby. Some thought he was madly attractive. Privately, Penelope thought he looked like the devil. That was not the dark and dangerous air she found appealing. In fact, it was more like menace.

"Mrs. Jennings was looking for you," Penelope went on in the same obliviously cheery tone. "She was admiring the bonnet you wore the other day and I believe she meant to ask where you got your trimmings." It was all a lie, and Olivia would know that; neither of them knew anyone called Mrs. Jennings.

Olivia glanced at Clary. Her face was dead white. "Thank you," she said, very softly. Clary made a noise like a growl, and she leapt backward. Her eyes glittered, and Penelope realized it wasn't anger or fear driving her friend, but hatred. Without another word Olivia whipped around and all but ran out the door, clutching her skirts.

Penelope stared after her in amazement. What in blazes? She took a step after Olivia, but was brought up short when Lord Clary seized her arm.

"You're a forward wench," he said quietly.

"I'm not a wench, I'm a young lady," she returned. "And I didn't think it was forward to speak to one of my dearest friends, which Mrs. Townsend is."

"Mrs. Townsend was engaged in a private conversation—which you interrupted."

"Did I?" Penelope made her eyes very round and wide like a ninny. "Good heavens, sir, I had no idea! I'm dreadfully sorry."

He stared at her for a moment. "Are you?" he murmured at last. "How sorry?"

Not as sorry as I am to be still talking to you, she thought. "Profoundly sorry. In fact, I'm quite prostrate with shame and regret. I feel faint from it, in fact—oh dear, I may swoon! I'd better find my mother at once!" She tried to pull out of his grip, thinking it was time to retreat.

"We wouldn't want that." Lord Clary reached past her to push the door closed. "You must sit down." With an iron grip on her arm, he yanked her across the room to an armchair, spun her around, and shoved her into it. And as Penelope tried to catch her breath, he went down on one knee in front of her and braced his hands on the arms of the chair. "Did she bid you follow her into this room?"

"Who? Mrs. Townsend?" Penelope forced herself to stay calm, when she really wanted to poke him in the eye and run for it. "Of course not."

"Hmm." He leaned closer. "Your arrival was quite . . . inconvenient."

"Was it?" She blinked innocently. "It did look as though Mrs. Townsend had a prior engagement, though, so your conversation would have soon ended anyway, don't you think?"

He leaned closer yet, until his face was very near hers. Up close she could see the veins beneath the pale skin of his temple. He lowered his head and inhaled a long breath. "You smell delicious," he whispered.

For the first time a frisson of alarm went down her spine. "How kind of you to say so. The perfume was a gift from my father. My mother is very fond of it, too." Somehow, frequent and repeated mentions of her parents seemed necessary, so he would know she wasn't without protection. Unlike Olivia.

"You don't smell like a virginal little girl." He traced one finger down the ribbon edging her bodice. "Nor act like one."

"Take your hands off me," she said, firmly but quietly. "I am not a little girl, but a young lady capable of screaming very loudly if assaulted."

"Assaulted?" A smile slowly curved his lips, making him look almost demonic. "I haven't touched you." Giving the lie to his words, his finger bumped over the ribbon, brushing her skin more than once.

"And you'd better not," she replied. "Let me pass, sir."

"Not yet." He lightly touched the brooch pinned at her bosom, right between her breasts. "You've got a bit of a reputation already, Miss Weston. A bit daring, a bit scandalous, far too adventuresome for a proper young lady . . . But perhaps that's to be expected of an upstart schemer."

She struggled to contain her temper. "I shall overlook your general ignorance of my reputation, to say nothing of your repulsive true nature, if you stand aside and let me go at once."

"Who would believe you over me, anyway?" he went on. "I have connections your father can only dream of. If you—or he—were to accuse me of anything, well . . ." He shrugged. "But your friend Mrs. Townsend promised me something this evening, and you prevented her from giving it to me. Perhaps I ought to collect it from you instead."

Penelope didn't move, but she glared at him with icy hatred. "You don't deserve the slightest thing from her, or from me."

He raised one brow. "Deserve? Who said anything about deserving it? But now that you have, perhaps you should learn what happens to curious little girls who interrupt assignations."

Her shock upon learning that Olivia had, in fact, made an assignation with this disgusting man was quickly put aside when Lord Clary suddenly ripped the brooch from her gown. The lace at her neckline tore off with it, to her outrage.

"Let's just have a touch," he said, and grabbed her breast in a rough squeeze.

Acting on advice from her brother, Penelope brought up her knee, right between Lord Clary's legs. She didn't manage to do it as hard as Jamie had suggested, but apparently it was enough. Clary cursed and rocked back, just enough for her to get her other foot against his chest and kick for all she was worth. He tumbled over backward and she scrambled out of the chair. Her voice seemed to have fled; her heart was racing so hard her hands shook. Outraged, appalled, and furiously frightened, she tried to run for the door, only to feel his hand clamp around her ankle.

"The bitch likes a bit of a scratch and tumble, eh?" He yanked, sending her crashing to the floor so hard she saw stars. "I can play at that."

"You disgusting pig!" Penelope kicked again, but her dancing slippers didn't have the impact she wanted.

Lord Clary thrust his other hand up her skirts, seizing her knee in a painful grip. "Disgusting? I just want what any man wants. If you're the only female around to provide it—"

"My father will kill you!" Penelope twisted, but he had her. All her wriggling had thrown up her skirts, and as Lord Clary plowed his hand farther upward, her petticoats were being tossed aside as well, baring her legs.

"I don't give a damn about your father," muttered her assailant—for that's what Penelope was rapidly realizing he was. "Nor your bloody brother nor cousins."

"How about me?" The voice rang through the

room, deadly calm and icy cold. Penelope looked up through the locks of hair that had fallen over her face, and her heart leapt. Benedict Lennox, Lord Atherton, stood in the doorway, very tall and dark and angry. Or so it appeared from her position sprawled on the floor.

"I said, do you give a damn about me?" he repeated when no one spoke. He stepped into the room and closed the door behind him with an audible click. "On your feet, Clary."

Lord Clary gave Penelope one last malevolent look before shoving her away and rising to his feet. Penelope scrambled to safety behind the armchair, and watched with speechless gratitude as Atherton, one of her least favorite people in the world, advanced on Lord Clary. For a second his gaze flickered her way. "Are you hurt, Miss Weston?"

Wordlessly she shook her head. It wasn't true. There would be bruises on her knee, and she probably wouldn't be able to sleep for days, with the memory of Clary's repellent touch and intentions fresh in her mind. But the thought of what hurt she would have suffered in a few minutes left her mute with relief.

"Good." Atherton turned back to Clary, who was straightening his jacket and looking furious. "Get out of this house."

Clary's lip curled. "Mind your manners, young man."

Atherton began unbuttoning his regimental coat. "You may address me as Atherton, although I'd rather you didn't speak to me at all. Get out of this house, or I'll ruin you."

Clary laughed. "How? By insinuating I had a liaison with her? Try it. I'll not hesitate to tell everyone she met me here, eager for a little adventure. No one else in town will have her, even with her father's coal-tainted millions."

A hot ball of rage burned in Penelope's chest. What the devil had Olivia been thinking to meet such a man? If Penelope hadn't followed her, it would be Olivia here, with bruises and most likely worse. Clary was angry to have been interrupted, but he hadn't been treating Olivia much more gently, in the glimpse Penelope had seen.

"Try it." Atherton straightened his shoulders. "But I wouldn't recommend it. I'll tell them you had something more like rape on your mind."

"I didn't rape her." Clary's eyes glinted as he faced Penelope again. "No one will believe you."

"But if I say that you tried to force yourself on me . . ." Atherton paused as Clary's face blanked in shock. "It will explain why I did this." And before Clary could react, Lord Atherton punched him in the gut, not once but twice.

The viscount must have had considerably more power in his punch than Penelope had in her kick. Lord Clary went down on his knees, turning green and gasping for air. Atherton grabbed the man's cravat and yanked, forcing Clary's head upward until he looked as though he was being hanged. "Take your leave or take your chances," Atherton said in the same even tone.

From where Penelope huddled behind the armchair, Clary's chances didn't look good. Lord Atherton loomed over him like the Angel of Death, his free hand still in a fist. She gazed up at him with a little bit of awe. It was mildly astonishing that he had come to her rescue, particularly in such a gallant and primal fashion. It was almost enough to make her forget that she disliked him, and instead notice how strong and tall and spectacularly handsome he was . . .

She closed her eyes and turned away, whispering a bad word very softly. She did not want to notice how tall and strong and handsome he was. He'd been that way since she met him, and had quickly proved himself undeserving of admiration. She still felt like a fool for being so taken in by his appearance and charm. Thank God her sister hadn't married him. Thank God no one knew that her first feelings toward him had been so decidedly opposite the intense dislike she now felt for him . . . most of the time.

She kept her eyes averted as Lord Clary hissed something profane before rising to his feet. From the scuffling sounds, Atherton didn't make it easy for him, but then footsteps crossed the room. Penelope looked up just in time to receive one last poisonous glare from Clary before he left the room, leaving her alone with Atherton.

Chapter 7

For a moment the silence was deafening.

"Are you positive he didn't hurt you?" asked the viscount again.

Penelope flinched. "I'm not lying!"

He gave her a curious look, no doubt wondering why she was snapping at him when he had just saved her from being mauled. "I didn't say so." He put out his hand.

This time she blushed, ashamed of herself. "I'm sorry," she mumbled as she pulled herself up, using the chair for support instead of his hand. "I can't believe he—" An unexpected swell of tears caught her by surprise. She swiped at her eyes in horror.

"Sit down." Without waiting for a reply, Atherton pushed her back into the armchair and went down on his knee. "What did he do to you?" His gaze dipped, taking in her ripped bodice and tumbledown hair.

"He grabbed me and tore off my brooch. He trapped me in this chair and wouldn't let me leave." She tried to shove her hair away from her face, but it flopped back every time. Her hands had begun shaking so hard she could barely feel them. "I started to run, but he grabbed my foot and then—then—" Her throat closed as she remembered the brutal grip of Clary's fingers on her knee.

Atherton's eyes darkened. He took a handkerchief from his pocket and offered it without comment. "Why were you here with him?"

She wiped her eyes with the handkerchief, using it as a shield against his scrutiny. "Chance. I didn't intend to meet him, if that's what you're implying."

"I certainly thought you were cleverer than that." He glanced down as Penelope gaped in astonishment. "Is your foot harmed?" She tried to wiggle her foot, stopping at the sharp pain that ensued. The viscount heard her intake of breath. "May I feel the bone, to see if it's broken?"

Penelope wanted to say no, but now her ankle throbbed hard enough to bring renewed tears to her eyes. She nodded.

He didn't look at her as he took her foot in his hands. She felt a bit light-headed as he pushed aside the flounce of her skirt and ran one warm palm up her shin. For a fraught moment she imagined his hand would keep sliding upward, not cruelly like Clary's but tenderly—seductively. She jerked her gaze away from his dark head, telling herself she was vastly relieved when his fingers slid back down to her ankle, where he gently pressed and prodded the bone. His touch eased when she whimpered. "I don't think it's broken, but you'd better rest it a few days."

"Thank you." She ought to take her foot out of his hand, but somehow she didn't.

"Your stocking is ripped, too." He raised his eyes. They were the deepest blue she'd ever seen. "What set Lord Clary off?"

"His evil nature," she whispered.

"No doubt. But I've never heard a breath of reproach about him; I find it hard to believe he makes a habit of attacking young ladies at balls, especially not when they struggle and try to flee." Penelope bit her lip as he studied her, his brilliant gaze far too keen and watchful. "What did you say to him? He looked rather vengeful when he left."

"*You* punched him."

"In your defense."

Penelope looked away from the pointed truth of that. "I can't say." He released her foot and sat back. "Please don't think I'm not grateful," she added in a rush. "I am—enormously. But I can't tell you why Clary was angry at me." She refused to mention Olivia's name in connection with Clary, and to be honest, she hardly knew anything anyway. Yet.

"I suggest you take care to avoid him, then." Atherton sighed. "Should I fetch your mother?"

"No!" she exclaimed. "No, I—I'm perfectly fine." Penelope wouldn't be sorry for her mother's company, but she did not want to explain how she'd become such a mess.

"You look like you've been riding to hounds in a hurricane," he said bluntly. "Your hair is all falling down."

For some reason a flush warmed her skin. She

hoped he didn't notice. "How gallant of you to remark on it." She reached up and began feeling for pins, irrationally wishing he would go even as she didn't want to be alone. It was just so strange, so unsettling for Lord Atherton to be on bended knee before her, gazing at her with such intent concern.

Atherton watched her for a moment. Penelope could feel it even though she kept her face averted as she wrestled with her hair. Half of it had fallen from the pins, while the other half felt like one large knot. Her fingers were still trembling and his nearness wasn't helping. "Here," he said at last. "You're making it worse." And without asking for permission, he combed his fingers through her hair, brushing aside her hands.

Penelope held very still. She clenched her hands into fists in her lap and stared fiercely at them, as if that could help her ignore the feel of his hands running through her hair, extracting one pin after another, almost like a husband or a lover would do. Inside her mind she called herself every sort of fool for not standing up and regally thanking him before sweeping from the room like a confident, sophisticated woman who had no reaction to his touch. Instead she resolved to avoid him for the rest of her life and muttered again, "Thank you for coming to my aid."

One corner of his mouth curled. "You sound surprised that I did so."

A thick lock of hair came free, drooping over her face. Penelope hoped it hid her guilty blush. "I hardly expected you to."

"Oh? Why?" Startled, she jerked her head up,

meeting his gaze as the rest of her hair tumbled down her back. He withdrew his hands and held out the pins he'd removed. "You don't like me, do you?"

It was as bracing as a slap. Penelope straightened in the chair and took the pins. "Don't be ridiculous, my lord." She swept up her hair and twisted it into a simple knot. "Whatever made you think that?" With each pin that went in, her poise began to return, at long last. "Thank you again for your invaluable assistance." He'd done her this service—a rather enormous one, she fully admitted—which proved he had some basic decency and chivalry, but nothing more. She would be grateful to him, especially for punching Lord Clary, then return to keeping her distance from him.

"It was entirely my honor," he said wryly. "I suppose this is yours?" He picked up the brooch Clary had ripped from her dress, a bit of lace still snagged in the clasp.

"Yes." Penelope looked down at her damaged gown, shuddering again at the memory of Clary's repulsive touch on her breast. She pressed one hand against the spot as if to rub it out. "He tore my gown."

"Indeed." There was an odd hitch in Atherton's voice. Penelope glanced up. Clary hadn't torn the bodice itself, only the lace flounce at the neckline, and yet . . . Lord Atherton was staring at her bosom. And there wasn't a trace of disgust in his face. It was very like the way he'd looked at her the other night, when he was trying to put her in her place by saying a man must consider all a woman's charms . . .

There was a sound from the other side of the room. Still somewhat disconcerted by the focused interest on Atherton's face, Penelope didn't identify it at first. The viscount, though, spun around, coming to his feet in an instant. "Yes?" he snapped.

"There you are, sir!" cried Mrs. Lockwood. "I've been looking everywhere—" She stopped abruptly.

Penelope sat frozen in the armchair, afraid to move. All too clearly, she could picture what Mrs. Lockwood saw: the man who was courting her daughter leaning solicitously near a wildly disheveled woman. She said a quick frantic prayer that it was too dim in the room for anyone to recognize her.

"What did you want with me?" Atherton seemed to be the only one with any wits about him. He had stepped squarely in front of Penelope, impeding Mrs. Lockwood's view.

But not, it turned out, enough. "You," breathed Mrs. Lockwood. "You—you scheming, brazen trollop!" Each word grew louder and more indignant.

Penelope cringed. Hoping desperately this was all a nightmare, she peeked around Lord Atherton, who still stood protectively in front of her. Frances's mother was in the doorway, silhouetted by the light of the corridor. Shock and fury were written in every line of her taut posture and expression.

"Why were you looking for me, Mrs. Lockwood?" asked Atherton again, his voice a little colder.

That seemed to jar the woman out of her

speechlessness. She yanked someone next to her and thrust out an accusing finger in Penelope's direction. "See, Frances," she exclaimed, "see how silly you were? I told you that girl was up to no good, filling your ears with nonsense. Do you see now that I was right?"

With deep mortification Penelope met Frances's stunned gaze. The younger girl looked like she'd been crying; tears still glistened on her cheeks. Now she stood staring in openmouthed shock, and whispered, "Miss Weston?" as if she couldn't believe her eyes.

"It's not what it looks like," Penelope burst out. Finally jolted into action, she scrambled out of the chair and across the room, putting as much space as possible between herself and the viscount. "Frances, please don't be hasty—"

"Hasty!" Mrs. Lockwood seemed to quiver with outrage. "Frances, don't be a fool! Do you see now that she schemed to disrupt your engagement to Lord Atherton because she wanted him for herself?"

"No," gasped Penelope. Good Lord—of all the things to be accused of! "That's a lie! I would never!"

Atherton crossed the room in two strides. "What do you want, madam?" he bit out. "Just this evening, your daughter told me she never wanted to see me again, so I expect it was something terribly urgent that made you seek me out."

"I was bringing her to apologize for that, but now I see that I was wrong to make her reconsider." Her gaze raked scornfully over Penelope. "I understand *perfectly* now why she gave you the answer she did. She must have seen what I did not: how very faithless you are!"

"That wasn't the reason she gave earlier." He turned a hard look on Frances, who blanched.

"Nevertheless . . ." Mrs. Lockwood gave her daughter a shake. "She did not suspect such scheming interference and betrayal from Miss Weston, who pretended to be her friend."

Penelope wanted to strike the woman. She shook her head at Frances, pleading for understanding—surely Frances knew that wasn't true—but it was too late. Frances pulled loose of her mother's grasp as betrayal settled over her expression.

"No, Mama." She glanced at Penelope. "I don't believe Miss Weston schemed to get Lord Atherton for herself. She hates him."

Oh Lord. The viscount turned to her, one brow slightly raised. Penelope blushed scarlet. Even if it helped her case, she would rather Frances hadn't said that, not so soon after Atherton had been so unquestionably heroic to her. She wet her lips and avoided his eyes, praying she could talk her way out of this as skillfully as Abigail would. "This is all a terrible misunderstanding. I fell down the stairs, you see, and was quite disheveled as a result and Lord Atherton happened to discover me and he so kindly helped me to this room to repair myself. There's really nothing else at all in it . . ."

Her voice trailed off as Frances pointedly looked from her tumbledown hair to her ripped gown to her bare foot. Penelope closed her mouth in humiliation. Combined with Atherton's similar state—his hair rumpled and falling over his brow, his jacket unbuttoned—the appearances were very, very damning.

"No." Now Frances sounded hurt and accusatory. "I don't think I misunderstand, not anymore. All the time he was only pretending to court me but really he never wanted me at all—he wanted you."

Mrs. Lockwood gasped loudly. Penelope's eyes nearly popped from her head. *"Atherton?"* It was ludicrous—so ludicrous she gave a hysterical little laugh. "That's absurd!"

"He always talks about you," Frances went on bitterly. "'Did Miss Weston tell you that?' 'What did Miss Weston say?' 'May I dance with Miss Weston?'"

"Is this true, sir?" demanded Mrs. Lockwood, her face almost purple.

"Of course it isn't! It can't be!" Penelope turned to the viscount in panic. "Tell them! For goodness' sakes, you proposed marriage to Frances—"

"And was promptly told to go to the devil," he replied. He hadn't looked away from her since Frances blurted out that Penelope hated him—curse it, she knew she ought to have held her tongue around Frances—and it was starting to unnerve her. Why wasn't he protesting? He most certainly did not want to marry her! He wanted to marry Frances, yet was just standing there watching the nightmare unfold with a curious, almost speculative expression.

And then it got worse. With two spots of color burning in her cheeks, Frances Lockwood drew herself up. "I refused you because you aren't in love with me. You didn't do anything a man in love would do." She thrust an accusing finger at Penelope. "You're in love with her, aren't you?"

"Don't be an idiot," retorted Penelope before she could think better of it.

Frances paled, then flushed a deep, sullen red. "That must be what you think I am. Telling me you hated Lord Atherton and then sneaking off with him the first moment you can!"

Mrs. Lockwood swept her daughter into her arms and turned a venomous look on Lord Atherton. "Well! I must say, I quite understand my daughter's actions now!" Her glare moved to Penelope. "And as for you, miss, I knew all along you were a bad influence. Low breeding always shows itself in the end, I say, and it certainly has in this case."

"You're wrong," Penelope said once more, uselessly. "It's not what it looks like . . ." She glanced at Lord Atherton, wishing he would do something to stop this, but he just raised his shoulder in a faint shrug, as if he had no idea what to say, either.

This time Mrs. Lockwood's glance held some pity. "You never think the rules apply to you, do you, miss? Well, I assure you, they most certainly do." She took her daughter's arm in hers. "Come, Frances. Let us find more worthy companions."

Penelope stared after them, numb. She was doomed. The Lockwoods would ruin her out of spite—oh, why hadn't she kept her mouth shut the other day? Frances had broken off with Lord Atherton, and her mother blamed Penelope as the cause. As if *she* had compelled Frances to tell him to go to the devil. Good heavens, had Frances really said that? She shook her head, her thoughts still tangled and jagged.

Slowly she turned toward Atherton. He, too, was staring out the door, although with a more distant expression, as if he was lost in his own thoughts. What remained of Penelope's goodwill toward him bled away. So much for a heroic rescue. All it would have taken was a few soothing words to Frances, or some exaggerated exclamation over Penelope's turned ankle, and Mrs. Lockwood would have been distracted. Instead he just stood there looking rumpled and beautiful and guilty—all of which made Penelope hate him all over again. Even worse, he turned toward the mirror on the wall behind them and began buttoning his coat, just like a man might do after an illicit, scandalous rendezvous.

"Why didn't you stop that?"

He cocked one brow without looking away from his reflection. "How?"

"By snatching Frances into your arms and making love to her!"

"Is that what I ought to have done?"

Penelope flushed at his dry tone. "It couldn't have hurt!"

"No?" He pivoted on his heel and strode toward her until she stepped back in alarm. "Speak for yourself. If I had 'snatched Frances into my arms and made love to her,' as you so delicately suggest, her mother might have insisted I marry her. And as you know by now"—his tone grew harder—"she turned my proposal down flat."

She had guessed as much. "But if you proposed,

that means you want to marry her," she tried to argue.

"Not any longer." He pulled loose the end of his cravat and began retying it.

That was understandable. Penelope switched to the next most pressing problem. She planned to pretend Frances had never said anything at all about Atherton being in love with her, which was just unthinkably stupid. "But now Mrs. Lockwood thinks we had an—an—assignation!"

His gaze ran down her figure, just once, but it was enough to make her skin prickle and burn. "Would you rather she have seen you with Lord Clary?"

She shuddered at the name, and wrapped her arms around herself as a chill shot up her spine. "*No.*"

He finished with the cravat and did the last buttons on his coat as he faced her. "Then I suggest you repair your appearance and carry on with your evening, as I intend to do." Again his eyes flickered downward. "Are you certain you don't want me to send for your mother?"

Penelope gaped at him. He was going to go back to the rout and smile and dance as if nothing had happened? "Are you mad?" she demanded in a constricted voice. "She's going to gossip—tell tales—"

"I doubt it."

Her temper snapped. He had rescued her from one terrible fate, true, but then done nothing to save her from the other, possibly worse, scandal. Before she could stop it, her hand was swinging toward his face.

He caught her wrist just before the slap landed. Jerked to a halt, she stumbled toward him, then into him as her injured ankle gave way. His arm went around her waist to steady her, and Penelope froze. For a moment they both seemed frozen, in fact, her wide-eyed gaze locked with his steely one.

"Don't," he said quietly, giving her upraised hand a slight squeeze. "We might well need each other."

Her stomach twisted into a hard knot. His body was tall and hard and so strong against hers. The scent of his shaving soap made her light-headed, because his clean-shaven jaw was so close she could see every line of his firm, sensual mouth. Penelope fought down the heat spreading through her veins; her attraction to him was a fatal weakness, but she refused to succumb to it.

She pushed against his chest and backed away, no longer caring what her hair or dress looked like. "We should stay far away from each other," she said, hating her voice for being shaky and breathless. "Give her time to reconsider—to realize it was all a misunderstanding—or perhaps simply to find another suitor and cease caring about either of us—"

"Do you really hate me?" he interrupted.

She flushed again. "Have you really been in love with me all along?"

Neither said a word.

"See?" she said grimly. "We've both been horribly misrepresented. Thank you for saving me from Lord Clary, but I beg you: Do not speak to me again, do not seek me out, do not do anything that might turn any of my other friends against me—" Her voice broke on the last words. "I hope you won't say a word about this to anyone." She waited, and after a moment he gave a slight nod. "Good-bye, sir." Head held high, she retrieved her lost slipper and limped out the door, hoping desperately that an injured ankle was the worst that happened to her tonight.

Benedict watched her go. He wasn't quite sure what he'd just done, but he damned sure wasn't going back to the rout now. When Penelope had had sufficient time to escape, he went into the hall and sent a servant for his things.

On one hand, his actions were perfectly defensible. It wasn't exactly admirable to follow Penelope because he wanted to argue with her about the way she'd incited Frances to lunacy, but finding her struggling on the floor with Clary had superseded that intention and prompted him to intervene; what gentleman wouldn't? And he stayed to make certain she was unhurt because she was a young lady, very near the age of his youngest sister, and if Samantha ever were in such a position, he hoped someone would do the same for her.

But then . . . He ought to have fetched her mother at once, no matter what she said. He ought not to have touched her hair, even though that, too, was done in the spirit of trying to help her. Her trembling hands had disproved her protest that she was perfectly fine; he admired her fortitude if not her ability to lie. But it had been a mistake because it put him much too close to her. With his hands tangled in her silky hair he had an all-too-intimate view of the flush on her cheeks, the rapid beat of her pulse at the base of her throat, and the ripe swells of her breasts above her ripped bodice. And just like the other night, he'd been jolted by the reminder that Penelope Weston was a beautiful young woman.

For a moment he thought of her wild suggestion that he ought to have seized Frances and kissed her to distract both Lockwood ladies. It might have worked . . . except he no longer wanted to marry Frances. Somewhere between her impassioned outburst and that strangely fraught moment when Penelope looked up at him, her face shining with joy and gratitude, from where Clary held her down on the floor, Benedict's interest in wedding Frances Lockwood had withered away. Otherwise he might have explained to Mrs. Lockwood immediately that *he* hadn't been the cause of Penelope's ripped dress, disheveled hair, and missing shoe. He could have supported her far-fetched tale of falling on the stairs that portrayed him as nothing more than someone of good manners who happened by.

Instead he'd said nothing of the sort.

Benedict reached into his pocket. The brooch was an oval agate surrounded by pearls, pale and perfect in the dim light. The clasp still had a bit of lace stuck in it—fine, expensive lace. From Bannister's report the other night, he knew each Weston daughter had a dowry approaching forty thousand pounds. It was more than any other heiress he'd met in two Seasons, and more than twice Frances Lockwood's. That dowry, paired with Penelope's brilliant looks and keen intelligence, was a considerable temptation. At her best, Penelope was exuberant and amusing, with a sparkling wit; she was loyal and fearless in her devotion to those dear to her. With her hair tousled and her color high, she was a smoldering temptress, and all her words in praise of passion ran through his mind in sinful suggestion.

On the other hand, she hated him. There was no mistaking the guilty blush that stained her face when Frances blurted that out.

He tucked the brooch back into his pocket as the servant returned with his hat and gloves. His father was fond of saying that it was often to one's advantage to sit back and see what opportunities emerged from a scandal. Much as Benedict hated to admit it, perhaps this time his father was correct.

Chapter 8

Penelope's ankle was red and sore the next morning, and instead of protesting that it was fine, she let her mother fuss over her. The encounter with Lord Clary had given her a real fright, and the subsequent scene with Frances and Lord Atherton hadn't helped.

She told her mother none of it. If she confided in Mama about Lord Clary, she would have to explain why she'd been alone with him. If she did that, Mama would send for Olivia at once and interrogate her, and if Olivia admitted having an affair with him, there was a real chance Mama would forbid Penelope from seeing Olivia again. Not only was Penelope determined to protect her friend—who had obviously been in great distress about the assignation, if that's even what it was—she was wild to know why Olivia would speak to such a man, let alone slip off to meet him. And if she tried to warn her mother about what Mrs. Lockwood or Frances might say, she would have to explain what had led to that, which would mean explaining about Clary. On the whole, Penelope didn't see how she *could* tell her mother.

So she let the physician examine her ankle, nodding meekly when he pronounced it slightly turned and in need of rest. As Lord Atherton had said, it wasn't broken, even though it hurt like the devil. Mama showed the doctor out after getting his instructions for poultices and wraps, and then came to sit on the edge of Penelope's bed.

"Quite an evening," she remarked.

"Not my finest," Penelope murmured.

Mama studied her. "Merely because of a slip on the stairs?"

Penelope creased her skirt. She'd told her parents she fell on the stairs to account for her disheveled state, but suspected her mother wasn't completely fooled. "I wasn't enjoying it before that, either."

Her mother squeezed her hand. "Things haven't been the same since Abby wed, have they?"

"Not at all," Penelope muttered. If Abigail had been there last night, Penelope would have stayed in the ballroom gossiping with her, and none of the nightmare would have happened.

"I knew it would be hardest on you," Mama went on. "The two of you have been so close, ever since she peeped into your cradle and demanded to play with you."

She gave a halfhearted smile. "I'm very happy for her."

Mama smiled. "As am I. But I miss her, too." She leaned over to press a kiss on Penelope's forehead. "As I'll miss you, when you decide to settle down like Abigail did."

"She met the right man," Penelope protested. "The man of her dreams! You make it sound like she decided it was time and the perfect husband was just standing there, waiting for her."

"I know very well it wasn't like that," said Mama wryly. "Your papa still grumbles about it from time to time. Do try to make things easier for him when you fall in love, Penelope."

"I never try to make things difficult."

"It just happens naturally?" Mama rose. "I'm sure he'll come to tease you about being an invalid. Can I fetch you anything to pass the time?"

Penelope shook her head, and her mother left. She lay back on her pillows, staring at the ceiling for a few moments. Did she make things difficult? Certainly not on purpose. The debacle last night had been a pure accident.

Still, there would be nothing to worry about if Mrs. Lockwood could keep her mouth closed. Hopefully she would reconsider, once the heat of her shock and outrage passed, and decide it was better to say nothing. No matter how overwrought Frances was, she would be a complete ninny to tell everyone Lord Atherton had courted her while he really wanted someone else. Best of all would be if Atherton and Frances somehow made up their quarrel and became engaged, but that seemed highly unlikely. She wondered what, exactly, the viscount had done; it must have been something terrible if Frances had said she never wanted to see him again. Frances had been eager to accept him when Penelope saw her at the Venetian breakfast. Perhaps he'd been rude or somehow revealed his coldhearted self, and Frances slapped his face before storming out on him. The thought cheered Penelope immensely.

Unfortunately that did nothing to ameliorate the horrible scene after. Frances couldn't really think that Atherton was in love with *her*. Why, if he had been, he could have pursued her last summer in Richmond, or more recently in London. Instead he'd never given her a second glance and spent his time courting other young ladies, dancing with them and calling on them and listening to them play the pianoforte.

Penelope lurched out of bed. Wincing and swearing under her breath, she hobbled to her desk, where she took out some paper and opened her ink. Enough of Atherton; the man had caused her almost nothing but misery. Meanwhile, Olivia was in trouble and Penelope was dying to know what it really was. Why had Olivia met Lord Clary? Why had she let him hold her even as it made her cry? Penelope dashed off a note to her friend and rang for a servant to deliver it right away.

After that, the hours dragged. She reread all her magazines, and even her few issues of *50 Ways to Sin*. She had learned it was dangerous to keep them for long—her mother must have ordered the maids to look for contraband when they tidied the room—but now she had no one to pass them to. A few months ago she would have shared the issues with her sister or Joan, but they were both gone. Having no one with whom she could discuss Constance's shocking behavior took away some of the thrill. Still, she expected to find some pleasure in the reading, and was unhappily surprised that there was none.

Her father came to see her, as her mother had predicted. Penelope braced herself for any hint of trouble or gossip, but Papa was in good spirits. He teased her about being out of the races, and pretended to console her on the bad luck of twisting her ankle on the stairs instead of while dancing with a handsome nobleman in want of a bride. Penelope laughed with her father, although mention of being caught and saved by a handsome lord did make her face grow hot. She *had* been in the arms of a devilishly handsome man who'd saved her from disaster last night, though she could hardly tell either parent about it.

Thankfully Olivia came that afternoon. Penelope was settled on the window seat, staring broodingly out the window at the sunlight dappling the trees in the square, when she saw her friend walking up the street. With an exclamation of relief, she hobbled downstairs as fast as she could to whisk her friend into the morning room, where she barely managed to wait until the maid had brought the tea tray and left them alone.

"What in the world were you doing, meeting that wretched man?" she burst out.

Olivia avoided Penelope's gaze as she took a sip of tea. "Please don't ask me that."

"Don't ask?" Penelope goggled at her. "After I saved you from him?"

"You should not have followed me."

Penelope frowned. Part of her agreed. If she hadn't followed Olivia, Lord Atherton wouldn't have followed *her*, but then Olivia would have been left alone at Clary's mercy. Neither outcome could really be called preferable to the other.

"What would have happened if I hadn't? Lord Clary meant to do vile and immoral things to you, didn't he?"

Olivia's jaw tightened. "I can't tell you."

"Why not?" Penelope protested. "Why did you meet him? He said you had an assignation with him—is that true?"

"No!" Olivia grimaced. "Yes. Of a sort."

"What sort?"

The other woman took a deep breath. "I can't tell you that, either."

Penelope scowled in alarm. It wasn't like Olivia to be this mysterious. "Could you tell Abby? I can write to her today and tell her to come at once—"

Olivia raised one hand. Her face was composed, but that upheld hand trembled, betraying the intensity of her feeling. "*Don't.* That is, I can't tell her any more than I can tell you, so there's no need to bring her back to town."

"Oh." There was something about Olivia's implacable expression that Penelope did not like. It left her feeling shut out and helpless, and she hated feeling helpless. It was enraging and frustrating and terrifying. "You can't tell her, or you won't?"

Olivia curled her hand into a fist before lowering it to her lap. She stared across the room, seeming to search for the answer for a moment. The sunlight slanting through the window cast her face into harsh relief, picking out the lines around her mouth and the faint dark circles under her eyes that made her suddenly look years older. "I won't."

"But why not? I won't tell a soul. I can see you're

violently distressed—as anyone would be, if Lord
Clary had any influence over them. I know I'm not
sensible like Abby but I want to help."

A wry smile twisted her friend's mouth and
she reached out to squeeze Penelope's hand. "You
are sensible. You're the dearest friend I could ask
for, and every bit as trustworthy and clever as
Abigail. But this . . ." She hesitated, then released
Penelope's hand. "This is my problem, and I won't
drag you into it. I never wanted you to know about
it, and if Lord Clary did anything to you in retali-
ation, I would never forgive myself."

"He already did," Penelope told her. A dim
voice—which sounded a great deal like her
sister's—sounded in her mind, protesting that
she was about to be brazen and manipulative,
but she ignored it, as she usually did. "He was
angry I'd interrupted your—your *assignation*
with him."

Olivia's face went dead white. "What? I—I
thought you left the room right behind me. What
did he do to you?"

"He grabbed me and wouldn't let me leave
the room. He said that if he couldn't get what he
wanted from you, he'd have it from me." The protesting little voice sounded again. Penelope men-
tally cursed at it to be quiet; there was a greater
good at stake here, and she felt it was more important to find out what trouble her friend was
in. Olivia was determined to be noble and self-
sacrificing, and Penelope wasn't having that. "He
shoved me into a chair, he ripped the brooch off
my gown, and he seized my foot and twisted it.
He's the reason my ankle is injured." She didn't

have to fake the shiver of revulsion that went through her at the memory.

"Oh my God." For a moment it looked like Olivia would be ill. She set down her tea and pushed it away, so violently the cup rattled against the saucer. "*Why* did you follow me?" She pressed her hands to her temple and gave a sharp shake of her head. "No, that's unjust—I am at fault. I should have made certain you left. I was stupid, I . . . I was just so grateful to be free of him, I ran and—" She looked up fearfully. "Did Clary— What did he—?"

"I kicked him between the legs, as Jamie taught me to do, and then someone else came into the room and got rid of Clary."

"You kicked . . . ?" Olivia's mouth dropped open in disbelief. For one fleeting moment a smile of pure vengeful delight flashed across her face. Then her brow creased. "Who came in and sent Clary away?"

"Lord Atherton." Penelope said it as if the name meant nothing to her.

"Atherton?" Olivia's eyebrows went up, and her face went blank with astonishment again.

Penelope stirred her tea and lifted one shoulder. "He was quite gallant, actually."

"Viscount Atherton? The one who courted Abby last summer?" Olivia went on incredulously. "The one about to propose to Miss Lockwood?"

She gritted her teeth. "The very one." She was growing very tired of discussing Atherton's romantic intentions. "I'm sure Clary learned his lesson and will keep away from me, but I suspect he won't do the same for you—and I also fear he'll take out his fury on you." She watched closely for any sign that this shocked Olivia and saw none; the other woman had clearly already thought of it. "You have to tell me. Or someone. Tell Jamie! He'll be glad to put a dent in Clary's smug face."

Olivia had the tense look of someone thinking very hard. "No, don't tell your brother."

Penelope wanted to rip out her hair in frustration. Why were some people so amiable? If someone like Clary was compelling her to meet him in secluded spots for vile reasons, she wouldn't hesitate to tell anyone who might help her—or at least lend her a pistol, so she could see to Clary on her own. "Why not? Jamie won't think badly of you," she argued, trying to make her friend see reason. "He's stiff and dull but he's not an idiot, and he's been your friend since . . . longer than I can remember! He'll keep your confidence, I know he will."

"I know he would, too." For a long moment Olivia hesitated, her mouth working subtly as if struggling with what to say. "It's not that I don't trust him—or you or Abigail. You simply have to believe me when I say there's nothing any of you can do to help. I don't want you caught up in my problems. Promise me you'll stay far away from Clary, and even from me if he's nearby."

"Promise me you'll do something to save yourself from him, then." Penelope threw up her hand when Olivia said nothing. She thrust her teacup back onto the table and leaned toward her friend. "There must be something you can do, or someone you can ask to help you. I promise I won't tell a soul, not even Abby, if you wish," she said in a low, fierce voice. "But you have to see that Clary is a monster! If you could handle him yourself, why haven't you already done it?"

"I know!" burst out Olivia, losing her composure at last. She rubbed her hands along her skirt, and bright red spots burned in her cheeks. "I know that, Penelope! But . . . he's not easy to refuse, and I just need time. But you must promise me that you'll stay far, far away from him. *Please*."

"If you let me tell Jamie so he can keep close to you," replied Penelope quickly. She had no qualms committing her brother to being a watchman.

Her friend sat back, her expression closed and hard. "Absolutely not." She inhaled a deep breath. "I know I have to do something about—about him. I promise you that I am thinking, frantically, and when I construct a plan that will work, I will come to you at once for any help I need."

"Olivia . . ." Penelope gazed at her in worry, at a loss for words. "How did you get tangled up with him in the first place?"

The other woman didn't answer for a long minute, then simply said, "Henry."

Oh Lord. Henry Townsend, Olivia's late husband, had been the sort of man who couldn't avoid trouble if he sat alone in a locked room. Penelope bit back some very rude words about Henry. "Then I give you my word I won't say anything. But I won't stop thinking about it. If I had known he was hounding you so horribly, I would have told Lord Atherton to punch him a few more times."

"Lord Atherton punched him?" Olivia blinked in confusion.

Penelope cleared her throat. She hadn't really meant to mention him again. "Yes. When he saved me from Clary, he might have punched the earl in the stomach once or twice."

Instead of looking pleased, Olivia paled. "Once or twice?"

"I wish he'd done it a dozen more times," Penelope added, repressing the primal thrill that went through her at the memory of Atherton standing over Clary, fists at the ready to defend her. "Clary deserved it."

Her friend swallowed hard. "But it means he'll remember you—both of you."

"That can't be helped now, so I choose to relish the fact that he did punch Clary, and not lightly, either." Penelope relented at the worry in Olivia's expression. She reached for her friend's hand. "Don't fret. I'm sure Atherton won't tell anyone; do you know, I think he rather enjoyed it. And he never saw you there at all, so he knows nothing of your involvement." *Which is about how much I know,* thought Penelope, wondering what Henry Townsend could have done that was so vile, Clary would expect to violate his widow—and that Olivia would feel she had no choice but to allow it.

Olivia grasped her hand and squeezed. "I'm very grateful he happened by when he did," she said with a trace of her usual smile. "You must have been so happy to see him."

"Er . . . yes." Penelope smiled uncomfortably and eased her hand free. "That once." If only he'd left immediately after sending off Clary.

"It sounds quite heroic, Pen. Surely this will

help you think better of him, should he marry Miss Lockwood."

Penelope was quite certain that wouldn't happen now, but she didn't feel like volunteering the information. The less said about the Lockwoods, the better. She was still praying Mrs. Lockwood might suffer a feverish delirium that would erase her memory of the Gosnold rout entirely, or that Lord Atherton's regiment would be posted suddenly and immediately to northern Scotland. "Surely," she mumbled in agreement.

Olivia sighed, with a sympathetic smile. "Well, I for one am very grateful to him." She hesitated. "Just as I am very grateful to you. I wish Clary had never set eyes on you, but I must confess I was very happy when you opened the door."

Penelope smiled cautiously in reply. "Then I'm not sorry I did it. I—I do know how you feel. When Atherton appeared I almost thought I could kiss him." Olivia blinked, then snorted with laughter at her exaggerated grimace. Penelope grinned, immensely relieved to see her friend happy again. "You are sure you're all right, Olivia?"

Still smiling—although a little bittersweetly—Olivia nodded. "I'm sure." She rose. "Be careful of Clary," she said again. "For me, if not for your own sake."

"He's the very last person I ever want to see again," Penelope assured her with complete honesty. "Just remember you can count on me for any help you need."

"I will." Olivia gave her a quick embrace. "Thank you, Penelope."

Chapter 9

Benedict's sense that his encounter with Penelope would yield an unexpected opportunity was confirmed within a day.

It was not, however, the one he had expected.

"Atherton, you sly dog." Hollander sidled up to him in the officers' common room the next night. "Very cleverly done."

"I have no idea what you mean," he replied, pouring a glass of port.

Hollander snorted. "No idea! You were so indignant: *I refuse to discuss a lady!*" He chuckled. "Now I see why—but good Lord, you might have let some of us in on the secret."

"Is it secret?" Benedict sipped his port, pretending not to care even as his attention sharpened.

"Not any longer." Hollander glanced over his shoulder and lowered his voice. "The rumors are true, aren't they? You certainly seemed eager to squash Cabot's interest in her the other night."

Benedict lifted one shoulder. His mind raced; what were these rumors about Penelope? He'd expected there would be some—it was too much to hope that both Mrs. Lockwood and Frances would be completely discreet—but from Hollander's avid expression, they were more salacious than expected.

As expected, his disinterest provoked his fellow officer. "You won't say?" Hollander's eyebrows went up. "Ah, I see. You've enjoyed her and don't want any competition, do you?"

"Competition at what?" Cabot dropped into the chair opposite Benedict. He looked between the two of them. "What are you whispering about, Hollander?"

"Atherton put one over on all of us, it seems," the man replied, never taking his eyes from Benedict's face. "Not very sporting of him. I daresay he's been having the Weston girl all this time, and warning the rest of us off to preserve his place between her—"

Benedict was out of his chair and had the man by his collar. "Not one more word," he said through his teeth.

Cabot seized his arm and hauled him back. "Bloody hell, Atherton! You can't attack a Guardsman!"

Benedict released his fellow officer with a small shove and glanced around the room. Hollander's eyes were wide, but his mouth curved in a slow, delighted smile. Everyone had gone silent, staring at them in a mixture of astonishment and anticipation. He straightened his shoulders and kept his voice low. "That's arrant nonsense, Hollander, and I'll thank you not to repeat it."

Hollander smirked as he got to his feet. "That you've been having her, or that you're warning us lot off?"

"Having who?" asked Cabot. His face blanked. "You don't mean—?"

"The Weston girl. It turns out she's even less a lady than she pretends."

Cabot gaped a moment before recovering himself. He waved them toward the door. "Step outside, gentlemen. This is a private conversation," he barked as men started to follow them. "Are you brawling over a woman?" he demanded once they reached the courtyard.

"Not brawling at all," said Benedict in a flat tone. "Hollander's gossiping like an old woman."

"Oh?" The corporal leaned forward, arms folded over his chest. "Have you heard that gossip? Every woman and man, young or old, will be repeating it soon."

"No, what is it?" asked Cabot, to Benedict's private relief. He was dying to know but did not want to ask.

"That Penelope Weston is little more than a whore," replied Hollander. "They say she can be tumbled for the asking, at any ball or rout. They say she left a rout early the other night, in significant dishabille, after a particularly vigorous rendezvous." He stared defiantly at Benedict, who somehow managed to keep his own expression fixed and unresponsive.

Cabot frowned. "Are you sure? That sounds unlikely. She's an heiress, and a pretty one at that."

Hollander shrugged. "She's no lady."

"And the only two things a female can be are a lady or a whore?" Benedict asked coldly. It took some doing to keep his fists at his sides, even though he doubted Hollander was really the one to blame for this.

"Just reporting what I was told," retorted Hollander.

"Peace!" Lieutenant Cabot threw up his hands. "Hollander, that's a vile thing to say about any woman without hard proof. Atherton . . ." He hesitated. "Don't strike him for repeating gossip, no matter how unbecoming it may be for an officer of the Guards to repeat such sensational and defaming whispers." He glared at Hollander. "Good night, sir."

Hollander snorted and walked away. When the door of the barracks had closed behind him, Cabot turned to Benedict. "Not after the girl, eh?"

He flexed his hands. They were stiff from being clenched into fists. "Not willing to be labeled a despoiler of young women, no."

"Trying to strangle a man who suggests you want her makes it appear you want her."

"Hollander suggested I knew she was a whore and kept it secret so no one else would have a chance to ride her." Benedict glared at his mate. "If he accused you of murdering your father, would you look guilty if you tried to close his mouth?"

Cabot inclined his head, acknowledging the point. "I still say it's better not to fly at his throat. Hollander loves a good fight; it will only encourage him."

Benedict gave a nod of grudging assent. The door behind them opened again, and this time it was Bannister.

"I hear I missed the bare-knuckle brawl," he said with a faint smile. "Do relate it blow by blow!"

Cabot sighed and squared his shoulders. "There was no brawl. I'll go tell Hollander to hold his tongue." He went into the barracks.

Bannister twisted to watch him go, then glanced at Benedict. "Defending a lady's honor, are you?"

Benedict gave him a hard look. "How bad are the rumors? I assume you've heard them."

"You haven't?" Bannister studied him thoughtfully when Benedict shook his head. "I'd call them scandalous—or even worse. The tale I heard was rather detailed as to the young woman's depravities."

He hesitated, then just asked. "With whom was she supposed to have been so wicked?"

Bannister shrugged. "No one in particular—or rather, everyone in particular. I heard she wasn't discriminating. Poor Hollander must have felt left out and wanted under her skirts as well."

Benedict bit back the urge to growl at that. Hollander was the least of his concerns. He muttered a farewell to Bannister and turned toward the stables, wanting some space to think.

These did not sound like the sort of rumors Mrs. Lockwood or Frances would start. Benedict had fully expected some little tattle to emerge from that, women's gossip about a shameless attempt to steal poor Frances's suitor or something similar. If Hollander had given him an amused, pitying look and asked which girl he was really courting, he would have been prepared to wave it aside with a weary sigh about female theatrics, and hope that ended it.

But tales of wicked depravities meant the rumors had to be from Clary, although it was very curious that Benedict's name didn't seem to be part of them. As Penelope had pointed out, Benedict was the one who had punched him—and yet she alone was about to be raked over the coals in every drawing room in London.

Why the devil would Clary want to do that? He'd obviously been angry at Penelope, but he'd already put a terrible fright into her, and there would be consequences to spreading lies about her. Thomas Weston might not be a gentleman, but he also wasn't a foolish or weak man. If Clary ruined Penelope's reputation, Weston had the funds and the drive to hound the man forever. Only an idiot would invite that sort of vengeance, and Clary wasn't stupid. Benedict's father had once called Clary a worthy adversary, which was the highest show of respect the Earl of Stratford could give.

He let himself into the stable, waving aside a groom who stepped out of the tack room in inquiry, and went down the dim block until he reached the next to last stall. His horse nickered quietly at his approach, and he ran one hand absently along Achilles' neck.

He wondered why Penelope had been alone with Clary in the first place. She'd been quite adamant about not telling him, and perhaps it was none of his concern. No matter her reason, he hoped she'd learned a lesson from the experience. Whatever had happened before he arrived, Clary's intentions had been quite obvious when he pushed open the door to see the man pinning her to the floor. For a moment his mind lingered on that image: Penelope sprawled on her back, her hair tumbling down, her skirts tossed up above her knees, her bosom heaving, her blue eyes glowing with passion . . . Benedict gave himself a mental shake; her eyes hadn't been glowing with passion but with fury—first at Clary and then at him, when he was apparently to blame for Frances and her mother drawing fairly logical conclusions.

But now . . . Now Penelope was in no position to be furious at him. If Bannister's report was true, everyone in town would be watching her to see if the rumors were accurate. Even this late in the year London was filled with gossip-hungry people eager for the next delicious scandal. If they got their teeth into a beautiful girl known for her adventurous nature and sharp wit, they would devour her. The fact that she was a nouveau riche heiress would only add to their pleasure. Mr. Weston's ambitions were widely known, and frequently mocked in private. Some people would be only too eager to believe his daughter was shameless and immoral.

Which meant the competition for the hand of one heiress would be greatly lessened, just at a moment she would find herself most in want of marriage.

Benedict's hand slowed to a stop on Achilles' nose as that thought sank deep into his brain. "That's madness," he said softly. The horse whickered back at him as if in agreement. It *was* madness, and yet . . . The feel of her hair sliding through his fingers. The way the color came up in her face. The mesmerizing swell of her breasts straining at her bodice. And the fierce flash of joy in her face when he stepped into the room and stopped Clary from assaulting her. Penelope was a beauty. When she laughed, it made a man stop and listen. And once upon a time, he and she had got on quite well together—splendidly, in fact.

He inhaled unevenly. He did not want to want Penelope. From the beginning he'd seen that she was not the sort of girl he wanted to marry; she was passionate and tempestuous and liable to drive him mad. But now he couldn't stop thinking about the feel of her legs in silk stockings, or the scent of her perfume, wild and sweet and perfectly Penelope. He tried to force his mind back to all the times they argued, and only managed to imagine all that blazing temper transformed into passion as the argument ended in a rough coupling against the nearest wall. And even though Benedict told himself that was not what he wanted, the mere thought of her arms and legs wrapped around him as he drove himself inside her made his skin turn hot.

"Damn it," he muttered, trying to repress the instinctive reaction of his body. "*Think*, man." Think of all the reasons he needed a bride, not all the wicked things he wanted to do to Penelope Weston. Marriage was far too important to be based on anything as common or fleeting as desire and passion. Marriage was meant to be based on a practical evaluation of multiple factors that would ensure a secure, companionable alliance.

First, he needed a bride with money.

Penelope Weston had a dowry of forty thousand pounds.

Second, he didn't want to become a laughingstock. He wanted a wife of sense and discretion, not a wild hoyden who would constantly be the subject of gossip and innuendo.

Of course, to his knowledge Penelope had never been involved in a scandal until now, and he had already seen how deep and unwavering her loyalty could be, once engaged.

Third, he wanted a wife soon. Two humiliating rejections were quite enough, and he had hoped to be married by now in any event. His moment of opportunity to find a bride on his own terms was quickly passing, and he never knew if or when he'd get another one. When Abigail Weston had asked for his help in clearing Sebastian's name, it had led his sister Samantha to confess that she, and not Sebastian Vane, had once stolen four thousand guineas from the Earl of Stratford. Their father's rage had been implacable. Stratford blamed Benedict for trying to hide his sister's deception, and banned him from the estate in addition to cutting off all communication and funds. Benedict could withstand the financial pinch this time, but banishment was a golden chance he could not ignore. As long as his father remained furious at him, he was somewhat free—but sooner or later, Stratford would set about bringing him back to heel. And then only a wealthy bride would render him immune to the earl's demands.

And Penelope Weston—wealthy and beautiful—was about to find herself in desperate want of salvation . . . such as a respectable marriage.

"Tell me it's a bloody stupid idea," Benedict said to his horse. "Tell me I'm an idiot." Achilles huffed out a breath and shook his head before pushing his nose against Benedict's shoulder.

"No, I didn't think so," he murmured, taking a carrot from the bucket behind him and snapping it into pieces for the horse.

It was like fate was throwing her at him. And even if it was a mad idea, reason and logic hadn't won him a bride, either. Penelope might claim to hate him—might think she hated him—but if that fervor could be turned into a different sort of passion . . . It wouldn't be the sort of marriage he had wanted, but there could be other compensations. Without meaning to, he imagined making love to her, and a bolt of pure lust shot through his veins, straight to his groin. Benedict closed his eyes and inhaled raggedly. He was no better than Hollander, it seemed—except that he was willing to marry her.

But he would have to play his cards just right. Logic and sense might win over her parents, but Penelope herself would require more dramatic suasion. What had she said the other night? A woman wanted a man to be half mad with passion for her. Benedict's mouth crooked wryly. Half mad was a fair description of how he felt around her. It wasn't strictly desire, though desire was unquestionably part of it. And if he could make her want him, too, there was a chance that theirs might be an incomparable union.

Not to mention one that would save them both from ignominy.

Chapter 10

For once Penelope was not at all sorry to be unwell. She kept to the house that night, thinking it best to give Frances and Mrs. Lockwood time to cool their tempers, and to give herself time to think of an appropriate response. Sooner or later she would see them again, and she hoped to have something conciliatory to say when they did meet. Even if Frances's friendship was lost forever, Penelope did not want anyone to think she had schemed to steal the other girl's suitor. No good explanation had come to her yet, but surely something would.

A package arrived from Olivia the next morning. Penelope opened it to find the travel journal of Italy she'd bought in Madox Street. "I expect you are imagining yourself anywhere but home by now," read the enclosed note, "and I enclose this to aid in your imaginary wanderings. I am feeling much better about the vexing matter we discussed yesterday, and have every expectation of a solution soon."

The gift made her smile and breathe a sigh of

relief. Olivia was no fool, and even though it had looked very bad with Clary, Penelope was hardly in a position to judge by appearances.

But she was not made to be an invalid. The day was bright and sunny and it seemed the walls of the house were closing in on her. When her mother mentioned after breakfast that she was going shopping, Penelope asked if she could go as well. It took multiple assurances that her ankle was strong enough, that the swelling had entirely subsided, and that she would be very careful when she walked, but finally Mrs. Weston consented.

Shopping with her mother was not the same as shopping with Olivia or her sister, but on this day Penelope didn't care. It was bliss to be outside, with the sunshine on her shoulders. She followed her mother into various shops and amused herself by trying on fur tippets and admiring the latest style of bonnets. For the first time in two days she was able to forget about Frances Lockwood and Lord Clary, and apparently it was obvious.

"You seem restored," remarked her mother.

"Restored? What do you mean?"

Her mother gave her a thoughtful look. "You seem your happy self again, as if you've shaken off some great worry."

Oh heavens. Had her mother noticed? Penelope ducked her head, uncomfortably aware that she had not shaken off anything; she had merely forgotten it for a little while, until now. She picked up a carved fan and fluttered it in front of her face. "It's just lovely to be out of the house again."

"I imagine." Mama sent the shopkeeper to wrap up the gloves she was purchasing, and then she and Penelope left the shop. "Shall you feel well enough to attend the Crawfords' soiree tomorrow?"

Oh dear. That was a conundrum. Mrs. Lockwood was nearly as close friends with Mrs. Crawford as Mama was. There was a strong chance Frances would be there. For a moment the word "no" hovered on her lips, but then Penelope swallowed it. *Be brave*, she told herself. "I believe so, Mama."

"Very good." Her mother's eyes flickered, then widened. "Good heavens. Is that—?"

Penelope tensed. Oh no; she said a quick prayer it wasn't Mrs. Lockwood, descending on them with vengeance in her heart. "Who, Mama?" She didn't even dare look but kept her bonnet brim tilted to hide her face.

"I believe it's Lord Atherton," murmured her mother in wonder. She was almost staring, which meant she missed Penelope's cringe of horror. Hastily Penelope revised her prayer. She would much rather see Mrs. Lockwood than him, especially in view of her mother. "And he is coming directly toward us."

Grimly Penelope eyed a nearby shop. Could she plausibly pretend a sudden desire to dash inside? Unfortunately it was a tobacconist. Her mother would never believe she wanted to go in there. She dared a peek around her bonnet brim.

It was indeed Atherton, his gaze focused and intent on her. It was eerily reminiscent of the look he'd given her the other night, the mesmerized expression that hinted at real interest. That was dangerous; it tempted her mind to wander off and wonder what might happen if he really did look at her, long enough to truly see her for the first time, and realize . . . And realize that she saw through him, and that she wasn't fooled by his charming facade and perfect face. Penelope squeezed her eyes shut for a moment and reminded herself that she'd seen Atherton's true colors last summer, when he allowed Sebastian Vane—a guest in his family home who had once been his dearest friend—to crawl home unaided after his own father had caused Sebastian to fall on his crippled knee. She'd seen Atherton's real measure when he persisted in pursuing her sister, Abigail, even when it was clear Abigail was in love with someone else. She'd known what the viscount really was when she learned he had allowed accusations of murder and theft to endure for years against Sebastian, without speaking a word of support or protest. Atherton might be the handsomest man in all of England, and he had saved her from Clary, but Penelope really didn't want to see him.

Naturally her prayers were not answered. "Mrs. Weston," he said, his voice as rich as caramel. "How delightful to see you again." His blue eyes settled on Penelope. "Miss Weston."

"The delight is entirely ours, sir," replied Mama warmly. Penelope dipped a stiff curtsy and said nothing. What did he want? He looked magnificent today in regular clothing instead of his uniform, with a charcoal coat and dark blue trousers that outlined his form exquisitely. It was really unfair for a man to be that beautiful and yet a complete fraud as a person.

He laughed. "I flatter myself to hope it's even

half as great as mine! I've worried over Miss Weston since the other night, and it gladdens my heart to see her on her feet again."

She jerked her head up. Mama was regarding her with surprise, and Atherton with an expression of warmth and concern and . . . determination. What the devil? "Yes, thank you, sir," she said politely.

"I was very fortunately close at hand when she suffered her mishap the other night," he told Mama, still radiating charm.

"How very kind." Mama sent Penelope a probing look. "You didn't tell me Lord Atherton assisted you when you slipped on the stairs."

She widened her eyes innocently. "Didn't I? Oh dear, I must have forgotten. I was very shaken, you know."

"No doubt," murmured the viscount.

She flushed, reminding herself to be more polite. He could expose her as a liar with just one word. "I must thank you once again, my lord. Your help was both timely and considerate."

"Not at all! I was very distressed when I discovered you after your fall, and have worried ever since that you would suffer a lasting injury."

Penelope clenched her jaw. She'd heard his slight hesitation before the word "fall" and knew he was calling her a liar. She gave a carefree little laugh. "Not at all! A slightly sore ankle. The more I walk on it, the better it feels."

"Oh?" His blue eyes gleamed. "How fortunate we met. I was on my way to take a turn in the park. Perhaps you would care to accompany me?" He turned to her mother before she could utter a word. "With your permission, Mrs. Weston."

"Of course," said Mama at once, pleasantly surprised. "It will be good exercise, and spare you standing around waiting in the upholsterer's shop."

She could almost hear what her mother was thinking. Lord Atherton—and his parents, the Earl and Countess of Stratford—had every reason to dislike her family. It had been a thorn in her father's side ever since Abigail rejected Atherton, dashing Papa's hopes of a noble connection. But here Atherton was, smiling as charmingly as ever. A chance to restore the goodwill between the viscount and the Westons would delight both of Penelope's parents beyond description. Even more, Atherton had fixed his attention on her in a way that implied he held no grudge over the things she had said to him. Of course, Mama couldn't know about those things, but Penelope did, and it all left her very ill at ease. What was he plotting? A public stroll in the park was the last thing they should do together. Really, after the way they parted last, she thought he would never want to see her again. He did not like her; he had all but told her so the other night when they danced together. So why was he here watching her with an unwavering attention that made her skin feel taut and warm?

Penelope writhed inside, but saw no way out. He'd better have a good reason for this. She forced a smile to her lips. "That would be lovely, thank you."

She put her hand on his arm and let him lead her off, across Pall Mall and down a side street into St. James's Park. She waited until no one was within earshot to demand, "To what do I owe this honor, my lord?"

He smiled down at her, although now it seemed more ominous than before. "I wanted a private conversation."

Oh Lord. That stamped out the unwanted but unmistakable thrill that had shivered over her when he drew her to his side. A chill of apprehension went down her back. About what? Mrs. Lockwood, most likely, or even worse, Lord Clary. She wet her lips. "How very mysterious of you. I'm sure we haven't anything private to discuss."

"Are you sure? Very sure?" He dipped his head closer and murmured in her ear, "Perhaps you should hear what I have to say before you answer."

Her heart seemed to leap into her throat—in anxiety, she told herself, not in reaction to his breath on her cheek. "Go on, then," she said coolly.

"I wanted to warn you."

She tensed. "About what?"

"You can't guess, after what happened the other night?"

"Oh, that." She flipped one hand and pretended a great interest in the shrubbery they were passing, to hide the sudden thudding of her heart. She had hoped for more time . . . but perhaps it was best to hear it now and absorb the blow in private. "What is Mrs. Lockwood saying?"

"How interesting you would think of her. What have you got to fear from Mrs. Lockwood?"

Penelope gave him a guarded look. Why did he sound amused? "You know what. She saw—"

"Us?" he finished when she didn't. "Alone

together, in extremely suggestive disarray—what some might even call a compromising position? Certainly. But I suspect she also saw the young lady who's been keeping company with her own daughter for several weeks. What, pray, does it gain her to go about accusing that young lady of impropriety? It might make some people wonder how much of it rubbed off on Miss Lockwood."

That made sense and yet . . . If Mrs. Lockwood hadn't been causing trouble, what did he want to warn her about? Suddenly she wished whole-heartedly that Atherton was teasing her, that Mrs. Lockwood or Frances was the problem, because if his warning about that night didn't involve either of them, it would have to be about . . . Lord Clary. "She could say she was deceived! She could say she regretted allowing me to speak to her daughter, and . . . and . . ."

Atherton nodded once. "She could. But I somehow doubt she's behind the rumors I heard."

Oh Lord. Penelope steeled herself. "Why is that?"

"Because they are rather vile—far worse than anything I would expect Mrs. Lockwood to say."

"What?" she demanded at once. He wanted to tell her, so he ought to tell her, not draw it out and make her want to shake him.

He turned them into the Birdcage Walk. The trees were losing their leaves, which crunched and rustled underfoot. The sun was warm but the breeze was brisker here, and Penelope had to fight off the urge to press closer to her companion. Her arm, tucked against his side, was deliciously warm, while the rest of her was acutely aware of the chill in the air.

"I believe there's no question that Lord Clary is responsible." He glanced down at her. "Why *were* you in that room with him?"

Penelope flushed. "I can't tell you."

"Can't?" repeated the viscount. "Or won't?"

"Very well, I won't." Her face still burned, but she met his eyes without flinching. "I swore not to."

"Ah," he murmured. "Swore to whom?"

"I can't tell you that, either." She shot a defiant glance his way and added, "Nor will I."

He shrugged. "As you like. I recommend you avoid him from now on."

"Huh!" She snorted. "As if I ever wanted to speak to that vile pig."

"And yet you were alone with him, in a room far from the other guests. Why?" he asked again. "Did someone send you?"

"I already told you, I didn't mean to be alone with him," she snapped. "I won't tell you more, so please stop asking."

Something flashed in his eyes, but only for a moment. "Whatever led you there was a foolish instinct. I hope you won't give in to it again."

She shuddered at the thought. "I don't plan to." She took a deep breath. "You said you wanted to warn me. Please just tell me what he's saying. I promise I shan't faint or weep or have a hysterical fit."

Atherton took his time replying. "I thought you might like to know before it reaches your family's ears. Your reputation is about to take a public flogging. The rumor I heard is that you've been little more than a whore, slipping away for liaisons during every ball and soiree this year."

It took a moment for the awful words to sink in. The blood roared in her ears; her stomach dropped, and then heaved. "That no-account, lying, disgusting *villain*," she managed to gasp. "That's—that's a slanderous lie!"

"Indeed."

She wrenched loose of his arm and paced away. She pressed her hands to her stomach, both to still them and to keep from casting up her accounts. And she had been worried Frances would call her a sly schemer—nothing pleasant, but not on this scale. If people believed this about her—tears prickled in her eyes—if her parents heard this—

Atherton followed her. "I suppose Clary means to ruin your chances of a decent marriage."

Her lungs felt tight. Whether Clary intended that or not, he had achieved it. "Surely—surely people won't believe it," she whispered.

"Perhaps not," he said after a moment.

Of course they would. Not everyone, but enough to stain her name forever.

"I do have a suggestion for how you can preserve your reputation." Penelope started as the viscount's voice came again, softer and closer than before. Gently he eased her shawl up around her shoulders again. "You could spike Clary's guns before the gossip takes root, if you already had a suitor."

"But I don't . . ."

"You could." His fingers ran down her arms.

Penelope jumped forward as if he'd prodded her with a fork and whirled around. *"You?"*

He smiled, the intimate, seductive expression that he'd never directed at her before. "I'd be delighted, my dear Miss Weston."

"I wasn't asking!"

"But I am offering." Penelope just gaped at him in horror. Slowly Atherton started toward her, his eyes never leaving hers. "Think for a moment. What sort of attention will you attract from now on in London if you don't have an apparent suitor at your side? There are any number of disreputable rogues who would be very interested in testing your willingness—and a few who wouldn't be much bothered by unwillingness, either."

Her skin crawled at the thought. "I could leave town. I'll go stay with my sister in Richmond. If I'm not here, no one will have any joy in destroying my name."

"Fleeing town will imply that every word is true."

"I won't flee. I'll tell everyone I miss my sister and wait a few days before leaving."

"And in those few days you'll face a frenzy of whispers at every turn."

Curse him, he was right. And it wouldn't solve the problem of her parents hearing it all. Her face felt damp with perspiration. How could she possibly explain this? Mama would never believe her story about slipping on the stairs if they heard this hideous rumor. And once Mama knew she had lied, Penelope would have to confess what had really happened. Unfortunately, she feared that would only drag Olivia down and do nothing to save her.

"It would be a storm of gossip," Atherton

went on. "Clary's tale is so salacious, some might have trouble believing it, but if a lady like Mrs. Lockwood confirmed that she'd seen you disheveled at a ball, just as the rumor described . . ." He didn't finish, but he didn't need to. On her own, Mrs. Lockwood might be able to hold her tongue, but if she was offered a chance to ruin Penelope with just a few words, with no real danger to her daughter, it might prove irresistible.

Her mouth thinned. "So! Through no fault of my own, people will think terrible things about me, but the moment *you* stand up beside me, all will be forgotten. What is the world coming to, when a woman can be accused of—of—*that*, and her reputation can only be redeemed by the approval of a man? And of course people will believe the most terrible things about any woman if a *man* says them! Lord Clary deserves to be run down by a poultry wagon! I wish—" She stopped, her bosom heaving as she seethed. With an effort she recovered herself. "It is a very kind offer, my lord, but I must refuse."

He cocked his head. "What better plan do you have?"

None. She pushed that thought aside. "I simply don't think a false courtship between us would stop the rumormongers. If anything, it will make people suspect you were . . ." *The man making love to me.* Her face grew hotter than the Yule log blaze at Christmas. That was the last thing she needed to think about. "Involved," she finished lamely.

"I disagree. There isn't a breath of scandal attached to my name."

Penelope blinked. "No? Then Clary didn't . . . ?"

Slowly Atherton shook his head. "Not one story includes my name."

"But you punched him!" she exclaimed. "Why is he angry at me and not you?"

"I only punched him because he was mauling you."

She wet her lips. "That was extremely gallant of you, and I heartily approved. But that makes it even clearer that we should stay far away from each other. We might even go on as if we violently disliked each other, to negate anything Mrs. Lockwood might say! There's no reason at all for you to make such a sacrifice for me."

He looked at her for a long moment. Penelope unconsciously took a step backward under his unwavering scrutiny. "Was Frances Lockwood right? Do you truly hate me?"

She wanted to say yes. She hated so many things about him: the way he had turned his back on Sebastian and allowed rumors of murder and thievery to persist for years; his cold-blooded approach to marriage; the effect he had on her despite all her wishes to the contrary; the fact that he had never once noticed her attraction to him or felt any similar pull. But he had saved her from Clary, and even after the appalling scene with Frances and Mrs. Lockwood, he was offering to help save her again. The lie wouldn't even come to her lips. "Of course not, my lord," she muttered.

"Then don't trouble yourself about any sacrifice on my part. I offer freely and unreservedly. Don't underestimate Clary; he's a cold and vindictive man. He already tried to force himself on you. If I'm by your side, you'll be safe."

Another shudder went through her. "My father and brother can protect me, thank you."

"Indeed," he replied dryly. "And yet they were nowhere to be seen when you most needed them, and it doesn't appear you've even told them about the encounter."

That was true. Penelope groped for another reason. "Why would you do this? If you're dancing attendance on me, it will spoil your chances with any other lady you might wish to court in truth."

He leaned toward her, very slightly, but enough for her to see the different striations of blue in his eyes. His lips curved in that mesmerizing smile that generally reduced women to sighs and blushes. "What if that lady is you?"

She snorted. "Don't be ridiculous! You tried to marry my sister." Saying the words aloud restored her sense. Atherton's proposal—as mad as it was—had an insidious appeal that had begun to weaken her resistance.

"But I didn't," he replied, unruffled. "Once we got on quite well together, you and I. I would like to see if we might be able to rediscover that . . ." His gaze flickered down for a moment. "Affinity."

She took a step back, feeling a little saner as the distance between them increased. "I wouldn't."

He took a step forward, closing the distance again. "Why not? What are you afraid of?"

"The apoplexy I might suffer if exposed to much more of your company, my lord."

He raised one brow. "Apoplexy! I've never brought a lady to one of those."

"How can you know?" She widened her eyes.

"Perhaps that's why they all refuse your marriage proposals."

That barb struck home, she could see it in his face. His eyes flashed, and his sensual smile faded. "I think the next one will be accepted," he said evenly.

Penelope felt at once better and worse. Better, in that she was accustomed to dealing with Atherton this way; he probably thought her shrewish, but it kept her from succumbing to his charm. Penelope was not about to be the next young lady he set his sights on, the next female who swooned under the influence of his charm and handsome face and knowing smile. She didn't trust Lord Atherton, even when he was ostensibly coming to her aid.

But at the same time . . . a small part of her twinged in regret. What if he did want to court her? What if he did want her? What if he'd been attracted to her all along but tried to deny it and now no longer could? What if those were the real reasons behind his gallant offer?

Ruthlessly Penelope squashed that wistful little voice. Only a fool would give in to it. That little voice knew nothing at all of what Lord Atherton might actually think and feel, and she would not give in to its pathetic longings. "I wish you the very best of luck," she told the viscount. "I'm ready to return to my mother now."

Without another word of protest he escorted her out of the park to the upholsterer's shop where Mama was still choosing fabric. "Thank you, sir," she said. "I do appreciate your kindness in warning me."

Atherton studied her for a moment, no longer

radiating charm or tense with irritation. It was the most considering look he'd ever given her. "If you should change your mind . . ."

"I won't." Penelope curtsied to avoid his probing gaze. "Good-bye, my lord."

To her surprise he took her hand and raised it to his lips. "For now," he murmured. He turned on his heel and strode away. Penelope watched until he disappeared around the corner, and told herself she'd done the right thing.

If only it felt more rewarding.

Chapter 11

Benedict returned to the officers' barracks in a turbulent mood.

He hadn't expected Penelope to seize on his proposal with protestations of relief and gratitude. He knew her better than that.

However, things still hadn't gone the way he anticipated, or hoped. He'd meant to charm her, persuade her, even woo her, just a little. For a moment it had seemed he was making progress. When he'd asked if she really hated him, she couldn't bring herself to say yes. When she said Clary ought to be run down by a poultry wagon, he'd almost laughed aloud. Whatever her other faults, Penelope had a quick wit.

Of course, in the end she exercised it on him, and then she turned him down flat.

Was he mad to pursue this? Yes, they had once got on well together, but perhaps that had been merely a mood of hers. He thought of the summer day when they had gone with a group to Hampton Court. Benedict had remarked that the palace supposedly had ghosts, and Penelope immediately wanted to see the haunted corridors. It was exactly the sort of lark he'd loved as a boy, so together they set off while the rest of the party strolled in the gardens. For a moment it was crystal clear in his memory: the hazy warmth of the day, the hushed quiet inside the corridors, the gleeful look on her face when he'd put a finger to his lips, taken her by the hand, and led her down a corridor not open to visitors. For an hour, he and Penelope had trespassed and whispered and laughed together, sometimes hand in hand, as they sought out quieter and dimmer corridors to investigate for possible specters. That day there had been no trace of dislike or even disinterest in her manner. That day she had made him not just smile, but laugh out loud. That day she hadn't wished openly for his absence, she'd gone off alone with him, happily and willingly. And for the first time he wondered what would have happened had he fixed his attention on her, and not on her sister . . .

Well. Perhaps he ought to give her some time to think about it. Whether she liked him or not, Benedict suspected her resolve to brave it out would waver once the gossip hit full stride.

It was just after dinner when that moment arrived, symbolized by a note from Thomas Weston. Benedict unfolded it, raising his eyebrows when he saw the signature at the bottom. It was short and terse, requesting a meeting the next morning in Green Park but giving no hint of what he wanted to discuss.

Benedict regarded it for a few minutes. It was possible Penelope had regretted her answer to him and told her father, who wanted to discuss the offer he'd made today. But in that event, he would expect a more solicitous and tempered query. This peremptory summons hinted at something else.

He might well end up married to Penelope after all, and sooner rather than later.

He reached the park early, but Thomas Weston was already pacing along the Queen's Walk, head down and hands clasped behind his back. Benedict dismounted and gave his horse a long rein. "Good morning, sir."

Weston looked up. "Atherton." He made a sweeping motion with one hand. "I felt the need to walk." Benedict fell in step beside him and waited.

"I expect you know why I wanted to see you," said the older man after a minute.

Benedict murmured that he had some idea.

"I've thought of a dozen or more things I'd like to say," said Weston, his gaze fixed ahead of him. "Most of them aren't fit for female ears, and in my house there's always a female listening, somewhere, somehow. The park seemed safer." He shot a dark look at Benedict. "Frankly I never thought I'd have to have this sort of conversation with a gentleman of your caliber, but if there's one thing I've learned as the father of two daughters, it's that I shouldn't expect anything to go as I think it ought to go. Our conversation some months ago, when you asked for Abigail, was exactly as I had anticipated such a conversation would be." He threw up one hand. "That ought to have been my first warning. Abby's a sensible, intelligent girl but even she has a way of setting her heart on something and doing whatever it takes to get it. I completely overlooked her determination." He gave Benedict another look. "I won't make the same mistaken presumption about Penelope."

Perhaps it was best to clear the air. "Sir, when I asked for your daughter Abigail's hand, I did so with the noblest intentions."

"I always thought so." Weston stopped and turned to face him, and for a moment Benedict wondered if he'd been summoned to Green Park so Weston could shoot him and dispose of his body in some remote corner. The man certainly looked capable of it at the moment. "But here we are, because of the decidedly *less* noble intentions you seem to have toward Penelope."

"I beg your pardon?" Bloody hell. Had Clary decided to draw him into the mud as well? That would be the surest way to attract his father's notice—and wrath. Benedict had hoped to avoid it.

"I heard what's going around London." There was a tic in Weston's jaw as he spoke. "I know what people are saying about her. And I heard from my wife that you were with Penelope the night of—" He broke off. "I am not a fool, Atherton."

"Of course not, sir." He met Weston's black glare evenly. "I heard the rumors, too. I warned her what might happen."

"Tell me truly," said the other man in a voice that trembled ever-so-slightly with anger. "Are they even remotely true? Did you seduce my daughter and expose her to the grossest humiliation?"

It was on the tip of Benedict's tongue to tell Weston about Lord Clary, right now; *he* hadn't assaulted her and saw no reason why he should take the blame for it. But he bit it back. Breaking her confidence was the wrong way to win her over. "No. I give you my word that I did not."

"And yet that is the tale sweeping London," retorted Weston. "That she was caught in the most compromising of positions. Your name is not publicly linked with the episode—yet—but I doubt it will take long."

Benedict hesitated. It was unthinkable not to defend himself at all, but the wrong word now could spoil his chances. A different sort of father would have summoned him here to face him over pistols at dawn. Weston wasn't that sort of father, apparently. "The person who started the rumor did so out of pique. Miss Weston was in some disarray, after her . . . fall when I came upon her and offered to help."

"Her fall," repeated Weston dourly. "I saw her. That disarray, as you so politely name it, was not from any slip on the stairs." He saw Benedict's quickly suppressed flicker of surprise, and jerked his head in a nod. "Yes, I know she lied to us. Penelope does that. Most of the time her little lies are harmless, and the Lord above knows I told my father enough of them as a young man that I deserve to hear a few from my children. And I admit, I allow it; she's my youngest, and I've always had an extra weakness when it comes to her. But I would do anything to protect her, Atherton, and hang the consequences."

Benedict heard that warning loud and clear. Thanks to his own father he was well attuned to veiled threats, and it was very easy to slip into the deferential mode that usually worked on the earl.

"I completely understand, sir, and admire you all the more for it. But I fear . . ." This time he hesitated for effect. "Miss Weston didn't wish to alarm you, but I fear in this instance she was mistaken in keeping the truth from you."

"She usually is," grumbled Weston. "What really happened?"

"I would tell you if I hadn't given her my word that I wouldn't," he replied. "But—gentleman to gentleman—the culprit is not someone to cross lightly."

Weston glared at him for a minute. For once Benedict was grateful to his father; the scrutiny of this man was nothing to that of the earl's, who would ruthlessly pry any crack in his composure into a gaping wound. Weston loved his daughter; he tolerated her foibles and wanted to protect her, even though she'd lied to him, and that explained his glowering demeanor today. Benedict found he admired the man for it. It was nothing to face him calmly and patiently. For a moment he wondered if Penelope truly appreciated her father. She must not, if she'd not trusted him enough to tell him how Clary threatened her.

"I feared as much," said Weston at last. "The story I heard wasn't the usual tattle of idle ladies. My wife tells me the amusing rumors; how some forward wench tried to cozen a man into marrying her by letting the poor fool steal a kiss or put his hands on her, and the fortune hunters who try to trick silly girls into thinking they're in love, just long enough to get them to Gretna Green. Penelope's not that sort, nor would I be so quick to hand over my daughter to anyone who tried such nonsense. But this story . . . Atherton, I can't let it go. It accuses my daughter of debauchery that would make a sailor blush. She'll be the target of every rake and scoundrel in London. No respectable man will have her."

Benedict just waited.

"Who started this tale?" demanded Weston after a moment. "You know who it is—tell me and I'll deal with him until he publicly retracts this slander."

"I don't think he would." He had a feeling Clary would never retract the story, no matter what Weston did to him. "I fear any attempt to get him to retract would only make people talk about it more."

Weston growled under his breath, striding along with barely contained fury. "I don't like my other options."

There were most likely only two. One was for Penelope to leave town for an extended time. That had the disadvantage of making the rumors appear true, or close enough to true that it wouldn't matter. Even though Penelope had suggested fleeing London herself, he doubted she would really do it. He had an easier time picturing her attacking Lord Clary with a fireplace poker than slinking off to the country in shame.

The other option was marriage. Since Benedict had never been Thomas Weston's confidant before today, he guessed the man was leaning toward that second option, with Benedict doing the honorable thing. Given that this aligned perfectly with his own desires, he had no real objection. It wasn't how he'd hoped to achieve his goal, but perhaps the end justified the means . . .

"The trouble is, Penelope doesn't care much for you." Weston stopped and faced him again. "Or so she says. I can't bear to give my child to a man she doesn't want, but neither can I sit idly by and let her sink into ruin and shame. You, sir, are the solution to my quandary, one way or another. Either give me the name of the blighter who's telling lies about my daughter, or persuade me that you can make her happy."

"I cannot do either before I speak to Penelope." But Benedict's heart skipped a beat. He remembered Penelope's laughter as he whispered to her about the naughty Tudor ghosts. He remembered the way she'd blushed bright red when Frances Lockwood accused her of wanting him for herself. Somehow he didn't think her antipathy ran as deep as she claimed.

Not that it mattered much. She was in a desperate spot, and he was her only ally.

Weston gave a curt nod. "Very well. But you'd best come out of that conversation prepared to do one or the other. I promise you won't like the consequences otherwise." He waved one hand. "No time to waste."

Penelope would not willingly have admitted it, but she was immensely grateful to Lord Atherton for one thing. He'd warned her, privately, about the nightmare that was about to destroy her life, and given her time to brace herself.

She'd dashed off a frantic letter to her sister as soon as she and Mama returned from the shopping expedition, with the result that Abigail reached Grosvenor Square almost at the same time the horrid rumors did. When she heard Abigail's voice in the hall, Penelope lurched off the sofa and ran from the room as fast as she could on her still-tender ankle. "Abby!"

"Oh, Penelope." Abigail opened her arms and let Penelope fling herself into them. For a moment she just wallowed in the relief. Abigail was only a year older than she, and they had been the closest of friends before Abigail's marriage. Only when her sister was gone did Penelope realize how much she depended on her.

"Thank you," she said, finally releasing her sister and stepping back. "I'm so glad you came!"

Abigail smiled. "As if I wouldn't! I've never received a letter with more exclamation points and underscored words."

"I've never written a more desperate one," Penelope replied. "If I could have made it burst into flames when you finished reading it, I would have done so."

Her sister laughed. "Then let's have a cup of tea and you can explain it better. Some parts were indecipherable."

Penelope grimaced as they went back into the small parlor. Given her state of mind when she wrote that letter, it was a small miracle Abigail could read any of it. "I don't know that I can explain it any better now."

"Try," said her sister with a patient smile. "What have you got yourself into, Pen?"

"A great lot of trouble," she admitted. "I didn't mean to!"

"You never do. What happened?"

Penelope made a face, but she let it go. The whole wretched story, from Frances Lockwood's infatuation to Lord Atherton's actions and warning, came rushing out. The only part she withheld was how Viscount Clary had been mistreating Olivia, and that only because Olivia had explicitly begged her not to tell Abigail. Her sister listened intently, with only an occasional question. By the time she finished, Penelope felt as if a great weight had lifted off her—probably only for a few moments, but it felt so wonderful to unburden herself, she didn't care.

"My," murmured Abigail at the end. "That is quite a tangle. And Mama doesn't know?"

Penelope shook her head.

Her sister sighed. "You'd better tell her. You know she'll hear it eventually."

"Agreed—but I would rather have a response in mind when I tell her, to spare me from being murdered on the spot." Abigail gave her a doubtful look, and Penelope flushed. "And I also kept hoping I wouldn't need to tell her."

"Not a good gamble, Pen."

She groaned. "So what should I do?"

Abigail took her time fussing over another cup of tea. That alone warned Penelope that she wouldn't like her sister's response. "Did Lord Atherton tell you precisely what the rumors are?"

She shuddered. "They're terrible; every sort of wicked lasciviousness you can imagine. Worse than Lady Constance's stories. But he said his name wasn't part of them," she added, with a silent sigh of relief that she'd been spared that.

Abigail's brow wrinkled. "But you said Frances Lockwood accused you of stealing him. How long do you think before she repeats that, especially when the other rumor spreads?"

Penelope's throat felt tight. It still hurt, deeply, that Frances would think that of her. She pleated a fold of her skirt and stared out the window until she could speak. "May I come live with you? For the rest of this year, and perhaps next as well?"

Abigail snorted. "I remember how well you liked Richmond when we spent the summer there. Now you want to spend the winter there as well? But this time at Montrose Hill House, where workmen are busy repairing everything from the roof to the stables."

"I could endure," Penelope assured her, although privately she wasn't so certain, now that Abigail reminded her about Richmond. When their father had bought a country estate there, it had seemed like the end of the earth to Penelope, a good ten miles distant from London and as quiet as a country village. The only excitement had been Abigail's romance with Sebastian Vane, which had involved clandestine meetings in the woods, a public argument in the middle of Richmond, a daring jaunt through the woods to solve an old mystery and recover lost treasure, and, best of all, a romantically thrilling night when Abigail fled the odious Lord Atherton's advances and spent a night of passion in Sebastian's arms.

Penelope was imagining that last part, as her sister had refused to tell her anything about it, but from Papa's furious reaction both before and after

Abigail returned home, she thought it must be reasonably close to the truth.

Her sister only smiled. "What's wrong with Lord Atherton's suggestion?"

The part about his presence. Penelope managed not to say it aloud. "Don't you think it unlikely that people who are calling me all kinds of vile names today will welcome me with approval and respect tomorrow if only Viscount Atherton is standing beside me?"

"I doubt the gossip would reverse course that quickly, but we both know it would eventually. Especially if people thought you would marry him. He'll be an earl one day, and not some penniless, indebted one."

A red flush blazed up her face. "I'm not going to marry him!"

"I didn't say that. I said people would regard you differently if they *thought* you would marry him." Abigail tilted her head and studied her shrewdly. "But that was quite an adamant exclamation."

"I just don't want you to get any ridiculous ideas," she retorted. "Atherton is the last man on earth I would ever marry."

"The last man?" Now Abigail gave her a look of such skepticism, Penelope flushed even hotter. "A handsome, wealthy, charming viscount. Really, Penelope? You'd rather have a bricklayer or a chimney sweep?"

She scowled and fiddled with her cup. "You know what I mean."

Abigail was quiet for a moment. "I know that when he first came to call at Hart House, you were much more approving."

Penelope rued the day she had ever admitted that to her sister. "That was before I knew his true character. And I only admitted then that he's very handsome, which I have never denied."

Her sister raised her brows. "His true character. Which facet do you mean: the bit of him that came with us to search the woods for the money Sebastian was accused of stealing, quite probably defying his father's orders? Or perhaps you mean the bit where he let his sister confess that she actually had taken the money? That was horrible of him, I grant you. No, I know: you must mean the impulse that drove him to get a letter from Lord Stratford exonerating Sebastian, so Papa would let me marry him." She shrugged as Penelope glared at her. "You're not making a good argument so far."

"He didn't protest when his father started those evil rumors about Sebastian," she pointed out. "And he kept the secret for years. He turned his back on a friend."

Abigail hesitated. "It's not as simple as all that. Sebastian has told me a great deal more about him, and I think you judge him too harshly."

"Oh? What would pardon letting everyone think his dearest childhood friend was a thief and a murderer?" Penelope widened her eyes. "To say nothing of leaving Sebastian to crawl home after falling on his wounded knee—when Sebastian was an invited guest in his home?"

"I'm not saying he's been above reproach in everything," her sister countered. "But I suspect his lot hasn't been as easy as it appears. Lord Stratford is neither a kind nor a loving father. Sebastian says he used to beat Atherton regularly."

Penelope pressed her lips together, unwilling to feel sorry for the viscount. It was not difficult to believe Lord Stratford was a cruel father, but Atherton was a grown man; if he couldn't stand up to his father now, what did that say about him? "He schemed to marry Frances, just a few weeks after he was courting you."

"Thank goodness," said Abigail, to Penelope's astonishment. "I would have felt terrible if he'd been truly hurt."

"*Schemed*," she tried again, emphasizing the word and making it sound as noxious as possible. "He wasn't in love with her any more than he was in love with you! What do you make of a man who would do that?"

"I would guess he's trying to find a wife," her sister calmly replied. "You said she was a very sweet girl; did she have other admirers?"

"Yes," Penelope muttered after a moment.

"Does she have some connections? A dowry?"

"Yes," she growled.

"It sounds very ordinary to me. A handsome gentleman of his age and rank will want a bride, and she sounds just the type a gentleman would prefer. What did you do to disrupt it?"

Penelope, already sulking, did not see that question coming. She gaped, then blushed, and mulishly set her chin. "Nothing."

"Really?" said Abigail so dryly, Penelope flushed deeper red. Her face would be permanently scarlet after this conversation.

"She asked what sort of man I wanted to marry and I told her. I encouraged her to be sure Atherton cared for her before she accepted him. That's all," she insisted.

"And what happened?"

She cleared her throat. "I don't precisely know. I saw them dancing, looking in good charity with each other, and then I left the room. After the—the *incident*, when Mrs. Lockwood was glaring down her nose at me, Atherton said Frances had declared she never wanted to see him again. But I swear, Abby, I have no idea what happened. He didn't tell me, and Frances . . . I don't think Frances will ever speak to me again." And that hurt. Penelope was aware of her own faults, but disloyalty was not one of them. Frances was—had been—her friend, and she never ever would have tried to attract any man who was courting her friend. The unvarnished betrayal in Frances's eyes when she accused Penelope of lying about that cut very deeply.

"Not to be harsh, Pen, but that seems like the least of your worries at the moment."

She knew it. Unfortunately she had no idea what to do about Clary. Hopefully he would tire of telling lies about her quickly. Hopefully a duke's daughter would elope with a footman, or two peers would come to blows in Parliament. Any of those things would give people something far more interesting to talk about. "I know, although I miss having her friendship. But what am I to do about the rest?"

"Short of following Lord Atherton's suggestion?" Penelope made an impatient gesture, and Abigail sighed. "You could marry someone else. You could persuade Jamie to take you to Italy for a few years. Or you could cut off your hair and live as a man for the rest of your life."

Penelope's jaw sagged open. "I meant within reason!"

"It would be very reasonable to marry someone else."

"But who?" Real alarm stirred in her breast. Somehow she had been sure her sister would have a sensible yet acceptable alternative, because Abigail always did. Penelope would have spent her entire childhood being punished if not for her sister talking her into schemes which were just as exciting, yet somehow less dangerous, than her own ideas. Spend a few years in Italy with her brother? She'd rather live as a man, if it came down to that.

"Penelope, I don't know," Abigail said. "Since you haven't got a more appealing suitor at the ready, I think your best choice is to graciously accept Lord Atherton's proposal and make the best of it. You might come to revise your low opinion of him. Try to remember how you liked him when he first came to Hart House. Remember how entertaining he was when he took us to Hampton Court and tried to find a ghost for your amusement." Penelope opened her mouth to protest, and Abigail held up one hand to stop her. "Sebastian doesn't hold his behavior against him, and Sebastian was the wronged party. How can you be less willing to forgive? Not only has he done you no wrong, he's offering to do you a very great favor."

Penelope clamped her mouth shut and stared down at her hands. She couldn't very well tell her sister that it was for her own peace of mind that she clung to her dislike. Abigail might decide that constituted permission to meddle.

As she was searching for a reply, the door opened to admit their mother. She was pale and held herself stiffly erect as she closed the door, very carefully, behind her. "Penelope," she said, her voice low and shaky. "I have heard the most dreadful thing—your father just told me—did you . . . ?" She paused, visibly fighting for composure. "Did you behave as people are suggesting?"

It was all there in her mother's face; Mama knew, and apparently Papa did, too. She was doomed. "No, ma'am," she whispered anyway, shrinking into her chair.

Mama gave her a look of pure disbelief, although that faded quickly. With jerky steps she crossed the room and sank into a chair. "I am completely at a loss. I can tell by your face that you know exactly what I'm referring to." Cowed, Penelope gave a tiny nod. Mama's throat worked. "And yet you chose not to tell me."

Never had Penelope felt such searing shame, or such regret that she'd put something off. She'd had no idea how to bring it up; she'd had no idea how to respond.

Abigail stepped into the charged silence. "We were just discussing how to deal with it, Mama—"

"When I want your advice, I will ask for it, Abigail," said her mother icily. "This is about Penelope, and why she did nothing even though she knew there were rumors out there calling her the very loosest and immoral of women!"

"I didn't know how to tell you, Mama," she said softly. "I'm sorry."

"And so you said nothing?" Mama's eyes flashed with wrath, and her voice rose with each word. "Not even a hint? Not even in confidence? How could you?" She shook her head. "You lied to me. A slip on the stair at the Gosnolds' party. A turned ankle. I trusted you, Penelope, and I believed you. What a foolish thing!"

Her mouth was dry. "I didn't want you to worry . . . I didn't think anything would come of it . . ."

"And what do you think now?" snapped Mrs. Weston. She took a deep breath and closed her eyes, raising her clasped hands to her chin. Penelope knew that look; it was the Praying for Patience look, and her mother was only driven to it in dire situations. A frisson of alarm went through her. That look meant the worst was yet to come.

And then it did. The door opened and her father stepped into the room, followed a moment later by Lord Atherton.

"Abigail," said Papa. "I need to speak with your mother and sister."

His tone brooked no argument, nor any reply at all. Her sister all but ran from the room, with only a brief sympathetic glance at her. Penelope got to her feet, feeling like Joan of Arc must have felt when she saw the bonfire prepared for her. Atherton was watching her far too closely for comfort. The fact that he was here at all was very bad.

Papa turned to her. "What were you thinking, child?"

Her father's disappointment crushed whatever defiance she had left. Penelope adored her father, and the expression on his face was utterly disillusioned. "I'm sorry, Papa. I didn't know what would happen . . . I was going to tell you . . ."

"You might have guessed that it warranted telling me or your mother, in warning if nothing else!" He ran one hand over his face. "Not that it matters. The only question now is how to mitigate the disaster."

Penelope avoided looking at Lord Atherton, though facing her parents was no better. "I'm thinking of running away to the West Indies." At this moment, any far-off colony, even with tropical insects and cannibalistic natives, sounded inviting.

"Do not be smart with me!" warned her father. "Who started those malicious rumors?"

She couldn't resist a shocked peek at the viscount. He hadn't told. At her glance, he raised one brow slightly and cocked his head toward Papa, as if in invitation for her to denounce Clary. She hovered in horrible indecision; if she told Papa, it might save her. But then again, it might not. Clary had disdained her father. What if Papa called him out and they fought a duel and Clary killed him? Penelope pictured her mother, weeping brokenheartedly over her father's body lying dead in the grass on Hampstead Heath, and bit down on her lip. Oh God. She'd made a thorough mess of this, and she couldn't let her father suffer for it. "I can't, Papa."

"Yes, you can, and you will."

Her mind was running feverishly. Maybe she

could say something, if not quite the truth, that
would let her slip free of the noose. She could say
Clary had been drunk and accosted her in the
hallway, and was now lying to cover his own rude
behavior. She could say it was some other man
whose face she never saw. She could even blame
Frances and suggest it was done out of pique, just
a fit of female jealousy—she gave her head a shake
to dislodge that idea. Too late she realized there
was no good explanation, and if Papa had brought
Lord Atherton here, he knew it, too. "I don't think
it would do any good to tell you, Papa," she said
softly. "Even if he would retract it, the damage has
been done."

Her father exhaled and then slowly lowered
himself into a chair next to her mother. He hung
his head, and when Mama reached out her hand,
he clasped it as if it would save him from drowning. Penelope looked away, painfully aware of
how deeply she had disappointed both her parents, and caught sight of Atherton. He was watching Mama and Papa with an odd expression, but
he must have felt her gaze on him; with a jerk he
turned his head and met her eyes. She had the
strangest sense that he was looking at her in a
completely different light, almost as if he'd never
seen her before.

"Mr. Weston," he said. "May I have a word with
Penelope?"

It was the first time he'd said her name.
Penelope gulped and concentrated on her hands,
wishing she hadn't heard it. Then he made it
worse by adding, "After all, this involves us most
intimately."

Papa nodded, and he and Mama left. The room seemed very small when it held just her and Lord Atherton. She wet her lips. "Yes, my lord?"

He sat down in the chair next to hers. "I've just had a very pointed conversation with your father. At the end of it, he offered me a choice, which really depends on you."

"Which is?" Her heart lifted; a choice?

"He wants the name of the man who started the rumors."

She bit her lip wretchedly. "I can't tell him." She couldn't drag Olivia into it; whatever trouble her friend was in, drawing Papa's fury onto her wouldn't help. As it was, she was growing very alarmed for Olivia; if Clary would ruin Penelope this way, what would he do to Olivia? And then there was that horrible image of her father lying on Hampstead Heath, covered in blood, while Clary stood gloating over him, a smoking pistol in hand.

Atherton let out his breath as if he'd been expecting that. "Why not? Who are you protecting?"

She flinched. "No one."

"Is it another man?" he pressed.

Penelope blushed. "No!"

His shoulders eased. "Then there's no reason you shouldn't marry me."

"Except that I don't want to!"

"My tender feelings are crushed," he said dryly.

"Huh! We don't even like each other," she muttered.

"Not true, and you know it." He held out his hand. "Come here."

Her heart tried to jump into her throat for a moment. "Why?"

"Trust me a moment." When she still didn't move, he took hold of the arms of her chair and tugged, dragging it toward him until their knees touched. Penelope sat frozen in her seat as he leaned forward. "I don't dislike you," he said in that buttery-smooth voice. "On the contrary. From the moment we first met I thought you were enchanting."

"No, you didn't," she said, trying not to stare at the way his hair fell in dark waves over his brow. It was romantic and poetic and rakish. Damn him for being so attractive, especially close up.

"And we got on splendidly," he went on, ignoring her protest. "At first."

"First impressions are very unreliable." One lock fell in a perfect curl right above his left eye. She wondered what it felt like, and then she squeezed her fingers into fists to punish them for wanting to know.

"Penelope," he murmured, "we're both in a very bad spot." He lifted her hand, handling it as if it were fragile, and smoothed her fingers straight. He bent his head and brushed his lips over the pounding pulse in her wrist. "Fortunately we can save each other."

She felt the room sway around her. Her heart seemed to be choking her. His breath was warm on her skin, and he kept her hand cradled against his cheek, where she could feel the faint scratch of stubble. Heaven help her, but something inside her thrilled at the contact. Her dislike of him had been the bulwark protecting her from her own wicked urges to fling herself into his arms and beg him to do scandalous things to her, and now he was dismantling that disapprobation, brick by brick. Soon she would be defenseless.

"I don't think we should," she said by way of one last effort, but her voice had lost its vigor and defiance, and become soft and almost regretful instead.

He tilted his head, peering up at her with those vivid blue eyes from beneath the rumpled waves of his hair. "I do."

Penelope swallowed. He was still holding her hand, but barely; if she pulled, she would be free. Unfortunately she seemed unable to do anything remotely sensible when he touched her. She had never seen this side of him . . . because of course he'd never wanted to marry her before. The thought gave her a small burst of courage. "Is this how you proposed to all the other girls?"

"No," he said. "But I think I did it all wrong before. There was something missing . . ." He eased his weight forward, sliding off the chair and onto one knee. Penelope knew what he was going to do—she even caught her breath as he leaned ever closer—and there wasn't a single thing she could do to stop him. Indeed, some treacherous part of her seemed to burst into life at the prospect, until she had to grip the chair arm with her free hand to keep from reaching for him. His mesmerizing gaze never wavered from her; Penelope could only assume she was staring at him like a simpleton, unable to move or think or even breathe as his lips dipped toward hers.

She quaked at the first brush of his mouth. Like evil pixies unleashed from captivity, her thoughts spilled out in a tortured mess. How she'd imagined him falling in love with her the first time he sat in Mama's drawing room and turned his dazzling smile on her. How she'd been so stupidly silly trying to get his attention during a barge expedition by tossing her hat overboard, and how he'd gallantly rescued it. How she'd dared him into taking her off to look for ghosts at Hampton Court, all the time hoping he might steal a kiss. How ecstatic she'd been when he sent her flowers . . . until she realized he'd also sent flowers to her mother and her sister. And even how jealous she'd been when he focused his attention on Abigail and gave everyone to understand that it was the kind, sensible Weston girl he wanted, not her.

Except . . . he wasn't kissing Abigail now, or Frances Lockwood, or any other young lady. He was kissing *her*, his lips moving over hers lightly yet teasingly, until she barely realized that her own mouth had softened and responded. Apart from her hand, which he still held clasped in his own, he wasn't touching her anywhere else, but Penelope felt nailed to her chair. Or perhaps she simply didn't want to move, to interrupt this breathtaking moment of unexpected tenderness.

"Marry me, Penelope," he whispered, his mouth still brushing hers.

Her resistance was rapidly waning. "I don't think I should," she whispered back in honest apprehension.

"Nonsense. Trust how you feel," he breathed, and his lips settled on hers. Penelope inhaled in surprise, and he touched her chin, nudging her lips apart and proving beyond all doubt that there was far more to kissing than she'd thought.

"Do you want me?" It was a weak basis for marriage, but she was trapped and she knew it. Any little comfort would be very welcome.

"I do." He glanced at the door. "Enough to commit every last wickedly pleasurable act we're accused of, right here on this sofa, if only your parents weren't outside the door."

Heat flooded her face, and not at the thought of her parents. If she married him, he'd make love to her. "What acts?"

His eyes glittered and one corner of his mouth curled upward. "Marry me and find out."

She wavered and then gave in. It wasn't as though she had much choice anyway. She nodded once.

A fierce grin crossed his face, and he leaned in and kissed her again, harder this time. "We'll be good together."

Penelope wasn't so sure, but it was too late. Atherton was heading for the door to tell her parents. Even as she covertly—and unwillingly—admired the way his trousers fit as he walked, she worried that she'd made a terrible mistake. If he hadn't kissed her—if he hadn't managed to hit on her one great, inexplicable weakness, her attraction to him—would she still have given in? She smoothed her shaking hands on her skirt and tried to hide her anxiety. Once upon a time she had daydreamed of him kissing her and telling her he wanted her. And deep in her heart, she admitted it had been a lovely kiss, soft and seductive and far too short. She wanted him to kiss her again.

But now something her mother used to say echoed around her brain, with a particular sharpness this time: *Be careful what you wish for, Penelope. You may get it.*

Chapter 12

Within a few days the deed was done.

Mrs. Weston decreed it would be a small but exquisite ceremony. Abigail was still in London, but otherwise it was just Mr. and Mrs. Weston, Atherton, and her.

Not Atherton, Benedict. She was entitled to call him by name now.

Because he had been living in the officers' quarters, Atherton had taken a suite of rooms in Mivart's Hotel until they could locate a house. It was very near Grosvenor Square, but Penelope still found herself hesitating as the day wore on and her trunks were brought down, ready to go. Lizzie, her maid since she was twelve, would be going with her, and she left with the trunks to make everything ready at the hotel. That left nothing for it but to bid her parents and sister farewell, and let Atherton hand her into the carriage for the short ride to Mivart's, which was accomplished in complete silence.

She was almost relieved when a few Guardsmen were on hand to greet them. Almost, because it was apparent they had already been drinking and were intent on bearing Atherton away for a few more rounds at the nearby tavern. With hardly a glance at her, he left with them as the porter showed her up to the suite.

The hotel was blessedly quiet. Penelope had never stayed in a hotel, so she walked through the rooms curiously. Lizzie had already unpacked her things and retired, so she had the suite to herself. There was a sitting room, with windows overlooking Brook Street. She peeked out, marveling at the view, so different from the elegant expanse of Grosvenor Square she'd seen from her bedchamber at home. Even at this late hour carriages were coming and going, and if she listened very carefully, she imagined she could hear the Guardsmen carrying on at the pub. That was certainly not like home.

Well. Home was not home now. She was no longer Miss Weston but Lady Atherton. The mere name made her cross her arms protectively over her chest. How the devil had she got herself into this mess? She didn't look, but she knew the door to her right led to a bedroom. As hard as she tried not to, she couldn't stop thinking of the myriad pleasures Lady Constance had written of. Would Atherton do any of that to her? Would he want to? And even more importantly, would he do it as well as Constance's lovers?

Whatever her other failings, Penelope was a realist. She saw nothing wrong with trying to direct her own fate, but she didn't see the point in crying over unhappy circumstances; time spent crying would only be time spent not plotting how to improve her situation. And if any situation needed improvement, it was this one: married, till death parted them, to a man she didn't much know, let alone love. A man, no less, who had wanted to marry first her sister and then her friend. A man who'd visibly lost his patience with her on more than one occasion. A man who'd nevertheless kissed her so persuasively, her sense had flown out the window and she'd somehow agreed to marry him, meaning she had no one to blame for this but herself.

For a moment she wondered why he'd been so determined to marry her. No mistake about it, he had wanted this marriage. She knew from eavesdropping on her parents that Papa had been reluctant to agree, because he didn't think Atherton was a good match for her. Mama had disagreed, but Penelope had been more interested in her father's words. He'd told Atherton there would be no wedding if Penelope didn't agree to it. He'd told Atherton he would be watching carefully to see that Penelope was happy. It warmed her heart to know her father wanted her to be happy, but it also made her feel very small and selfish that she hadn't gone to him earlier, before things went so terribly wrong.

No one to blame but herself.

Penelope took a deep breath, telling herself she also had no one to look to but herself for making her marriage happy. Atherton had wanted to marry her, for some as-yet undetermined reason, so he should be amenable. He'd looked at her bosom the night of the *incident* with undisguised interest. He wanted her. Despite valiant efforts not to, she wanted him—and now there was no reason to fight it. That was a start.

She circled the room again, investigating every little luxury and convenience. Her opinion of hotels was vastly improved when she finished, but her husband still had not returned. The clock on the mantel indicated she'd been waiting an hour. *What was he doing?* she wondered in some irritation. It was his bloody wedding night.

That thought led to another, and Penelope realized she was a married woman. Married women could read whatever they wanted, and no mother would take it away or punish her. She all but ran into the bedroom and dug through her valise until she uncovered an issue of *Ackermann's Repository*, which held between its pages not one but two issues of *50 Ways to Sin*. Abigail had given her the missing thirty-third issue with a whispered assurance that it was a particularly delicious one. Penelope devoutly hoped so; the one with red silk ribbons had been mesmerizing. Perhaps she should leave it out where Atherton could find it . . . But before she could sit down to enjoy it, she heard the creak of the door in the sitting room. On instinct she stuffed the pamphlets back into her valise and crossed the room in time to see Atherton close the door by stumbling backward against it. His jacket was askew and his hair rumpled, and when he saw her, his mouth curved in a sly, predatory grin unlike his usual polished charm. "Good eve, lady wife," he said, his voice rough with laughter.

She looked him up and down. "It seems as though you've enjoyed it thoroughly."

"So far," he agreed, shoving himself away from the door and ambling into the room. "Have you?"

Her brows lowered in pique. She'd been sitting here waiting for him while he was out drinking with his mates. The closer he came, the more she could smell the spirits. "Not as much as you, it appears."

He laughed. "There were a few rounds of toasts. How was I to say no?" He pulled out a chair at the table and dropped heavily into it before taking a flask from his pocket. "Are you jealous?"

"Of drinking until I can't walk a straight line?" Penelope sniffed. "No."

He cocked his head and studied her. That roguish smile still lingered on his lips. "So what noble activity were you engaged in whilst waiting for me?"

"I was contemplating how on earth we're going to make each other happy for the next several decades." She looked pointedly at the flask hanging from his fingers. "Strong spirits will be required, obviously."

"You think so?" With one booted foot he kicked another chair out from under the table. "Let's have a drink, then."

"Ladies don't drink."

He leaned back and picked up two glasses from the tray on the table behind him. He tipped his flask and poured a small amount in each glass. "Ladies don't drink because they aren't allowed by their proper and respectable mamas. You're a married woman now. Have a drink with me."

"Is it whiskey?" Penelope eyed the glasses in

unwilling interest. Whatever he wanted her to do must be a bad idea, and yet . . .

"It's an excellent French brandy." His faint grin seemed to simmer with wicked intentions and hint that he wasn't such a shallow prig. "You're not afraid, are you?"

She hesitated a moment longer, then defiantly seated herself. "Not at all. I simply hate the smell of whiskey and wouldn't drink it if you forced me to."

He caught up his glass and raised it in the air with a grand sweeping motion. All his movements were loose and sweeping. "To our marriage," he said, watching her with glittering eyes.

Penelope raised her glass. "If you insist." She took a dainty sip. It was strong but smooth, and although it made her gasp and blink a few times, it felt warm and soft once it reached her belly.

The corner of her husband's mouth crooked. He tossed back the entirety of his drink with one flick of his wrist, and poured more. He reached across the table and refilled her glass. "To our future."

Better endured when foxed, she thought, but obediently took another sip. "Are you drunk?"

"A little," he said without guilt. "Are you?"

She licked her lip for a stray drop of brandy. "Of course not."

"Drink up, then." He raised his glass and tossed down his liquor as before.

"Why should I get drunk?"

Atherton shrugged and tugged at his cravat. His jacket was hanging off one shoulder, and his waistcoat was already half undone. Penelope watched from under her eyelashes as he pulled the cravat free and threw it on the floor. His shirt flopped open at his neck, giving her a view of skin all the way down his throat. He looked rakish and dangerous, unlike his usual buttoned-up self. "You don't have to get drunk. I thought you would relish the chance to live a little dangerously."

Penelope took another sip. It went down very easily this time, silky smooth. She took another longer drink, until the glass was almost empty. "I had hoped for something more exciting than sitting in a hotel room drinking brandy."

He draped one arm over the back of his chair and slouched elegantly. His eyes slid over her in blatant appraisal—and hunger. "What else have you got in mind?"

When her brother, James, got drunk, he would say anything. He often wouldn't remember half of what he'd said the next day, but Penelope had learned a variety of very interesting and useful things when he was three sheets to the wind, things she was sure even her parents never knew. She'd learned that Millie the upstairs maid had been sent away to the country not for her lungs but because she'd been carrying George the stable hand's baby, and that George had taken a beating from the head groom before being given a wage increase and allowed to marry Millie. She'd learned that James's mate at university, Edward, had been sent down for lewd behavior—with a male porter. She'd learned that Mr. Wilford had been a suicide and not the victim of a housebreaker as publicly believed, and that Lady Barlow's child, born after years of barren wedlock, was really the offspring of her husband's valet.

How James knew some of that, Penelope couldn't imagine, but it was all fascinating. Sadly her brother had given up most heavy drinking, at least when she was around, but it struck her that Atherton might be similar. This could be her chance to get truthful answers from him on questions that had tormented her for months.

"We could talk," she suggested, pushing her glass back across the table. "Get to know each other."

"We could get to know each other in other ways," he replied with another searing glance at her bosom, but he tipped the flask over her glass again. "What should I know of my wife?"

She thought for a moment, sipping her brandy slowly. Lord Almighty, no wonder men drank it by the cask. Bloody lovely stuff. She felt bold and clever and fairly invincible. "You asked me once what you'd done to earn my dislike. I denied it but I doubt you believed me, particularly since I was lying." That got his attention. His eyebrows went up, and the hand holding his glass paused in midair. Penelope shrugged. "I haven't been able to work out in my mind how an honorable man would turn his back on a friend of many years' standing and allow him to be condemned—even shunned—by everyone in town." She cocked her head and kept her expression artless. "Why did you?"

Atherton finished his drink in one swallow. "I never intended that to happen. I never wished Sebastian ill."

"But you accused him of scheming to run off with your sister," she pointed out.

He let his head fall back, as if he'd faced this question a hundred times and was weary to death of it. "She disappeared in the middle of the night. She was deeply infatuated with him, and I knew he was very fond of her. There were few other places she could have gone in Richmond. It wasn't unreasonable to think she had gone to Bastian."

Bastian. Penelope had never heard that, not even from Abby; it must have been Sebastian's childhood nickname, and it hinted at the depth of the friendship he'd betrayed. "So you went looking for her at his house. But why did you assume he'd seduced her into an elopement?"

He gave his flask a shake, and then held it out and closed one eye, squinting into its depths. "I was fairly crazed with fear when I went after her, and said things I didn't really believe."

"Crazed with fear?" she exclaimed in surprise. "Why?"

His eyes flashed at her, and she got the sudden sense that he wasn't anywhere near as foxed as he seemed. Then his face eased and he thumped the flask down on the table before reaching behind him for the bottle on the sideboard. "She might have fallen into the river. She might have been set upon by highwaymen or kidnappers. She was only sixteen. I already admitted I was wrong, didn't I?"

Penelope watched him pour a generous amount of brandy into his glass, then into hers. He was crazed with fear for Samantha, but he hadn't gone to the river with a hook, he'd gone to Sebastian's house. There was more to that than he was telling, but she let it go. "Then why didn't you say anything to dissuade people from believing he murdered his father?"

He made a face. "What could I have said? I didn't know where old Mr. Vane was. I never repeated the rumor and I never agreed with anyone who did."

"But you never came to his defense, either, did you?" she couldn't stop herself from replying.

Atherton's eyes darkened, and his fingers tightened around his glass. Penelope tensed as well. "I was a young man," he said after a moment. "Neither as sensible nor as noble as I ought to have been. I asked Sebastian's pardon and he gave it. I never wanted him to be miserable or shunned, and I'm delighted he's found happiness." There was a definite note of warning in his voice.

Penelope heeded it—somewhat. There was still much more she wanted to know. She tilted her head and arched one brow. "Even though he got the girl you wanted to marry?"

He stared at her a moment, then gave a sharp bark of laughter. "Even though."

"Were you very miserable when Abby rejected you?"

He sat back and shook his head, still wearing a humorless smile. "Must everything be a storm of passion and emotion with you?" He reached for his glass again. "I wouldn't have asked her if I didn't hope to be accepted." He paused thoughtfully, glass raised, then added, "And the same went for Miss Lockwood, if that was your next query." He tossed down the brandy.

Penelope's face burned. "You didn't love either of them."

"No," he readily agreed. "There are many reasons a man asks a woman to marry him. Love is only one possibility."

She scowled, then quickly wiped it away. Her glass sat in front of her, untouched for some time, so she snatched it up and took a quick gulp, barely noticing the heat of the liquor this time. "But it's a vital one. And you couldn't even muster up a pretense of affection. That's why my sister sent you packing, and that's why Frances declared she never wanted to see you again, isn't it?"

This time he looked irked. "Are we going to revisit every humiliation I've ever suffered at the hands of a woman? There was a tavern wench when I was at university who never would grant me a kiss . . ."

"Huh! I'm not surprised," she muttered.

"And then there was a woman who bedeviled me for months," he went on. "When we first met, she was charming and delightful, but she soon grew fickle. She'd dance with me one night, and then the next day look as though she'd like to skewer me with my own sword. Even though I tried to make amends—often for sins I hadn't even committed—she said she'd rather I kept far, far away from her and told everyone I violently disliked her." Penelope jerked up her head in shock. "I suppose I put paid to that suggestion this morning, though, eh?" he added with a suggestive wink.

She pressed her lips together. This had been a bad idea. He wasn't as voluble a drunk as Jamie was, and his answers were only stoking her temper in spite of her efforts not to allow that.

"You ought to have given it a try," she said coolly. "It would have benefited us both."

"But then we wouldn't be here, savoring our wedding night together."

"No, we could each be doing something far more pleasurable," she snapped back. "Perhaps mucking out the stable stalls, or blacking grates. It would have spared us this pointless conversation at least."

"Mucking out stables! Perish the thought." With surprising speed he went from sprawled in his chair to leaning over the table toward her. "Very well." He glared at her, rakishly dangerous with his dark hair falling over his brow and his blue eyes searing with intensity. "You ask why I courted your sister and Miss Lockwood. You really want to know why I paid them attention."

Dimly Penelope thought there was a more strident warning there, but her blood was running. Her nerves were tingling, and she felt reckless and uncaring of what might come. "Yes, if you're not too cowardly to admit it."

"Cowardly?" He arched one brow. "Someday I'd like to know how your mind works. But if you want to know, you shall know. My sister recommended Abigail."

That was utterly unexpected—and just as unsatisfying. "Your sister?" she repeated incredulously. "Samantha? You courted *my* sister because *your* sister took a fancy to her?"

Atherton poured more brandy, watching it slosh into the glasses. Some spilled on the table, but neither of them paid it any mind. "No, although Samantha's good opinion means a great deal to me. She met your family and immediately wrote to me, saying she'd met the most delightful girl: sensible, kindhearted, independent without being wild, and lovely to look at." He tilted the glass to his lips again as Penelope gaped at him in outraged shock. "Oh yes—the young lady had one more appealing attribute," he added with a cynical twist to his lips. "An immense dowry."

Penelope found her tongue. "The money? It was all about the money, not my sister or what she wanted, or even what you wanted? I could have forgiven it, you know, if you'd been bowled away with love for her, but I knew all along that had nothing to do with it—"

"Forgiven it?" His laugh was harsh. "You've never forgiven a single thing I've ever done."

"Some of them don't deserve to be forgiven," she retorted, lurching to her feet. The room swayed dangerously around her, and she clutched the edge of the table to keep her balance. "I'm leaving, and I intend to tell my father to sue for repayment of my dowry—which was every bit as immense as Abby's, as you would have known had you cared to ask."

"I knew," he said, watching her with glowing eyes. "Sit down."

It struck Penelope like an arrow between the ribs. Her hands shook and her lungs seemed to have frozen. He knew. He knew it was just as profitable to marry her as it was to marry Abigail, and he'd still chosen Abigail. She was sure it wasn't possible for one person to feel more humiliated and stupid than she did right now. "It makes me wonder what Samantha said about me," she said, somehow managing to keep her voice steady.

Slowly her husband raised his eyes to hers. His head tipped to one side, casting his chiseled face into sharp relief in the firelight, and for a moment she thought he would roll right out of the chair, drunk as a lord. If he did, she intended to leave him in a heap on the floor.

"Vivacious," he said softly. "She said you were spirited, intelligent, strong-willed, and beautiful."

Penelope blinked, her slipping opinion of Samantha arrested. That didn't sound terrible. "So why didn't you want me?" The wretched words fell out of her mouth before she could stop them.

He shrugged. "Because I wanted a peaceful marriage. Because I didn't want a wife who would bedevil me and torment me and turn me inside out. A sensible, pleasant, pretty girl with a dowry: those were my hopes."

She swallowed. Why did it hurt so much that he didn't think she was any of those things? She ought to be enraged that he'd labeled her sister so slightly, but instead she felt as though he'd slapped her. "I'm sorry you didn't get what you wanted."

He looked up at her without moving. "Don't be so sure of that. Come here."

She recoiled. "Of course I won't, Atherton."

His moody gaze dropped to her mouth. "My name is Benedict. You should use it, Penelope. Now, come here."

Again the sound of her name in his voice sent a little shiver of delight through her. "Don't be ridiculous. We hardly know each other, marriage notwithstanding, and we both know you don't care for me, nor I for you."

"We have a lifetime for that to develop." Without warning he turned his dazzling smile on her, the one that always made her feel weak in the knees. Although perhaps that was the brandy this time; she had drunk an awful lot of it, now that she looked at the bottle and saw how low the level of amber liquid was.

Penelope took a step backward, until she almost tripped on her chair and had to steady herself on it. The floor seemed to be tilted. "You must be very drunk if you think that. Good night, sir. I'm going to bed." She turned toward the bedroom door, but the damned chair was in her way and she had some trouble getting around it.

"Come here, Penelope," said her husband. She started when she realized he was right beside her; how had he done that? "You can barely walk." He caught her as she wobbled precariously.

"I can walk!" She pushed at him, but that only sent her staggering away. He was much bigger and heavier and immovable, and she had to put one hand on the wall to brace herself.

"So I see." He strolled after her, propping one hand above her head. "Not much used to brandy, are you?"

"Did you think I was?"

"No. I was astonished when you sat down and took a drink."

She gaped at him. "Then why did you offer it, you rotten blighter?"

He burst out laughing. For some reason, so did she. That upset her equilibrium even more, and she ended up leaning against the wall, holding her sides as the laughter wouldn't stop.

"I have no idea," said her husband, still laughing. "It seemed like a fine idea at the time."

"We're both going to regret it in the morning," she gasped, wiping at her eyes. "Brandy gives people terrible headaches . . ."

"I'm sure it will," he agreed, his voice low and amused, and then he kissed her.

Chapter 13

There was still a smile on her lips, and her brain seemed to have been scrambled—by the brandy, no doubt—and that was surely why Penelope kissed him back. This time his kiss was neither gentle nor soft; this time it was insistent and compelling, and somehow the feel of his tongue stroking hers sheared away all her inhibition. She pressed against him, clinging to his shoulders. His arm was around her waist, dragging her off her toes and into his kiss. Before she knew it her back was against the wall, her arms were around his neck, and he was kissing the side of her jaw as his hands roamed over her body with shocking assurance.

"Don't kiss me," she whispered even as she tipped her head to let him do just that.

"Only if you don't kiss me." His breath was hot on her skin.

Penelope threaded her fingers through his hair, ostensibly to pull his head away, but she got distracted by the feel of his hair around her fingers. How many times had she wondered what it felt like, and now here she was, plowing both hands into the silky, coal-black strands as he sank to his knees, his head bent over her bosom. His hands slid around her ribs, right beneath her arms, arching her back while his thumbs stroked the sides of her breasts and his mouth whispered wicked things over the low-cut neckline of her gown. "You should stop," she said weakly.

He glanced up, eyes gleaming like lightning. "If you want that, you'll have to say so with more conviction." His thumbs traced maddening whorls over her skin. His hands slid, until he was nearly cupping both her breasts in his palms. As she stared at him, speechless from the brandy and the intense craving of her body finally slipping its leash, he hooked one thumb inside the neckline of her dress and tugged, just until her nipple popped free. Penelope's whole body went rigid as he languidly touched his tongue to the pink pearl of flesh and then took it between his lips. Just the sight of his mouth on her breast was arousing, and when he began to suckle—

She would have fallen over if not for his weight bearing her against the wall. She turned her head away and closed her eyes, unable to meet his glittering, knowing gaze as he made short work of her resistance. Not that anyone would suspect she was resisting; her hands were still tangled in his hair, and the word "no" had never crossed her lips. And really, what reason did she have to resist? She'd dreamt of a man—of *this* man— looking at her as if he would go mad without her. She'd wished he would kiss her. She'd wondered, with equal parts fascination and disgust, what it would be like to make love to him. Now it looked like she was about to get all three wishes at once, and really, what motivation was that to protest anything?

Her gown loosened even more under the inexorable tugging of his thumb. Dimly she realized his other hand had gone behind her back and worked free the buttons. He released her nipple after one last strong pull, leaving it glistening and engorged, and Penelope seized the momentary respite. "Stop," she gasped, shocked to realize that she was panting and her heart was racing. "For a moment. *Benedict*."

He raised his eyes, although his thumb continued rolling idly over her breast, sending little shocks through her nerves. "Yes?"

What had she meant to say? It took her a moment to remember. Oh yes. "If you mean to make love to me, there are a few things you should know."

His lips quirked. "Such as?"

Penelope forced her eyes up and away. She stared fiercely at the vase on the mantel, trying to keep her composure. "I don't intend to sit quietly by while you take a mistress," she announced. "If you didn't want to be married to me and keep your vows, you should have taken advantage of my suggestion to avoid each other. Now you've lost your chance."

"So I have," he murmured, not sounding at all upset. Penelope shuddered at the gust of his breath on her breast. "As long as your next decree isn't that we shall sleep apart, I see no cause for concern."

"No?" Without thinking she met his gaze.

There was something unsettling about the way he was watching her, without a smile or a grin, just a focused intensity that scrambled her thoughts. What had she been saying? "Well—good. I always expected to share a bed with my husband. I hope you know what you're doing there."

Leisurely he peeled down her gaping gown and shift, exposing her other breast. "Indeed. I'll do my best."

"I expect it to be pleasurable, you know," she went on, her voice rising as his lips hovered tantalizingly close to that untouched nipple. "Wildly, passionately pleasurable."

"Based on what?" he asked, his voice a low rumble.

Penelope quaked at the first lazy stroke of his tongue. "I've read stories."

That seemed to amuse him. She felt him chuckle silently. "What every man longs to hear. But in that case, what are we waiting for?"

She didn't know. Her body was a writhing mass of taut nerves, all hungry for him. The prospect of the pleasures Lady Constance recounted—and the considerable amount of brandy she'd drunk—had dulled her worries about love for the moment. He was her husband. He didn't love her, but Penelope could no longer deny that she wanted him. She wanted him to seize her in his arms and take her to bed and ravish her senseless. Hadn't their marriage vows included something hinting at that? Perhaps it would be so good, so blissfully satisfying, she could forget about the rest, at least for a while.

He rose to his feet, looming over her. "Tell me

about these stories," he said, turning her away from him and setting to work in earnest at her dress's fastenings.

A furious blush warmed her face, even though he couldn't see it. "They're about men of astonishing prowess."

"Oh?" He was amused again, she could tell. "And innocent maidens?" There was a swish of fabric as he untied the long sash around her bodice.

"No, there's no innocent maiden." She let him push the sleeves down her arms. "One brazen lady."

"Intriguing. How brazen?" Her gown slid down to puddle at her feet, followed by her petticoats.

Penelope thought of the issue where Constance had allowed her lover to bind her to the bed with ribbons. And the one where she'd tested the limits of a closed carriage. And the one where she'd brought two men to her bed at once, and the one where she'd given herself—blindfolded—to a stranger. Just thinking about them made her pulse pick up and her blood surge. Would Benedict do any of that? She imagined him tying her to the bed with silk ribbons and had to press her knees together to stay on her feet. "Very brazen," she choked out.

"Really," he said in a speculative murmur. He was plucking at her stays' lacing with both hands. Penelope shivered as it came loose. "What do you particularly like about these stories?"

The fact that there was no shame. No blushing embarrassment or tears. Even though Constance took a different lover in each story, she was completely free with them. She had no horrible secret lodged in her breast, like Penelope did; she had no hidden longing for more from her companions. She never feared she would fall in love with any of them.

But Penelope couldn't say that to Benedict, who had married her without one word of love. He had wanted Abigail, who was kind and sensible—not like her. He had wanted Frances, who was sweet and anxious to please—not like her. He hadn't wanted passionate love in his life. He was probably like the men Constance found, able to take any willing woman to bed and then walk away without a backward glance, while Penelope was realizing she might not be much like Constance at all. She wanted passion and excitement, certainly—but not without love.

Still, there was no doubt that her body was responding to his touch and the talk of all the ways Constance found pleasure in *50 Ways to Sin*. She felt hot and restless and desperate to discover the truth of lovemaking.

"The passion," she whispered in belated answer to his query.

He began pulling pins from her hair. She heard each one plink as it hit the polished wooden floor beside her. It had taken Lizzie an hour to perfect the arrangement of braids and curls, and it was coming down in a matter of minutes at his hands. "What do you mean?"

She had no idea. "Desire," she managed to reply. Now he was running his fingers through her hair, undoing all the plaits, and it made her want to arch her back in wordless pleasure. "A wild, desperate desire to throw off restraint and . . . and . . ."

"I see," he said when her voice failed her before she could name the wicked act. He coiled her unbound hair around one hand and tugged her head to one side. "I can do that." And he pressed his mouth against the curve of her neck.

Penelope sucked in her breath. Her skin seemed to come alive at his kiss; tendrils of sensation coursed, lightning-quick, through her nerves as his lips moved over her nape. His hands teased her waist before gliding up her ribs and shaping themselves to her breasts. Her shift felt coarse and thick now, a barrier between her skin and his, and her hands, braced against the wall, balled into fists as he kissed his way down her shoulder and played with her already swollen nipples until she found herself swaying in time with the strokes of his hands.

"I am agog to know more about these stories," he murmured. His tall, strong body pressed against her, his boots bracketed her feet. She was hemmed in, trapped in an infernally hot cocoon of sensation, and she only wanted more.

"They're wicked," she whispered back.

"Tell me," he growled. His teeth nipped her earlobe, and Penelope shuddered. "What does this brazen lady do?"

"It varies." She gulped as his fingers ranged lower, over her belly. He was handling her body with a bold assurance that she thought she ought to protest, if only it hadn't been setting her every nerve ablaze.

"Does she ever touch herself?"

Oh heavens yes. In one issue, a mystery man had blindfolded Constance and bade her touch herself all over while he watched. Penelope gave a weak nod.

"Have you ever touched yourself?" Benedict whispered, his lips brushing the skin below her ear.

She blushed scarlet. "What?"

"Intimately." His wayward hand nudged between her thighs. "Here."

There was no question about it: she was drunk. That was the only explanation for her response, which was a soft moan just before her knees—and the last of her resistance—gave out. He held her up easily, and his hand slid fully between her thighs and cupped her sex.

He inhaled sharply, still nuzzling her ear. "Have you?" he asked again. "Have you brought yourself to climax?"

"A—a few times . . ." She ought to be mortified that she'd just admitted that to him; she tensed a little in anticipation of him being shocked or displeased. But his fingers were circling, stroking between her legs, sparking feelings that were very different from the little shocks of pleasure her own fingers had wrought. She would be on the floor right now if he weren't holding her against him. Her breasts felt swollen and sensitive, and the brandy must have vanquished her power of speech along with her legitimate worries that this was a bad idea.

Instead he gave a low growl of satisfaction. "Excellent. I like a woman unafraid of pleasure."

A riot of images streamed through her mind.

Of herself, naked as the day she was born; of him, also naked. Of his face, taut with hunger—for her. Of him touching her, everywhere—with his hands, with his mouth, with his naked body. Of him driving himself inside her until they both expired in ecstasy.

No, she wasn't afraid—at least not of pleasure. She forced all her other fears into a dark corner of her mind and closed a door on them. Tomorrow she would sort through her tangled new circumstances; tonight she wanted euphoria, bliss, mindless desire. She threw back her head, arching her spine to press against the marvelous feel of his fingers on her breast, and gave herself over to the sensations surging through her.

Her shift loosened; he had pulled loose the ribbon at the neckline. Penelope blushed again as he tugged it down until it puddled on the floor around her feet. "That's better," he murmured, running his hands over her shoulders, her breasts, her belly, her hips. Two more quick tugs and her pantalets came off as well. She was naked except for her stockings. "Come here, wife," he said once more, swinging her into his arms in one quick motion.

Disoriented, she curled her arms over her chest. The facings on his regimental coat scraped her, and she squirmed. "Aren't you going to take off your clothes?"

"As quickly as possible," he assured her as he dropped her on the bed. Penelope pushed herself up and watched in avid interest as he stripped off his coat and waistcoat. His shirt came over his head and her eyes grew round. No wonder Mama had never wanted her to see the statues at the museum. Without taking his eyes from her face, her new husband yanked off his boots and unbuttoned his trousers, shoved everything down and kicked it away.

And then she stared. She had read so many descriptions of a man's privy parts, but nothing compared to seeing them. And even though Constance wrote approvingly of men who were amply equipped, Penelope suddenly wasn't sure she agreed. His erection was quite a bit larger than she'd expected, and when one thought about where it was meant to fit—

"Alarmed?"

She jumped at his question, and made a face. "I was merely trying to judge it objectively."

"Were you?" He took her hand and brought it to his lips, which were shaped into a sinful half smile. To her astonishment, he licked her palm, once, twice, then each finger. It felt wicked and debauched, his tongue on her skin, and she could only stare in dazed fascination as he sucked one fingertip between his lips for a moment. Then he carried her hand lower, lower, and wrapped her fingers around his rigid member, his own hand closing over hers to keep it in place.

Penelope inhaled a strangled breath. He was thick and hot; his skin was as soft and smooth as silk. Leisurely he slid her hand down the length, right to the black hair that grew at his groin, then back up. Then he repeated the motion, his fingers tightening around hers. She felt his blood surge and his flesh quicken beneath her palm, and when a fine shudder went through his body, she instinctively smiled in female satisfaction.

"Impressed?" he rasped, stroking himself yet again with their combined grip.

She barely heard him, but managed to nod. Her skin seemed to burn where he touched her and shiver like frost where he didn't. There was a relentless, maddening throbbing between her legs, and she couldn't take her eyes off his erection.

"Good," he muttered. He released her hand and pushed her shoulders. Startled, Penelope lost her balance and sprawled on the bed. Her knees came up as she tried to catch herself, but Benedict didn't seem to mind. He pushed her thighs apart, hiking one of her knees a little higher around his waist as he did so, and then he settled the head of his cock against her and pushed.

She flinched at the invasion. Now he felt very thick and very hard, and some of the restless throbbing inside her faded. She tried to lever herself up but he put his hand, fingers spread, on the middle of her chest and held her down. "It will be easier this way," he said, his voice ragged. Dark hair fell over his face as he loomed over her, holding her in place, forcing himself into her. Penelope gasped and wriggled as the stinging stretch grew uncomfortable. He paused for a moment, even pulled back a bit to her relief, but then he pushed forward harder than ever. She bit her lip to keep from crying out, furious with herself for being disappointed and furious at him for hurting her. He noticed; his jaw clenched and his grip on her thigh grew almost painful. He pulled back again, then drove forward so fiercely she did let out a little cry.

"That's it," he said, sounding as if he was holding his breath. His head sank and for a moment he just held her hips, refusing to let her wriggle away. "That's the end of the pain." He opened his eyes, and they seemed to blaze like blue fire. "Now it's only pleasure, from here on." And he laid his hand on her heaving belly and dipped his thumb into the blond curls below.

If she had thought it felt intense before when he touched her, it was nothing to this. Her body, smarting from being stretched to accommodate his, was raw and defenseless. He touched her and she shivered; he stroked her and her limbs spasmed. She writhed without thought, exquisitely conscious of him inside her, slipping in and out just a little with every movement she made. After a moment she realized he was also rocking back and forth, magnifying the advance and withdrawal. And a moment after that, she realized each thrust seemed to feed something inside her, like a clock spring being wound tighter and tighter. She focused on his face, and discovered with a mild shock that he was watching her, his attention unwavering.

"You like this," he said, his voice a rough rumble.

She could only nod once. A dark, dangerous smile crossed his lips, and the strokes of his hips grew longer, slower, harder. His thumb still played lightly over the aching nub of flesh. He bent over her and cupped one breast, teasing her nipple with his tongue. Penelope gripped his shoulders, trying to anchor herself as the bed ropes creaked beneath their coupling. He overwhelmed her, above her, inside her, across every inch of her skin. The delicate strokes of his thumb grew firmer and more demanding. Heat seemed to be rolling through her in waves, each one stronger than the last—

And then they broke. She shook and let out a gasping moan as her body convulsed, far more powerfully than it ever had alone in her spinster's bed. Benedict said something under his breath—it almost sounded like a curse—and pushed himself impossibly deep inside her before dropping his head right onto her bosom and shuddering.

The first thing she became aware of was the sound of her own breathing. It was harsh and labored, and sounded as if she'd run a mile. The second thing she heard was her husband's breathing, which was even rougher than hers. She opened her eyes—which took some effort—and gazed up at the ceiling, somewhat overwhelmed. So that was making love. No wonder Constance felt ill and out of sorts when she went a fortnight between lovers.

Slowly her husband raised his head, and for a moment their eyes met. He was still inside her, still gripping her hip with one hand and her shoulder with the other. Penelope realized that one of her legs was looped over his back, and she was clutching his arm. She had never been so exposed, so uninhibited with another person, and yet felt only a vague amazement that it was with him. It must have been the brandy.

"Is that how it is in your stories?" he asked quietly. "Was that what you crave?"

A tiny tremor went through her; she could feel the vibration of his voice all the way inside her. "All that and more," she said, feeling reckless and wild.

His expression was fierce—and satisfied. "As you wish, madam wife." He ran one fingertip over her breast. A dark smile crossed his lips as she quivered when he gave her nipple a light pinch. "I wouldn't want to disappoint you."

Some of her haze of good humor dissipated. "There's more to a happy marriage than one successful bout of lovemaking."

He seemed amused. "The devil you say."

"You might as well know now." She brushed his marauding hand away and tried to scramble away. "I shall be a demanding wife."

"Is that so?" Before she could protest, he freed himself from her splayed legs and rolled her over, so she was fully on the mattress. "Perhaps I shall be a demanding husband."

I wish you would be, she thought on a sudden moment of yearning. *I wish you would fall desperately in love with me and never want to be apart from me.* There was no reason not to admit it—to herself only—now that she was married to him, had just made love to him, and wanted him more than ever. If only he would want *her*, passionately, physically, emotionally . . . For a moment he looked down at her, desire etched on his face. The lone lamp in the room was turned down low, and the shadows in the bed made him look almost savage. It was nothing like the polished, urbane image he usually presented, and she found it inexplicably, unbearably, exciting. "You once accused me of watching you like a cat stalking a mouse."

Penelope scoffed. "I don't remember that . . ."

"You do," he said, all arrogant assurance. "You said I looked like a cat watching a mouse, contemplating breaking its neck. Do you recall my reply?"

"No." She did, but denial sprang automatically to her lips.

"I said a cat would eat the mouse if he caught it." He untied the ribbon on her garter and began rolling off her stocking. "And now it seems I've caught you."

"Just as much as I've caught you," she retorted.

He laughed softly. "Absolutely. And I think we're going to enjoy each other a great deal."

That treacherous longing spiked again. Penelope tried to ignore it. If he could be satisfied with the purely physical pleasure of lovemaking, she could be, too. She would have to be, for it might be all she got. She lifted her knee for him to remove her other garter and stocking. "You mean we might as well make the best of things."

"Yes," he agreed, sliding over her and easing between her legs. "The very best." He pressed into her again. Penelope caught her breath in apprehension, but the sting was only a muted memory. Her flesh still felt hot and swollen, but now it easily parted for him. "What does my demanding wife want this time?" he whispered against her lips.

Penelope sucked in a shaky breath and closed her eyes as he kissed her more deeply, his tongue mimicking the slide of his hips between her legs. Yes, she wanted him—oh how she wanted him, here, hard and ravenously hungry for her. She wanted that, but also so much more, so she told him the truth, though she doubted he realized it. "Everything."

Chapter 14

Benedict had always been an early riser, and the morning after his wedding was no exception. He slipped from bed when the light outside the windows was just beginning to turn from gray to pale pink. There was a pounding in his head, but it was mild; all the more reason to rise before the sun became blinding. Penelope still slept, stretched out half on her side, half on her stomach. Her golden hair was a glorious mess, spilling over her pillow and one arm, although her shoulder peeked out, soft and bare. He reached out, then stopped himself before his fingers brushed her skin; better to let her sleep. God knew she needed it, after he'd kept her awake until the small hours of the morning.

What a brilliant decision pursuing this marriage had been. Not only the fortune he needed but a wife he couldn't seem to get enough of—and better yet, she had none of the virginal hesitation he'd expected, even though she had most certainly been one. No tears, no alarm, no complaints, no matter what decadent desire he whispered in her ear. She'd blushed scarlet but denied him nothing. His eyes tracked down the curve of her hip and the line of her leg. She must read the notorious Lady Constance's stories. That woman was a bloody genius. Half the women in London were so aroused by her naughty adventures, they could be tumbled by any man bold enough to ask. Benedict, searching for a respectable bride, hadn't availed himself of any coy invitations, but the men of the King's Life Guard would probably vote Lady Constance an annuity if she asked them. It went without saying that she could have had nearly any man in the regiment for the asking. Sir Perry Cole, a retired captain of the Guard, had had her, despite losing his left hand in Spain. He denied it in public, but in the officers' mess, he would give a wink and say that a man needed only one hand, if he knew how to use it.

But as Penelope said last night, there was more to marriage than making love, even if that proved an exceptionally pleasing aspect. He'd been drunk last night, but not too drunk. He hadn't really expected an inquisition on his actions toward Sebastian Vane—or rather, he hadn't expected it on his wedding night. The questions were inevitable, since her sister was married to Vane and must have told her some of the ancient history between his family and the Vanes, and also since Penelope seemed incapable of keeping her curiosity to herself. It would have been better to have that conversation in a more sober state, but he wanted to win his bride over; brushing aside her query would have been a wasted opportunity. No doubt she would hear it all eventually. Stratford family affairs were private, always, from everyone, but now she was part of the family.

That thought flattened his mood for a moment. Her family was so very different from his. He'd been struck, more than once, by the way Mr. Weston relied on and trusted—even valued—his wife. The earl, on the other hand, didn't care a whit what his countess thought. Her purpose was to obey his dictates and to look lovely doing it. Mr. Weston knew his daughter lied to him but he didn't whip her, as Lord Stratford had whipped Benedict many times as a boy. Just the memory of that willow cane on his back made Benedict's shoulders tense. Penelope obviously didn't have that reaction, not even to her father's anger. He gently lifted a stray lock of her hair away from her face, and silently vowed to be the sort of father whose children slept the way she did, knowing they were loved and protected.

But today he had business to attend to. Silently he made his way into the dressing room and se-lected his clothes for the day. It would be a long day in the saddle, ten miles to Richmond and ten miles back. Penelope's valise was in the dressing room as well, standing open where the maid must have left it last night. Mildly curious, he peered inside and saw a familiar pamphlet, crumpled up. A slow smile curved his mouth. Not every man would be pleased to find *50 Ways to Sin* in his wife's possession, but Benedict only found him-self wondering which issues were her particular favorites.

He washed and dressed, then let himself out after one more brief look at Penelope. He went downstairs and sent a man for his horse, leaving instructions with the staff and dashing off a quick note to be delivered to his bride when she woke. Then he headed out to face his father.

The miles passed quicker than they ever had before. Before he knew it he was boarding the ferry at Richmond, a crossing he had made a hundred times at least but never more easily than today. Another mile, and then the familiar gates came into view. The gravel drive leading to Stratford Court was just as he remembered it, and yet somehow everything looked different. Benedict let his eyes roam over the aged red brick, the precisely clipped hedges and shrubberies, the carved statues that lined the path like sentinels. His horse slowed to a walk and he did nothing to spur it on. He was in no hurry; time seemed to have stopped today. For all he knew, this might be the last time he came here.

Well—the last time before his father died. When the earl finally breathed his last, Benedict would inherit everything that came with the Stratford title, including this prison of a house. He watched dispassionately as he passed through the wrought-iron gate in the brick wall, and the whole of the building loomed before him in all its Jacobean glory. Perhaps someday he wouldn't hate it. Perhaps one day it would be a real home, no longer a monument to his father's pride and arrogance. For a moment an image of children playing hide-and-seek among the topiary flashed through his mind. A towheaded boy, with stains on his knees and grass in his hair. A girl with long black curls and dancing blue eyes, leading him on a merry chase through the garden, unabashedly shrieking when he found her.

He drew an unsteady breath. His children by Penelope. It shocked him how much he wanted to see them.

A groom ran out to take his horse when he reached the stables. "Welcome home, my lord," he said, taking Achilles' reins.

"Geoffrey." Benedict swung down and gave the man a nod. They were of an age, but he barely knew the man's name. Benedict had been ordered to remember his dignity at all times, even as a child, on pain of a whipping. He was very sure even the stable boys had pitied him those thrashings.

The groom bowed and stood at attention as he walked away. Benedict followed his routine at Stratford Court and counted the steps. It took twenty-six measured strides to cross the courtyard to the main door. There a footman swept open the door and took his hat and coat. Eleven steps through the hall. Forty-four stairs up. Eighteen strides to the north, then thirty-one to the east, where he reached his mother's suite. He knocked, feeling the first bit of pleasure. His mother, at least, would be pleased with his news.

"Benedict!" The countess rose from the sofa at his entrance and came to him, her face alight. "I didn't expect you!"

"A surprise, but not unpleasant, I hope." He kissed her cheek.

She laughed. "Never! Come, sit. It has been so quiet lately. Tell me all the news of London. Have you seen your sister?"

He grinned. An indisputably joyful topic. His youngest sister had recently married Lord George Churchill-Gray, son of the Duke of Rowland, a talented artist and an excellent fellow. Even though it was a brilliant match, Stratford had had other plans for Samantha and initially refused to allow the marriage. Benedict was fiendishly glad Rowland had intervened and changed Stratford's mind. Samantha deserved to choose her own husband, and Benedict had never seen her happier. "A fortnight ago. Gray bought a house near Green Park, and Samantha has been refurbishing it. She had dust on her nose and a cap on her head when I was there, and all she could speak of was the mural Gray had threatened . . . that is, offered to paint on the dining room wall."

His mother sighed, a faint smile softening her lips. "Is she happy?"

"Blissful," he said, remembering his sister's glowing face.

Lady Stratford's shoulders eased. "I'm so pleased. The young man must be very fond of her."

Benedict hesitated only a moment. "Yes, he is."

"And you?" His mother touched his hand where it had clenched into a fist on his knee. "What brings you to Stratford Court again?"

She didn't need to say the rest. *What brings you here after your father threatened to whip you off the property the last time you came?* Benedict took his mother's hand. He sincerely hoped he wasn't about to add to her worries. "I have news," he said, summoning a determined smile. "Rather happy news. I am married."

Her blue eyes went wide, and her lips parted in astonishment. "To whom?"

"To someone you've already met. Penelope Weston."

He spoke confidently, hoping to convey that all was well, that she should be happy for him. The last thing he wanted was to cause his mother more anxiety. But as feared, the color drained from her already pale face, and she glanced worriedly at the door. "Why, Benedict?" she asked in a whisper.

"I met her in London," he said, choosing his words carefully to avoid lying. "I came to her rescue one night, actually, and it threw us together a bit. She's a beautiful girl, Mother, and as clever as anything. I admit, I find her . . . entrancing."

The countess was already shaking her head, though. "But why? You must know it will infuriate him . . ." Her voice trailed off as awareness dawned on her expression. "But she's just as much an heiress as her sister was, isn't she?"

To say nothing of twice as impertinent, four times as maddening, and a thousand times more alluring. He veered between wanting to snarl at Penelope's provocations one moment, and wanting to carry her off to bed the next. And to think, all he'd wanted was a friendly, kindhearted wife. Instead he'd got a fiery temptress who might well drive him mad in more ways than one.

"I married her because I want to make a life with her," he said, not untruthfully. "I hope you are happy for me—for us."

She still looked upset. "If you are happy, you know I am happy for you. And I suppose now it's too late, but Benedict, are you certain? Her family didn't maneuver you into it, did they?"

"No," he said, not adding that Mr. Weston would never have agreed to the match if not for the brewing scandal.

"And the young lady admires you for yourself?" his mother pressed. "Forgive me for impugning her, but it was clear to see her father was very moved by Stratford Court—"

"It was not her father's idea," he said. "I was not tricked. I asked her to marry me, and she accepted. If anything, I suspect it was a bit of a surprise to her family, after last summer."

Lady Stratford gave him a disbelieving glance. "And no less to me! You convinced me you truly admired Abigail Weston. I believed you offered for her hand out of an honest desire for the lady herself."

"I did," he said thinly.

"But when she turned you down . . ." She threw up her hands. "Did I imagine you saying you were done with the Westons?"

Benedict realized his hand had balled into a fist again. Carefully he relaxed his fingers. "No. But I spoke in a moment of disappointed pique. Now I have changed my mind, I have married Penelope, and I would like your blessing, even if not your approval."

She was quiet for a long moment. "It's not that I don't approve," she said at last, very softly. "I recognize it's a good marriage for you in some ways. She's a very pretty girl, and while her family is ordinary, they obviously have one great advantage. But you must know it's going to enrage his lordship, and it worries me that you went ahead anyway."

For the first time in years, the knowledge that he had done something that would enrage his father didn't make Benedict's stomach sink and his shoulders tense. He didn't have to dance around the earl's temper anymore. If he had to choose between enduring his father's rages and deciphering Penelope's actions, he'd take his lovely young wife any day. At least there was the prospect of pleasure with her, whereas he knew the earl would never change, never admit fault, never soften his attitude. Just knowing that he was free of his father inspired a small burst of affection for Penelope in Benedict's heart, because she had made it possible.

There was only one blot on his freedom. This marriage would enrage his father, and with Benedict out of his grasp, the earl would have just one person to vent his displeasure on: Lady Stratford. Even if he never raised a hand to his wife, the earl could make her life misery. He had probably done so for the last thirty years, in all honesty.

"I hope he would wish his only son joy," he said to his mother, "but if he cannot, so be it." He reached for her hand. "Mother, I've spoken to Samantha and Elizabeth. You are always welcome—warmly—in our homes. For as long as you might ever wish to visit us."

She appeared frozen for a moment, her lips parted—in hope? shock? He didn't know. But then she straightened her spine and smiled her remote, formal smile. "You are very kind. No mother could be prouder of her children, for their loving generosity. But my place is here with my husband, of course."

"Of course it is," said the earl's chilly voice from the other side of the room. He stood in the doorway, where he must have been listening. Benedict wondered how long he'd been there. "Where else would you go, my dear?"

Benedict rose and bowed. "Only to visit her children, sir."

"She has no need to visit you, you have come to her." He gave Benedict a piercing look. "Against my wishes, no less."

Benedict nodded once. His heart had begun to thump a little harder now that the moment was at hand. It was ridiculous; he was nearly thirty years old, a soldier, and a married man—yet he still felt like a boy, small and scared, even though he was a few inches taller than his father now. "I have momentous news and wished to bring it myself. I am married, sir."

The earl's eyes narrowed. "Oh?"

"To Miss Penelope Weston."

The earl said nothing. His expression conveyed it all. Benedict almost enjoyed seeing the contained fury in his father's face. Stratford knew exactly what the marriage meant. For a moment Benedict thought he might just walk away in silence, but then Stratford closed the door and came into the room.

"How surprising!" he said. "You must be a man of very great humility, to wed the sister of the woman who spurned you. But perhaps I underestimated Thomas Weston. He was determined to have a viscount for a son-in-law, and now he's got one."

"I like to think I was accepted for my own charm as well," said Benedict, keeping his confident expression fixed in place. Any sign of uncertainty and the earl would tear him to shreds. "By the lady as well as by her father."

Stratford harrumphed. "Is she breeding?"

"Perhaps," he replied, refusing to let himself think about that. "But she was innocent when I married her."

The earl's lips thinned. Benedict knew he'd been about to suggest Penelope had coerced him into marrying her. The thought almost made Benedict laugh. How furious would his father be if he knew that if anything, it had been more the other way around? "A rare feat in girls of that class."

"She is a rare girl," he agreed. "In the best way."

"Take care you don't get coal dust under your fingernails when you take her to bed."

He knew his father was trying to provoke him. Insulting his bride was just another way of insulting his own judgment and taste, but it offered Benedict the first real opportunity to show the earl that things were different now. Everything had changed, and he wasn't ceding an inch back to his father. "Her father was never a collier. He was an attorney who made a considerable fortune through shrewd investment. I hope my children have as much acumen."

"So you can spawn a future earl who deals in trade?" sneered Stratford. His temper was beginning to fray, and his face was dull red. "Stratford Court will become a counting house!

The bookkeepers and lawyers will overrun everything of grace and nobility your ancestors built over three hundred years."

"You gave your blessing when I wished to marry Abigail Weston." Benedict had long suspected that had happened because his father sensed Sebastian Vane wanted Abigail, too, and not because of anything Benedict had said to persuade him. Why the earl hated Sebastian that much, Benedict didn't know, but his hunch seemed confirmed when Stratford's eyes blazed with fury.

"And instead of recovering from your peculiar desire to wed a girl of common stock with nothing but her dowry to recommend her, you simply took her sister instead. Well, why not, I suppose; neither one is much of a beauty, but the fortune is worth as much either way."

Benedict opened his mouth to defend his wife—to defend himself. But then he realized it was pointless, and so he just raised his chin, savoring every tiny bit of height he had over his father. "Yes. It's good for a man to have an independent fortune."

Stratford made a motion, quickly restrained, as if he meant to strike Benedict. Somehow Benedict didn't flinch away. In fact, he almost wanted the earl to do it, to raise his hand and hit him. For the first time in his life, he felt able and ready to hit back. No, it was more than that—he *wanted* to strike his father, to pay him back for all the whippings and thrashings he'd endured in his life, for offenses as trivial as being late to dinner or not reciting his Latin lessons enough times. Benedict wanted to repay the earl for all the punishments he'd taken for his sisters and mother, for the belittling remarks and impossible demands and random acts of petty cruelty they had all suffered over the years.

But the reason he dared not do it—his mother—rose from her seat. She wore the distant, composed expression that hid her thoughts and feelings, which Samantha had once called "her ladyship's countenance." "What God hath joined together, no man may put apart. I would not wish anyone to suspect a rift in our family; Benedict, if you bring your bride to visit, I will receive her. It would be unbecoming to snub the next Countess of Stratford. My dear, will you join me in wishing our son well in his marriage?"

Her words gave the earl time to master his temper. He still glowered at Benedict, but he drew himself rigidly erect and bowed. "Of course. I trust he knows his duty to Stratford by now."

Benedict met his father's freezing stare. "Perfectly, sir."

"Time will tell. You would do well to keep from my sight until sent for. Remember it this time, and don't come slinking back under pretense of visiting your mother." With that contemptuous dismissal, the earl turned and left.

Neither Benedict nor his mother moved until the sound of his footsteps had faded away. Then the countess sank onto the sofa once more. "I wish you every happiness," she said softly. "Truly I do. No matter what impelled you to marriage, I hope she makes you very happy."

It took him a minute to reply. He hated to leave her here, uncertain of when he would see her again, but for himself . . . for himself he felt fully free of Stratford for the first time in his life. "Thank you, Mother." He bent and kissed her cheek. "So do I."

Chapter 15

It was an immense relief that Benedict was not in bed when she woke.

Penelope lay quietly for several minutes, trying to untangle her new circumstances. She could still smell him, and if she closed her eyes she could still feel his hands on her skin and hear the murmur of his voice in her ear. He'd made love to her three times, including waking her once in the middle of the night. Thinking about what he'd done that time brought a fiery blush to her face. Whatever other faults she laid at his feet, he was a very adept lover.

She supposed that was a good thing, since she was well and truly married to him. All her threats to leave last night were hollow, even before he'd made love to her. As much as she didn't want to admit it, part of her thrilled at the idea that he was hers. Part of her exulted in his attraction to her, and all of her was bowled over by his lovemaking. That had been every bit as exciting and powerful as Lady Constance had led her to believe it would be.

As for the rest . . . there was still hope. She now had a lifetime to loosen him up and make him fall in love with her. Penelope didn't really see any other option; they were married, and she wanted her husband to be madly in love with her. It seemed only fair, after all, since he obviously wanted her and she was already helplessly attracted to him. Just thinking about it made her pulse speed up. He'd taken her to bed and done wicked, wonderful things to her, and probably would again. She thought of all the acts described in *50 Ways to Sin* and wondered if Benedict would be amenable to trying any of them. Or perhaps he had other, equally thrilling, ideas of his own. She blushed all over her body at that possibility. Who could do those things and not develop tender feelings?

Oh—Lady Constance, that's who. She found pleasure with her lovers but never anything more, no matter how arousing or wicked their amorous encounter. Penelope had always dreamt of sharing a great passion with her husband, not just in bed but in everything. Instead she found herself married to a man who was a mystery to her, who admitted he'd wanted to marry a completely different sort of girl—her own sister!—who freely admitted that she bedeviled and tormented him. Unlike Constance, who sent her lovers away and rarely saw them again, though, Benedict would still be her husband tomorrow and the day after and the day after. How could she endure decades of a marriage with no love? How could she bear it if there was no passion between them—or worse, if there was a great deal of passion but nothing deeper? Could she be like Constance and simply enjoy making love with her husband, without caring that he didn't love her?

No. She was sure she couldn't. Sooner or later it would drive her mad; she'd run off with a lover, or maybe just run off.

With a shake of her head she flung back the covers and got up. Benedict was already gone from the suite. She could tell even before a peek into the sitting and dressing rooms revealed his absence. For a moment she hovered between disappointment that he'd left so early, and relief that she had time to compose herself before facing him again, and finally decided on relief. Perhaps he'd gone out early in search of a house to take. They obviously couldn't live in the officers' quarters. Or perhaps he'd just gone for a ride.

When Lizzie brought breakfast, the tray held a note from Benedict, left with the porter. Penelope tore it open with interest and even some delight, although that was dashed when she read it. He'd gone to Richmond to see his parents.

It sent a chill down her spine, and she threw the note onto the table with a slight shudder. She'd completely forgotten about the Earl and Countess of Stratford, her new father- and mother-in-law. The countess, she supposed, was merely cool and remote, able to look right through people with her pale blue eyes and distant smile, but the earl was another story. Tall and austere, he was the most forbidding man she'd ever met, and if she never saw him again she would be exceedingly grateful. And now she'd gone and married his son.

A nightmarish montage of future dinners and

events streamed through her mind, with the earl staring down his hawkish nose at her in barely veiled distaste. The Westons had been invited to Stratford Court once, when Benedict was trying to impress Abigail by showing off his family home. Sebastian had been invited as well, and that was the night Penelope had known for certain he was going to marry her sister. Abigail had fairly glowed with happiness when Sebastian asked her to dance, despite his crippled knee. But shortly after that dance, Sebastian and Benedict had disappeared, along with Lord Stratford. The next time Penelope saw the gentlemen, Sebastian had been on the verge of fainting, barely able to walk, while Lord Stratford—and Benedict—had watched him hobble painfully along, and done nothing to help. The earl had even looked pleased.

Just thinking of it revived some of her antipathy for Benedict. He'd done nothing, although he had looked troubled. What sort of man could walk away from any guest in obvious pain? It took a few deep breaths to restore her determination that she was going to make a happy life with him, curse him. And in her house, no guest would ever be mistreated that way.

Her mood considerably darker, she dropped into the chair nearest the window and glared blindly out at the street below. What was Benedict telling his parents? *I've gone and married the coal heiress*, she imagined him saying. That was what he'd wanted, after all: a sweet, pretty girl with money. Penelope studied her reflection in the glass. She was passably pretty, she supposed. Was that enough to overcome her other characteristics, which were—if she remembered correctly—bedeviling, tormenting, and turning him inside out? Those weren't necessarily bad qualities, but he hadn't looked very enchanted when he listed them.

A thought struck her, and she sat upright in relief. Samantha would know. If his sister had written to him in the first place about the Westons, she would know what he wanted in a wife. Penelope had always liked Samantha, even admired her, and now they were sisters. Surely a sister would give her good advice, as Abigail had always done. Penelope wasn't quite sure how she would react if Samantha confirmed that Benedict really did want a quiet, sensible wife, but it was a start, and it might give her greater insight into the family she'd somehow joined.

Before she could dress to go out, the porter came to say she had a caller. The card he presented made her gasp aloud. "Yes, I'll go to her at once," she told him, then called her maid to hurry through her toilette. As soon as the last hairpin went in, she rushed downstairs to the private parlor the porter had mentioned.

Olivia Townsend almost pounced on her. "Penelope!" She seized Penelope's arms and scrutinized her face worriedly. "You look well. Thank goodness."

For some reason Penelope's mind summoned up the feeling of her new husband's hands on her skin and his voice in her ear. "I'm perfectly fine," she said, hoping she wasn't blushing. "Why do you sound so worried?"

Olivia released her, raising her eyebrows in

disbelief. "Worried! Of course I was worried! I returned home last night to a note mentioning, in a very casual and almost careless way, that you had married Lord Atherton." She threw her hands out wide in entreaty. "Would you kindly explain how *that* came about?"

"I wasn't prodded to the altar at knifepoint, if that's what you mean." Penelope winced at Olivia's air of horror. "It was strongly urged upon me, but I did consent of my own free will."

Her friend gave a muffled gasp and whirled away, pacing to the sofa. Penelope followed her. Olivia yanked open her reticule and rummaged inside. "It was Clary, wasn't it? It's too much coincidence that you and Lord Atherton would be forced to marry after your encounter with him." She sniffed, still searching almost angrily in her reticule. "That evil man. I should have shot him—then he wouldn't have assaulted you, and Atherton wouldn't have had to save you, and you wouldn't have ended up married to a man you hate." She looked up. "What did he say about you?" she demanded. "Tell me, Pen!"

Penelope had never seen her friend so angry. Olivia's face was pale except for the spots of red in her cheeks, and her eyes flashed with fury. "What does Clary want from you?" she asked softly instead.

For a moment Olivia didn't seem to hear her. Then with a start she looked away. "Never mind about me. Is—?"

"I will not 'never mind,'" said Penelope indignantly. "What's wrong, Olivia? Is Clary hounding you again?"

"Again." The other woman gave a despairing laugh. "I fear he'll never stop."

"How?"

Olivia's expression closed. "I refuse to put you in any more danger from him. I—I cannot tell you, Pen. Partly because I don't know everything myself, but I know you are too loyal a friend to stay out of it unless I don't tell you. So you must trust me: I won't tell, for your own good." She forced a thin smile. "And for mine, because I cannot bear to worry about you anymore. Is—is he kind to you? Lord Atherton."

Penelope stirred uneasily. She'd been in some vile moods when she discussed Benedict with Olivia, now that she thought back on it. "Yes."

Olivia seemed to wilt a bit. "Thank God. Everyone I spoke to said he's a gentleman, but I know how much you dislike him, and when I think that I might have cost you your chance at love and passion and all the things you want in marriage—"

Thus far Penelope didn't feel deprived of passion. She cleared her throat. "You mustn't blame yourself. Papa didn't force me to marry him. I hope to make a success of our marriage." Olivia's mouth trembled, and Penelope realized she sounded rather tragic and martyred. She reached for Olivia's hands. "Truly. I have mostly myself to blame, and I hold myself responsible for making it turn out well. Atherton . . . he encouraged me to behave sensibly and I shied away from it. But he stood by me when he could have walked away, and I hope we'll be content." She really hoped for much more, but there was no reason to go telling everyone that so early.

"All right," murmured Olivia. She reached out and squeezed Penelope's hand. "I wish you much happiness—and Lord Atherton as well. How could he not love you? After a few weeks, he'll be madly smitten, I'm sure."

Penelope summoned a limp smile. She wished, rather than anticipated, that Olivia was right about that. "Where were you?" she asked, changing the subject. "The wedding was very small but Mama did say I could invite you. I was sorry you were out of town."

The smile faded from Olivia's face. She seemed to hesitate, then drew herself up as though embarking on something unpleasant. "Yes, I was away. It's not important where I went, but I was working on the solution to my . . ." She grimaced. "My problem with Lord Clary."

Penelope sprang to alertness. "What is it?"

"It's not fully formed," Olivia warned. "And I won't countenance your involvement in any way—I've learned my lesson on that score." Her chin wobbled. "Oh, Pen, I shall forever blame myself if you are not happy. Clary never would have noticed you if you hadn't come to my aid. No such act of decency should be repaid as I've repaid you, with evasions and lies." Penelope frowned in surprise; lies? But Olivia went on. "I know you deserve better from me, but unfortunately I've only come to take advantage of your friendship once more."

"You are not taking advantage! I want to help you, Olivia, if you'll only tell me how I can."

Her friend gave a firm nod. "Henry . . ." A flicker of pain crossed her face. "Henry was involved in things he ought not to have been. You've already guessed Clary plays some part, I'm sure." She darted a wary glance at Penelope, who nodded in encouragement. "I knew nothing of it before Henry died, but the people he was involved with refuse to believe that. Even worse, Henry left very few clues, and deliberately obscured what he did leave. I have to see if I can discover more, and I must leave London to do it. I don't want anyone to know where," she added at Penelope's expression. "There's a chance it will lead to nothing. But this is my best hope of putting Clary off forever."

"Olivia, that's lunacy," she protested. "Run off with Clary nipping at your heels, and refuse to tell anyone where?"

"I don't intend for him to follow me," she said bitterly. "Not him, nor any one of his—" She stopped, to Penelope's frustration. "I would prefer no one know; the truth about Henry, if my suspicions are correct, is shameful, and I would rather not brave the scandal if it became well-known." She took a deep breath. "But first I need two hundred pounds."

Penelope blinked. "For what?"

Olivia flushed. "I would ask anyone else if I could."

"I don't have two hundred pounds," Penelope told her. "I would give it to you if I did . . ." She frowned. "Did Henry owe Lord Clary some debt you have to pay back?"

That seemed to fluster Olivia. "Oh no, no, it's

not that, not precisely . . ." She got to her feet. "Forget I asked. It was a mad idea."

"I'll ask Jamie," Penelope said quickly. "He'll give it to me." Her brother would want to know why, but she could make up some story to persuade him. At least he knew Olivia and could be trusted to keep her secret.

Olivia turned away. "He's not in London," she said, her voice higher pitched than usual. She sighed. "I'm sorry, Pen. I shouldn't have asked it of you."

"No, wait!" Penelope scrambled after her as Olivia turned toward the door. Reluctantly Olivia stopped and waited. "Will it truly help free you from Clary?"

Her friend nodded. "I think it's my only chance."

"Then I'll get it," Penelope promised, even though she hadn't the slightest idea how she would accomplish that. Jamie would be the easiest person to ask, but it appeared Olivia had already tried him. Abigail might have it, but she might well not, with all the repair needed at Montrose Hill House after years of neglect. She shied away from asking her father; she had disappointed him enough already of late, and didn't need to make him think she'd been hiding other ignoble deeds from him.

And that left Atherton, her husband of less than a day. Did she dare ask him? Her jaw firmed. He'd wanted money, and he had it because of her. It was only fair that she be allowed to have some of it, and since the money came from her family, she didn't even see why she owed him an explanation of what she meant to do with it.

"I will repay it," Olivia began, her voice breaking, but Penelope waved one hand.

"I don't care about that. Just swear to me—swear it—that you won't let that toad Clary harangue you anymore. Promise me you won't endanger yourself to protect Henry's good name. And promise me that if anything goes wrong with your plan, you'll ask for help immediately," she said, adding once more for emphasis, *"immediately."*

Olivia was still for a moment, her eyes soft with gratitude. "You're the most loyal friend I have, Penelope."

"Huh! You mean the most devil-may-care," she said, trying to tease, but her friend didn't smile.

"Perhaps that, too. I don't know who else I could turn to."

Any glib reply about Abigail being as trustworthy died in her throat. Olivia meant it, which gave Penelope an odd feeling. All her life she'd been Abigail's younger sister, the wilder, less polite Weston sister. No one considered her more reliable than Abby. But instead of saying any of that, she just nodded. "You can always count on me."

Olivia's smile was wistful. "I know." She threw her arms around Penelope. "Thank you. I hope I can be as helpful to you one day."

"You could shoot Lord Clary," Penelope suggested. "That would please me immensely."

"I wouldn't mind doing it, either," said her friend wryly. "But neither of us deserves to go to prison for shooting a viscount, so I fear we'll have to settle for something less."

"When—when are you leaving?"

Olivia paused, hand on the doorknob. "As soon as I can."

Penelope nodded. She'd have to get the money quickly.

After her friend had left, once Penelope promised not to call on her but to send the funds by a reliable messenger, she went back up to her room, considerably less eagerly than she'd gone down.

What was Clary holding over Olivia's head? And what had Henry done? Henry had been a scoundrel, and not terribly clever, but surely even he knew better than to tangle with that horrid man. For the first time she felt real fear for Olivia's safety. Before she could think better of it, she sat down at the desk and dashed off a note to her brother, James, asking him to call on her the moment he returned to London. Papa would know where he was. Penelope sealed the note and set it aside, feeling a bit better already.

It was odd that Olivia hadn't turned to Jamie at the start; they were nearly the same age, and had been playmates as children. Penelope's first memory of Olivia was of Jamie bringing her home and announcing that he'd found someone to play at dolls with them, sparing him the indignity. Once upon a time, she'd even thought Olivia would marry Jamie, mostly because she couldn't imagine any other girl wanting her staid, unimaginative brother, but Olivia had married Henry instead.

Still, things would be so much simpler if Jamie were in town. She was confident he would give Olivia the money she needed, or failing that, he'd give it to Penelope for her. He might be dull and obstinate, but his heart was as loyal as Penelope's. All she would have to say was that someone deserving needed it and that he must trust her. Jamie might tease her, but he would help her.

Atherton, on the other hand . . . She worried at a loose ribbon on her dress, trying to plot how she should approach him. Asking him to trust her might not go over well. Demanding the money was probably not the best choice, either. How did Mama get something from Papa? She probably just asked, Penelope thought sourly. Papa was so easygoing and indulgent, and he'd adored Mama from the moment he saw her, at least in his telling. If he'd ever denied her anything, Penelope had no memory of it.

Very well; how would Abigail persuade Sebastian to give her money if she needed it? Penelope thought of her sister and her brother-in-law, and concluded that Abby would likely explain everything simply and honestly, and then Sebastian would move heaven and earth to give her whatever she wanted. Because he adored her.

This was not helping. She prowled about the room, straining for any other inspiration. She needed an idea that did not rely on a husband who adored her, because Benedict did not. She needed a plan that also didn't require complete disclosure, because she'd given her word to keep Olivia's secret. Perhaps if she could get him drunk . . . and in a good mood . . . and distracted . . . Slowly her restless feet came to a stop. That might not be such a bad idea. It had worked out rather well the previous night, and if she had time to plan and scheme . . . Once again she thought of the red ribbon issue. Yes, that might suit her very well indeed.

Chapter 16

It was late when Benedict reached Mivart's. He took his weary horse to the stables and trudged up the stairs, hoping Penelope was still awake. He hadn't meant to be this late, although he also hadn't rushed back. It had proven harder than expected to leave his mother and Stratford Court, knowing explicitly that he was no longer welcome to return. For all the bad memories he had of the place, it was still his childhood home, where he'd been born and raised. And he could only hope he hadn't caused a dangerous rift between his parents. His mother didn't deserve to suffer for his actions.

He let himself into the suite and unbuttoned his coat, wondering how long it would take to have some supper sent up and if he could stay awake that long. A shower of dust drifted out of the folds of his coat; his valet would have a real job, cleaning his clothing and boots. He had shrugged off his jacket and begun untying his cravat when he realized he was not alone.

His bride was curled up on the small settee,

her hair down around her shoulders and her bare feet peeking from the folds of her white dressing gown. One arm was draped over the side of the settee as she watched him.

"You're awake," he said in surprise. Almost at once he shook his head. "Obviously. It was a long ride, forgive me."

"I waited up." She shifted, and some of her dressing gown slid off the cushions to pool on the floor, baring her ankles.

Benedict tried, and failed, to look away. She had very finely shaped ankles, and legs, and breasts, all of which he'd seen the previous night. He undid his waistcoat and pulled off the cravat, feeling much less tired all of a sudden. "I'm glad."

"Really?" She put her head to one side. "Why?"

"It's a pleasure to come home to a beautiful woman."

Her lips pursed up in that tempting, kissable way. "Flattery, sir."

"But true," he countered.

She lowered her eyelashes, though not before he saw her roll her eyes, and a small smile curved her lips. "Thank you." He almost blinked in astonishment at the peaceful exchange, and then she added, "May I pour you a drink? You must want one after your journey."

Wordlessly he waved one hand in assent. She got up and went to the sideboard, where she poured a generous glass of wine. "How was your ride?" she asked as he took a long sip.

"Long."

"And how did your parents take the news?"

Benedict took another drink. It was hardly fair

to tell her his father's reaction. Someday he would have to explain about his family, but tonight . . . It was too long and grim a story, especially when there were much more promising possibilities at hand. "With some surprise." Penelope waited expectantly, but he led her back to the settee. "It's not an interesting tale. I hope I didn't wake you when I left."

She laughed, sitting on the settee like a child, with her feet tucked under her legs. "Oh no. My ability to sleep in the morning is unrivaled. Abigail used to swear it would take a cannon shot outside the window to wake me."

"I'll keep it in mind." He was still holding her hand. She had lovely hands, exactly how a lady's hands should be. He stroked his thumb over the gold ring on her third finger. His ring; his bride. His beautiful, wealthy, suddenly friendly bride. "You deserved to sleep."

Her glance was sly. "After all that brandy, who would not?"

Benedict shifted, turning more to face her. "Yes, after all that brandy . . . among other things."

She widened her eyes. "Other things? I don't remember aught after the brandy."

"Truly?" He leaned forward until their noses almost bumped. "You don't remember this?" He touched his lips to hers.

"Why, no!" she said in affected surprise. "Did you kiss me last night?"

"More than once."

"Oh my." She tipped her head to one side. "It must not have been as bad as you expected."

His brow wrinkled. "What?"

"You used to look at me as though you'd like to strangle me."

His gaze drifted down to her neck. The pulse at the base of her throat was quick. He brushed one finger over that point, then let it slip down her breastbone. "If I ever thought that, it was so long ago I can't remember it." His finger met the edge of her dressing gown, which he nudged aside. "No, I don't think I ever wanted to do that."

"Then what were you thinking when you glared at me?" For all her challenging questions, Penelope wasn't doing a thing to hinder his exploration; she even leaned back into the arm of the settee.

"Doing something like this." He lowered his head and pressed a kiss to that pulse.

"That's what you thought of? You wicked man," she murmured.

He could feel her fingers in his hair. All thought of food and sleep fled. "Isn't this what you want?" He angled his body more over hers. Penelope slid down the cushion, under him, her eyes gleaming under half-lowered lids.

"What do you mean? Are you implying I'm wicked?"

He grinned at her pretense of indignation. "Isn't anyone who reads Lady Constance?"

She froze. "What? I mean, who?" A deep pink suffused her face. "I've no idea what you're talking about."

"Which was your favorite issue?" He pulled loose the peach ribbon that held her dressing gown closed and spread the gown open. Her night rail was so thin, he could see her breasts beneath the fine cotton.

"You—you know about them?"

"Doesn't everyone in London?" He thumbed one pink nipple and nearly growled as it peaked rosy and firm. "And you left a copy in plain view in the dressing room."

Penelope stared at him, then let her head fall back and laughed until her shoulders shook. "And you don't disapprove?"

Benedict had taken advantage of her outburst of humor to find her ankle under the folds of her dressing gown. Now he just gave her a rakish grin as he slid his hand up her shin. "If her stories amuse you, who am I to deny?" He tugged at her knee, lifting it up and apart from its mate to rest against the back of the settee. "If they inspire you, why would I forbid?" He drew her other leg across his lap, sliding down the cushions to rest more snugly between her thighs. "And if they arouse you . . ." He shrugged, plowing his hands under the dressing gown to move her hips to a better position. "I rather approve."

Penelope lay against the side of the settee, her lips parted and her eyes glittering. Lust flowed through him like molten steel, igniting every nerve. "Are you?" Beneath her night rail, he swirled his fingertips over her belly. "Aroused?"

The question seemed to startle her. She swallowed, then licked her lips. Her muscles quivered beneath his fingers, drifting slowly upward. "Perhaps."

"Oh dear," he murmured in mock concern. "What would decide the matter?"

She licked her lips again. "Would you let me on top of you?"

He was already primed, but the thought of Penelope riding him on the settee made him so hard he could barely move. "Yes," he managed to say.

Something sparkled in her eyes. "Then come to bed."

"No." He stopped her as she made to scramble off the settee. "Right here."

She glanced at the door in shock, then at him with growing excitement. "Here?"

"Take off your dressing gown." He shucked his waistcoat and yanked the shirt over his head. A bright blush stained her cheeks as she disrobed, but it was eagerness and not maidenly reserve. By God what a brilliant marriage this was, he thought as he unbuttoned his trousers. "Come here."

"Will this work?" She gingerly put one knee beside his hip. He took her hands and drew her toward him, settling her astride his lap. Her breasts were right in front of his face, barely veiled by the thin cotton of her night rail, and he couldn't resist licking one plump nipple through the cloth. She flinched and gasped, then cupped one hand behind his neck. "Do it again," she whispered.

He'd meant to all along. He caught the little bud between his teeth and swirled his tongue over it. In response, she shuddered and surged against him, her body pressing exquisitely against his erection. Blindly he rolled up her night rail—it seemed to be composed of hundreds of ells of fabric now—until her legs were bared to the waist and he could feel the soft, damp curls between her thighs, just a few inches from where he wanted them.

"You're on top," he rasped, barely able to speak. "What do you desire now?"

Her gaze dropped. His erection strained between them. Penelope shifted her knees, studying it, then licked her palm and wrapped her fingers around his cock.

"Holy Father," he choked, his back arching involuntarily even as his hands clamped down on her hips.

"Isn't this the proper way?" She flashed a coy smile at him as she continued to glide her hand up and down.

The witch knew very well that it was damned perfect, Benedict thought, but he managed to nod.

"I like it," she whispered, watching the motion of her hand with a fascination that nearly sent him over the edge. "I always wondered what it would feel like, and exactly how big it was . . ."

He was going to come in her hands, even before she circled the head with two fingers and pulled, applying exquisite friction. Shaking, he seized her hands. "Touch yourself. Show me how you do it."

Again she blushed bright pink, but obediently she laid one hand over her mound, smoothing her nether curls out of the way. She closed her eyes and turned her head away as her fingers began to stroke, circling and rubbing.

There was a faint ringing in his ears. He watched her fingers raptly, mesmerized by her willingness to let him watch. He hadn't really thought she would, but now her spine was softening—he could see a ripple of gooseflesh over her arms—her lips parted and a breathy moan escaped—

He pulled, raising her hips. "Take me," he said, his voice a guttural rumble. Penelope's eyes flashed at him, feverishly bright, but she did as he commanded. Benedict had to hold his breath for a moment as she positioned herself, but then she was sinking down, and he was sliding into the hot, wet grasp of her body. "Spread your knees," he told her, and his breath escaped in a hiss as she did so and impaled herself even further.

"And now I . . . ?" She sounded as breathless as he felt.

Benedict nodded once and gripped her hips again. "Like posting a trot. Put your hands on my shoulders—" He stopped speaking then as she put together what to do, and rose up on her knees before slowly sinking down. His head fell back in a silent groan of excruciating pleasure.

"I feel quite in control of you," she whispered in delight, repeating her motion. "As if you're under my spell—"

He grinned, tautly, and moved to forestall her talking. Not that he minded, but he wanted her as delirious as he was. He wanted her to lose control and sense and feel the same drowning ecstasy that simmered all up and down his spine. He slipped one hand around her hip and nestled his thumb in the blond curls between her legs. Every time she fell, he could feel himself as well, and the sight and sound of his flesh plunging deep into her made it difficult to breathe.

"Oh—oh—" She went still, her fingernails digging into his shoulders, when he touched her there. "Oh, wait," she begged, her voice wheezing. "That feels so—so—"

"Good?" he supplied, forcing his eyes open to watch her face. Her hair fell around her in shining disarray, her eyes were wide and unfocused, and her breasts quivered with every breath she sucked in.

"Yes," she gasped. Her legs were shaking.

He urged her hips downward, tilting his own upward to drive himself deeper. "Both at the same time."

The pace was neither as smooth nor as even as it had been before, but Benedict thought it would break his mind. Arms braced on his shoulders, she rode him roughly and eagerly, her hair swinging around her shoulders. He focused on her face, memorizing every flicker of her eyelashes, every flick of her tongue over her lips, every little sign of impending climax. He wanted to know her inside and out; he wanted to know exactly how to bring her to this brazen wantonness, so he could do it again and again.

When he felt the first convulsions of her release, he pulled her close, holding her to his chest as she shuddered and cried, and the storm gathering along the length of his spine broke at last. It felt as though part of his soul poured into her, and for a moment he could only cling to her, robbed of speech and thought.

And then . . . *This is what she wants,* came the insidious thought. This was passion and excitement, which he knew she craved. His arms tightened around her. God, she'd been right. He couldn't imagine almost passing out in any other woman's arms. And silently Benedict said a fervent prayer of thanks to every busybody in London who had helped precipitate his marriage. He'd promised Mr. Weston he would do his damned best to make Penelope happy, and if this was part of that, it would be the truest vow he'd ever made.

"I guess it works," she said faintly, "on a settee."

He laughed, making his chest hurt. "Better than I expected, even."

She raised her head. He thought she'd never looked more lushly beautiful than she did now, with her color high and her eyes glowing and a pleased smile curving her lips. "Really?"

"Didn't you think so?" There seemed to be a permanent grin on his face. "Perhaps we'd better try it again, if you're not sure."

"Hmm." She arched one brow speculatively. "But I have other ideas."

God bless Lady Constance, Benedict thought. "I am all attentiveness." But then he ruined it by yawning. It was nearly midnight; he'd been awake since dawn and ridden almost twenty miles, with the last heady gallop the most thrilling—and exhausting.

His bride only smiled. She ran her fingers through his hair, smoothing it over his temple, and his eyes almost closed in pleasure at the caress. "Perhaps tomorrow. Shall we go to bed?"

Benedict could barely raise his head. The servants would be aghast at the state of the rooms in the morning, with clothing everywhere, but at the moment he couldn't be moved to care. It seemed to take an inordinate amount of time to get off the settee, make his way to the bedroom, remove the rest of his clothes and boots, and wash up before finally—blessedly—falling into bed. Penelope was already there, since she'd been ready for bed. Benedict snuffed the lamp and stuffed the pillow under his head, pleased and mildly surprised when she snuggled against him.

"Benedict," she whispered.

He brushed his lips across her forehead. Marriage was turning out to be better than he'd ever hoped. By God, if he came home to Penelope like this every night . . . "Hmm?"

"I have something to ask you." Her voice was silky and low. She sounded as relaxed as he felt, and the feeling of easy companionship made him draw her just a little closer. Her hand flattened on his chest, and her fingers began a lazy stroking motion that was shockingly soothing. "I know it's very early in our marriage, but you did say you want us to be happy together, and that means we must come to trust each other and try to help each other, doesn't it?"

"Indeed." Another yawn cracked his jaw, and he felt himself slipping into sleep.

"Then if there is something I need, I should be able to ask for it without hesitation, shouldn't I?"

He smiled faintly, wondering what she wanted. Most likely a new bonnet. Women and their fashions. "What is it?"

"I need two hundred pounds, and I need it tomorrow morning."

Benedict opened his eyes. "What?"

"Two hundred pounds," she repeated in the same careless way. "Can you get it for me in the morning?"

He pushed himself up onto one elbow. "Why the devil do you need two hundred pounds?"

"I just do."

He stared at her incredulously, unable to see her expression in the weak moonlight. "And you expect me to hand it over for the asking?"

"Well, why not?" She sat up, too. "You wouldn't have that money if not for marrying me, so I see no reason why I shouldn't have a little bit if I need it."

It was true, and yet stabbed his temper to life. "What are you going to do with it?" A thought struck him. "Are you in debt to someone?"

"No."

"Are you being blackmailed?" he demanded. The Earl of Clary lingered at the back of his mind; the man carried a grudge and he hated Penelope, for reasons Benedict still hadn't discovered.

"No!"

"Then why do you need two hundred pounds?"

"Does it matter?" she exclaimed. "I daresay you won't be asking *my* permission every time you want to withdraw some funds."

Of course he wouldn't. A deep scowl settled over his face.

She was quiet for a moment, though he could hear her breathing heavily. "You promised my father you would be a good husband," she said in a low voice. "You said you wanted us to have a happy marriage. I'm only asking this small favor, and it is important to me. Why can you not trust me?"

"It's quite a large favor," he shot back. "Tell me why you need it." Before she could answer, another thought struck him. "Did you just seduce me on the settee so I would give you money?"

"Seduce?" She leapt out of bed. "Who seduced whom? You kissed me! You untied my dressing gown! You started it!"

"And you were bloody eager to carry on, weren't you?"

He regretted it the moment the words left his mouth. By now his eyes had adjusted to the dark enough to see her mouth drop open. Without a word she turned and marched to the dressing room, closing the door behind her with a firm bang.

He stared after her in disbelief. What the devil? Two hundred pounds! Why could she possibly want that much money? And without a word of explanation or justification. The thought of her sneaking around behind his back caused an instinctive snarl of denial in his throat. Why wouldn't she tell him?

Ah. Right. *Can't or won't tell?* echoed his own question in his memory, along with her response: *Won't.*

His mouth thinned. He'd suspected for a while that she was protecting someone who was involved with Lord Clary. Penelope hadn't gone to meet him on her own; she either went with someone, or at someone's behest, and it had almost ended in her being violated and abused. Everything he'd warned her about Clary rang through his mind, and his hand curled into a fist at the thought that she was ignoring him—still. Perhaps this other person was being blackmailed by Clary, or owed him money. For all Benedict knew, the money was to hire an assassin to kill Clary. That last seemed unlikely but he would wager her request was connected to Clary in some way. And he had warned her and warned her to stay away from that man.

With a muttered curse he went to the dressing room door. "Come back to bed, Penelope."

"Not if you're in it" was her cool retort.

Benedict braced his arms against the door frame. There was no lock on the door. He could open it and drag her back to bed if he so desired. Not that he did desire that—he much preferred Penelope as she'd been earlier, soft and welcoming and willing—*eager*—to let him make love to her on the settee. "I don't want to argue with you about this."

"I don't want you to, either."

His fingers curled into fists. "I am responsible for your safety," he said evenly, trying to check his temper. "I refuse to allow you to involve yourself in something that may cause you harm. If you won't tell me who or what the money is truly for, I cannot make you. But neither will I give it to you without being satisfied that you won't be endangered by whatever you're plotting."

There was a pause. "I'm not plotting anything, let alone anything dangerous. If I could have asked anyone else for it, I would have."

Benedict scowled at that. "Really. Yet you won't offer me even a token explanation. I am your husband, Penelope."

"And you think so little of me, you accuse me of seducing you for money!"

Benedict rubbed his eyes. God, he was tired; that must be why he'd accused his bride of something dangerously close to whoring. "I should not have said that."

"No, you shouldn't have. But you don't trust me, so perhaps it's no surprise." Her voice was muffled by the door, but he could still make out the angry hurt. "Stupid of me, really, to think you'd believe I must have a good reason for needing money, and an equally good reason for not telling you every thought in my head."

Benedict's jaw tightened. Part of him wanted to take a stand, put down his foot, and exert his will. His wife would not make a fool of him. If he gave in to this demand, who knew what she would ask next? Better to establish his marital authority now before she ran roughshod over him. His father would never have countenanced such a thing.

Slowly he let out his breath. *Christ.* The last person he wanted to emulate was his father. He made himself soften his tone. "Can you give me your word that this money won't cause trouble for you?"

After a brief pause, the door creaked open. *Tell me*, he silently urged her as she regarded him somberly. *Tell me who you're protecting from Clary.*

"I give you my word," she said, and nothing more.

He let out his breath and went back to bed. Exhaustion was making him short-tempered and stupid. It was better to go to sleep before he made things worse. "You should trust me. I have a duty to you now."

"I might say the same," she muttered. "You hardly tell me all your secrets."

"What secrets?" He rolled under the covers, his

muscles aching with relief at the prospect of sleep. "There's nothing to tell."

"Huh," he thought she said under her breath. "'How did your family take the news of our wedding, which none of them attended?' Who would wonder about that?"

She climbed back into bed a moment later. He listened to her yank the covers into place before she went still. It was peace, though a fragile one. But she never rolled back across the bed into his arms, as he privately wished she might do. And he fell asleep before he could work out any words of conciliation.

Chapter 17

Penelope stared out the carriage window as they drove through the busy streets of Mayfair. Benedict sat beside her, inches away and a vast gulf apart. Scarcely a dozen words had been exchanged so far today, all of them cool and polite. She'd woken to a bundle of banknotes on his pillow beside her. He had been gone. Even though he'd given her the money she wanted, Penelope felt no triumph or delight. She sent Lizzie to deliver the money to Olivia, and then sat brooding over her cooling tea for an hour.

Had she just spoiled everything? His charge that she seduced him only for money bit into her like a burr under her clothes. *That wasn't the only reason*, she argued fiercely in her own mind . . . although it wasn't unreasonable for him to draw that conclusion. She'd waited up for him and poured his wine, determined to be sweet and engaging. When he began kissing her and teased her about Lady Constance, it had only seemed like she was succeeding beyond expectations. And then he invited her to make love to him, which had been thrilling and daring and so arousing, there weren't even words to describe it. For the first time it had seemed possible her marriage would become what she'd always dreamt of: Benedict, wild with desire for her, daring her to be wicked and brazen, the pair of them finally forging a bond that would spawn a deep, abiding love.

Naturally that had been wrong.

Still, how could he demand that she trust him when he told her nothing? He went all the way to Richmond to tell his parents, the day after the wedding, then wouldn't tell her how they received the news. Penelope hardly wanted to face the Earl of Stratford personally, but she was still warily curious to know his response. Would he bring himself to be gracious, now that she was Benedict's wife, or would she be the shame of the family, the nouveau riche coal heiress who'd only caught a husband because she couldn't keep out of scandal? Unfortunately she had a feeling it was closer to the latter, by the way Benedict dodged her question. And if the earl disdained her, she would probably lose whatever affection Lady Samantha felt for her as well. Benedict's other sister, Lady Turley, and his mother the countess had only ever been polite to her, so she probably hadn't lost much there, but . . . She heaved a soundless sigh. It would have been lovely to feel welcomed by someone.

The carriage stopped, jolting her out of her thoughts. Benedict pushed open the door and jumped down before holding out his hand for her to follow.

She stepped out of the carriage, covertly

surveying the surroundings. It was a pretty little street, lined with attractive homes, though none was large. He hadn't told her a thing about where they were going, and she hadn't paid attention during the drive, so she had no idea where they were.

A gentleman waiting on the steps of the house in front of them hurried forward. "Good day, m'lord," he said, bowing. "My lady. Thomas Grace."

Benedict shook the fellow's hand as he peered up at the house. "Good day. Shall we go in?"

"Indeed, sir, I was just examining the house, and the front rooms get very good light. I think you'll be pleased." He went up the steps into the open front door.

"I thought we should find a house." Benedict offered her his arm. "A lady deserves a proper home."

"As does a lord," she said, gingerly setting her hand on his arm.

"A married lord, at any rate. But if this one doesn't suit you, we'll find another." He led her after Mr. Grace.

As the man had said, the front rooms were wonderfully bright. The dining room was elegant and spacious, with columns at both ends. The back parlor was charming and cozy. The drawing room on the first floor was nearly as large as the one in the Westons' Grosvenor Square house, and Penelope instantly liked it. It was a handsome house, suitable for entertaining. Mr. Grace escorted them through the first few rooms, extolling the virtues of the house, its craftsmanship, and its setting, but then he excused himself and let them explore in privacy.

"What do you think?" Her husband had barely said a word to her during the tour of the other rooms, but now his attention was fixed on her.

Penelope ran her fingers along the windowsill. They were in the master's bedchamber, another large room overlooking the street. Thus far they had shared a bed, meaning this would be their bedroom if they took the house. Or perhaps only his, or only hers. There was another bedroom, though not as spacious or as bright, and there was a dressing room between it and this room. After last night, it seemed far more likely they would do better apart.

Her glove came away gray with dust. She tried to brush it off, then just folded her hands. "It's very comfortable."

"Do you like it?" He had propped one shoulder against the wall beside the window and folded his arms. The sunlight gleamed on his dark hair and caught his eyes, making them seem brighter than ever. But his expression was carefully neutral, as if he didn't want to discuss what had happened the previous night.

"It will do."

"So you like it?" he prodded. "There are hundreds of houses in London; I want you to be pleased."

As if a house could make up for everything lacking in their marriage. "Yes, I like it." She turned away from the window and headed for the door.

"Penelope." His voice was low. "Stay a moment."

She stopped but didn't face him. "Last night . . . I didn't want it to end that way."

She hadn't, either. It had begun so splendidly, and then suddenly burst into flames and exploded. That was partly because she hadn't thought it through well enough; she hadn't considered how manipulative her actions might look to him. She was new to this, and marriage was turning out to be more complicated than expected. Or perhaps the problem was that she didn't really know him, and he was far more reserved. Hadn't she called him coldhearted and arrogant? For a while, on the settee, he hadn't seemed so at all, but as soon as she asked for the money, his demeanor became chilly and imperious. "I made a mistake," she said quietly. "My only hope was to be warm and welcoming, and not start an argument as so often happens with us. It was not my intention at all to—to *seduce* you in order to get money—"

"I should not have said that." He exhaled loudly. "I was tired and caught off guard, and I spoke without thinking. Forgive me."

After a moment she gave a nod. It *was* the sort of thing one said without thinking, in a temper. Lord knew she was prone to the same misjudgments from time to time. As for whether or not he was only sorry for saying it aloud . . . she preferred not to know. "Thank you for giving me the money."

"You made a reasonable point; you should have some claim on the funds that came from your family. It was the amount, in banknotes, that startled me, and that made me fearful of your reason for wanting it." He paused. "I hope that someday we can trust each other more. Our marriage didn't begin under the best of circumstances, but we have equal roles in making it a pleasant one."

Penelope thought about that last bit. In the happy marriages she knew, there was trust between husband and wife. She had told herself that Benedict was shallow and arrogant, but he'd been chipping away at that image for some time. Abigail had hinted there was more to his story than met the eye, and that she should give him a chance; while her sister might be more trusting, she was also usually right. And no one could question Abigail's loyalty or motives. Moreover, Olivia wanted her to be happy with Benedict, and keeping Olivia's secret was becoming a serious obstacle to that.

"I gave my word not to tell a soul," she began. "You must give me the same promise, or I cannot tell you why I needed the money."

"I give my word," he said slowly.

Penelope took a deep breath. Surely Olivia would understand. "The money is for a friend—a friend in desperate trouble. I don't know exactly why, but Clary has some hold over her. He's a vile, despicable man, you know, and I would do anything to help her get free of him. The night you intervened so fortuitously, I had gone to try to rescue her from him. I—I believe he meant to compel her to—to—to allow him—" She bit her lip, blushing. Benedict's eyes darkened and he gave a nod of understanding. "He caught me and refused to let me leave with her." She stopped, then added, "I was never so happy in all my life to see anyone as I was to see you, when you opened the door. I almost gave a huzzah when you punched him in the stomach."

"He deserved far worse."

She had never seen his face so still and dangerous. "I heartily agree," she said. "If I thought I could get away with it, it would give me great pleasure to shoot him." Benedict's mouth curled, but the grim smile didn't reach his eyes. "My friend came to me in great distress, saying she had discovered a way to end his influence over her. It requires some funds, though, and she didn't have them. So I offered to give her the money." She raised her chin. "I don't care if she ever repays it. Just knowing she's safe from that horrible man will be payment enough."

He studied her with a curious expression. "You're very loyal."

"Because I gave the money without knowing what she means to do with it?"

Slowly he shook his head. "Because you kept her secret, at great cost to yourself, though you don't even know what it is. What if you discover it's something trivial?"

"I'm sure it's not," she said at once. "I've known her all my life, and she's not the sort to make a fuss over something minor."

He inclined his head, ceding the point. "Why wouldn't you tell your father it was Clary who tried to ruin you?"

"I couldn't explain about Clary without confessing her part as well. If Papa knew about that, he would forbid me to see her again, and now more than ever she needs a friend."

"And she has no one else?"

"What does that matter?" Penelope exclaimed in surprise. "Should I leave her to Clary's mercy, hoping someone else will help her to spare myself the chance of getting in trouble?"

"No, I—" He seemed taken aback by her words. "I mean, has she no one else better able to help? Someone able to challenge or rebuff Clary?"

Penelope heaved a bitter sigh. If only Jamie had been in town and not taken himself off to places unknown. Jamie was the only person who might have come to Olivia's defense, particularly if Penelope persuaded her to confide in him. But her useless brother had gone off, and not even Papa was certain where he was rusticating at the moment, or so he'd said when she asked him to send her letter to Jamie. "Not at the moment, no. So I did the best I could."

Benedict looked at her for a long, long moment. "I see."

It wasn't quite a declaration of support and understanding, but it also wasn't a scolding. And now he knew. She was surprised to feel some relief at having told him. "I don't plan to make a habit of giving away large sums of money to everyone who asks," she said. "In case you were worried I would beggar us."

This time his smile looked real, if a little rueful. "I wasn't." He hesitated, then added, "Thank you for telling me."

"Yes, well." She made a show of looking around the room once more, as if the woodwork was of great interest to her. "I don't want to spend my life arguing with you. That's not really the sort of marriage I want."

"Nor I." He strode across the room, but instead of going out to call Mr. Grace as she expected, he closed the door. "I want to make you happy."

"I don't think my father would really kill you if you didn't, despite what he told you." He blinked and she waved one hand. "I listened in when you came to sign the marriage contract. I wanted to know what he was saying about me."

"Ah. He did warn me about that," said Benedict wryly. "But it isn't because of your father that I want to make you happy."

Against her will, something hopeful fluttered in her chest. She tamped it down and forced a disinterested expression to her face. "Then why? Your vision of marriage is quite different from my own, as I recall. You wanted a quiet, sensible wife who wouldn't torment you, while I . . ."

"Want passion and adventure and love," he finished for her, when she simply ended with a shrug. "I remember. I thought you were mad, but the strange thing is . . ." He reached out and took her hand. "Now I find myself thinking it's not such a deranged idea after all."

Penelope gave him a measured look. "Now you want love and passion and adventure, too?"

That lazy, dangerous smile crept over his face. "I think I've found part of it already."

She knew he was going to kiss her. She tried to tell herself that he meant he'd found passion, which was very different from love, and that she was still offended by his remarks the night before. But somehow she didn't move away or say something smart as his head dipped toward hers. Unfortunately for her, she liked it when he kissed her. She liked it when he dug his fingers into the back of her neck. She liked it when he nudged her jaw open so he could kiss her deeply. She liked it when his arm went around her and pulled her onto her toes, forcing her to cling to his shoulders and neck for balance as he sucked hungrily at her tongue, and she absolutely loved it when she gently bit his lower lip and he growled in approval.

"Do you truly like this house?" he whispered against her lips.

"Hmm?"

"Can you imagine making love in this room?" His hands went down her back to cup her backside. He pulled her against him, and Penelope gulped back a moan at the feel of him growing harder against her stomach.

"Right now?" She'd never seen another man's erection, but she was continually impressed by his. "There's no furniture . . ."

He cupped one hand over her breast, raking his thumbnail over her nipple. "I didn't mean to— right now—but now that you mention it . . . Lack of furniture is no obstacle . . ."

"Really," she said, intrigued. "On the floor?"

"Against the wall." His voice had gone guttural. "I'll show you—" The sound of a door slamming somewhere in the house made them both jump. Penelope blushed, then choked on a giggle, and something like shock flashed over Benedict's face before his expression eased.

"Mr. Grace will be wondering what we're doing."

"No doubt." He kissed her again, lightly this

time. "And for the future . . . If you ever wanted something like a new bonnet or gown, seducing me on the sofa would be an excellent way to ask."

Slowly Penelope smiled. "I'll keep that in mind."

"Do that." Her husband grinned. "Shall we take the house?"

"I think we must." She smoothed his cravat where it had gone awry. "So you can show me about the wall."

Benedict's mood was irrationally buoyed by Penelope's confession, to say nothing of the kiss that followed. For a woman who was remarkably open and free about expressing her thoughts and feelings, she'd kept a friend's secret even when it damaged her own reputation. He had a guess who the friend was. Penelope had introduced him to someone once. Little about the woman herself remained in his brain, because he'd been so focused on Penelope, but after a while he decided her name might be Townsend, or Thompson, or something that began with T.

Still, it sounded like a significant entanglement this woman had with Lord Clary, and for a few minutes Benedict debated calling on Clary to remind him to stay far away from his wife. He stole a glance at her from the corner of his eye. She was sitting next to him in the carriage, her brow clear, watching out the window with idle interest. *I almost gave a huzzah when you punched him*, she'd said. He wished he'd known that at the time.

Not only would he have relished punching Clary a few more times, apparently it would have won Penelope's esteem earlier.

On impulse he laid his hand over hers and entwined their fingers. She went abruptly still, then relaxed. A hesitant smile curved her mouth, and she gave his fingers a little squeeze. He leaned forward and thumped on the carriage roof. "Stop here," he told the driver.

"Is there another house to view?" Penelope asked as he helped her out.

"Of a sort. My sister's house is there."

She shielded her eyes with one hand and peered in the direction he indicated. "Where?"

"On the other side of Green Park." He took her hand in his. "Care for a stroll?"

"Will she be expecting us?" She hung back.

"I think I can visit my own sister without advance warning." He grinned. "If we're not welcome, she'll have no trouble closing the door in my face." Still Penelope looked doubtful, and he remembered her muttered remark about his family from the previous night. "She'll be delighted to see you, even if not me. Samantha will be so pleased to be your sister. She didn't come to the wedding because she and Gray— her husband—were out of town for a few days. It will be years before she forgives me for marrying while she was away."

Finally she began walking, though slowly. "I hope you're right."

"I know Samantha. I'm right." He tugged her hand around his arm. Penelope walked beside him in silence, but he could tell from her expression that she was thinking hard about something. Not only did she grow quiet when she did that, but her gaze grew focused and dark. He wondered what it was, and prayed she would wait to ask what he didn't want to discuss: his family.

"Did your father really beat her for her part in stealing the money?" she asked abruptly.

Benedict stiffened. "No."

"You said he would."

He thought back to that night when Penelope had sent him an almost taunting note, daring him to come look for four thousand guineas that Sebastian Vane had been accused of stealing from Stratford Court some seven years previously. By then they both knew that Samantha had actually stolen the money in a foolish attempt to help Sebastian, but Penelope wasn't content with the truth; she wanted to find the money, and she'd offered him a bribe to come help search for it. Benedict had told himself he went to help because he really wanted the bribe, namely the location of the long-lost grotto of Hart House, which he had spent his childhood seeking. It allowed him to pretend it wasn't guilt that sent him out into the woods, just as he told himself he helped break into a mausoleum as part of the search because Samantha was determined to confess to their father, and Benedict hoped that recovering the money would temper the earl's fury. Instead . . . He sighed. "I feared he might. He was furiously angry when she told him."

"Did he beat you?"

"No."

She glanced at him. "Your father's not a very kind man, is he?"

"No," he agreed shortly.

"What did he do?" she asked, her voice very carefully neutral. He could tell now when she wasn't being completely herself. "You tried to prevent Samantha from telling me and Abby the truth. You said you expected to be horsewhipped for helping us. You—"

"I didn't know exactly what Samantha would confess," he interrupted. "I didn't know it was about the money. I thought—I feared she had planned to elope with Sebastian. If our father had heard that confession, I shudder to think what he would have done to her." Penelope gave him a sideways look, as if wondering whether he was exaggerating or not, and Benedict said a silent curse. There was no way to put it off. "You suspect me of being a terrible friend, not without cause. You believe I turned my back on Sebastian for years, and you're right. But the more complete truth is that my father—" He stopped, at a loss to explain something he'd never before put into words.

"I know he despises Sebastian," Penelope said. "That much was clear."

He smiled grimly. "He does. He ignored our friendship when we were young—I suppose it was too trivial for him to worry about—but when Mr. Vane went mad, my father lost all tolerance for the Vanes. Madness taints the blood, therefore the son must be avoided as well. Sebastian had gone into the army by then. When old Mr. Vane came around begging to sell his lands, my father was only too happy to relieve him of the property."

"Begging?" she repeated, her voice rising.

He gave a brusque nod. "For a pittance. Mr. Vane was mad, Penelope. He looked like a wild man and spoke to people who weren't there. He pleaded with my father to take the land."

"Who could take advantage of a man in such a state?"

"A man who has no pity for others." He gave her a very serious look of warning. "I mean that. Stratford has none."

She frowned. "But why did you defend him when Sebastian appealed to you for help?"

This, he realized, was the real sticking point for her. A woman who went to a friend's aid and kept her secret, even when it rebounded disastrously on her, would not understand why he'd acted that way. "If I had taken Sebastian's side, what could I have achieved? Protesting to my father would not have changed his mind, and would only have made him angry with me. On the other hand, agreeing with Sebastian would only have encouraged *him* to continue asking, which I knew would be pointless. You have to understand," he said, seeing her frown deepen, "Sebastian didn't make the most diplomatic approach. He arrived in a state of outrage, and it only got worse. There is one way to handle my father, and arguing *anything* isn't part of it."

"But you could have let Sebastian know you disagreed!" she exclaimed. "You could have explained to him that you knew he was right, but his cause was hopeless . . ."

Benedict tried not to feel a surge of resentment. Why did she ask if she didn't want to know the truth? But perhaps he shouldn't be surprised; how could Penelope understand what Stratford was like? Her father was of a far different breed. Thomas Weston had given in when Abigail wanted to marry the penniless son of a madman. Neither of Benedict's sisters would have dared broach such an unthinkable request with the earl. Indeed, Elizabeth's first choice of husband had been summarily rejected because he was merely a gentleman, even though one of excellent family and handsome fortune. She'd pleaded with Stratford to reconsider, gently, nervously, and been confined to her room with only bread and water for a week. Benedict remembered it well, for he'd been whipped for sneaking her a pair of oranges.

This was why he never told anyone about his family. No one else quite understood, or even knew, the firmness of the earl's resolve or the quickness of his temper. And really, what did it matter to Penelope? Stratford had banished him for marrying a woman of common origins; there was no reason to bring the two of them together. It wouldn't change Stratford's mind—nothing did—and Benedict's lot was cast with his wife. To his mind, it was better for everyone if Penelope and Stratford never met.

"Perhaps I could have," he said at last, answering her demand about Sebastian. "Perhaps I should have. But I didn't, and I can't change it now."

"Weren't you sorry at the time? He was your friend," she went on in growing agitation. "When he needed you to support him, you told him his father was a madman and deserved what he got. You abandoned him!"

For some reason that snapped his temper. Sebastian Vane has his own wife to stand up for him; why must Benedict's wife do the same? "I? He abandoned me first," he retorted. "He bought a commission and rode off with his regiment. What was I to do? Does nothing change in three years? He was not the same when he returned home, and neither was I. He never asked for my help, before he came to Stratford Court. I would have told him not to come, but once he had done it and enraged my father, yes, I knew he had wrought his own fate. It might—*might*—have been possible to wrest the land back from my father, over time, with the right persuasion, but after the blazing row they had . . ." He shook his head. "My father wouldn't sell it back to him now for all the paintings in Rome. Yes, I thought it was kinder not to leave Sebastian any hope of regaining that land, because he has none."

"But he told people Sebastian was a thief," she said, although with less indignation than before. "And you didn't say a word of protest . . ."

"Who would have believed me?" She had let go of his arm some time ago. Now Benedict backed away from her and threw out his arms wide. "If I had gone around Richmond telling people Sebastian was innocent, it would have been the same as calling my father a liar—and I had no proof of anything, mind. I would have been caned within an inch of my life for such disrespect. Until a few weeks ago, I had no idea where the money was. For all I knew, Sebastian did take it. He threatened something very like that, you know; I heard with my own ears. He shouted that 'Stratford would pay' for swindling his father out of that land. He might as well have slapped a glove in my father's face and called him out, Penelope."

Her eyes were perfectly round. For once it seemed she had nothing to say. He sighed and dropped his arms. "I don't mean to shout at you," he said wearily. "You don't know my father. And to be honest, I hope you never do." Still she stared at him, not cowed but decidedly taken aback. He looked over his shoulder. The handsome little house Gray had bought for his sister was visible across the street. "Here is Samantha's house. Let's go in and see one decent member of my family."

Chapter 18

Penelope really didn't want to pay a call after that conversation, but Benedict seemed determined. He rapped the knocker and stepped back to her side. As he did so, everything about him changed. She noticed it because she was still staring at him in confused anger and hurt. His shoulders went back, and his spine straightened. All hint of tension and displeasure dropped away, and he looked as serene and composed as the King out taking a walk.

Penelope was flabbergasted. They had been arguing, heatedly, just a few minutes ago. He'd raised his voice and told her off. Now it was as if the conversation never happened.

"Is Lady George in?" he asked the servant who opened the door.

"Yes, my lord." The man held the door wide.

He left them waiting in a small parlor. Benedict strolled to the window and appeared fascinated by whatever was outside. Penelope fidgeted with a button on her glove, not sure what to say. Perhaps it was for the best that she keep quiet;

everything she said today seemed to be wrong. Hadn't Mama warned her that she must overcome her tendency to speak her mind, and become more sensitive to those around her? Abigail had told her Benedict's father whipped him. Penelope had seen with her own eyes how cold and uncaring the earl was. It was hard to think of anyone choosing Lord Stratford over Sebastian, who was as decent and kind as the earl was not, but Lord Stratford was Benedict's father. It was very easy for her to choose, but perhaps not for him—and she'd only thought of that too late. She slipped the button through its silk loop, then back again. She ought to join a convent, one with a vow of silence.

After a few minutes the footman returned. "My lady asks you to join her in the dining room, my lord."

"Ah, the mural," murmured Benedict as they followed the footman. He once again offered his arm, and Penelope, feeling like a very poor wife, took it. If he wanted to present a facade of marital contentment, so be it. "Samantha said Gray was threatening to paint one."

"Paint?"

"He's an artist; quite a good one, I understand."

And so he was. When they reached the dining room, an incredible sight greeted them. One wall had been whitewashed, in jarring contrast to the rich red surrounding walls. A tall man with untidy dark hair was on a ladder, painting a goddess whose face bore a striking resemblance to Samantha's. That lady herself came hurrying toward them.

"You've come to me, when I should have come

to you!" She threw her arms around Benedict, who returned her embrace, before turning to Penelope. "I do hope you can forgive me. I shall never let Benedict forget that he didn't tell me of his own wedding!"

Penelope smiled uneasily. "He didn't tell you?" This was not the way she remembered Samantha. Three months ago, when they last met, Samantha had been quiet and sad, relating her terrible part in the disappearance of Stratford's money and Sebastian's father. Now she was like a new woman, her face flushed with happiness, her eyes bright, and there was no trace of fear or stiffness in her motions.

"Not in time!" Samantha cried, swatting Benedict's arm. "Gray, did you know Benedict was to marry?"

"No," said the man on the ladder without turning around.

"It was a very small affair, and you were away from town." Benedict spread his hands. "What was I to do?"

Samantha gave him a reproving look. "You could have waited." She turned back to Penelope. "I wish you great happiness. My brother needs a woman of firm mind, and I think you'll be very good for him."

"Thank you," said Penelope. "I hope to be." That caught her husband's attention; he raised his brows at her. Penelope ignored him. Did he think one argument would change her mind about such a fundamental thing?

"Gray, do come down now and meet your new sister-in-law," called Samantha. Her husband waved one hand, a paintbrush between his teeth, and she sighed. "He'll stay up there all day. Shall we go to the salon?" She linked her arm with Penelope's and led them to a private parlor. "Tell me about the wedding. Was it beautiful?"

"Yes, lovely," said Penelope.

"I'm so glad." Samantha beamed. "And have you taken a house yet? It's time Ben left the officers' barracks."

"Only this morning," Benedict told her. "We were there just now, in Margaret Street."

"So near! We must have a dinner party. Elizabeth will want to come with Turley, of course. Would your sister wish to come?" she asked Penelope. "I do hope she is well, and Mr. Vane also."

Penelope, who had expected all of Benedict's family to avoid any mention of the Vanes, was startled. She looked at her husband in mute appeal, but he said nothing, his expression politely pleasant and utterly opaque. "They're both well, thank you," she murmured.

"I'm so glad to hear it!" Samantha gave them a sparkling smile, which died away after a moment. "What's wrong?"

"Wrong! Nothing," scoffed her brother. "Do you accuse all visitors this way?"

"Ben." She sighed. "What have you done?"

He looked at Penelope for a long, fraught moment. "I told her about Father."

"Oh dear." Samantha's voice dropped to a whisper and for a moment she went pale. "Is he— Has he—?"

"He banned me from the house, so there's no worry of that." He summoned a smile again, bright and confident. "I don't suppose you've got any refreshment, do you, Samantha?"

"Of course." With a worried expression she rang the bell and asked the servant to bring a tray. "Are you terribly shocked?"

That was addressed, very hesitantly, to Penelope. "He sounds very exacting," she replied cautiously.

A fine shudder went through her hostess. "Yes." There was a moment of awkward silence.

Penelope began to resent her husband a little. Why did he only tell her about his father as they were walking up to his sister's house? Didn't he suspect she might need a chance to absorb what he'd said? Now she felt out of place and tongue-tied, and still smarted from the feeling that she had been callous and unthinking. On no account was she going to say anything that would upset Samantha, but then what did that leave for conversation?

"I gather your parents are very different from mine," she began, praying she wouldn't make things worse. "In many, many ways. It's one of my great failings to presume others might share my own feelings and perceptions, and I had made assumptions . . . But I shall endeavor not to act or speak thoughtlessly when I meet Lord and Lady Stratford again."

The siblings exchanged a glance Penelope couldn't interpret. Samantha mustered a smile. "Yes, I believe our parents are very different from Mr. and Mrs. Weston. Still, I imagine our mother was delighted to hear Benedict has settled down at last."

Benedict relaxed. "Indeed she was! She wished us both great happiness, and begged me to bring you to call on her, my dear."

Since Penelope remembered the countess as a cool and distant woman, she was in no hurry.

"Well." Samantha visibly shook off her tension. "I must plan my dinner party for you. Not a large one, only dear friends and family, to celebrate your marriage. Do say you'll allow it. I promise Gray will have completed his work on the wall by then and we won't have to dine amid the paint pots."

"What do you say, Penelope?" asked Benedict. "Shall we indulge her?"

"Indulge! Oh, you terrible man," cried his sister. "You owe me this, Benedict!"

Penelope met her husband's eyes. He wore a teasing grin as he bantered with Samantha, but there was something more tentative in his gaze. What had he said when they arrived? *Let's go in and see one decent member of my family.* Perhaps he'd told her about the earl deliberately, as if to temper the recounting of his father's cruelty with the evidence of his sister's kindness. "That's very generous of you," she said to Samantha.

"It would be my pleasure," Samantha assured her eagerly. "It will be our first party. Oh, what fun—I've long looked forward to having another sister!"

"It must have been quite a surprise to learn of it," said Penelope wryly.

Her hostess laughed. "Of the best sort! I wish you every happiness, Penelope—I always thought Ben would make some girl a wonderful husband,

and I'm so happy he chose someone I'm already fond of."

Penelope smiled uneasily and murmured a vague thanks. She was burning to know more about Samantha and all the Lennoxes. What had Benedict been trying to say as they walked over here? Was his father truly a monster? She didn't want to think her husband was a liar, but it was hard to reconcile the various aspects of his personality. He abandoned his friend out of loyalty to his father, but warned her the earl had no pity or kindness in him—not the sort of man to inspire blind loyalty. He claimed he'd acted to protect Samantha, but his sister hadn't been beaten, and had even ended up married to a handsome man who clearly adored her—what had Benedict feared would happen to her? There had been a moment when Samantha had seemed genuinely alarmed at the mention of Lord Stratford, but then both she and Benedict went on as if nothing was wrong. Even now Samantha was chattering about the dinner party she planned to throw, when all Penelope could think was: *What sort of family have I yoked myself to?*

Over the next fortnight, they settled into something resembling peace. Penelope didn't argue with him anymore; she didn't roll her eyes at anything he said. If anything, she became more reserved and compliant—just like the wife Benedict once thought he wanted—and instead of reassuring him that this marriage had been the right choice, it unnerved him. Why had he ever thought a sweet, pleasant companion would be enough? Instead he wanted the girl with the sharp wit who seduced him on the sofa, but that girl seemed to have closed herself away from him. It put him on guard, and as a result he and Penelope became almost two strangers, orbiting each other with uncertain watchfulness.

Benedict felt a certain injustice in that. He had hoped it would improve things between them if she finally heard the whole story behind his history with Sebastian Vane. Penelope had clearly decided that he'd been callous and spiteful to Sebastian, who was Abigail's husband now and must have told the Westons his version of the tale—a version which understandably did not reflect well on Benedict. He'd shrugged it off as none of her concern before, but now she was his wife and deserved to know his side. He had even imagined Penelope's reaction when he told her: astonished, contrite, deeply sorry for the way she had blamed him for every travail in Sebastian's life. He had probably spent a little too much time imagining her making amends for her previous scathing remarks. Instead she seemed skeptical at first, and then almost distant.

He could guess why. Penelope didn't believe him, or didn't understand. Most boys were whipped for bad behavior from time to time; most fathers expected their sons' loyalty. To the outside world, Lord Stratford presented an intelligent, urbane, and precisely controlled persona. He was renowned for his art collection and his impeccable eye for statuary, and publicly acclaimed for his patronage of rising artists. He could be ruthless in business, but that was generally admired as well. In public, he expected his wife and children to be the epitome of grace and charm, worthy of the illustrious Stratford name—and they didn't dare act otherwise. Benedict doubted one person in one hundred would believe the truth. He was probably a fool to have hoped that his wife would be that one person.

Still, he told himself it was not insurmountable. Very rightly, Penelope had no interest in meeting the earl, just as the earl had little interest in her. He ought to take that as a blessing from heaven and be content never to bring them together. Trying to explain his family only made her doubt him more, so the less said about Stratford, the better. It certainly wasn't a subject that gave him any joy.

They took up residence in their new house in Margaret Street. For a while he hoped it would revive the spirit of honesty that had surfaced during their viewing of the house. He recalled quite clearly a promise to show her how to make love against the wall, and he wanted to keep that promise, but once there was a large bed in the room, it seemed contrived, and Penelope never mentioned it. As long as they continued making love in the bed, he reasoned, he had nothing to complain about. In bed she never denied him, but she didn't curl into his arms afterward. He began to wish she had never asked to ride him on the sofa, because now he knew what he was missing.

As the days passed in this perfectly dull and respectable way, it began to gnaw at him. Every time she politely agreed to accompany him on a walk or a drive, he wondered what had happened to her spirit of adventure. What was the matter with her? He never struck her; he treated her with the utmost courtesy. He'd been initially relieved when she stopped asking uncomfortable questions, but then he began to miss the arguments . . . and the reconciliations . . . that ensued.

When he caught her watching him one evening in the carriage, her expression somber and contemplative, his frustration boiled over. "What is it?"

She blinked. Benedict realized he had spoken rather tersely, and tried to ameliorate his words. "What are you thinking, my dear?"

She turned to look out the window. "Nothing much. I was attempting to puzzle you out."

He tensed. "What a poor use of your time! I'm not so great an enigma to cause you such consternation."

"Consternation!" She whipped around, the old fire sparkling in her eyes, and Benedict was shocked by the surge of anticipation in his chest. But then her ire faded. She turned her face back to the window. "If you insist, my lord."

He felt like an ass. Without thinking he covered her hand with his. "I spoke hastily. You looked quite grave, and I hope I don't inspire such feelings."

His wife watched him from the corner of her eye, as if she didn't quite believe him. "Benedict," she began, just as the carriage halted and a footman swept open the door.

"Yes?" He held up a hand to stay the servant, his gaze fixed on his wife.

"We've arrived," she said, and he had no choice but to step down and lead her into the assembly rooms.

For the first time in years he felt conscious of keeping a public face at odds with his feelings. As the Earl of Stratford's son, he had been raised never to show any upset or fear; a viscount did not lose his temper or his poise in public. A viscount—heir to an earl—must be conscious of his surroundings at all times, to give a good account of himself. No one must ever suspect him of having any weakness or uncertainty, of being unprepared or unequal to any situation. For years he had played the part almost without effort. He wasn't a hot-tempered man by nature, and people liked a charming fellow much better than an aloof one, or one who complained all the time. Benedict rather liked being liked, even when being agreeable took some effort—as it did tonight—but this evening he felt surly and restless, and uncaring of who noticed it.

The assembly room held a more varied mixture of society than he was accustomed to. London society had thinned considerably as the weather grew colder, but those hardy souls who lived in town all year were determined to enjoy themselves. The parties were smaller, the crowds not as intimately acquainted. This didn't seem to dim Penelope's interest; on the contrary, she soon abandoned him to dance almost every set.

Benedict didn't share her inclination toward activity. He sipped a glass of cheap wine and broodingly watched his wife clasp hands with a man he didn't know, and flash her wicked smile at him.

It wasn't that he didn't trust her. It was that he wanted her to look that openly happy in his company. What did she expect him to do?

Penelope's partner turned her left, then right, their raised hands drawing them almost face-to-face. She wore a gown covered with gilt embroidery, and literally sparkled in the candlelight. The neckline hugged her bosom lovingly, and the skirt swung up to reveal tantalizing glimpses of her silk-clad ankles. He drank more wine. She'd dance with him if he asked her—she never said no—but she wouldn't look at him that way.

"She's very beautiful," said a female voice beside him.

He glanced to his left and saw a rather plain woman, dressed in brown velvet, watching the dancers. He had no idea who she was. "I beg your pardon."

"The lady in the silk net gown with the gold embroidery. You've been watching her all evening."

"Yes."

She tilted her head closer. "She's been watching you as well, although I suppose you know that. Is she your lover?"

Benedict would have walked away except for the intriguing remark that Penelope had been watching him. Against his will he wanted to hear more. "She is my wife."

The lady gave him a sly smile. "Even better!" She turned back to the dancers. "Have you had a dreadful row, to avoid each other as you're doing?"

"No," he said stiffly.

"No?" She looked deeply disappointed. "What

a pity. I was imagining all the ways a man and his lover—or even his wife—could mend a quarrel. Perhaps she spends too much; perhaps he has a mistress she's just discovered. Perhaps—"

"There was no quarrel," he repeated testily. "And I don't believe she's looked twice at me all evening."

"Oh, but she has," the woman almost purred, giving him a quick appraising glance, from the toes of his shoes to the top of his head. "No wonder, too. You're a handsome one, sir."

He stared at her in affront and shock, but curiosity won out. "When has she been looking at me?"

"Every time her partner turns the other way. A quick glance from under her eyelashes, nothing more. But I daresay she knows you're speaking to me this moment."

Benedict turned his head to watch Penelope. Her attention seemed fixed on her partner; they joined hands once more and skipped lightly down the set as the other dancers clapped. Her cheeks were pink and her face was alive with excitement.

"You'll think it impertinent of me, but I believe she's waiting for you," murmured the woman beside him. "She's trying to make you jealous."

"Jealous!" He was so astonished, he forgot to take umbrage. He glared at the back of Penelope's partner's head. The fellow was tall and fit, and he seemed very taken with Penelope. The conniving, seducing rogue.

"Is it working?" The woman's voice had grown soft and almost gentle. "If it is, you ought to take her home and make wild, desperate love to her.

That will show her you don't really care for your mistress, and that you don't care how much she spent on that gown because it makes you want to tear it off her. That's what every woman craves, you know, at least every now and then. A man driven out of his mind with passion for her."

The thought set his blood simmering. "I haven't got a mistress," he bit out, "and I've no idea how much the gown cost."

"All the better." She edged slightly closer, and without thinking he dipped his head. "She looks like a passionate one . . . I hope you're able to fulfill her fancies. Ravish her, my good man."

"Madam." He recoiled. "What cheek!"

Her smile was a little caustic. "Because I can see what a woman craves? Very well. Go on with your brooding. Ride home with her in toplofty silence and stare at the ceiling all night in frustration, all because I spoke the indelicate truth." She shrugged. "Be like every other stuffy man in England, and don't be surprised when she does take a lover."

Benedict felt his very bones seethe with frustration and longing as she spoke, each word like the pricking of a dagger. Damn it, he didn't want Penelope to take a lover. None of his visions of marriage had included that, even before he married a spirited, vivacious minx who seemed to be roasting him on a spit in the heat of his own desire. "My private life is none of your concern," he said coldly. There was no response. When he turned his head and looked, the lady in brown velvet had disappeared. He frowned and scanned the room for her, but saw no trace. Who the devil was she, and why in God's name was she wandering a public ballroom offering unwanted and unsettling advice? Who did she think she was?

A thought struck him then. Could it be . . . ? This time he searched for her in earnest. He scraped his memory, trying to recall her exact appearance. Dark hair, though not too dark. Nondescript features, so ordinary he would be hard-pressed to describe them. Her dress was simple, neither luxurious nor shabby. But there was only one woman in London that audacious, and if she'd just advised him on his marriage . . . He strode across the floor almost before the music ended. Penelope was still thanking her partner when he took her hand. "Say farewell," he murmured in her ear. "We're going home."

She gaped in astonishment. "It's not late at all!"

He leaned close, pressing his cheek to her temple. "I never said we were going home to sleep." And he flicked his tongue over her earlobe.

Penelope jumped. Color flooded her face. She turned to her partner and gave him a dazzling smile. "It was a great pleasure dancing with you, Mr. Greene, but my husband and I must return home. Good night."

In the carriage he took the backward-facing seat, all the better to feast his eyes on her. Penelope flung the edges of her cloak open and crossed her legs, letting her slipper slide along the curve of his calf. "Why must we leave in such a hurry, Lord Atherton?"

Curse that mysterious woman. Or maybe bless her. Benedict was so twisted up with wanting his wife, wanting her to want him, wanting her to *like* him, he couldn't think of any elegant or polite way to put it. "I need to make love to you."

Penelope's eyes widened. "Now?"

"Yes, but I'm going to wait until we reach home."

Her eyes flitted from side to side, measuring the carriage. "Why?"

His smile felt feral and hungry. "Because it will take much longer than the short journey home."

And Penelope only raised her brows and smiled her familiar, coy smile that only dug those little needles of lust deeper.

When they reached home, he undressed to his shirt and trousers, then dismissed his valet. Through the door he could hear the murmur of Penelope's voice talking to her maid. Benedict prowled the room restlessly. He felt vital and alert, as tense as a soldier on patrol at the front lines. *Ravish her*, whispered the unknown woman's voice in his ear. He paused at the writing desk by the window and opened the top on impulse. Sure enough, there lay a copy of that wicked, wonderful pamphlet. He flipped it open and began to read. Penelope must favor this one, for she'd left it close at hand.

And no wonder. God Almighty.

Lady Constance—if that's who the lady in brown velvet had been—was right. He really needed to ravish his wife.

Chapter 19

It was only through an act of great patience that Penelope didn't tear off her dress and run naked into the bedroom.

Lizzie chatted idly as she took away the lovely gilded gown, the one that cost the earth and which Penelope had worn in frustration tonight. She didn't think the embroidery would dazzle Benedict, but she hoped the low, wide neckline would give him pause. For weeks now he'd retreated into an enigmatic manner that drove her mad. There was no complaint she could make about his behavior; he took her to parties, he danced with her, he made love to her, he dined with her. They even talked, about any topic but the thing that seemed to hang like a dark cloud over them. It was a small cloud, as these things went, but it was there and Penelope could never forget it. She'd called on Samantha twice now, and each time her sister-in-law had kept things determinedly cheery, as if she felt the same compunction as Benedict not to discuss their family.

For a while Penelope had tried to convince

herself that it didn't matter. It wasn't her business if the Earl of Stratford was a terrible father, or if he never wanted to see her. She didn't want to rip open old wounds by asking. But it remained at the back of her mind that Benedict had something he wasn't telling her, something that had played a vital role in his upbringing, and she couldn't ignore the hurt that he wouldn't tell her. It didn't help that she had an active imagination, capable of filling in a multitude of terrors and horrors that might have beset him as a boy. She was sure the truth couldn't possibly be that bad . . . and yet he wouldn't tell her and acted as if she had no need to know. Perhaps it wasn't an actual *need*, but she was dying of fearful curiosity. Sooner or later it would come out, as terrible secrets always did, and she would rather know and be prepared for it.

But by far the saddest thing was that it threw up a wall between the two of them. She sensed a watchfulness in him, a wariness, even when they were alone in bed. There was none of that warmth and closeness that had enveloped them the night after their wedding, when he held her in his arms and kissed her so affectionately. That had ended when he accused her of seducing him on the sofa for money, but for those few precious moments, she'd thought she had the true Benedict, without his guard up or any scheme in mind.

But perhaps tonight would change that. As soon as she was in her nightgown, Penelope sent Lizzie away and slipped into the bedroom.

Her husband was standing at her writing desk, something in his hand. He looked up at her entrance, and her stomach leapt at the fire in his gaze. Then she registered what he held, and a tide of heat rolled through her.

"You like this one, don't you?"

Penelope pressed her knees together as she remembered the wicked story in sharp detail. "Yes."

Benedict fingered the pages, then dropped it on the desk. "Take off your nightgown."

She blinked, but raised her hands and began pushing one button after another through its hole until the garment gaped open to her belly. His eyes followed every movement of her hands; even in the dim room she could see his face was taut with want. Boldly Penelope ran her fingertips along her collarbones, flicking the nightgown from her shoulders and letting it slide to the floor. He made a choked sound, but didn't move. "And now?" she asked when he didn't speak.

He inhaled roughly. "Now undress me."

She had never walked around naked before, but she sauntered across the room as wantonly as Lady Constance might have done. Her husband's gaze was fixed on her in hungry fascination, and she'd never felt more beautiful, more powerful. Whatever had been wrong or missing in her marriage seemed to have receded from view. This was the way he'd looked when she settled herself astride him and caressed his cock with her hands before he taught her how to ride him. Penelope was ready for all that to happen again—only this time, she meant for things to end better.

He had already shed his cravat, but she took her time undoing the buttons at the neck of his shirt. His skin felt scorching hot beneath the shirt as she pushed the braces off his shoulders. When she pulled the shirt free of his trousers, she could feel the thudding of his heart. But he didn't move, except to duck his head when she tugged the shirt over his shoulders.

She touched the fall of his trousers, strained by his obvious arousal. "All the way, my lord?" she whispered. His jaw flexed as he gave a single nod. A thrill of excitement ran through her, all the harder when he cupped one hand around her breast as she worked at the buttons.

"Were you trying to make me jealous by dancing with other men tonight?"

Penelope looked at him through her eyelashes. "Were you jealous?" She'd seen him watching her with a dark, stony look on his face, but until that last moment when he all but dragged her from the floor, her actions hadn't seemed to affect him much.

"Yes." His thumb and forefinger curved around her breast and gave her nipple a firm pinch. "I'm always jealous when you smile at another man."

"Always?" The buttons were undone; she ran her hands around his hips beneath the trousers, dislodging them as she blatantly felt his arse. It brought her chest against his, and she tipped back her head to look him in the face. "What are you going to do about it?"

His eyes darkened before a seductive smile curved his mouth. "I'm going to make love to you until my touch is branded on your skin and you never want another man's hands on you. I want you enough for ten men."

"Really?" She pushed his trousers down, and

fingered the tie of his smallclothes before pulling it loose. "Ten men?"

He kicked aside his clothing, making no effort to hide his jutting arousal. "Hold out your hands." Intrigued, Penelope did. He reached over and plucked something from the desk behind him and wrapped it around her wrists, binding them together. Her heart stuttered as she watched him wind the scarlet ribbon around and around before looping it between her hands to hold them tight. "Go to the bed."

The blood rushing in her ears, she went. At the bed she paused; it was a big one, and with her hands tied it would be awkward to climb up. But Benedict's hands were at her waist. He lifted her, holding her against him for a moment before letting her down on the mattress. She started to scramble forward, but he threw the end of the ribbon over the top rail of the bed and pulled. Penelope forgot to breathe as he pulled until she was stretched up, bound hands raised to the ceiling. He let out a little slack, until her knees rested on the bed again, and then he knotted it, fixing her there.

She held perfectly still, except for the jarring beat of her pulse. A polished silver vase stood on the table across from her, and she could see herself reflected in it. And then she saw Benedict, darker and larger, behind her.

His hands brushed her waist. "I never wanted to want you," he whispered next to her ear as his hands idly stroked up. "I knew you would be like a sickness I could never recover from." At her elbows, he switched from fingertips to fingernails, and lightly scored down the tender undersides of her arms, over her shoulders, around her breast. Penelope writhed and twisted, shocked by the sensation.

"And I was right." His hands gentled again, flowing down over her belly and around her hips. He moved closer, and she felt his erection nudge between her thighs. Wordlessly she flexed her spine, and he pulled back, only to push forward again, his rigid flesh gliding over her feminine core. "You're a fever in my blood, the lodestone of my madness. You dazzle me, you delight me, you infuriate me, and I only want more of you." Leisurely, almost accidentally, his fingers drifted lower, passing through the curls that were already wet. "And I want you to want me the same way." He swirled one finger around, and Penelope's eyes rolled back in her head.

"This—this is a good start," she managed to gasp.

"But only a start." His hand withdrew from between her legs, leaving her throbbing with thwarted desire. "How does one enslave a woman? Shackles are worthless. The only way to keep her attention is to sate her—to fulfill her darkest desires—to leave her as fascinated, and as hungry for more, as I am."

She was leagues away from sated. "I do want you."

A low laugh made her ears burn. "I can tell." Again his fingers slid between her legs, a light, passing stroke that made her pull against her bonds and whimper. "But this is no ordinary love affair. We are bound as one until death do us part, and there's no reason to rush to hasty climaxes."

She bit back a plea for just one hasty climax. Even as it surprised her, this play enthralled her. What would he do? He was dark and almost intimidating now, running his hands over her body as if probing for her most sensitive spot. It was Benedict and yet not like himself, and Penelope could hardly see straight for the craving he inspired.

She had told herself he must be scheming at something, that he never showed his true face to the world. Whatever he was playing at now—whether he meant anything he said about being dazzled and delighted by her—she was sure of two things: first, that he was as aroused as she was, and second, that he had found her great weakness and was ruthlessly exploiting it. Tied up, stretched and exposed, helpless to escape or return his sensual touch, she had never been more excited in her life. If this was to be the new way of things between them, she would never notice another man.

"Spread your knees," he murmured, sliding his hands down her inner thighs and helping her do as he commanded. "Lean forward." Her shoulders ached as she did, and he reached up and adjusted the knot, giving her a few more inches of play. She barely managed to breathe a sigh of relief—for her shoulders—when he slid his other hand back up her thigh, delved into the intimate folds there, and began to stroke her, more boldly and forcefully than ever before.

It was as if lightning struck her. Sparks seemed

to crackle over her skin. The feeling threatened to swamp her, drown her, but she dimly heard her own voice, goading him on, and his guttural answers. The rail above her head creaked as her body undulated, almost independently of thought. Benedict raked one hand down her spine and she nearly sobbed in pleasure.

His hand settled at the small of her waist, pressing down. She arched her back, holding her breath as he took his erection in hand and rubbed the blunt head against her, where his fingers had tormented her just a moment ago. Back and forth he moved, gliding over her slick flesh until she trembled with need.

"I want you," she repeated, her voice shaking.

"Do you?" He pushed deep inside her. Penelope shuddered. He pulled out.

"Yes," she moaned as he resumed stroking that raw, tender spot.

"Desperately?" He slid deep again.

"Madly," she choked.

He stroked her for another minute, then took hold of her hips. "Then we're equal." And this time when he thrust into her, it was only the beginning. His strokes were long, hard, and wickedly deep. He held her hips, controlling the pace and denying her the rapid ride she wanted.

Tears leaked down her face; she could hardly breathe. Everything inside her bore down, hard and tight and hot, on his increasingly urgent thrusts. Then suddenly he stopped, leaving her stranded on the precipice. He gripped her hip so hard his fingers trembled. His other hand reached back between her legs and touched her, and that delicate touch sprang the trap. Penelope gasped, then shook as release roared through her. In time with the pulse of her body, Benedict thrust again and again, hard and sure, his breath a feral grunt against her shoulder, until he put his head down on her back and growled in climax.

She thought she would never move again. Vaguely she noticed that her arms had gone numb, but she didn't care. Would that it could always be that way with them.

He reached up to the knot, then hesitated. Gently, reverently, his hands slid once more the length of her body. "You are so beautiful," he whispered, almost wistfully. "So open and honest." One arm closed around her waist and his forehead touched her shoulder. "I want to make you happy." He pulled loose the knot and caught her as she sank down.

She turned her head and laid her cheek against his temple. "I want us both to be happy. I just . . . I just feel we don't understand each other."

He gave a sad laugh. "I fear not. But I don't know how to fix that."

Penelope felt like she was glowing. No doubt the pleasure still lingering in her veins made her reckless, but she ignored the little voice that had been hissing in her ear for the last few weeks, sowing insidious doubts about him and their future together. "Just talk to me," she said softly. "I want to know you, and you to know me. Not just which carpet to lay in the drawing room, but what you really feel. Between us there need be no secrets, no shame. I warrant I have enough faults of my own to balance any of yours, and if I cannot trust you with my deepest, darkest thoughts, whom can I trust?"

He didn't answer for a moment. She felt his breathing on her skin and wondered if again she'd said the wrong thing. Perhaps he didn't care for that sort of marriage; perhaps he wanted too much to keep his own secrets.

"If you feel differently, I wish you would just tell me," she went on. Better to get it all out now while she felt bravely rash. "I have tried to hew to the model of discretion and civility you seem to embrace, but I cannot keep it up. I don't want to demand something you aren't willing to give me, but—"

He squeezed her. "Don't say you'll turn to someone else. I don't want that."

"I don't, either," she whispered. "But it's killing me to live as strangers."

"Strangers!"

Penelope twisted until she faced him. "Aren't we? Aside from this, I mean."

"This?" He cupped her cheek. "You mean our passion for each other."

"I just wish it could be like this always between us," she said.

His face changed. For a moment he just looked at her, his eyes deep and searching. "Like this . . ."

She blushed. "Well—nothing barred, I suppose. This—this was so exciting, so wanton and unrestrained. There was no thought of propriety or dignity." She gave an unsteady laugh. "At least not on my part."

He smiled in turn. "Nor on mine." He hesitated, then laid her down on the bed before lowering himself atop her. Gently he unwrapped the ribbon from her wrists. "I cannot change what I did to Sebastian."

Penelope blinked. He thought she held that against him? "I know. He's forgiven you, so I have as well."

Benedict raised his head. "You have?"

"Of course." She traced the line of his collarbone with one finger. "My sister ordered me to, but I would have done so anyway. As you said, it can't be undone, and it's foolish to let the past ruin the future."

"Then what caused the distance between us?" he asked slowly. "Is it about my parents?"

"No." She touched his lower lip. "I would like to know what made you the man you are, but if you don't wish to see them or talk about them, I can accept that. I gather they are not like my parents at all, and I confess your father isn't anyone I'd like to dine with."

For a moment his eyes were shadowed. "My father . . . I don't think we'll ever dine with him, and that suits me. You wouldn't like him."

She had already sensed that, quite strongly. "Then he is banished from our marriage."

A spark of surprise lit his face before he kissed her. "So he is. My duty—my life—is with you now." He hesitated. "I would like you to know the man I am."

"And can it be more like this all the time?" She wound her arms around his neck.

"Yes, darling, it certainly can."

"Can I ask . . ." She hesitated. "What inspired you tonight? Was it the neckline of my gown? Or were you jealous of Mr. Greene?"

"Fishing for compliments?" He grinned. "I do like the neckline of that gown, very much. And Mr. Greene had better keep his distance." Then he chuckled. "But if you must know, I was advised by someone to carry you home and ravish you as you wished to be ravished."

"Advised!"

"By a woman I've never met." He smiled again at her astonished expression. "But one whose name, I suspect, we both know. She was bold, with an eye on all the dancers, and her conversation was very daring and suggestive. She said you were tormenting me, trying to provoke me, and that my best course of action would be to make desperate, passionate love to you."

Penelope frowned in thought, then her mouth fell open in disbelief. "Lady Constance?"

He shrugged. "Perhaps."

She seized his shoulders. "What does she look like? Where did she go? What a coup it would be to recognize her! Did you know there's a bounty on her name? Oh, did she mention any hint of when her next story will appear?"

"No, to every question. She was the most unremarkable-looking woman I've ever met, and she melted into the crowd before I could inquire into her publishing schedule." He turned onto his side and pulled her against him. "I'd much rather think of you than of her."

"And so you should." Penelope wiggled a little closer. "But I wish I could thank her, all the same."

Chapter 20

The evening of Samantha's dinner party arrived, crisp and clear. Samantha greeted them warmly. "I hope you will be pleased," she said, leading them through the drawing room. "I thought it would be lovely to receive the guests in the garden, since the weather's been so fine. Gray teased me that I was inviting rain, but thank goodness he was wrong." She threw open the French windows into the garden. "But if you disagree we can easily remain in the house."

Benedict glanced at Penelope. Surely this would reassure her of Samantha's regard. His sister had turned her garden into a fairyland. Lanterns winked in the trees, and small lamps glowed along the path that circled the small fountain. Streamers of silk fluttered in the light breeze, although thanks to the garden's high brick walls, it was surprisingly warm. And sure enough, Penelope's expression was one of amazed delight. She looked at Samantha. "It's wonderful!"

Their hostess beamed in relief. "Oh, I'm so glad you agree! It was such fun decorating—Gray wanted to put fish inside the fountain but there wasn't time. This is my first dinner party and I want to do it well."

"I believe you'll set a trend."

Samantha laughed. "Wouldn't that be a fine thing!" She excused herself to go answer a hovering servant's question, and Benedict offered his arm to his wife.

"I told you Samantha would be pleased by our marriage."

"It would be quite rude of her to act otherwise."

"She's not just being polite," he said in a low voice. "I hope you know that."

She was quiet for a minute. "I'm very glad to hear it. I always liked Samantha, and I did feel very sorry when . . . Well, last summer."

"That's all over," he said firmly. "The past is over and done with."

She looked grateful. "Thank goodness."

The guests began to arrive soon. One of Gray's brothers with his wife, an amiable, good-natured couple. Another couple who were good friends with Samantha, Lord and Lady Roxbury. A neighbor, Mr. Wayles-Faire, who was also an artist, and his sister, who kept house for him. Abigail and Sebastian had not been able to come after all; nor had Elizabeth and Lord Turley, but Samantha passed on their congratulations and an invitation to visit at the soonest opportunity. Everyone was friendly and warm. Benedict was both pleased and surprised that his sister had such a circle of friends, and greatly touched that she had arranged such an evening for him and Penelope.

They strolled about the garden chatting. It was

a magnificent evening, and more than one lady discarded her shawl in the cloistered warmth of the garden. From time to time someone would exclaim over a newly discovered figure painted in some hidden spot, causing Samantha to exclaim in astonishment and hurry to see. Gray's satisfied grin got bigger each time she laughed at the lizard painted on a stone bench, or the frog painted on the rim of the fountain.

"What a prankster you are," Samantha scolded her husband with a fond smile.

"Of the best sort!" Penelope wanted to see each little gem, too, and the four of them had congregated over the tiny image of a hummingbird painted on the bricks above the roses. "Such whimsy! What have we overlooked?"

Gray just winked at her. Samantha gasped. "Oh, there are more? Where?"

"You'll have to keep looking for them," he told her. "Inside the house and out."

"Inside the house?" Samantha turned shining eyes on Penelope. "We must search it from top to bottom!"

They were all still laughing when the butler appeared in the drawing room doorway, looking ill at ease. He hesitated, his eyes roaming the garden before lighting on them. Then he all but ran to Gray's side. "My lord," he murmured, and whispered the rest of his message in his employer's ear.

Gray's eyes narrowed. He gave a curt nod and turned to follow the butler back into the house, but his wife stopped him with a hand on his arm. "What is it?"

He glanced at Benedict, then leaned down

and told her, too softly for anyone else to hear. Samantha was already facing him, so Benedict had a good view of his sister's face as it went ashen. "Father's here?" she whispered, almost numbly.

Benedict felt the same stab of alarm. Instinctively he reached for Penelope's hand and pulled her to his side. "Why?"

"I don't know!" Samantha looked to her husband in worry. "What should we do?"

"Invite him to call another time," suggested Penelope after a moment of frozen silence.

"Brilliant thought! I concur." Gray no longer looked jovial or pleased.

"Oh no, we couldn't dare!"

"I could," muttered Gray. "What say you, Atherton?"

Benedict felt the weight of three sets of eyes on him: his sister's anxious, his brother-in-law's measured, and his wife's wary and curious. Why the devil was Stratford here? He wasn't invited. He barely acknowledged Gray, and he'd banned Benedict from his sight. Whatever had brought him to town, to this house tonight, couldn't be anything good. Tonight, when he and Penelope were in good charity, when Samantha was so happy, the earl was the very last person he wanted to see. "Turn him away," he said in a low voice.

Gray clapped his shoulder. "Excellent decision. Crawley, tell his lordship we are engaged, and ask him to call another time—" he began telling the butler.

"Too late," whispered Samantha, facing the house.

As one, the rest of them turned toward the house. Framed in the well-lit doorway stood the Earl of Stratford, as dark and grim as the specter of death. As if he'd been waiting for their attention, he came down the few steps and strode toward them, his gaze never wavering. The other guests withdrew at his approach as if they felt a chill, and the hum of conversation grew noticeably quieter.

Gray muttered something to his butler, who hurried off, and stepped forward as Stratford reached them. "Good evening, sir," he said with a bow.

Stratford barely looked at him. "Indeed."

Samantha wet her lips and stepped around her husband, who immediately put his arm around her. "Good evening, Father." She curtsied. "I had no idea you were in town."

"Only just arrived." He glanced around at the lanterns, the streamers, the now-quiet guests. "I trust I'm not intruding."

"Obviously not," said Gray evenly. "We're delighted to have you join us."

"How gracious." Stratford turned his hooded eyes on Benedict. "Is there a special occasion being celebrated?"

"Indeed," said Samantha, beginning to recover her poise, although she never released her husband's arm. "My brother's marriage. I'm delighted to have another sister, and we wanted to wish Benedict and his bride joy."

"Indeed," repeated the earl. He finally turned to Penelope, giving her a brazen up-and-down inspection. "Here is the bride, I take it."

Benedict felt as if he'd just been smacked in the face. Samantha gasped softly, and Gray's face grew dark. Penelope smiled her sunny smile as if the earl had just paid her a lavish compliment, and dipped a graceful curtsy. "Thank you, my lord. I'm very honored to receive your blessing on our marriage."

Stratford's mouth firmed. Benedict was torn between wanting to applaud his wife's response and the urge to whisk her away before the earl could berate her for impertinence. "I had not thought it would take this long to give it."

Penelope nodded sympathetically. "We were so sorry you and Lady Stratford didn't attend the wedding. I hope to make her ladyship's acquaintance soon."

Samantha was staring at Penelope in wide-eyed awe, Gray in open approval. Far from being cowed or even muted by the earl's presence, Penelope seemed more fearless than ever. Every word she said was utterly true, perfectly polite, and absolutely guaranteed to infuriate Stratford. He preferred people respectful and accommodating, and instead Penelope had just told a garden of people that Stratford hadn't approved his own son's wedding. Benedict considered waiting for the earl's reply, but the watching assembly of guests dissuaded him. At least in public, he preferred to maintain some civility. "Has Mother accompanied you to town, Father?"

Stratford watched Penelope with a curious expression. Benedict had long been a student of his father's expressions, attuned to any clue to his mood, and he had no idea what this one meant. It was unnerving. "She has not."

"What a terrible pity," Samantha put in, catching his eye. She was trying to follow his lead. "I hope Mother is well?"

"Yes."

Thankfully the butler rushed up, walking as fast as he could without running. "My lord, my lady, dinner is ready."

"Excellent!" declared Gray at once, giving Benedict the strong impression that he'd sent the butler off to rush dinner along as soon as Stratford appeared. He had noted the way his brother-in-law stepped in front of Samantha as the earl approached, and the way he kept her close to his side. "Crawley, set another place next to mine for Lord Stratford."

Stratford's smile was cold. "That won't be necessary. I will dine at my club." He glanced at Penelope again. "I shall call upon you tomorrow, Lady Atherton."

"Of course!" She beamed at him again. "I look forward to it, sir."

"It would be our pleasure," added Benedict evenly. "Until tomorrow, Father."

A muscle twitched in the earl's jaw. Without a word he bowed, turned on his heel, and left.

No one spoke until he was gone. Samantha let out her breath. "What does he really want?"

Benedict felt Penelope at his side. Somehow he had a bad feeling Stratford had come because of her, although he couldn't see any reason for that. "I expect we'll find out tomorrow," she said, seemingly unconcerned. "Is he always so stern and grim?"

Samantha shuddered. "No," she murmured. "Sometimes he's worse."

"Enough about him." Gray took her hand again. "I refuse to let him ruin this evening. Shall we go in? I told Crawford to announce dinner even if it was still raw from the butcher, but I am personally quite ready for the wine."

Samantha's worried gaze flitted around, taking in her curious, expectant guests. She gave a strained smile. "I am as well. Perhaps we could begin with a toast in the drawing room to give Cook a little more time for dinner."

"Wine sounds ideal," said Benedict. "But would you allow us a few moments alone?"

His sister nodded, and he seized his wife's hand. Through the garden, into the house, into a small salon away from any prying ears. He closed the door and paced the length of the room, plowing his shaking hands into his hair. "I hope you didn't provoke him."

"Oh," she said airily, "no more than he provoked me, I'm sure."

Benedict looked at her in amazement. "What? Why, Penelope?"

She opened her mouth, then closed it, obviously struggling to choose the right words. "Do I understand this correctly? Your father arrives, unannounced and uninvited, well into the evening, to look me up and down like a piece of furniture. He deliberately insults me, by your admission. He slights Samantha and Gray in their own home. He announces he will call upon us tomorrow, and then he walks out after barely acknowledging the invitation to stay to dine. And I'm the one at fault? Was I not polite?"

"That's not the question," he began.

"What ought I to have done?" she exclaimed. "Cowered in fear and whispered my thanks when he deigned to glance at me? That's not my nature."

"I know." He sighed and reached for her. "But it would have been better—"

She stepped back out of his reach. "Better? So he would think he can bully me as he's done to you?"

Benedict stood motionless, his hand still outstretched. "I will never let him touch you."

"Then I regret nothing. Perhaps it's time someone stood up to him."

He gave a bitter laugh and let his arm drop. "'Perhaps it's time.' As if no one else has ever tried."

"Then why does he still do it?" This time she reached for him. "You're a grown man, independent and able. Why can't you? Why can't Samantha? I wager Gray would be happy to defy him, but you and Samantha—"

"Stop," he said in a low voice.

"I know he's not a kind father, and never was," she barreled onward. "I know a child can't easily defy his father. But you're no longer a boy to be punished for impertinence. What can he do to you now? Why do you and Samantha both still live in fear of him?"

"Who told you that?"

She waved one hand impatiently. "Sebastian told Abby, and she told me. And more potently, Samantha's reaction proclaimed it clearly. If my father had behaved that way, I would have fled at the first opportunity and never looked back, let alone received him in my house."

"Very easy to say when your father treated you with particular kindness and indulgence."

Penelope snorted. "He punished me—"

"It was not the same," he cut in savagely. "Just . . . don't presume you know what it was like for us."

Her face changed, becoming more frustrated than indignant. "Then tell me! I keep trying to understand you, and you never let down your guard. We are married! Why must you keep so many secrets from me?"

"My secrets." He threw up his hands. "I've no idea what you want me to tell you."

His wife stared at him for a long moment. "The simple truth would suffice." She took a deep breath. "I'm going to rejoin the guests. If you have any other critical remarks on my actions or inexplicable commands for me to follow, I will hear them tomorrow morning."

He caught her arm when she started past him. "I *have* told you. You don't want to hear it. You want me to fall on my knees in abject regret because I didn't stand by Sebastian, or apologize for things beyond my control."

"No," she protested, "I want to know why your father exerts such control over you that you dare not contradict a word he says!"

"Because he can," he snarled. He'd thought it would be better for Penelope not to know, but now she had to know, before she unwittingly brought the earl's wrath down on herself. The look in Stratford's eyes as he studied Penelope had put a chill in Benedict's heart. "He always has. It didn't matter what the offense was; if we defied him, we were punished, harshly. No matter is beneath his notice. My mother dares not order so much as a new bonnet without his approval. Elizabeth once went riding without express permission, and he sold her horse; she was forbidden to ride again except in public. One must keep up appearances whenever society might be watching, but the rest of the time . . ." He shook his head. "Samantha was nearly married off to a dangerous lunatic because she stole those guineas from him." He smiled humorlessly at her wide-eyed start. "You wanted to know what he did to Samantha? He had a marriage contract with the Marquess of Dorre's middle son—the mad, dangerous one—drawn up, ready to be signed, before Gray's father, the Duke of Rowland, interceded on his behalf. Samantha's pleas meant nothing to him, nor did Gray's. I still don't know what Rowland said to persuade Father to allow it, but I would be astonished if he didn't threaten some awful reprisal—and even then my father cut Samantha's dowry almost to nothing."

Penelope searched his face for a moment. "What did he do to you?"

"Anything he pleased."

"How bad?" she whispered.

Benedict sighed. "Whippings. Scathing lectures. Confinement to my room with only bread and water." He released her and ran his hands over his face. "Suspension of allowance. Words with my superior officers. He once canceled my lodgings at university so I'd have to live in the charity ward for a term. He made me sack servants who had been with the family for years. When I returned the guineas Samantha took, he told me to leave his house, and when I told him I was married— without his permission and blessing—he banned me from the grounds and forbade me to visit my mother."

"But now he can't do anything to you," she said slowly. "Because . . ."

"Because I married you." He touched her face, unspeakably relieved when she let him. It gave him a jolt to realize that he'd feared she would recoil in disgust or horror.

Her eyes were shadowed. "But you would have preferred Abby or Frances Lockwood."

"No," he murmured, drawing her closer. "I would have regretted it to the end of my days."

"Both of them would have been deferential and polite to your father."

"Neither of them would have made me want to give a huzzah like you did tonight."

She raised her brows. "When was that?"

"When you told him you look forward to seeing him tomorrow." He brushed his lips against her. "No—I think it was when you said you wouldn't let him bully you." He slid his arm around her waist. "Actually, I think it might be right this moment . . ."

She framed his face in her hands. "He won't bully either of us. Promise me."

He had endured the earl's tyrannical demands his entire life, not only for his own actions but to spare his mother and sisters. None of them had ever told him to stand up to Stratford. On the contrary, they had all begged him at various times not to provoke his father's temper. Penelope didn't know the earl, but that left her unafraid of him. Even though he knew a little fear could be a good thing when it came to Stratford, her undaunted spirit brought a smile to his face. "I promise."

Chapter 21

Despite Benedict's fervent hopes, his father called on them the next day.

"I have come to issue an invitation," the earl announced almost as soon as they had uttered the usual niceties. "To Stratford Court. As Lady Atherton, you will be the next mistress there. I hope you will fill the role creditably."

"Goodness," said Penelope in overly solicitous tones. "What are the qualifications for the position?"

Stratford paused. Benedict waited with interest. "Poise. Beauty. A gracious, retiring manner." His dark, thin smile flashed for a moment. "But no; those were my qualifications for a countess. My son must have others."

As if she didn't feel the sting in his words, Penelope simply gave a sparkling smile. "Indeed he did! He told me himself exactly the sort of bride he had in mind, and I don't recall any of those qualities."

Oh God. Benedict tensed as his father's cold, faintly pitying gaze moved to him. "My only memory of that conversation is the realization that you surpassed every ideal I had, my dear," he said lightly.

She laughed. "Goodness, you'll make me blush, sir!"

"Surely he did not intend to do that. It would be unseemly to embarrass a lady." Stratford turned back to Penelope. "You will be welcome to visit Stratford Court tomorrow. I am prepared to convey you there on my yacht."

Benedict's tension grew worse at this inexplicable command. The yacht was one of the earl's most treasured possessions. It was sleek and fast, and Stratford had won many a race with it; others were rarely invited aboard. That Stratford had come to London specially to offer to sail them to Richmond boggled his mind. It also alarmed him. His father's attention had been fixed on Penelope in a surprising and unsettling way, and he wanted to refuse the invitation just for that reason.

But his wife seemed to have no inkling of his unease. "How very kind and thoughtful," she exclaimed. "Is it a pleasure boat or a racing craft?"

Few things annoyed the earl more than hearing his yacht called a common boat. "It is for my personal pleasure," he replied thinly, "although it is quite fast as well."

"It's rather late in the season for sailing," Benedict said, trying to squelch the idea. "Lady Atherton would be more comfortable in a carriage."

His father turned to him, his expression like granite. Benedict felt the wild elation of knowing the earl could not compel him to travel by yacht, as he once would have done. "I would be pleased to have your company aboard the *Diana*. Lady Stratford is most eager to make your bride's acquaintance."

The mention of his mother was deliberate, and unfortunately effective. He tried to ignore it. "And I'm keenly anticipating the chance to present my wife to her again. Perhaps in a few weeks we shall be able to make a visit."

Because he was so attuned to it, he noticed his father's furious disbelief at this response. The earl's breathing paused for a moment before growing deeper and more controlled. He flexed his hands, lying flat on his knees, until they looked like claws. Not a muscle moved in his face. But when he spoke his voice was as even and commanding as before. "This week would better suit. Tomorrow, in fact." He turned back to Penelope as if probing for weakness.

Penelope's gaze flickered toward Benedict, but to her credit she didn't quail from the earl's intense stare. "I would hate to give any offense. But we could only manage a short visit at this time, and I fear it would be insufficient to make Lady Stratford's closer acquaintance."

Stratford bared his teeth in a victorious smile. "I am sure you can arrange something later, as a filial obligation to her ladyship. I depart tomorrow from the dock above Vauxhall."

"It is kind of you to be so eager to welcome me to the family seat . . ." Again Penelope looked toward Benedict.

He could hardly say that Stratford's veneer of solicitous attention was what made him want to deny it. Stratford never did anything without a reason, a reason that was generally calculated to benefit himself and very rarely took any account of the impact on others. For some unknown motive, Stratford wanted them to sail with him to Richmond, although Benedict was unable to think of a single good explanation. That could only be an ill omen, and he had learned too well that ignoring those omens was extremely foolish.

But Penelope didn't know that, and now the earl turned her words on him. "Surely you don't want to disappoint your mother," he said, watching Benedict like a bird of prey. "After the way she worries about you . . ." He made a quiet *tsk* and shook his head. "When she only wants to see that you have made an agreeable match."

Now he didn't know what to think. He had promised his mother that the marriage was his choice—even desire—and that was more true than ever. His instinct said that the earl didn't care one whit what the countess worried, and this was merely a way to manipulate him into capitulating. But . . . he hadn't received a single letter from his mother since his visit to Stratford Court. That was unusual; she wrote to him once a month, even when he was out of the earl's favor. Her letters were mundane, polite accounts, but they let him know she was well. He was somewhat ashamed to realize he hadn't thought of his mother much lately; he'd been too distracted . . . and consumed . . . by his bride. "As ever, I'm deeply moved by her concern for my happiness. I hope you will assure her that I am very content." He glanced at Penelope. "We shall make a proper visit to Richmond in a few weeks, since Lady Atherton also has family there."

Stratford's anger was nearly a halo around him. "You are refusing to come, then."

"I'm delighted to be invited," he began, but his father cut him off.

"No, I see you are not." He gave Benedict the contemptuous look that never failed to make his skin crawl. "Perhaps my invitation was an insult to your new status. Perhaps you have forgotten your family duties, as soon as your family connections helped you wed an heiress. Perhaps you no longer need or care for a mother's tender feelings, now that you have a wife to comfort you. I shan't impose on you again, Lord Atherton." He said the last with an acid edge, a pointed reminder that he himself was the true Viscount Atherton; Benedict only used the title by courtesy of being his heir.

Benedict said a dozen curses inside his head. What to do? He was being manipulated again, despite all his resolve and efforts to put himself beyond the earl's reach. He could give in now, or risk never being allowed to see his mother again. Would Stratford stick to it? He'd never threatened it before. He glanced at Penelope, trying to buy a little time. She had grown quiet during the increasingly tense exchange, but her eyes were alert and wary. It was almost a relief to see. Perhaps now she would understand a little better about his father. This was one of the few times Benedict could recall the earl showing his true colors to someone outside the contained world of Stratford Court.

"It's a very kind invitation," he said, still trying

to delay. "The sudden notice gives me pause, not the visit itself. There are some matters I must attend to, and others I must put off if I'm to leave town for a few days. Will you allow me a day to make arrangements?" A day to analyze the offer for any hidden traps, and the chance to refuse by letter instead of in person.

He ought to have known better. Any sign of wavering was a sign of weakness, and the earl pounced on it. "Of course," he said with exaggerated civility. "A day to examine your fidelity to your birthright; a day to delay disappointing your mother and refusing your father. I understand perfectly."

Benedict clenched his teeth even as he smiled. "I knew you would. I'm no longer a bachelor, free to follow my whims. I have financial affairs to manage and servants to instruct. And, as you have noted, I have a wife to consider now. She hasn't had time to plan for a trip to Stratford Court, and I wouldn't want her to be inadequately prepared for her first official visit as the future mistress."

There was nothing Stratford could say to any of that, and they both knew it. Stratford gave him an icy look before turning to Penelope. "Nor would I ask it of you, my dear. But I assure you that you need not worry about ceremony overmuch in this instance." Another rapier-sharp glance at Benedict. "After all, we are family."

"We are indeed." Penelope rose to her feet, and the gentlemen followed. She gave the earl another dazzling smile. "You are so considerate to indulge my female vanity. I would be mortified to arrive ill prepared and unable to do credit to the Stratford name."

"No doubt," said the earl dryly. Benedict wondered again how his father was able to stand all Penelope's praise of his finer feelings—feelings he knew very well the earl did not possess, or wish to possess. Stratford bowed. "I depart for Richmond tomorrow afternoon. I trust you will see fit to join me, Lady Atherton." Without another glance at his son, he left.

Neither moved until they heard the door below close behind him. Benedict let out his breath and dropped back into his chair, rubbing his hands over his face.

Penelope went to the window. "He's gone," she reported. "What an odd call."

He closed his eyes. That didn't begin to describe it.

His wife's hand on his arm made him start. "Is that the way he usually is?"

Benedict gave a short, bitter laugh. "No, that was exceedingly kind and solicitous, compared to how he usually is." He met her eyes. "He's very interested in you."

His somber air weighed down the words. She didn't make a face or roll her eyes. "Why?"

"I have absolutely no idea." Absently he took her hand and rubbed his thumb over her ring. "I fear it's not a kindly interest."

A faint frown touched her brow. "Then what? Would he not want me to be presented to your mother?"

"I doubt he much cares one way or the other," he said, still thinking about the earl's demeanor.

"The last time I saw him, he threw me out and said I wasn't to come back, even under pretense of visiting her. If he didn't want us there, nothing she said would matter."

"Perhaps he really worries I'll be a terrible countess," she ventured. "Perhaps it's pride, and he wants your mother to instruct me . . ."

Slowly he shook his head. "Possibly, but that wouldn't be enough for him to come to London himself—and to take us on the yacht, no less. The yacht is his private sphere. I've only been on it twice, and my sisters have never been invited aboard."

"Never?" Her voice rose in astonishment.

"He's not like your father," he told her. "Daughters are not important to him. The yacht is."

Her mouth thinned. "If you wish to tell him no, I have no objection."

"That would bring its own consequences." But what were the consequences of saying yes? That was a harder question to answer, and this time it involved not just himself but Penelope.

Her fingers squeezed around his, lightly. She didn't say anything. Benedict realized he was slipping back into the habit of keeping his thoughts to himself. "It strikes me as odd because he was not overly pleased by our marriage." He hesitated, then decided it was time to bare all. "He disdains your entire family; your father made his fortune, which is not a gentlemanly thing to do, even though that fortune is the only thing—in my father's opinion—that renders your family even marginally acceptable. And I married you without asking for his approval. He prefers a world of pride and privilege where all defer to him. He refused to let Elizabeth marry her first choice of suitor, and he only agreed to permit Samantha's marriage when Gray's father, the Duke of Rowland, intervened. For his heir to wed a girl he didn't prefer, let alone approve of, is unthinkable."

"Then why are you considering capitulating to his demand?"

It was the concern in her voice that got him. That note of compassion and worry slid through his guard and nicked him where he had no defenses. It meant she believed him, and more important, she supported him. Wordlessly he raised her hand to his lips and kissed her knuckles. "My mother is not the same as he is," Benedict said in a low voice. "She is kind and loving, and I can't leave her to face his temper. He's never struck her, but . . . There are other ways to wound and cripple a soul, and Stratford excels at them all."

They sat in silence for several minutes. When he finally dared steal a peek at her face, Penelope wore her deep thinking expression. Her gaze was focused on their linked hands with an unusual intensity, and there was a determined set to her jaw. "Do you think your mother would want us to go?" she asked.

"She would be delighted to make your acquaintance. Stratford was correct to say she worries about me, and about my sisters. Her greatest concern when I told her of our marriage was that I be happy with the match." He shook his head. "But I wouldn't be surprised if she has no idea my father extended an invitation. He doesn't consult her on things like that."

"Then perhaps we should go for her sake. I am perfectly capable of withstanding your father's disdain for a few days, and we can always decamp to Montrose Hill or even Hart House, although it's been closed up for the winter." She met his astonished gaze evenly. "It would be cruel to subject her to any more of that man's displeasure, and if we refuse, he'll have no one but her to take out his temper on, will he?"

For the first time, Benedict felt utterly unworthy of his bride. Here was her principled loyalty, extending not just to himself but to his mother, a woman she'd met only once, under difficult circumstances. "Penelope . . ."

"But I refuse to let that man browbeat me," she went on. "I cannot promise to hold my tongue if he's rude and belittles me or anyone I care about. You should know that before you send him your answer."

Slowly his mouth curved. "I never thought to ask you to." He tilted his head to look at her. "Do you mind going by river?"

"And miss out on what may be my only chance to sail aboard the exclusive Stratford yacht?" She fluttered her eyelashes. "How could one possibly chance it?"

Benedict laughed. She grinned back. "Thank you," he said on impulse.

"For warning you I may give a smart answer?" She pursed up her mouth in that kissable way. "Are you certain you wish to encourage such behavior?"

"I know you won't do it lightly," he answered. "And I've been warned for some time now. I like your smart mouth."

A sly smile played around her lips. "You didn't always."

"I've come to see the advantages." He leaned toward her. "Shall I describe them?"

"Please do."

He tipped up her chin. Her eyes shone like aquamarines under her half-lowered eyelids. Benedict felt a burst of intense gratitude to Abigail Weston and Frances Lockwood. If either of them had accepted him, he wouldn't have Penelope. Who else would have pushed him to confront his family's facade of civility? She wasn't cowed by the earl and didn't buckle under his glare. Unburdened by a lifetime of his punishments, she called him a bully and highlighted his veiled insults. Benedict watched her fend off the earl's sharp words as if they had no power over her—as in fact they didn't—with some awe. No matter how many times he'd told himself his father had no sway over him anymore, he knew it wasn't completely true. Stratford would always know his weaknesses, his points of pride, his vulnerabilities, and would never hesitate to exploit them.

Benedict still didn't want to go to Richmond tomorrow, but perhaps it was the better choice. Let Stratford—and his mother—see what kind of woman he'd married. Penelope's indomitable spirit seemed to wear off a little on everyone who knew her; perhaps her example would be just the thing to embolden his mother and set his father back on his heels. If it went badly, they need never see his lordship again. Stratford knew that. His parting speech had touched on every point of independence. Benedict was a married man with an independent fortune and a wife who cared little for the aloof pride that Stratford prized. Together he and Penelope could chart their own course, and nothing the earl did could touch them.

Or so he thought.

Chapter 22

In response to Benedict's note accepting his invitation, the earl sent a terse reply with the dock and time of departure. Depending on the winds, they should arrive in time for dinner, which was served fashionably late at Stratford Court.

Benedict advised Penelope to pack only enough for a few days' stay and to dress warmly for the sail. It was a rather raw fall day, and as he stepped out of the carriage at the dock, he squinted up at the steely sky. It looked like rain. The stiff breeze would be good for the sails, not as pleasant for the passengers. There was a cabin aboard the yacht, handsomely appointed, but Stratford considered it a sign of weakness to go belowdecks. Benedict resigned himself to being cold and probably wet for the next few hours.

That didn't mean his wife had to be, though. He tucked her hand around his arm and dismissed the carriage. The servants were already en route to Richmond with the baggage. "Don't let my father persuade you to stay on deck," he told her. "It looks to be an unpleasant journey."

She was studying the yacht as they drew near it. It was a small craft, relatively speaking, but everything was of the finest quality. *Diana* gleamed in golden paint along the hull. "Does he always sail in such abominable weather?"

"No, but once he makes his plans, he doesn't like to change them." He caught her looking at a nearby boat, lurching fore and aft on a gust of wind, and realized he'd made it sound dangerous. "This weather isn't too rough to sail in. It just won't be as agreeable as it would be on a fine sunny day."

"No doubt," she murmured.

Stratford appeared on the deck. Benedict raised one hand in acknowledgment. His father nodded once, then turned on his heel and walked toward the stern. Already regretting it, Benedict took Penelope's hand in his and led her down the dock.

"Punctual for a change" was the earl's greeting when they had stepped aboard.

"Atherton is always punctual," said Penelope brightly. "How fortunate my father shares that virtue and raised his children to be prompt as well. It has made married life so much smoother."

Stratford's sour gaze slewed toward him. Benedict just bowed his head, trying not to laugh at how his father must feel to be compared to Penelope's father in any way.

"I've not been on many yachts," Penelope went on. "And none so fine as this one. Will you show me the finer points, my lord?"

He wasn't sure if his father would agree, but the earl must be in an exceptionally accommodating mood today. He offered his arm and gave her a frosty smile. "Of course."

Benedict fell in behind as Stratford led Penelope away, her gloved hand pale on his dark sleeve. No explanation for the earl's sudden interest had presented itself, and slowly he began to imagine it might be nothing but raw curiosity. Perhaps Stratford had repented of banishing him, or perhaps he'd heard gossip from London. Perhaps pride had undercut his fury, and his interest was primarily in assuring himself that Penelope would be a fit countess. Not that Benedict much agreed with his father about what a countess should be, and he certainly didn't intend to allow his father to impose his rigid ideas on Penelope, but if Stratford cared for anything, he cared for his name and title. Penelope was nothing like his mother—she wasn't demure and retiring, or aloof and reserved, but undaunted. Adventurous. Valiant and bold. When the wind caught her bonnet and almost pulled it off, she merely put up one hand to hold it in place without a word of complaint. Stratford led them to a spot where they could watch the three-man crew work, raising the sails and maneuvering the yacht into the current. Penelope watched everything with undisguised interest, asking a few questions that demonstrated she had a little familiarity with racing. Once Benedict even caught a glimmer of respect in his father's face as he answered her.

When they were under way, Stratford left to supervise his helmsman. Benedict joined his wife at the rail near the prow, watching the city drift past. "I believe he likes you," he said with some surprise.

Her lips curved. "Because he hasn't pitched me overboard yet?"

"Because he answered your questions."

She caught a strand of hair the wind had whipped across her face and tucked it back into her bonnet. "I've been thinking about your father and why he's so commanding. Perhaps what he most respects is strength. His children could not oppose him, but I'm not his child and he has no sway over me. By standing up to him—politely, of course—perhaps I've set him back enough to convince him to give up trying to browbeat me."

Benedict privately thought not; the earl still held Gray, the son of a wealthy, influential duke, in very low esteem, and he'd never forgiven Samantha for marrying him. But Penelope's theory was more appealing, and for all he knew she was right. He never had truly understood his father. "If anyone could set him back, it would be you."

She gave him a rueful look. "Did you just call me a shrew, Lord Atherton?"

"On the contrary, darling. I called you a woman of uncommon determination and self-possession."

"Hardheaded," she said with a laugh.

"In the best way," he agreed.

"Hmph." She refused to look at him, but her eyes were shining and he was sure the pink in her cheeks wasn't strictly due to the wind.

Benedict glanced over his shoulder. His father stood behind the helm, watching with a critical eye. He edged a little closer to his wife. "There is one significant drawback to traveling on my father's yacht instead of in our own carriage."

She must have heard the note in his voice. Her head tilted and she gave him one of her secretive little smiles, as if she were contemplating something very naughty. "What would that be?"

"The lack of privacy." He traced the stitching on her glove where she held the rail. "I read the most intriguing account of a carriage journey the other day . . ."

Her lips parted. "Where did you read it?"

"In my lady's dressing room." He let his fingers slide between hers for a moment. "I've no idea where that coach was going, but I daresay most of the trip's pleasure was had en route."

"And you didn't find it . . . alarming? Or shocking?"

"Very shocking, but in the best way." He lifted her hand to his lips, watching her blush deepen as she stared at him in fascination. "Did you find it shocking?"

She ran her tongue over her bottom lip. "No. In fact . . . I believe that was one of my favorite stories by the author." Her pulse was rapid. "Have you any other knowledge of such a feat?"

"Not direct knowledge." He laid her hand back on the rail. "Yet."

"We're not returning to London by yacht, are we?"

"No," he said before she even finished the question. It was too cold and wet for sailing, in his opinion. One journey would satisfy his father; he doubted they would even be invited for a second.

"Well." She tapped her foot against his, still smiling coyly. "Perhaps we shall test the author's veracity."

If the earl hadn't been only a few yards away, he would have kissed her. As it was, he felt a fiendish eagerness to reach Stratford Court. After the journey, they would need to retire, to change for dinner and repair their appearances. Benedict thought an extra hour or so to restore their good humor as well was more than justified. And if his father made any snide remarks about the future Earls of Stratford, Benedict would simply smile and think of another pleasurable way they might try to conceive those heirs.

The sky grew darker. It began to rain, very lightly, as they passed the Bishop's Palace at Fulham. Benedict turned up the collar of his coat, glad of an excuse to leave the deck. "Do you want to go into the cabin?"

"Not yet." She raised her face to the rain as if in bliss. "It's more like mist than rain."

"It will still get us wet," he reminded her.

She only grinned. "And what is that to us? We'll soon be warm and dry."

"You're saying that because you don't want to give any ground."

"True," she admitted cheerfully. "But isn't it also an adventure? How many times can one claim to have braved a storm on deck? I feel rather like an explorer, facing dangers and terrors in pursuit of the unknown."

He smiled. "If only there was something more exciting at the end of this trip."

"I shall meet your mother." Penelope hesitated, pulling her cloak more securely around her. "I hope to make a good impression."

He squeezed her hand. "You will. When you first meet her, my father will be there. Don't presume that is her natural manner. You must see her when he's not nearby, to see the true lady of warmth and affection she is. She wants very much to like you, Penelope, and I know she will."

"I hope so." She didn't look entirely persuaded, but her fingers curled into his, and he felt a burst of warmth for her again.

The rain pattered on, never heavy but stinging when driven by the wind. For a while they walked up and down the deck to keep warm, but eventually it grew too slippery and they retreated behind the helm, where there was some shelter from the wind.

Stratford looked Penelope up and down. "You must want out of the weather, Lady Atherton. My man will have tea prepared in the cabin belowdecks."

Again Benedict was astonished. The cabin below was as finely appointed as the rest of the ship, and when Stratford went on longer sails, he took a complement of servants to provide all the luxuries of home. Benedict had just never heard—nor thought to hear—those comforts freely offered to anyone else. But Penelope only smiled. "It's quite brisk out, my lord, but nothing to blunt my enjoyment of the trip."

The earl arched one brow. "Quite a redoubtable woman, I see, unlike most ladies."

Benedict heard his real meaning: unlike *any* lady. First Stratford all but dared her to come aboard, and now he slighted her for not dissolving into a plaintive mess at the discomfort aboard.

But when Benedict glanced at his wife, he noted the sheen of rain on her skin and the dampness of her cloak. It was silly for Penelope to remain out here just to show the earl how much backbone she had. He leaned closer and murmured in her ear. "We're nearly to the dock. There will be a bit of a drive to the house, so you might want to seize this opportunity for a quiet moment alone."

She met his gaze, then nodded. "You are so kind, my lord," she said to the earl. "A cup of tea would be very refreshing."

Stratford bowed his head and swept out one arm. "The door at the bottom of the steps." Benedict turned to go, too. His father would think him weak and womanish and he didn't give a damn. "A moment, Benedict," said his father. "I want a word."

He hesitated. Penelope stopped beside him, her hand on his arm. A gust of wind blew the rain directly at them, and he spoke without thinking. "Can it not wait?"

Stratford raised one brow. He didn't say a word.

Benedict bit back a sigh. "Go get warm," he murmured to Penelope, releasing her hand. She gave him a sympathetic smile, and then she turned and made her way across the deck.

Penelope ducked her head and clung to the rail as she descended the short flight of stairs. The steps were wet, and the floor had a tendency to tilt suddenly beneath her feet as the yacht tacked from side to side, sailing upriver. A narrow passage

opened at the bottom of the stairs, with a brass
lantern swinging on a hook just barely above her
head. The wood down here was polished to a
glossy sheen; Benedict was right about his father
sparing no expense, she thought as she headed for
the carved door that must lead to the main cabin.
But what a waste, to have such a craft and never
invite others aboard. She thought of the barge her
father had bought solely so her mother could plan
parties on the river. Surely that was a better way
to use one's fortune. The Earl of Stratford might be
immensely wealthy and noble, but she was sure
her parents wouldn't change places with him for
anything.

She let herself into the cabin and untied her
cloak, hanging it on a hook by the door before
stripping off her gloves. Benedict had told her to
dress warmly, but the cloak hadn't kept her pelisse
dry, and she removed it as well. It was dim in here,
despite the lanterns, but also quiet and dry, thanks
to the small round stove bolted to the floor beside
her. After the whistling wind upstairs and the in-
cessant spray from the river, it felt like paradise.
Penelope removed her bonnet and set the damp,
heavy thing aside with a sigh of relief. No wonder
Benedict had wanted to avoid this. Why had the
earl insisted they go by river? It might be faster
than carriage but it was also considerably less comfortable. She'd been determined to hold her own on
deck, but now that she felt the warmth of the stove
and didn't have the rain in her face, she was grateful Benedict had urged her to go below.

"There you are."

The unexpected voice from the shadows made

her jump and give a little shriek. Then she wanted to shriek again as she whirled around and spied the speaker.

Three quick thoughts flew through her mind. First, that she was going back on deck, even if a hurricane broke over them. Second, she wished there was a fireplace poker handy. And third— and most unsettling—this was why Lord Stratford had contrived to get them on his yacht. Far from relenting or softening in his attitude toward his heir, the earl had had something very nearly evil in mind.

"I thought I'd have to come fetch you down. Stratford was bloody certain you wouldn't last half an hour on deck, and now it's been almost two hours I've been cooling my heels." A chilling smile on his face, Lord Clary managed to slam the door before she could run through it. "Won't you sit down, Lady Atherton?"

Chapter 23

"**W**hat a surprise," she said, trying to recover her poise and not show how rattled she was. "No one warned me we'd see monsters on the journey."

He laughed. "Still very free with your tongue, I see." His dark gaze slid over her. "And not such a virginal young lady anymore."

She glared daggers at him, retreating toward the stove. Her dress was wet, and since she'd unthinkingly donned a light-colored one, it was also more revealing than it should have been. "I am sure my husband, Lord Atherton, will be just as gratified as I am by your kind felicitations on our marriage."

"Will he?" Clary smirked. "He damned well owes the marriage to me, so perhaps he will be."

"Oh dear!" She widened her eyes innocently. "Here I thought he owed it to my acceptance of his earnest proposal."

"If Atherton had half a thought to marry you before that night, he's a bigger fool than I thought." Again his eyes moved over her figure with rude speculation. "Unless you gave him what you refused to give me."

No, Penelope thought furiously, she was the fool. Benedict had known Stratford's invitation was suspect, but she had said they should go. She hadn't believed a father could be so heartless, so uncaring; surely there must have been some kernel of affection deep in his breast. Surely he must have wanted them to visit for a reason that might, possibly, have been considered generous or concerned. Now she knew better. It was possible Stratford had no idea what Clary had done to her, or that he'd started the gossip that led Benedict to marry her. But there could be no good reason for the earl to have manipulated them onto this yacht with Clary concealed belowdecks waiting to waylay her. "What do you want?"

His mouth curled in derision. "So direct! Very well. Where is Olivia Townsend?"

Penelope blinked. Olivia? Not for the first time she wished she knew what he wanted with Olivia, but it didn't really matter. Under no circumstances would she tell him even if she did know. "She's away from town."

"I know that." He came closer. "Where?"

"Far away, I believe."

Clary's face darkened. "Don't toy with me," he warned in a soft voice. "I want something from her, very badly. When I want something badly, I get it."

"But she is a person, not a thing," she replied politely. "You cannot have a person just because you want her. And if she has something you want, you can only make an offer for it in good faith and hope to strike a bargain."

His laugh was ugly. "Bargain for it? No, my lady, I don't think so. Perhaps I wasn't clear—it already belongs to me. She knows this, and yet she won't give it to me. What would you call that? It sounds like stealing to me."

"I would say that it sounds like you're lying, because Olivia isn't a thief."

Clary went very still. "Watch your words, girl."

"You may call me Lady Atherton if we ever meet again—which I sincerely hope we do not. I think I will rejoin my husband now. Good day to you, sir." She turned toward the door, trembling with fury and fear. The last time she found herself in a room with him, it had almost ended very badly . . . But Benedict was only one deck away. She just had to get back to his side.

And after this, she would never argue one word against avoiding his father. Clary was a monster, but Stratford had schemed to put her at Clary's mercy, aboard a boat where she couldn't walk away, and for that she tossed out every notion she'd ever had that she ought to try harder to think better of the earl since he was family now. He would never be her family.

Clary didn't stop her from opening the door, but he followed her. "You can run back to your husband, if you think he'll save you," he taunted, crowding indecently close behind her. Penelope clutched her skirts and tried to walk faster, but the wet floors made it treacherous. "Of course, he may not take your side as eagerly as he did before. After all, he already got what he wanted from you. And Stratford wants to find Olivia Townsend nearly as much as I do. Why do you think he came to London to get you?" Penelope glanced over her shoulder in shock before she could stop herself.

Clary's thin smile widened, gloating. "You should be flattered. An earl and a viscount both hanging on your every word! A clever girl would think carefully about what that means, and about how she should answer their questions."

"Given the earl and viscount in question, I am sure it means nothing good for Mrs. Townsend, and that's why I won't tell either of you anything." She turned her back on him and grabbed the rail to climb the stairs to the deck. The rain had stopped, although the sky was thick with dark clouds. It might have been late twilight instead of midday. The wind was quieter, but she shivered as it cut right through her damp skirts. Her cloak was still in the cabin. It made her hate Clary even more; she ought to have been drying off in the snug, warm cabin, not rushing back out into the elements even less dressed for it than before.

Just as she reached the top step, Clary caught her arm. "Perhaps you ought to think of your husband instead of Mrs. Townsend." He tilted his head toward the helm, on the other side of the ship behind the billowing sail. "He'll tell you what it costs to cross Stratford—and be assured, refusing me in this is the same as crossing Lord Stratford. Do you want to bring down his wrath on your dear husband?" He sneered the last two words.

"I know my husband," she said, low and furious. "I know he wouldn't hand over a defenseless, innocent woman to your grasp, no matter what his father said."

A muscle twitched in Clary's jaw. "Where is she?"

Penelope twisted loose of his grip and started

across the deck. It wasn't that large a boat but she couldn't see Benedict; the sails, straining at the lines, obscured everything from this position.

Clary pursued her. "I won't ask again," he said, raising his voice. "Where is she?"

"Somewhere you can't hurt her!"

He swore. This time when he grabbed her, she couldn't wrestle free. The wind drove his hair straight back from his face, emphasizing the sharp hook of his nose and the point of his chin. He looked like a demon, and the cold hatred in his eyes made her suddenly afraid. "Last chance," he said, looming over her.

"Let me go," she said, biting off every word.

For a moment he didn't move. His fingers bit into her arms. "As the lady wishes." He released her with a little push, so that she staggered a step backward. Her leather half boots slipped on the wet deck. Penelope reached for the railing to catch her balance. The yacht was tacking hard, canted over at a good angle, and the rushing water was very near.

Then Clary put one hand in the middle of her chest and shoved, sending her head over heels backward into the Thames.

"**R**eally, Benedict, I'm disappointed. I trust her father paid you a pretty penny to take her. She's a stubborn, headstrong female with little delicacy about her."

Benedict tried not to let his father's careless

insult goad him. "I'm very well pleased with the marriage."

Stratford cut him a narrow-eyed look. "Not much of a beauty, is she?"

In spite of himself, a faint smile curved his mouth. Penelope might not be the earl's idea of a beauty, but she shone with vitality and verve and Benedict thought he'd never seen anyone more bewitching. "I couldn't disagree more."

The earl sniffed. "I take it that means she's as loose and wanton as gossip holds. I'm astonished you would make such a woman your bride."

"Every word of that gossip was a lie." Not that Benedict wasn't deeply, quietly elated by her wantonness in *his* bed. The smile lingered on his face.

His father saw, and it displeased him. Benedict realized that, but there was nothing he could do to stop it. In fact . . . let Stratford know that his marriage wasn't a disaster. Let him realize that Penelope was no shrinking violet to be cowed and intimidated. Let him be very aware that his influence was waning, almost to the point of nothingness.

Stratford faced forward again, into the wind. "I never thought I'd see the day a common chit got my son by the ballocks."

"Penelope," said Benedict, "is my wife, not a common chit. It doesn't become you to speak so coarsely of the future Countess of Stratford, sir."

"What a proud day it will be when a coal miner's daughter presides over Stratford Court."

"I quite agree," he said, as if the earl had expressed approval.

His father exhaled, his breath steaming faintly

in the cooling air. Penelope would probably say it was the smoke of brimstone. Benedict's lips twitched. He shouldn't find her irreverence as amusing as he did. "Then perhaps you will begin educating her on her duties."

Something about that word "duties" always made his shoulders tense. In Stratford's world, duty meant something beyond its ordinary meaning. Benedict had learned, through painful years of experience, that when his father brought up duty, it portended a disagreeable task or an unreasonable demand. "The only duty she has is to me."

"And your duty is to me."

Benedict's hands clenched. Everything always came back to the earl's demands. "I've fulfilled that duty many times over."

"And you would deny your own father a simple request?" Stratford raised his brows. "I find that hard to believe. It is a small thing; there's no need to grow snappish and petulant," he went on before Benedict could reply. "You need only exercise your husbandly authority over your wife and persuade her to be cooperative."

The unease that had hovered around him all day burst into full-blown alarm. "No."

"No." Stratford's eyes glittered with pique. "Really, Benedict? After all these years, you must know that is not an acceptable answer."

Once it would not have been. Once he would have been holding himself taut and still, praying that the request would be minor or at least easy to fulfill, never daring to refuse. Not that his father didn't usually find some fault in his actions, no matter how hard he tried to please. He no longer remembered every beating—they had blurred together by now—but he acutely remembered the feeling of placing his hands on the earl's desk, bowing his head, and bracing himself for the first blow of Stratford's thin wooden cane. It was supple enough to bend without breaking, landing one stinging blow after another. In his mind, Benedict could still see that cane, propped against the frame of the wide windows in the earl's study, an ever-present reminder of the consequences of defiance. Stratford's only mercy had been that he used it over clothing, preferring to leave bruises and aches instead of scars.

Benedict closed his eyes a moment and inhaled deeply. Those whippings were a thing of the past. "After all these years, I am a grown man, no longer subject to being beaten for disobedience. How I choose to exercise my husbandly authority is strictly my right, and any man—*any* man—who interferes with that right will find his interference turned back on him." He met his father's furious eyes. "I mean it, Father," he added, softly but with warning. "Leave her alone."

After a moment the earl turned away. "I don't wish to have anything to do with her. However, it appears she is in possession of some information I need. After she answers a single question, you may take your common strumpet of a wife and do what you will with her, far from my sight."

Damn it. "What information?" he demanded, racking his brain. What could Stratford possibly want from Penelope?

Stratford's expression revealed nothing. "See that she's cooperative."

Without another word Benedict turned to go belowdecks. He knew this had been a mistake; whatever Stratford wanted, he wanted badly. Benedict had known there was some unspoken reason the earl wanted them at Stratford Court, but he'd—stupidly—thought it would involve him. He was certain Penelope had no inkling of what Stratford might want. Benedict himself couldn't begin to imagine what his wife could possibly know that Stratford would be desperate to discover . . . And then a man—a man Benedict didn't want within ten miles of Penelope—came around the deck.

Bloody hell.

His heart bounded into his throat as he bolted across the slippery, tilting deck and flung himself down the stairs. Lord Clary's presence alone would be enough to put up his guard, but they'd been at sail for two hours. That meant Clary had been waiting below, in the cabin where Stratford had urged Penelope to go. Benedict threw open the cabin door, praying she was safely within, but what he saw was worse: her wet cloak and bedraggled bonnet, but no sign of Penelope herself.

The sails snapped loudly overhead as he pounded up to the deck again, shielding his eyes against the rain to search frantically for her. The *Diana* was not a large craft; there weren't many places to hide. He ducked under the boom to see around the straining sails, but she was nowhere.

His father and Clary were still behind the helm, having a fierce discussion. Benedict stalked up to them and seized Clary's coat. "Where is my wife?"

Clary tried to brush him off, his face taut with fury. "Unhand me."

Benedict gave him a hard shake. "Where?"

Clary wrested free and glared at him, then at Stratford. "She's an obstinate creature—"

"You said you could persuade her," cut in Stratford. "Must I do everything personally? Bring her up here and I'll get the truth from her."

A muscle twitched in Clary's jaw. "I've already dealt with her."

Benedict lunged at him again. "Where is she? The cabin is empty. *Where is my wife?*"

A hateful smirk spread over the man's face. "Lost your bride, Lord Atherton? How convenient for you."

"Fetch the girl, Clary," said Stratford coldly. "My patience is running thin."

Clary just kept smirking, and the reason dawned on Benedict with horrible certainty. He wheeled around, scanning the water off the starboard side of the boat, then off the port side. The river was choppy and turbulent, and the foaming of constantly breaking waves obscured anyone in it.

"Where is she?" snapped the earl.

"You should thank me, both of you," retorted Clary. "Atherton has her fortune, and now you can choose a proper bride for him. I'll find Mrs. Townsend another way."

Without hesitation Benedict drew back his fist and drove it into Clary's smug face. He didn't wait to savor the view of the viscount going down on his knees, blood streaming from his nose, but stripped off his greatcoat as he rushed back to the rail. His hat had fallen off already. Feverishly he searched the river, tearing off his coat and waistcoat. There—was that a head, bobbing above the waves? Penelope's dress was white, and there was something white in the water. He kept his gaze on it, not even daring to blink.

His father seized his arm as Benedict yanked off one boot, then the other. "What the devil are you doing?"

"I'm going after her. And when I come back, I'm going to put a bullet into your accomplice." His eyes stung from staring at the point in the water where he thought—he hoped—a figure was struggling against the current. *Please God, let that be Penelope*, he prayed. How long since she'd left the deck? The wind was whisking the yacht along at a good pace. The river wasn't very wide at this point but it could be dangerous, even on a clear, calm day. He'd swum across it more times than he could count as a boy, fleeing his father and escaping to the woods on Montrose Hill to pretend he was an orphan washed up on a wild and distant shore.

Stratford grabbed him again, this time forcing him around. "You will not go after her. I will deal with that idiot Clary—he knew I wanted to talk to her—"

"Yet instead he pushed her into the river."

The earl brushed that aside with an impatient jerk of his head. "And in this water she's lost. Don't be a fool!" His gray hair was wild from the wind. "You are my son—my *heir*. How dare you risk yourself?"

Here at last was the paternal concern he'd always imagined Stratford must feel, somewhere deep inside, and it made Benedict want to kill him. Feeling it would be the last time they ever came face to face, one way or another, he threw off his father's restraining hand. "I'd rather die trying to save her than live as your heir." He stepped up onto the rail and dove over the side.

Chapter 24

The Thames was shockingly cold. Penelope almost gasped out her shallow breath as the frigid water closed over her head. For a paralyzed moment, everything—including her own heart—seemed to stop. She could see the *Diana* gliding past her, almost right over her, blotting out the gray light of the sky. She could see Lord Clary turn his back and disappear, without even a flicker of regret that he'd tossed her into the river. Then the wake of the boat went over her, and she felt herself falling deeper into the cold, dark water.

With a jerk she thrust out her arms. Jamie had taught her and Abigail to swim, long ago. It was the summer she was six or seven, and they'd gone for an extended visit to her grandparents' home in Somerset. There was a pond where all three Weston children went to fish and wade, and their mother had charged Jamie with making sure his sisters didn't fall in. After he had to pull Penelope out—twice—Jamie declared that either they would learn to swim or he wouldn't take them to the pond. Penelope had loved swimming.

Abigail didn't want to put her head under water, but Penelope would strip off her dress and jump right in, reveling in the freedom of movement and the feeling of weightlessness.

But floating on her back, giggling with her sister and trying to surreptitiously splash her brother, was a very different thing than fighting the current in the Thames, fully dressed and several years out of practice. She managed to get her head above water, but only had time to take a single deep breath before another ripple of the wake submerged her.

Slowly, clumsily, her muscles began to remember. She kicked and circled her arms, trying to angle her body so it would naturally float. When she broke the surface again, she almost cried from the relief of it.

But now what? Her skirts were weighing her down. The current was dragging her farther and farther from the boat. She had no idea where she was, or how far away the shore was. When she flipped onto her stomach and began paddling, her heart sank at the realization that the riverbank looked very far away.

Then again, so was the yacht. As if nothing had happened, *Diana* was still sailing on. She spat out a mouthful of water and searched for any sign of alarm or concern, and saw nothing. "Ben," she whimpered. But he could have no idea. Neither of them had suspected Clary was on the boat, and as far as Benedict knew, she was safely warming her hands in the cabin. He might not realize she was missing until they reached the dock.

The waves were calming a little as the wake passed. Penelope squashed the flicker of panic in her breast; now was not the time. Her jaw firmed. She was not going to let that villainous snake kill her. She was going to save herself and then see Lord Clary in the dock for attempted murder. Whatever he wanted from Olivia no longer concerned her; he had tried to kill her and she would see him hang for it.

Her hair was a wet, heavy knot on her head. She managed to pull out a few pins until it collapsed into a long braid. Thank heaven she'd had Lizzie do a simple chignon. She made a few efforts to tear away her skirts, but the fabric was too sturdy. Realizing she could hardly feel her feet anymore, she scanned the shore for a mark—a tall tree—and began to swim for it.

Benedict cut through the water, driven by fear and fury. From the water's surface he lost his vantage point to look for Penelope, and every dozen yards or so he stopped to shout her name. His heart pounded like a drum in his chest; it must be keeping him warm, for he barely felt the cold of the river. Penelope had been in the water longer, and he didn't even know if she could swim. The thought that he might already be too late, that she could be sinking unconscious beneath the waves, drove him onward.

When he felt the current start to turn, he stopped to tread water and listen. "Penelope!" he shouted. "Pen, where are you?" There was no answer.

"Penelope! Answer me!" His heart twisted in anguish. She had to answer. "Penelope!"

A faint sound ahead of him caught his ear. He swam forward a few more strokes and stopped again. "Penelope! Keep calling so I can follow your voice!"

"Ben . . ."

Before he heard the rest of his name, he gulped in a breath and plowed under the waves. She was still alive, and damn it all, he meant to keep her that way. Every few feet he came up to exchange a shout with her, until finally he saw her face, deathly white but alert and alive.

"Christ." With shaking hands he pulled her to him, kicking hard to keep them afloat. She cupped his face in her hands and kissed him. Even though it was the wrong moment to delay, he kissed her back. "Thank God," he gasped when she released him. "Thank God I found you . . ."

"Clary." She could barely speak, but wheezed out the words. "He *pushed* me."

"I know." His cravat had come undone as he swam, and now he peeled the limp linen from his neck. "Lovely day for a swim, Lady Atherton, but can I persuade you to come ashore?"

She laughed, a weak, relieved sound. "Easily . . . my lord . . . Where is the shore?"

He craned his neck. "That way." He looped the cravat around her wrist. "Can you swim any more?"

Her face looked fearful, but she nodded. He tightened the loop, and forced her fingers to curl around it. Her skin was like ice, and he could tell she was struggling. That thick, warm dress was like an anchor around her body. "I can pull you. Do not let go, do you hear me?"

"I won't." A wave nearly rolled over her, and she spit out a mouthful of water. "I am not . . . going . . . to drown."

He grinned at the fierce determination in her voice. "That's the woman I know. Ready?" He knotted the other end of the cravat around his fist. When she gave a weak nod, he struck out for the shore.

Now that he had her, he had to be wise in using his energy. He could feel the cold creeping into his legs and shoulders, making them stiff. He swam a few strokes, then glided, letting the current propel them. Again he felt it start to turn, carrying them away from the shore he could see coming tantalizingly close. This part of the river was winding and picturesque, but Benedict realized he could use that to his advantage. In fact, when he stopped to get his bearings, he realized he knew exactly where they were. The current had carried them almost to the place where he had used to swim across as a boy. He knew this part of the river. And when he spied an exposed chunk of rock near the shore, he saw his opportunity. He dragged on the cravat to pull Penelope close.

"Do you see that large rock?" She searched for a moment. Her lips were blue and her eyes looked unfocused. He slapped her gently on the cheek. "We're going to swim toward it, do you hear me? The current will bend away before we get there, but the boulder will disrupt it. We're going to wait until we get near and then swim with all our strength for it. For now, just float along. Understand?" She just stared, glassy-eyed, at the rock, and he slapped her again, a little more sharply. "Penelope!"

The way she nodded made her head look heavy. "Swim for it."

He cupped his hand around her cheek and forced her to look at him. "We're almost there. Just a bit farther, love. Think of how Clary ought to die." Something sparked in her eyes. "I'm leaning toward disembowelment," he added.

"Drowned." Her lips tried to turn up. "In a privy."

He laughed. "Better!" She was exhausted. He could feel her fighting to keep her head up. Benedict revised his plan; let the current carry them. He had to keep her afloat, and if he saved some strength now, he should be able to tow her ashore when the moment came.

Soon, too soon, it was time. "Let's go, Pen," he said. "We're almost there." He didn't add that getting ashore was only the first obstacle. The land in front of them was wild and lonely. These were the woods he had once explored with Sebastian Vane, before Mad Michael sold the whole acreage to Stratford for a few pounds. They'd been virtually untouched for a decade, and that meant he and Penelope had a long, challenging hike to Montrose Hill House. He ignored the flicker of uncertainty about turning to Sebastian. Abigail would help her sister, and if they turned him out on suspicion of being in league with his father and Clary . . . As long as they took in Penelope, he wouldn't say anything except in thanks.

He let her float out to the length of the cravat. "Come on, Penelope, swim," he prodded her. "Just a few more yards."

She managed a faint nod and began moving her arms, and he struck out, keeping his eyes on the boulder. His shoulders burned; his right leg was beginning to cramp. His feet were numb. Every stroke felt like he was swimming through treacle, and the current was an insidious tug, trying to steer him off to the right. When he finally felt the welcome resistance of mud, he could barely stagger to his feet and reach for Penelope.

His heart seized as he pulled her to him. Hair lay in snaky locks over her face, her eyes were closed, and her lips were parted, and for a moment he couldn't tell if she still breathed. "Penelope," he said desperately, hauling her upright. "Wake up!"

For answer she bent at the waist and coughed up a good quantity of river water. "I am never going in the water again," she said faintly. "Nor on a boat."

He laughed, a painful, raspy gasp of incredulous joy. His arms tightened around her, and he kissed her forehead. "I don't blame you." Half carrying her, he slogged out of the water, pulling his foot from the sucking mud with each step. They were on land.

But that only revealed a new problem. The wind hadn't abated and it sliced through their wet clothes like scythes. Penelope began a deep shuddering, and he searched for any shelter at all. There was a dark crevice at the boulder, and he steered her there. "We have to get dry," he said, rubbing her arms roughly. "Then we'll walk up the hill and see if your sister is receiving guests."

"Are we close to Montrose Hill?" Her words were slurred.

"Very near," he lied.

The crevice turned out to be more than it appeared. He pulled away some vines and dead branches and realized it went farther back than expected. In fact, as he pushed deeper into the relative warmth out of the wind, he had the sense of space. He put out one arm and touched nothing. It was almost like a cave—and then he kicked something that skidded along the ground with a metallic clang.

"Wait a moment." He went down on his knee and groped around to discover a lantern and, a few fraught moments later, a flint and tinderbox. "Stay here," he told Penelope, barely able to make out her pale, drooping figure. "I'm going to try to light this."

It took several tries to find the right position that allowed enough protection from the wind yet enough light to see, but finally he coaxed a flame in the small, rusty lantern. Penelope was where he'd left her, slumped down against the rock. He lifted the lantern, and she raised her face greedily toward the light.

"We've got to get you dry." He turned her around and began undoing buttons. The once-white wool of her walking dress was now gray and swollen with water. He finally just ripped the buttons away, desperate to get it off. It was only chilling her further. She clumsily helped as he peeled off the dress, leaving her in translucent undergarments. He tossed the dress aside and took her out of the rest of her clothes, wringing out each piece as much as possible before putting it back on her. Damp clothes were only marginally better than wet clothes, but everything counted.

"Now yours." Her teeth chattered as she wrapped her arms around herself and sank back to the floor.

More to please her than for his own sake, he stripped off his shirt and wrung it out. There was a considerable pool of water on the floor now, and he looked toward the back of the crevice. The wavering light of the lantern pierced the darkness for only a few feet, and it wasn't revealing an end to the narrow opening. "Wait here," he said. "I'll be back in a moment."

"Where are you going?"

He went down on his knee for a quick embrace. "If there's a lantern, there may be something else useful here. It looks like a small cave."

"I can come with you . . ." She started to struggle to her feet but he stopped her.

"Rest," he told her. "Catch your breath. We still have a stroll uphill. I swear I won't leave you for long."

After a moment she gave in. Benedict let out his breath in relief—if she'd pleaded with him to stay, he didn't think he could have left her—and impulsively he kissed her. "Rest, love," he whispered again, then caught up the lantern and picked his way into the gloom.

It really was a small cave. The passage was narrow, but only for a few feet. He marveled; how many times had he explored this shore, on his own and with Sebastian, and neither of them had ever discovered it? For a moment he wondered if this led to the elusive Hart House grotto, but quickly discarded the idea. It was too close to the water, and would probably flood from time to time. And Penelope had promised to show him the grotto. His mouth firmed and he lifted the lantern higher. Once they were safely at Montrose Hill House, he'd be sure to remind her of that.

He trailed one hand along the wall to keep his balance. The ground was coarse sand, and more than once a sharp rock bit into the bottom of his foot, clad only in stockings. The wall at his side curved away, opening into a cavity of some size. Benedict swung the lantern in a circle, but couldn't make out much; the flame was too small, and the space too big. But there was something there . . . He raised the lantern over it. A stray piece of canvas. He shook it out, surprised by the size of it, and knocked something else over. A quick circuit of the space revealed a few discarded crates, broken open, and a pile of straw to one side. He stared at the odd collection, then scooped up the canvas and hurried back to Penelope.

"I d-don't know which is more frightening," she said, her voice shaking as he came back down the passage. "The wind, or the dark."

"The wind." He lifted her to her feet and wrapped the canvas around her. It was stiff and scratchy but it would break the wind. "There's nothing to fear from the dark."

Her blue eyes seemed to fill her face as she looked up at him. "There is. When I fell in the water, it was so dark. I've never felt so alone."

God help him, she had been. Thank God that wretch Clary had come up on deck. If Benedict hadn't realized she'd gone overboard when he had . . . He pushed the thought from his mind. So far all he'd done was get her out of the water. Without dry clothes and a fire, they were both flirting with terrible illness at the least. He pressed his lips to her temple. "You are not alone—not now, not ever. We're going to walk to your sister's house, where there will be a hot bath and tea and a warm bed." She nodded, slumping against him. He looped her arm around his neck, secured his arm around her waist, and started out into the night.

Chapter 25

Penelope was terribly afraid one of them was going to die that night.

The thought had been hovering over her mind ever since she hit the water. At first she had scorned it, filled with righteous fury and determination that Clary would never have the satisfaction of disposing of her so easily. When Benedict had found her, she'd been buoyed again; she was no longer alone, and he knew the river. His fierce promise that they would spend the night at Abigail's, warm and safe—along with his vengeful words about Clary—gave her renewed strength.

Still, that strength was nearly gone by the time they made it to shore. Despite telling him she could swim, her limbs had become leaden. Her mind seemed to be receding from her body, pulling away until her senses felt attenuated and muted. She barely heard Benedict's voice, urging her on, breaking in relief as he dragged her ashore. She was only dimly aware of her body moving, although she did feel the shudders that racked her from head to toe as the wind cut into her soaked clothes.

She had never explored as much as her sister had, but Penelope had walked in the woods. She knew Montrose Hill House was just that: a house atop a hill. A hill they would have to walk up, in this wind, sopping wet. Like a moth transfixed by a flame, her thoughts circled around those few facts. There was no strength in her legs; she could barely walk. Benedict, who had just swum across a stormy river pulling her weight behind him, must be even more exhausted.

And then he took the lantern away and left her. She pressed herself against the rock, trying to quell the horrible shivering, and closed her eyes to the darkness. The sky was as dark as night above her, and the weak lantern light vanished with Benedict. She knew he was only a few feet away and would be back soon, but it was hard not to feel utterly alone.

There was no denying that she had been wrong about a great many things. Lord Stratford was a far, far worse man than she had ever expected. It was one thing to be strict, and many fathers thrashed their children. When Benedict told her he'd been whipped as a boy, even as a young man, she'd blithely thought it was akin to the way her father had thrashed her brother on a few occasions. When Benedict said his father had no pity for others, she assumed it was wrapped up in the general arrogance associated with being an earl. When he said he hoped she and his father never met, a small part of her had wondered if that was because he was somewhat ashamed of her. She had been wrong, wrong, wrong.

Even if Benedict had wanted to keep her away from the earl because of shame over his marriage, she should have counted her blessings that she wouldn't have to deal with Lord Stratford. Instead she had convinced herself that it was best to stand up to him, to assert their—her—independence from the tight control he had always exerted over his family. If Benedict had married her because her dowry freed him from the earl's authority, she reasoned, shouldn't he demonstrate that? Showing weakness only encouraged a bully.

Instead the earl had schemed to lure her aboard his yacht so Clary could corner her about Olivia. Perhaps Stratford had been deceived about Clary's true nature; perhaps there was some honorable reason he wished to speak to Olivia. But every other time Penelope had given the earl the benefit of the doubt, she'd been wrong, so she could only believe that Stratford was as ruthless as Clary.

Tears leaked from her eyes and down her cheeks. She had contributed to this nightmare through her disregard for Benedict's warnings, through her arrogance that she would know better how to deal with the earl than his son did, and through her own stubbornness in not telling anyone and everyone that Clary had assaulted her in the first place. What good was keeping her promise to Olivia if it led to her death—or worse, Benedict's?

She heard his footsteps coming back, and the lantern glow pierced the gloom. Hastily she wiped her cheeks, hoping her generally soaked

state would hide them. The last thing she deserved now was any sympathy. But her guilt only
grew worse as he lifted her to her feet and murmured words of comfort. He had found something stiff and musty to wrap around her, while
he wore only his soaking wet shirt and trousers.
When he assured her that she was not alone—
now or ever—she knew he meant it. Penelope
sensed that if she faltered, he would try to carry
her and doom them both. She managed to get
her arm around his shoulders and swore a silent
oath to herself: she was going to make it up that
hill, for Benedict if not for herself. She loved him
too much to do any less.

Whenever she felt herself slowing or began
to think of suggesting they rest, she forced herself to make a smart comment. It made her feel
better that Benedict would worry less about her
if she seemed unaffected. But when they finally
climbed a small rise and saw the house in front of
them, she burst into tears.

"I know, love, I know." Benedict paused, letting
them both rest. He held her face against his chest.
"I told you we'd make it."

In spite of her tears she laughed a little. "It
seemed a rum bet until now . . ."

His arms tightened. "Then I suppose I just won,
eh?" He tipped up her face and kissed her, long
and deep. "I've never wanted to get you into bed
more than I do this moment."

She gave another weak laugh. "And I've never
been more eager to go! The only thing that might
tempt me away from it would be a hot bath."

"If Vane has a tub that will hold both of us at

once, I shall buy it from him immediately, hang the cost." He kissed her once more. "Shall we?"

Only by keeping her eyes fixed on the wide front door did Penelope stay on her feet. *Almost there*, she told herself with every step. Benedict was shivering now, although she had almost stopped. She hoped that was a good thing and refused to think about it anymore.

Benedict had to bang on the door more than once before it opened. A puzzled woman looked at them. "Yes?"

"Mrs. Vane," rasped Benedict. Penelope felt herself slipping from his grasp, but her hands wouldn't work when she tried to hold on to him. "Her sister . . . nearly drowned . . ." The canvas fell away as she slid slowly toward the ground, and the wind felt like an icy knife. She just wanted to huddle on the ground and sleep.

"Penelope!" Abigail's scream cut off the rest of his explanation.

She floated dimly through the next several minutes. There was a bustle of activity, and someone scooped her up and carried her inside and up a flight of stairs. "Ben," she cried weakly, reaching out. *Don't leave me now*, she wanted to beg. *Come with me. Forgive me for not trusting you more.*

"Sebastian is with him." Abigail was beside her, hurrying along to open the door for whoever held her. "Put her down, Mr. Jones, and see to Lord Atherton. What happened?" Her sister began stripping off what remained of her clothing as the door closed behind the man. "Penelope, wake up! Talk to me!"

"What can I do?" another woman's worried voice asked.

"Bring more towels and put them by the fire." Abigail was yanking at her boot, none too gently. "Prepare hot tea for both our guests and make up the bed down the hall. And fetch Mr. Vane's hunting knife; her boots won't come off."

She opened her eyes. "Ben—where is he?"

"No doubt Sebastian has nearly bundled him into the fireplace by now."

"No! No, he mustn't do anything to Benedict—" She struggled to sit up, but her sister held her down.

"To get him warm, Pen." Her voice gentled. "What happened?"

Tears stung her eyes again. Now that Benedict couldn't see her, she did nothing to check them. "We were on the yacht—Stratford's yacht. He wanted us to go to Stratford Court. Benedict didn't want to but I told him we should go for his mother's sake . . ." Mrs. Jones returned, and Abigail began sawing at her boot laces. "Lord Clary was on the boat and he pushed me off. He wanted to know where Olivia was and I wouldn't tell him so he pushed me into the river. And Benedict jumped in after me and then we had to swim and oh, Abby, the current is so strong." She was sobbing so hard her sister probably couldn't understand a word, but she had to get it out. "I didn't know if we would make it and then we had to walk up the hill and I'm so, so tired, I don't know if I can ever move again."

"Shh," crooned Abigail. She'd cut off both boots during Penelope's increasingly hysterical outburst. "You can walk, just a few more steps. Fortunately Mrs. Jones had already prepared a hot bath, and we're going to soak you in it until you look like a poached egg." She helped Penelope sit up, now wearing only her shift, and with her housekeeper's help they got Penelope into the bath. The water felt scalding, and she wept even harder as her feet and legs prickled painfully. Abigail folded a warm towel around her shoulders and pushed her down until her chest and arms were submerged.

Gradually her shivers began to ease, and with them her racking sobs. She rested her head against her sister's shoulder, weary beyond words.

"Tell me again," whispered Abigail, stroking her hair. "Who pushed you?"

"Lord Clary." Olivia would have to understand. Penelope was never keeping another secret again. "He's been threatening Olivia. She told me she had a plan to escape whatever hold he has over her, but then she left London and Clary wants to find her. And—and he told me Lord Stratford also wants to know." Her voice shook. "I don't know what they want from her, but I fear she's in danger—"

Abigail shushed her. "Don't worry about Olivia now. So Clary pushed you off the boat—are you sure it was deliberate?"

She nodded. He'd looked her right in the face as he did it, and she would never forget his expression.

"Did he also push Benedict? I cannot believe Lord Stratford would permit such a thing."

"I don't know." She blinked back a few more tears. "But he saved my life, Abigail. I never would have made it without him."

Her sister smiled. "I told you he was a better man than you credited him."

She stared at the flickering flames. He was. Yet another thing she'd been very wrong about. "I know. I . . . I love him, Abby. And I've wished he would fall in love with me almost since the first moment I saw him. I wanted to hate him for what he did to Sebastian, but even then I wanted him. And now—now I understand why he acted as he did. With that *monster* for a father, how could he have done anything else? And that makes me a terrible person for assuming I knew better than he did how he should have behaved, and how could he ever love me after the things I said to him?"

Abigail handed her a handkerchief as Penelope began sniffling. "I think you're too hard on yourself."

She sighed. "Perhaps." But she feared she had finally been truly honest.

After a long soak and two cups of hot tea, Abigail helped her out of the tub and into a thick nightgown. She combed Penelope's hair and put her to bed, waving aside Penelope's protest upon realizing it was Abigail's own bed.

"Mama gave me the furniture from my room at Hart House so we have plenty of beds now." She tucked the blankets securely around Penelope. "Sebastian and I will be down the hall." She banked the fire and tidied the room, pausing at the door. "Shall I make up another bed for Benedict?"

"No," she said at once. She could only hope he would want to come to her, once he'd recovered from being nearly drowned, thanks to her.

The door opened sometime later, startling her from a restless sleep. She'd been fighting to keep her eyes open, hoping he would come. "Ben," she mumbled, trying to push herself up even though her body felt like it had been turned to lead.

"Yes." He eased beneath the covers, curling himself around her body. His lips brushed her neck. "I'm here."

She went limp again. "Thank goodness. I was so afraid . . ."

"I had a moment or two of alarm myself." He kissed her again before drawing her snugly into his arms. "Who would have thought sneaking out to swim the river as a lad would prove so useful?"

She gave a wheezy laugh, which somehow turned into a sob. "I'm sorry, so sorry. It was my fault . . ."

"No." His voice was fierce. "Don't say that. It was Clary's fault alone . . ."

Not quite. Benedict's voice trailed off, and Penelope knew what he was thinking. It was also his father's fault, even if Stratford had had no part in shoving her over the side. She swallowed hard. "But I urged you to go on the boat. You were right, we should have refused—"

"I wish we had," he said with feeling, "but neither of us knew. Your arguments were logical; I agreed with them. If you're at fault for innocently suggesting a false course, I am even more at fault for consenting, for I knew all along what my father is."

"He wants to find Olivia," she murmured. "Olivia Townsend is the woman Clary was abusing the night you saved me from him, and she's the one who needed two hundred pounds so she could leave London. Clary demanded I tell him where she is, and he said your father wants to know as well."

"Both of them may go to perdition, with my compliments."

"He pushed me over because I wouldn't tell him . . ." She turned her head, trying to meet his eye. "Clary was waiting in the cabin."

"I know. Penelope, if I'd had any idea he was on board, we would never have set foot on that yacht, no matter what my father threatened."

She shivered. "What will they do now?"

Benedict's face hardened. "I don't know, but neither will ever have another chance to hurt you."

"What about your mother?"

He touched one finger to her lips. "Not even if it means I never see her again, either."

"You saved my life," she whispered.

"So surprised!" He smiled. "Did you think I wouldn't?"

She closed her eyes. "I didn't know."

"I jumped over the side as soon as I realized you were in the water, praying it wasn't too late. Thank heavens you can swim."

Penelope thought of all the times she had thought badly of him, all the slights she had cast on his character. Things had improved between them, but he'd risked his life for her. Her throat closed up at how close they had both come to dying. Wordlessly she gripped a fold of his nightshirt.

He must have sensed what she couldn't say. "I love you, Penelope." His arms tightened around her, as warm and strong as ever. "Enough to die for you."

She was motionless for a moment, then twisted to face him. "What?"

"I love you." He rested his forehead against hers. "You once told me it was the most important thing in marriage, after all . . ."

"But you don't believe in it."

Slowly he shook his head. "I had never seen a marriage based on love and respect. Nor did I expect to."

She avoided his gaze, and her hands braced against his chest as he tried to gather her closer. "You didn't even want to. I'm not the sort of girl you wanted to marry at all."

"No, but I didn't expect to love my wife, either. Don't you remember all of what I asked for? A pleasant, good-natured companion. Someone pretty enough to look at, sweet enough not to drive me mad, and gentle enough never to argue or oppose me." He gave a soft *tsk*. "What sort of idiot wants that?"

"One who doesn't want to be tormented and bedeviled," she reminded him.

"Ah yes," he murmured, a hint of smile curving his mouth. "Tormented by wicked, lascivious thoughts about you in my bed. Bedeviled by your forthright nature and spirit of adventure. But also charmed by your exuberance. Impressed—and humbled—by your devotion to your friends. And deeply moved by your ability to put aside your dislike of me and try to make a happy marriage, even after the terrible beginning we had."

Her face burned. "Oh—yes, that was quite a magnificent feat . . ." She stopped. "No," she said in a low voice. "I cannot tease about that. Did you really never know? I fell partly in love with you the first day you came to Hart House."

"Did you?" His voice warmed with interest. "Tell me more."

"You were the handsomest man I'd ever seen—"

"And now?"

She blushed. "You still are—even more so than then. I'd never seen you naked then." He growled in appreciation. "But you didn't notice me, even when I tried to flirt with you by badgering you to go hunting for ghosts at Hampton Court."

Benedict's eyebrows shot up, and then he gave a soft laugh. "And here I thought I'd have my head handed to me if I dared try anything!"

"Well, you didn't want me then."

He rolled on top of her. "After a logical, calculated analysis, I decided your sister would be a safer choice. I knew if I married you, I'd never have a moment's peace. I'd spend the rest of my life reading scandalous pamphlets"—he burrowed one hand under the blankets and began tugging at the hem of her nightgown—"and wondering how daring you were willing to be when making love"—she arched her back and wrapped her arms around his neck as he moved between her legs—"and going out of my mind wanting you . . . kissing you . . . even savoring the sound of you laughing at me." He kissed her.

Penelope inhaled sharply as his hand trailed down her belly. She should be sound asleep by now, worn out from the ordeal of the last few hours. Instead her skin seemed to sizzle where he touched her, and she wanted him inside her more than ever before. She wanted him to hold her down and make love to her until every other memory of this night was scoured from her mind and her body was exhausted with pleasure, rather than from life-threatening danger. She clasped her hands around his arse and tugged. "As long as you love me back, there is no reason to deny yourself any of those things."

He laughed and pushed forward, making them one. "And as long as you love me, I won't."

Chapter 26

Benedict woke early the next morning. Penelope barely made a murmur as he extricated his arm from under her and slid from the bed. His clothes lay folded on a chair near the hearth. He dressed, gratefully pulling on a coat that wasn't his. It was probably Sebastian's; the shoulders were a little tight and the sleeves were too long. The boots were also too big, but only a bit, and the very fact that they were there, freely given before he even asked, touched him deeply. After folding the blanket more securely around his sleeping wife, he went in search of his host.

A sonorous bark stopped him at the bottom of the stairs. Sebastian's enormous black boar hound clattered out of the sitting room, his ears pricked and a faint growl rumbling in his throat. Benedict stood motionless.

"Boris." Sebastian Vane appeared in the doorway and put one hand on the dog's head. "Sit." The dog's haunches dropped instantly. Sebastian glanced at him. "How did you sleep?"

"A good deal better than I would have at the bottom of the river."

Sebastian nodded. "And Penelope?"

His throat closed. "She's well—thanks to you."

His onetime friend tilted his head. "I didn't jump off a boat and save her life, then carry her more than a mile up the hill."

If only that could atone for the fact that he'd allowed her to be on the yacht in the first place. Benedict hesitated. "Would you take a walk with me? We'll want a lantern."

If Sebastian was surprised, he didn't show it. He fetched two greatcoats, handing over one without comment. Benedict shrugged into it, feeling very keenly every time he had failed Sebastian, every time he had retreated behind his father's domination and expectations and protested, *What could I have done?* He had been a coward not to try. Penelope had been right about that. From now on, he meant to act as he knew he should, without fear of anyone's anger.

"They'll be looking for you, no doubt," said Sebastian as they walked down the hill, Boris bounding ahead of them.

"Perhaps." Benedict squinted in the sunlight, dazzling today. "Perhaps not." He felt his companion's swift glance. "It's quite possible we're both presumed dead, if not outright desired dead."

"That sounds harsh even for his lordship."

Benedict heard the rest of Sebastian's mildly spoken comment. The earl would never want his son and heir dead. Without Benedict, the earldom would go to a distant cousin, a rather hedonistic fellow who cared only for horse racing. All of Stratford's carefully collected artworks would be sold to finance a stud farm, or lost outright at the races. To a man who couldn't countenance a nouveau riche heiress as the next countess, the idea would be unthinkable. All Stratford's punishment and cruelty had come with the explicit admonition that it would mold him into a proper earl, fit to take his father's place.

But he'd learned more from his father's lessons than the earl intended—some of it later than he should have, but with a depth of meaning Stratford could never have imparted.

"After our last words, I daresay my father and I won't be on speaking terms again soon. I have finally seen, with absolute clarity and certainty, how devoid of feeling he is. Any concern he ever had for my health and safety was solely for my position as the heir to Stratford." He hesitated. "And I am ashamed of what I did in the hopes of retaining his regard. I should have told you that I never believed you stole from him, or had any hand in your father's disappearance."

This time Sebastian couldn't hide his astonishment.

Benedict forced himself to go on. "I told myself I didn't know for certain, but the truth is that I didn't want to risk angering my father. And—and partly because I hated you then."

Sebastian stopped in his tracks. "Ben . . ."

"I hated you for being able to do what I could not," he went on, feeling the lash of guilt, and the insidious ache of envy, all over again. "God, how I wanted to ride off with you to fight the French! I'd even have taken a crippling bullet in the leg.

Instead I was stuck at home, where my father knew I didn't want to be, and he made me writhe for longing to be somewhere else. Three days after you left he sent me to sack Mr. Samwell."

Sebastian would remember Mr. Samwell, who had been steward at Stratford Court for years. Samwell had scolded them both many times for various pranks and transgressions. What neither of them realized—what Benedict didn't admit—was that Samwell had been trying to spare them the earl's wrath. The steward must have recognized the earl's controlling, abusive nature long before Benedict knew what to call it, and he'd tried to keep both boys out of trouble. When Benedict had gone to tell him he'd lost his place, the old man had only sighed wearily and said he'd expected it for some time. And even though Benedict had delivered the earl's message in full, that Samwell must be off the property by the next day or be chased off with a horsewhip, the steward didn't turn on him.

"Why?"

Benedict only raised his hand uselessly in response to his companion's incredulous question. "I don't even know. His lordship never explains. But it was only the beginning of what he demanded. By the time you returned I had learned very well what would happen if I defied him."

Sebastian's probing gaze grew more compassionate.

"Penelope was right about me," Benedict added in a low voice. "I was a coward for not standing by you. The sad truth is that I didn't know how to defy him." *Until now.*

"I suspect we both have much to regret," said Sebastian. "Fortunately it is in the past." He hesitated, then went on, "I never thanked you for your part in . . . everything."

Benedict dared a quick glance at his former friend and saw nothing but calm assurance. But then, Sebastian must feel much the same way he did. Penelope had taken great delight in telling him how much Sebastian adored Abigail, and for the first time he truly appreciated how much love could improve a man's outlook on life. "Thank you for taking us in last night."

"Did you think we wouldn't?"

Benedict shrugged helplessly. "I didn't know."

"Well." Sebastian cleared his throat. "We are nearly brothers now."

Benedict's head jerked up. "I suppose we are."

"Feels a bit like the wheel has turned full circle, doesn't it?"

Slowly Benedict grinned. "It does. Happily."

They walked on for a while. "Where are we going?" Sebastian asked as they drew near the water.

Benedict stepped down over a rocky ledge onto the narrow shore and held aside some saplings so Sebastian could negotiate the step. He shielded his eyes and looked left, then right. The sun sparkled off the river, and all the clouds had blown away. "When we made it to shore, I found a small cave. In all the years we explored these woods, did you ever know of one?"

"Never."

Benedict nodded. "It's not large—more of a gash in an outcropping of rock—but someone's been using it. I found that bit of canvas there, and just wanted to have another look in daylight."

Together they walked along the water's edge for about a hundred yards. Finally the hulking shape of the boulder appeared. From this vantage point it just looked like part of the woods, covered with creeping vines and more green than rock. Even when he walked right up to it, the crevice didn't become obvious until he could almost touch the stone. Exchanging a glance with Sebastian, who was a few steps behind, he carefully stepped into it.

There lay Penelope's discarded dress, still wet. He kicked it aside to clear the path and lit the lantern, opening the shutter all the way to illuminate the space. Boris, who had been sniffing along the edge of the water, barked from the bank behind them, but quieted at a word from his master. Benedict followed the narrow passage; it seemed far shorter this morning. He handed Sebastian the lantern and bent down to examine the crates in the small chamber.

"Who would have guessed?" murmured Sebastian, gazing around. "Do you think it's been in use recently?"

Benedict pushed over one of the crates. It was flat and wide, and when he checked the corners, there were bits of wool stuck to the wood. "I have a feeling it has been. The straw is fresh. I daresay the water doesn't come in except at high tide, but there's enough moisture for it to rot if left long enough."

Sebastian tapped his cane against the broken wood. "Odd shape for a crate."

Benedict stared at it. He'd seen that type of crate before, many times. All his life, a steady stream of pictures and statuary had come to Stratford Court. The earl had one of the finest collections of art in England. He was well-known for his eye for it, and just as feared for his ruthless pursuit of it. Stratford Court would have rivaled the Royal Academy in London if the earl had ever permitted anyone to see his collection. Of course he never did; in fact, he had his own private gallery where even his family was rarely invited. Heaven only knew what paintings were inside it. Benedict had seen it a few times as a boy. On occasion his father had brought him in to see a new masterpiece removed from its packing and installed for the earl's pleasure. Benedict had been about thirteen when his father decided he had no eye for art—a grave failing in the earl's eyes—and after that he hadn't been permitted in the gallery.

"Not if it's meant to hold a painting," Benedict said.

For a moment there was silence, save for the faint rushing of the river. "Smugglers, do you think?" asked Sebastian at last.

He didn't answer. His father owned this land. Despite it being eighty acres of good riverfront property, the earl hadn't done a thing to it; it was even wilder than it had been when old Mr. Vane owned it. Benedict had thought his father simply didn't care about it—why should he clear it and build on it when his own manicured estate lay just across the river?—but perhaps there was another reason. If a small boat were to stop here and unload crated works of art, perhaps at night, no one would notice. Skiffs crossed the river all the time, and besides, this was Stratford's own land . . . But why would the earl need to go through that subterfuge?

"Sebastian," he said, his voice loud in the enclosed space, "I don't suppose there was a lot of looting in the war, was there?"

"Only every chance that arose," was the wry reply. "The army looks the other way—in fact, they might even prefer that men find their own supplies."

"But what about finer things? Jewels, coin, valuables . . . ?"

"And paintings?" Sebastian finished when he didn't say it. "By the officers, certainly. Enlisted men had no way to carry much, but officers could ship baggage at will."

Benedict nodded. He didn't want to know more. The war had been over for a few years, but that didn't mean much. Napoleon's armies had relocated vast quantities of priceless art from all across the Continent; Stratford had spoken with distaste of the public exhibition of looted treasures in Paris. Even though the Duke of Wellington had ordered stolen artworks returned, it was a monumental task. If even some of that art had fallen into private hands . . . or slippery government hands . . . Benedict doubted his father would have any qualms in acquiring it through any means possible. When Lord Stratford wanted something, he was rarely denied. But smuggling?

He led the way back into the sunshine, dousing

the lantern. What was he to do? A few broken crates and discarded straw proved nothing. Benedict knew little about where Stratford's art came from; he'd never taken much interest in it, even before he was forbidden to see it. Even if he wanted to accuse his father, whom would he report it to? Stratford might be the coldest man in England, but he knew the value of alliances and connections.

"What will you do?"

He started at Sebastian's question, asked so neutrally. "What can I do? What do a few broken crates prove? I don't wish to protect him, or ignore any wrong he's done," he hastened to add, "but this is only suspicion, and I dare not act without proof." He grimaced; hadn't those been nearly the same words he used to excuse saying nothing on Sebastian's behalf years ago? "But if one were ever to spy a craft landing here, and discover what it left . . ."

His companion got a knowing look. "I daresay Mr. Weston wouldn't oppose a sentry or two on his property." He raised one hand and pointed. "The boundary is only there, around that curve."

A dark smile split his face. "Let's go see how good the view is."

They had made it a good distance along the waterfront when Boris began barking, and someone hailed them from the river. A longboat was gliding past, dragging the oars to slow its progress. Sebastian hushed his dog again and raised one hand, and the boat pulled nearer. Benedict stepped forward to see better, and the servant in the boat exclaimed aloud. "My lord!" He stood up in the prow and waved his arm so vigorously, the boat almost overturned.

"I knew they'd be out looking for you," murmured Sebastian. "The heir to an earldom doesn't just wash away."

Benedict's mouth firmed. He didn't give a damn about the earldom. If nothing else, Stratford's reaction to Penelope's possible murder had hardened his heart until no trace of weakness remained, dutiful or fearful or otherwise. "Yes," he replied coolly as the boat plowed ashore and the servant leapt out to splash toward him. "Here I am."

"My lord." The man gulped for breath. It was Geoffrey from the stables, Benedict realized. "Thank heaven, sir. We've been searching since dawn. Her ladyship will be overjoyed that we found you . . ."

Benedict ignored the mention of his mother's worry. "My wife and I were very fortunate to make it to land. You may tell the earl he shall remain disappointed." He turned away, intending that cryptic reply to be his final message to Stratford.

"But my lord," Geoffrey exclaimed. "I can't."

"If he sacks you, you have a position with my household," said Benedict without looking back.

"No, sir. I mean your father is dead. You are the earl."

Benedict froze. Sebastian inhaled sharply. "What?"

Geoffrey bobbed his head, as did the two men at the oars of the boat. "His lordship your father suffered a fatal attack last night. He expired shortly after he reached Stratford Court, sir. Her ladyship your mother sent every servant in the house to search for you and Lady Atherton—that is, the new countess—as soon as it was light." He hesitated, then added, "My sympathies, my lord."

Benedict glanced toward Sebastian, who looked as dumbfounded as he felt. Dead? But that was incredible; just yesterday his father had been as hale as ever. It flickered through his mind that it might be a lie, that Geoffrey had been told to say whatever it took to get him to return to Stratford Court, but it was incredible that Stratford would speak such heresy.

"Will you come with us?" Geoffrey asked again.

He roused himself with a start. "No. You may tell my mother Lady Atherton and I are at Montrose Hill House." He didn't want to go near Stratford Court yet. Surely the news about his father was a mistake of some sort.

But it was not.

Less than an hour after he and Sebastian returned to the house, a carriage rattled up the drive. Before the groom could dismount and open the door, the Countess of Stratford threw herself out. Benedict scarcely recognized her. Her hair was a disheveled mess, she wore a plain morning dress, and her cloak was in danger of falling off altogether. She stared wildly about. "Benedict—oh, Ben!"

"Mother." He strode from the house and caught her as she flung herself at him. "I'm here."

"They told me you drowned," she wept. "You and your bride both. They said you had been swept over the side of the yacht and vanished from sight!"

"We are both alive." He set her back. "But what's this about Father? Geoffrey said . . ."

She nodded. Her face was flushed and her eyes glittered as if with fever. It was the least composed he had ever seen her. "He suffered an apoplexy while still aboard the yacht. As soon as *Diana* reached dock, he was rushed to the house, but never regained consciousness. He expired before midnight; the doctor said it was his heart. There was nothing anyone could do for him." She touched his face, almost disbelieving. "Lord Clary said he turned white and clutched his chest when he discovered you had been swept overboard, and collapsed in a fit. He died thinking you were lost."

"Clary?" Benedict asked sharply. "Is he at Stratford Court?"

"No, he left for London early this morning."

"Why was he on the yacht?"

The countess paused at the urgency of his questions. "He said he'd come to look at a painting his lordship was considering selling. He expressed his sympathy and returned to town at once. Why?"

Benedict shook his head. Of course Clary would run; the bastard. There would be time to see justice done to Lord Clary later. "Father's really dead?" he asked in a hushed voice, as if to say it too loudly would cause the earl to emerge, lip curled in scorn, from the Stratford carriage.

She sobered. "Yes." To his astonishment, she tugged his head down and whispered in his ear, "He can never hurt you, or any of us, again."

His throat closed up. He'd never actually wished his father dead—not much—but he certainly felt no sorrow. It was more like numb amazement. He embraced his mother a little tighter. "I'm not sorry," he breathed.

A movement behind him caught his eye. Penelope stood watching in the doorway of the house. Everyone else had stayed tactfully away. But his wife was there, waiting, a thick shawl around her and an expression of watchful concern on her face. "But here—you must meet Penelope."

The countess hung back. "She must have no good opinion of me . . ."

He looked toward his wife and crooked his hand. Without hesitation she started toward them. "Mother, she is the fairest, most generous person I've ever known. Be yourself and she will love you."

She mustered a smile as Penelope reached them. Benedict drew his wife to his side. "Mother, you remember Penelope. Darling, my mother, the Countess of Stratford. Or I should say, the dowager countess."

Penelope's gaze flew to his. He'd told her Geoffrey's report about his father, but also that he didn't quite believe it. Without a word she dipped a curtsy. "I'm delighted to make your acquaintance again, madam. I hope this time we shall truly get to know one another and become friends."

His mother looked amazed; she glanced from one to the other. Benedict could see the moment she realized the truth. "My dear," she said in a voice that quavered with emotion, "welcome to the family. I can see that my son adores you, and I can do no less."

Penelope's lips parted in surprised delight. "Your ladyship is too kind . . ."

"No," said Benedict, grinning. He tipped up her chin and kissed her. "She is absolutely right."

Epilogue

Three weeks later

The gardens were still beautiful, even muffled by the first frost of the year. The air was sharp and clear, and Benedict filled his lungs with it. For the first time in . . . ever, he was glad to be here.

Despite the public observance of mourning for his father, the halls of Stratford Court had never seemed lighter. In part that was because they were filled. Both his sisters had come for the funeral, and stayed to rebuild the bonds of family. Samantha and Gray planned to return to London soon, but Elizabeth and her husband, Lord Turley, were staying until after Christmas, when Elizabeth's child was due. She had confided a wish to birth her baby here, with her mother by her side, something that would have been unthinkable a month ago. There was black crepe on the doors, but the house felt happier than he ever remembered.

Penelope came up beside him on the step leading down to the garden, and he slipped his arm around her waist. He'd begun doing it when she was still recovering from their harrowing swim through the Thames, and continued even after she insisted she was well because he liked it. Even better, *she* liked it. She rested her cheek against his shoulder and gave a small sigh of happiness. Benedict smiled. He loved the feel of her beside him.

"I've sold the yacht," he told her. "Lord Marsden had coveted it for some time, and he leapt when I offered it to him." Marsden was Scottish. If he bought the *Diana*, there was little chance it would sail up and down the Thames. Benedict didn't want to keep it, and he knew Penelope would never set foot on it again.

"I suppose that's a better use for it than chopping it into kindling," Penelope replied. "I hope you offered him a good price."

He gave her a sideways glance. "If he'd only offered a year's maintenance, it would have been a fair price."

"A shilling would have sufficed," she muttered, but then she smiled. "May he sail it in good health—his own and all his guests aboard."

"May he sail it in good health around all the isles of Scotland."

Penelope laughed, and together they walked out into the garden. The scent of lavender lingered. His mother had spoken of plans to cultivate more roses in the spring, and she'd drawn Penelope into her scheme. Together they had subjected him to a detailed description of the new garden arrangements until he put his hands on his ears and laughingly told them to do as they wished—which, he realized, had been what Penelope wanted all along. Her triumphant smile made up for any suspicion that he might have been manipulated. The budding friendship between his mother and his wife warmed Benedict's heart more than any horticultural inconvenience could offset.

"I've been thinking of selling some other things," he told her as they walked.

"Not our house in London," she protested. "After we'd just got it so well arranged?"

He laughed. "Not the house in Margaret Street." That was theirs, even if it was a bit small for an earl's household. He led Penelope off the path and threw open the garden door, holding her a little closer when the wind from the river hit them as they left the enclosed garden. "Some land."

For a moment she just stared at him, then her face softened in understanding. "How much land, my lord?"

"Close to eighty acres." Across the rolling lawns, on the other side of the river, rose the hill, still wild and untamed. Near the crest one could just make out the chimneys of Montrose Hill House.

"I hope you ask a fair price," she said again.

He smiled, his gaze lingering on those chimneys. "Fifty pounds is all I'll take, and not a farthing more." He glanced down at her. "Let Vane maintain his own side of the river. I've got enough here to look after."

The unanswered questions about his father still lingered at the back of his mind. He had inspected his father's gallery, but just entering the room made his skin prickle, as if the specter of the earl lurked in the shadows to protect his collection. After noting a number of pictures that would fit perfectly into the crates across the river, he'd left the gallery and locked it again. Perhaps Gray could help him sort it out. And if the gallery turned out to hold stolen or looted art . . . he would deal with that when he was sure. No one had approached the small cave across the river, let alone landed near it. He and Sebastian had set round-the-clock watches on it, all for naught.

The other possible actor, Lord Clary, had vanished. By the time Benedict went to London to swear a complaint against the viscount for attempted murder, Clary had left. Lady Clary was no help, saying her husband had told her he had some pressing business at his estate in Wales. A rider to Wales confirmed that Lord Clary was not there. Benedict doubted he was anywhere near Wales, but until his investigators located the man, there was little he could do. The moment Clary showed his face in society again, though, Benedict would be waiting, and ready.

By far the greater concern was Olivia Townsend, from whom no one had heard a word. Benedict agreed with Penelope that Clary had probably gone searching for her. But Penelope's letter to her brother, Jamie, had finally caught up to him; he rode out to Stratford Court two days after the earl's funeral and peremptorily declared that he would find Olivia. So far they'd received only two brief notes relating his progress—or lack thereof—but Penelope was confident Jamie was much cleverer than Clary and would track down Olivia first.

Benedict hoped she was right, as much as he hoped that James Weston left enough of Clary for him to exact his own vengeance.

"Thank you," said his wife softly, returning his attention to the opposite shore. "It will make things right again."

His arm tightened around her. "I could never think of that land as mine. If for some reason Sebastian won't take it back, you shall have to get your sister to speak reason to him."

"Oh, he'll accept your offer." She grinned. "Abigail is quite fond of walking in the woods, you know, and he'll want more woods for her to explore."

His mouth curved. "Indeed. I wonder if there were any other long-lost treasures in those woods. Perhaps we should explore them before selling them."

"What could you possibly mean by that?"

"What?" He stopped dead. "Don't tell me—have you truly forgotten?" A telling blush rose in her face but she merely widened her eyes curiously. "You do know," he accused her, winding his arm around her waist and anchoring her against him. "You owe me a debt, madam."

"It's too cold to go," she protested, revealing that she knew exactly what he meant. When she wanted his help clearing Sebastian's name, Penelope had promised to show him the Hart House grotto. He'd heard stories of it since boyhood, and despite years spent traipsing through the woods, usually with Sebastian, he'd never found it. But at some point Sebastian had, and he in turn had shown Abigail, who told Penelope. There had been a few distractions since she made the promise—a scandal, a hasty wedding, a fitful courtship that finally blossomed into love, to say nothing of the near-fatal yacht trip—but he hadn't forgotten, or lost his interest in seeing that grotto. "Abby said it was as cold as ice in there, even in summer. I can't imagine how frosty it will be now."

"A heavy cloak and warm boots will keep you warm."

"It's out in the woods. Quite deep in the woods, in fact." She made a face. "The last time I went looking for it, I fell in the mud and turned my ankle."

"I've walked in the woods hundreds of times and swear to protect you from any dangerous mud puddles." He raised his brows expectantly. "I've only been looking for it for twenty years. Are you really going to cry off a promise?"

She huffed. "And it will still be there in the spring!"

"Come, darling," he coaxed. "We could sneak across right now."

"Now! Are you mad?"

He laughed. "Perhaps. I used to dream of seducing a wench in the grotto, you know." He skimmed one hand up her waist to cover her breast.

A fine blush colored her cheeks. "I don't see any need to abandon the comforts of a heated bedchamber for that."

"No?" His lips whispered across her temple. "Can you really deny yourself the thrill of something so primal and untamed? What would Lady Constance advise?"

"A roaring fire to banish the chill."

"And risk a smoky end to my seduction?" He wrapped his arms around her, holding her close. "But I promise you won't be thinking about the cold."

She laughed, pressing a quick kiss on his mouth. "No, I'll be worrying about the child."

Benedict went still. "What child?"

Penelope hesitated, then took his hand and laid it on her belly. "The one who will be born next summer."

Benedict ran his fingers over her still-flat stomach. "What?" he said again, stupidly.

She nodded. "I spoke with your sister, my mother, and the midwife. Everyone agrees."

A child. The fleeting thought crossed his mind that he must be vigilant and not slip into his father's way of treating children, but then he banished it. The willow rod no longer stood in the study; he'd thrown it on the fire the day of his father's funeral. And Penelope would be quick to correct him if he ever erred in that direction. Rather, he would think about all the ways he wished he had been raised, and see to it that his child had a happier life than he had had—at least until now.

He drew his wife into his arms and kissed her. He was unspeakably glad to have her. He was even thankful to his father, for if Stratford had been a more benevolent parent, Benedict might be safely married to a woman of excellent breeding and mild temper who never would have captivated his heart and soul. "Then you *must* show me the grotto, so I'll know where our son's gone when he wants to avoid his tutors."

"Or our daughter."

He laughed. "Yes, with you as her mother, any daughter of ours would be just as daring as a son."

"You don't seem to mind my daring anymore," she said with a coy look.

"I adore your daring ways."

She smiled and tugged at his cravat. "Except when exploring grottos."

"Surely I can win you over." He gave her his best smile.

Penelope's face softened, and Benedict marveled anew at the unadulterated love shining in her eyes. "You already have."